SO-AXA-423

BEYOND THE MISTY SHORE

This Large Print Book carries the
Seal of Approval of N.A.V.H.

BEYOND THE MISTY SHORE

VICKI HINZE

THORNDIKE PRESS
A part of Gale, Cengage Learning

Detroit • New York • San Francisco • New Haven, Conn • Waterville, Maine • London

Copyright © 1996 by Vicki Hinze.
Thorndike Press, a part of Gale, Cengage Learning.

Thorndike Press® Large Print Clean Reads.
The text of this Large Print edition is unabridged.
Other aspects of the book may vary from the original edition.
Set in 16 pt. Plantin.

LIBRARY OF CONGRESS CATALOGING-IN-PUBLICATION DATA

Hinze, Vicki.
 Beyond the misty shore : Seascape Trilogy, book one / by Vicki Hinze. — Large print ed.
  p. cm. — (Seascape trilogy ; bk. 1) (Thorndike Press large print clean reads)
  ISBN-13: 978-1-4104-5189-7 (hardcover)
  ISBN-10: 1-4104-5189-5 (hardcover)
  1. Life change events—Fiction. 2. Maine—Fiction. 3. Psychological fiction. 4. Large type books. I. Title.
PS3558.I574B49 2012
813'.54—dc23   2012024888

Published in 2012 by arrangement with BelleBooks, Inc.

Printed in the United States of America
1 2 3 4 5 6 7 16 15 14 13 12

Beyond the Misty Shore

CHAPTER 1

T.J. MacGregor tried to leave Seascape Inn, but every time he crossed the property's boundary line, he blacked out.

For nine months now, he had attempted to find out why. Yet, after all this time, he stood alone on the misty shore, his feet wedged into crevices in the jagged rocks, without so much as a weak hypothesis.

Hoping for a miracle but fearing he'd used his ration of them long ago, he looked to the horizon. A wall of fog headed inland, rolling over the white-capped Atlantic. The frigid November wind soon would carry it onto the cliffs and it, too, would enshroud him. That had new resentment heaping onto the old and burning in his stomach. There had to be a reasonable explanation for this. *Why couldn't he find it?*

Angry waves crashed against the sea-jutting rocks forming the coastal barrier and the narrow strip of sandy beach below. The

7

smell of salt spray filled his nose. It tingled from the cold, as his nerves did from tension, and he looked down at his hands. They were red and raw and trembling. He rubbed warmth into his numb fingers, setting them to stinging and him to cursing at not having gloves. If he'd expected to winter in Sea Haven Village, Maine, he'd have had gloves. But he'd expected to be at home in New Orleans. He'd expected to be painting.

The resentment burned deeper, welled in his throat. His eyes stung and teared. He blinked, then turned away from the ocean, letting his gaze dart past the dead grass, brown and bent and broken under the weight of blade-clinging ice. Feeling equally burdened, he looked on toward the nest of firs and the hints of rooftops beneath the steely gray clouds in the sleepy village to the south, then up the western path leading back to the house that once had seemed to heal and now had become his prison.

Seascape Inn.

Across the road and atop a little hill, it looked so . . . ordinary. Just three floors of gray Victorian clapboard with stark, white shutters. A widow's walk. A wide porch strewn with rockers and a swing. A north tower stretching up into the heavy clouds.

Ordinary.

Yet no one knew better than Tyler James MacGregor that Seascape Inn was anything *but* ordinary.

During his time here, most guests had attributed Seascape's "special" assets to its caretaker, Miss Hattie, an angel if ever one walked the earth. But some had claimed Seascape itself the haven: a wonderful old house with seemingly magical, soothing powers where a person could come broken-bodied, or broken-spirited, gaze out upon the star-spangled sea, and heal.

On departing, three guests had seemed disturbed, though they'd refused to disclose their reasons, which could have been entirely unrelated to the inn. But the majority of the guests had said nothing out of the ordinary and had radiated silent contentment. A rare two guests, however, actually had called Seascape "The Healing House." With those particular two, T.J. closely identified. Though cynical now, he'd felt that same way years ago, on his first visit here.

Miss Hattie swore that during her lifetime Seascape had seen more than its fair share of miracles, and everyone in the village considered her word bankable. Forced to agree with them, T.J. rubbed at his neck. Pure and simple, the woman could never lie. But she could be a victim of distorted perception.

Living here as a prisoner for the last nine months had opened his eyes in a way only forced, constant exposure can. What he'd known about the seaside inn back then hadn't been the entire picture, and the entire picture had him wondering. Was Seascape a haven or Purgatory?

Still uncertain, he squinted up at the thin rays of weak sunlight seeping through cracks in the early morning haze. They slanted against the attic room window, and the glass sparkled gold like a cocky, winking sentry, mocking him. His stomach churned and, seething, he glared at the glass. How had he been so blind? So enraptured with Seascape's false sense of calm and peace back then that he'd convinced himself the house held the ability to heal? How had he been so arrogant as to truly believe it held magic and he'd captured that magic on canvas?

T.J. grunted. That was the trouble. He had believed. Gosh, had he believed. So much so he'd neglected to remember something very basic in art, and in life: every object casts shadows.

He'd once experienced Seascape's light, its healing magic — the object. Now, he experienced its dark side, its curse — its shadows. The light sucked a man in and

10

blinded him to his troubles. The shadows lured him, then tortured his mind and smothered him until the man inside threatened to wither and die.

Forgetting that basic truth had been a big mistake.

He kicked at a small stone and watched it skid over the rocks then plunk down into the ocean. Why had he forgotten it? He had no high-blown illusions about himself. He was an artist — in a sense, an atypical one because he wasn't atypical, just talented. No overestimation of his worth, by any stretch of the imagination. Ten world-class pros stood brush-in-hand right behind him, nipping at his professional heels and, at any time, he could be replaced by an up-and-coming. He was rich and made no bones about it. Why should he? Money was an accident of birth, useful only for the good that could be done with it — no less, but certainly no more. Only the way a man lived his life determined him a better or worse person than any other man. He reeked conservative. Definitely not-flashy in manner or appearance. He hated flash as much as he hated snobs, peach ice cream, government interference, closed minds, and garden-variety fanatics. And he never, never, used his personal clout to further his professional aims.

No, he shifted on the granite cliff and stiffened against a strong gust of wind, he had no illusions. In the physical sense, he was above average for a guy in his thirties, filling out a good forty-four-long suit just about right. Big men seemed to attract women and for that he felt grateful. He genuinely liked women. The way they walked, thought, sounded, and felt fascinated him. On the emotional front, well, he had a ways to go to get to average. But he loved those he loved, and he never lied to those he didn't. All things considered, he rubbed his jaw, he was a guy with dreams and the desire to become a better human being who happened to paint for a living just as other men happened to run corporations or to work in mills. He played straight with everyone, personally and professionally. Tried to live right. Heck he'd never even stinted and squirmed out of jury duty. So what had he done wrong?

Where had he failed?

This imprisonment had to be punishment for something. But what? What had he done to warrant — whatever in heck this was?

A lump of bitterness swelled in his throat. He swallowed it. No, even if Seascape were magical, it couldn't heal him again. Though his friend, Bill Butler, disagreed, T.J. clearly had gone too far for it to help him this time. Bill might be one of the best fishermen, the most sensitive poets, devoted family men, and trusted friends a man could have, but about T.J.'s situation the man was dead wrong.

Or was he?

The wind shivered through the pines down to the tree line and lifted whorls of sand on the rocks below. The tide was coming in, splashing higher and higher on the rocks, and the wind was bouncing off them, gushing up and over T.J.'s skin and whistling in his ears. Okay, there was logic in Bill's argument. If T.J. believed his art had caused him to become stuck here, then it did stand to reason that his art could free him. But could the mystery playing out here be that simple? T.J.'s gut instincts screamed that it couldn't and, when Bill returned from New Orleans with the painting and T.J. tried, and failed, to cross the boundary line and to escape while holding it, Bill would see that this situation had nothing to do with logic. Like everything else sweet that had soured in T.J.'s life, this had to connect to his gift . . . somehow.

His *gift.*

T.J. fisted his hands. Some *gift.* He never

wanted to paint again. Why in the world would he want to paint again? It had cost him everything. His parents. His fiancée, Carolyn. His freedom. And now, he feared, his sanity.

His nerves were raw, his muscles clenched into ropy knots. He squeezed his eyes shut. No. No, Bill *had* to be right. This strange phenomenon *had* to be psychological. T.J. couldn't fight insanity, but he could fight psychological. He was not insane. His attempts to leave here were not futile. He *could* fight.

He stiffened his spine, determined to regain control of his life. Despite the frigid chill in the air, sweat trickled down his temples, between his shoulders, over his ribs, and down his back. So many times he had attempted this challenge and every time he had failed.

But this time he would succeed.

This time he would cross the invisible boundary line and step off Seascape land. He would walk down the cliff to the winding road and then on into the village. From there, he'd hitch a ride with Jimmy Goodson, the mechanic, and drive up to Bangor, where he'd catch the first flight out and go home to New Orleans. He'd leave Seascape Inn and its mysteries to its caretaker, Miss

14

Hattie, the soft-spoken, iron-willed, and gold-hearted angel who for some unknown reason chose to spend her declining years as she had spent the rest of her life: residing here among the demons. This time, T.J. *would* leave. And he'd never look back.

Resolved, he opened his eyes, scuffed the toe of his shoe into the boundary line. While dragging it, lifting tiny stones and forming a ridge in the coarse, damp sand, he issued himself his standard pre-attempt reminder: *The sooner I get away from here, accept my loss, and bury everything that's happened here, the better off I'll be.*

Feeling an adrenaline rush, a surge of fear chipped away at his certainty that this time would be different, he lifted his foot and stepped over the line.

The temperature plummeted.

That familiar veil of freezing mist blanketed him.

Those hated, icy fingers of cold applied pressure to the hollow at his shoulder.

Dread punched into his stomach and warning spots flashed before his eyes. Panic seized his mind and, fighting the unseen demon for all he was worth, he swung his fists and screamed, *"Nooo!"*

Clipping only air, he swung again and again. His head grew lighter and lighter, his vision dimmer and dimmer. His chest throbbed. Oxygen-starved, his lungs burned and ached. He struggled to gasp, but couldn't find air. Fought hard, then harder, but the unseen demon wouldn't let go.

His strength drained. Helpless and weak, he crumbled onto the rocky ground, and despair settled in. Heaven help him, it was happening again.

And again there was nothing he could do to stop it.

Sensation dulled.

He ceased struggling.

And he sensed . . . nothing.

After two years in what amounted to a self-imposed prison, Maggie Wright stepped off the riverfront sidewalk and into Lakeview Gallery. A warm blast of heat welcomed her, and somewhere in the back of the building a bell tinkled softly, announcing her arrival. It wasn't cold in New Orleans — it was rarely cold in New Orleans — but it was raining, and she'd gotten wet hiking the three blocks from the closest available parking space, which didn't do wonders for her mood. At best, that mood bordered on grouchy, and it hovered too close for her comfort at downright scared.

Shoving aside the feeling she was forgetting something — being mobile and responsible only for herself again would take a little adjusting — she gave her shimmering teal raincoat a gentle shake and wiped her matching, drenched heels on the carpet in front of the glass doors. Why would anyone put white carpet in such a high-traffic area?

She looked around. The old warehouse had been remodeled by someone with an appreciable taste and talent that helped her recapture her confidence. She'd never been a wimpy woman — a *flaw* her mother had warned her against from the cradle. *Maggie, you've got to be less sure of yourself, hon. If you're too independent, you'll never snatch up the gold ring, much less the man dangling it.*

Maggie grimaced at the memory constant repetition had burned into her brain — not that she considered it credible. In her book, feminine or eligible didn't equate to helpless or dependent, and, even if it did equate, she lacked the panache to fake it. Who'd want a man who wanted a woman like that, anyway?

With a calmer eye, she scanned the gallery. Muted white satin benches circled the bases of tall white columns that stretched up to the high ceiling. The walls and ceiling, like the floor, were painted soft white. So was the long linear desk near the far south wall. In fact — she scanned the wide room — there was nothing present to detract from the purpose here. And that purpose was art. Visitors had to focus on the sculptures, on the paintings lining the walls, because there was nothing else to focus upon. Yet, the place didn't feel cold or distant. It felt . . . alive.

The marketing expert in her appreciated the clever design and decor. Maybe the white carpet wasn't so silly after all. The aesthetic gain far outweighed the hassle of dealing with a little dirt.

A black man stood across the cavernous room. His hand shoved into his slacks pocket had his suit jacket bunched up and pushed back at his hip. He had a kind, sensitive face, a tall, graceful body — clearly a runner — and, from his expression, the painting on the wall before him entranced him. He wasn't a collector. While nice and immaculately pressed, his suit wasn't expensive, and collectors who acquired art via Lakeview Gallery were notoriously as wealthy as the gallery was prestigious. More likely, he was an employee. Hopefully, one who could give herthe answers to questions she'd pondered on, wanted, and waited two long years to hear. Answers, now that the time had come, she half-feared.

Before she died, had Carolyn changed? Had she been capable of change? Maggie's mother insisted Carolyn had but, disappointed once too often, Maggie remained cautious and held her doubts. Still, she'd promised her mother she'd solve the mysteries surrounding Carolyn's death and find out what really had happened to her. After all her mother had been through, Maggie hadn't the heart to refuse her, and Carolyn, for all her faults, had been family. That alone, without the promise, made uncovering the possibly ugly, surely embarrassing, truth Maggie's responsibility. It helped that she wasn't going into this blind to Carolyn's flaws. Hoping for the better but prepared for the worst, she would keep the deathbed promise her mother had made to Carolyn's mother when Maggie had been twelve. And now that her mother had recovered well enough to again be on her own, Maggie would do her family duty.

To Carolyn's credit, she had been a master manipulator but never a thief. The police had insisted she'd stolen the Seascape painting, but it had to have been that MacGregor man. He was the hotshot famous artist with the world-class connections. Carolyn had just loved him. She'd been about to marry him. And if not for him, why would she have gone to Maine? From her address book and personal correspondence, she hadn't known a soul in Maine.

Questions tumbled through Maggie's mind. She couldn't answer them any more now than when Carolyn had been killed two years ago. A traffic *accident,* they'd said. But had it been? Really?

Maggie didn't know, but she intended to find out. The painting was here. Carolyn had worked here. Tyler James MacGregor's work was sold here. And Maggie's answers would come, *starting here.*

Trembling inside, she steeled herself then walked over to the man who still stared at the painting. "Good morning."

He turned, looking dazed, and smiled, as if a little embarrassed at having been caught dreaming. "Hello."

"I'm Maggie Wright." She hitched her purse strap up on her shoulder and extended her hand. "Carolyn Conners was my cousin."

He looked surprised, but clasped hands with her. "Bill Butler."

"I'd like to ask you some questions about her, Mr. Butler. Actually, about her and Tyler James."

"Tyler James?" Bill Butler cocked his head, looking even more surprised and now a little suspicious. She nodded, and he added, "I'm afraid I don't know much about the artist, other than information that's common knowledge."

"It isn't the artist I'm particularly interested in," she confessed. "I'm more concerned with T.J. MacGregor, the man." It was a calculated response. One meant to let Bill Butler know she knew of the artist, but also of the man who in the art world dropped the use of his surname. Hopefully, that insider tidbit would encourage Bill Butler to open up to her — without forcing her to open the family closet door and expose skeletons she'd really rather keep hidden.

A flicker of recognition shone in his brown eyes. He lowered his lashes and glanced down at the floor. "I know a little about him."

"I understand your reluctance to discuss one of your artists, Mr. Butler. Especially one of T.J.'s fame and reputation, but, I assure you, my interest is strictly personal. I'm not sure if you know it, but T.J. and Carolyn had been engaged."

"Yes, I was aware of that."

"Then you know she died two years ago." A droplet of rain dislodged from Maggie's hair and trickled down her cheek. She brushed at it. "A few of the circumstances surrounding her death are, well, frankly mysterious."

"Mysterious?" He arched a brow. "Then why have you waited so long to check them out?"

Valid question. And one, thank goodness, she'd anticipated. Still, something in his stance warned her to be honest. She gave him another once-over. Did she dare to ditch her rehearsed spiel?

"Until now I wasn't free to investigate." The truth. Another gut-instinct-based, calculated risk. One she prayed she wouldn't regret. "My mother suffered an injury right at the time Carolyn died, Mr. Butler. A severe injury that required extensive therapy. If you couldn't be in two places at once, wouldn't you give priority to the living?"

Silence.

Had she blown it already? Her palms grew sweaty. She dragged them down her soggy raincoat and let him see the concern in her eyes. "Please, I just want . . . I *need* to know what happened to her."

"I heard it was an auto accident."

He wasn't going to help her. Maggie's stomach muscles constricted, and her determination compressed with them. "I heard that, too. I also heard a painting was in her car." Squeezing her purse strap, she lifted her chin. "Carolyn was burned beyond recognition and the car exploded, but that painting wasn't damaged in the least. Doesn't that strike you as odd?"

He didn't look at her, but shrugged. "It's a big world out there, Miss Wright. Strange things happen in it."

Stepping back, he sat down on the bench and slid her a compassionate glance, then propped his elbows on his knees and laced his fingers together. "I'm sorry about your cousin, but I get the feeling you think T.J. was somehow involved with her death."

Too transparent! Fighting the instinct to stare at his shoes to avoid his eyes, she held his gaze, but she couldn't make herself outright deny his suspicions. She'd never been good at deception, and she'd been worse at half-truths. Had she been crazy to think she could pull this off?

He pursed his lips, thoughtful. "For whatever comfort it might be to you, my being here proves T.J. wasn't involved."

Her heart pounded a strong, hard beat that thumped in her temples. "I don't understand."

"No, you don't." He looked away, back at the painting. "But I imagine you soon will."

Confused, sensing sadness in his tone,

Maggie started to ask for an explanation, but her gaze drifted to the painting he'd been studying. Her thoughts dissipated. A sense of calm and serenity and peace she hadn't known since she was little and became suspicious at the goings-on at home seeped from the painting into her pores. Her insides warmed and a sense of balance, of rightness, flooded her.

The painting was of a house atop a hill near the shore. But not this shore. Nowhere in the South. The painting's shore was rugged and rockbound. She appreciated art, but never before had she reacted so vividly or intensely to it and, though she couldn't begin to explain it, she sensed something special about this painting. Something that whispered to her and lured. Something . . . *magical.*

She glanced down and read the signature: *Tyler James.*

The discreet brass plate attached to its frame: *Seascape Inn.*

"Oh Gosh." Her knees went weak. "That's it. That's the painting." Shaking, she leaned back against the column for support and forced her gaze back to the man. "It's in Maine, isn't it?"

Bill Butler sighed. He'd seen her reaction before — everyone who lived in Sea Haven

Village had seen one like it at some time or another. Still, he didn't know quite what to make of Maggie Wright.

She was pretty, about thirty, he supposed, with shiny red hair that hugged her shoulders and green eyes that at present pleaded with him. She was about as tall as his wife, Leslie, who topped out at his shoulder and long ago had mastered that tell-me-what-I-want-to-know look Maggie Wright leveled on him. She wanted answers, but should he give them to her? She'd lied to him.

He'd known it the second she'd said she wanted to know about T.J. the man. Her face had flushed red, she hadn't met Bill's eyes, and the pulse in her throat had begun pounding against her skin. Leslie'd had that same look thirteen years ago when she'd assured him she wanted to move from California to Sea Haven Village so he could build the Fisherman's Co-Op and be close to his Uncle Mike.

Yes, Maggie Wright had lied. And she radiated that scorned woman glow he'd learned to respect all those years ago. She suspected T.J. was involved in her cousin's death, and proving it was her bottom line.

If only she knew the truth.

Bill resisted shaking his head. Ridiculous. If it weren't, he'd be home fishing, not here doing T.J. a favor. Well, doing T.J. a favor, plus being paid by T.J. to come. Bill would've made the trip anyway, but with fish prices being down the extra money certainly would come in handy — which, he supposed, was why T.J. insisted on paying for the favor. A man capable of that kind of caring wouldn't be involved in anything shady. Would he?

He might. T.J. was in trouble. But what world-class artist who couldn't paint wouldn't be in trouble? Carolyn's death was tied up with *that* somehow, though Bill couldn't peg the connection — other than as a side-effect of T.J. having lost his fiancée. Loss could do terrible things to a man's mind. And the way T.J. was living up at Seascape wasn't helping either. Keeping himself locked in the Carriage House, sitting on the cliffs and staring at the ocean for hours on end . . .

Well, the man might be suffering from guilt, but guilt at having something to do with Carolyn's wreck? Ridiculous. And, yet, if T.J. somehow had been involved, even indirectly, that would explain his guilt feelings . . . and his blacking-out episodes.

Bill grimaced, feeling like a traitor. How could he even fleetingly doubt T.J.'s innocence? "T.J. didn't have anything to do with your cousin's death, Miss Wright."

"How do you know that?"

"I just . . . know." How could he not know? He'd watched the man suffer and struggle for nearly a year, trying to come to terms with his losses. Difficult to tell what all went on in T.J.'s mind — he held his feelings close to his chest — but Bill strongly suspected, and Leslie agreed, that Carolyn was but one of the losses that had sent the man into a tailspin. Bill also maintained the opinion that it would take a professional to help T.J. untangle his emotions and get him back to flying straight. A professional, or a miracle.

"That house" — Maggie pointed to the painting — "is in Maine, isn't it?"

From her doubt-riddled expression, the woman didn't believe him. She'd already tried and convicted T.J. Guilty. Bill chewed on his lip and considered his options. Never would he be so foolish as to think he could tell any woman her opinion on anything. There were things a person had to learn firsthand, and trust ranked among them. Living with Leslie had taught him that too. But he could see to it that Maggie had the opportunity to learn the truth.

He reached into his inner coat pocket, pulled out his business card and a pen, then wrote Miss Hattie's name and phone number down on the back of it. "It's in Maine." He passed the card to Maggie Wright. "The innkeeper's name is on back. You'll need to call and let her know you're coming."

Maggie looked at him, her eyes wide and round. "How did you know I intended to go to Seascape? I — I only just decided."

Bill shrugged. Her bewildered look, he'd also seen before. "Just a hunch."

Groggy, his head aching like the devil, T.J. groaned and opened his eyes.

Something bright white blinded him. He squinted and saw it was Miss Hattie's hankie. She stood over him, flapping the scrap of lace as if the cold wind whipping over the granite cliffs weren't strong enough to revive him without her personal assistance. Bill Butler's whopper-telling, tall, lanky, eleven-year-old, Aaron, stood next to her, his breath fogging the air. They both looked worried.

"Hey, Mr. James." Aaron blinked, his eyes bright in his warm cocoa face. "Did ya fall and bust your head on the rocks?"

This was *not* a dream. He was still here in this forsaken place.

Frustrated at yet another failure, T.J. looked at Miss Hattie. Her apron showed in the gap of her unbuttoned coat. It whipped around, molding with her dress to her plump calves. A blueberry stain near the pocket looked wet. He'd interrupted her making her morning muffins . . . again.

Miss Hattie stopped flapping her hankie and pressed it into her coat pocket. "Are you all right, dear?"

Her kind green eyes looked worried, and he hated seeing that, but he couldn't do a thing to ease her concern. He was plenty worried himself.

Reaching beneath his hip, he pulled out a stone that was digging into his side. His head ached like the dickens. So did his back. He pursed his mouth to tell her he was anything *but* all right — and he would have told her — had he not been looking at her.

The wind teased her white wispy curls that had come loose from her bun and sneaked out from under her blue woolen scarf to frame her tender face. Round and soft and lined with wisdom, it was chafed red by the wind and cold. A woman in her seventies had no business being out in this damp breeze. Miss Hattie thought she was invincible and if he'd reminded her that she wasn't, she'd only scoff, so he didn't. But he couldn't bellow at her either. It'd be like giving Mary Poppins or the good fairy a hard time.

"I'm fine." Unfortunately, he'd live. T.J. frowned and rubbed at the back of his head, pressing against a lump the size of a goose egg. Pain shot through his skull, and he winced. "Just fine."

"You don't look fine. You look a bit peaked. Doesn't he look peaked, Aaron?"

Aaron twisted his mouth and studied T.J. "Uh-huh, he surely does." He squinted up at Miss Hattie. "He looks just like Mrs. Johnson when Mr. Johnson dozes off in church."

"That bad?" T.J. muttered. If anything could be worse than dead, being equated to the stuffy, social-climbing Lydia Johnson was it. She'd been bad enough as co-owner of The Store, but when her husband, Horace, got elected mayor, the woman became a first-rate snob — or tried to. Frankly, she never quite pulled it off. His shoulder stiff, T.J. rolled it to loosen it up.

"Yes sir, you do — and that ain't no lie."

"I happen to agree with the boy, Tyler. You're as pale as a ghost."

Grunting, T.J. hauled himself to his feet, careful that not so much as his big toe crossed over the boundary line, off Seascape land. He'd already pushed fate far enough for one day. "I'm fine, Miss Hattie. Really."

30

Dusting the sand and dead grass from his jeans, he gave her a reassuring smile. "I just fell on the rocks, like Aaron said."

Aaron grinned as if pleased he'd been right. "Folks from away don't know it, but you gotta watch those rocks, Mr. James. They're slicker than spit."

"That's a bit graphic, mmm?" Miss Hattie patted the boy's coat-padded shoulder. "What are you doing running around up here anyway?"

"Mama sent me. She got a message from Daddy. He said to tell Mr. James that he's flying home with the painting today. The man at the gallery said okay."

Miss Hattie gasped. "He's secured the loan of the painting, Tyler! Isn't that wonderful?"

"Yeah, wonderful." The painting wouldn't work, but it could get Bill and Miss Hattie past believing that this situation was completely psychological. A little reassurance would be welcome to T.J. too. Doubts about his sanity were eating him alive. Still, being of two minds on the matter, he didn't know what to hope. Half the time, he wanted to believe that the problem rooted in his mind because dealing with that seemed more comfortable than accepting any other cause. But the other half of the time, he wanted an outside source to blame — even a bizarre one — because he hated that possibility less than the idea that even his psyche had turned against him.

"Aaron, you tell your mama not to risk the drive to Bangor. I'll phone Jimmy straight away." Miss Hattie looked at T.J. "Leslie's from California, you know. She's only been here thirteen years. Not at all used to driving on snowy roads."

Carolyn hadn't been either. T.J. nodded, solemn. Then what Miss Hattie had said hit him. *Thirteen years?* Well, this was Maine. Maybe in another generation or two, the Butlers wouldn't be considered *from away.*

"There's something else too." Aaron scratched his dark head, as if it'd help him recall exactly what.

The boy's glove was a little large, frayed at the wrist, and bunched at his fingertips. But at least he *had* gloves. T.J. grimaced.

Remembrance lit Aaron's eyes and, clearly pleased with himself, he looked at Miss Hattie. "A lady's gonna be calling, Daddy said. Maggie White. No, that ain't right." He grinned. "Maggie Wright. That's it. Maggie Wright."

"Thank you, dear." Miss Hattie gave the boy a smile. "You'd best get home now and help your mother with your brothers."

32

"Yes, ma'am." Aaron turned and started down the path to the road.

T.J. didn't watch him. Though he couldn't put a finger on it, there was something odd about Miss Hattie's reaction to Aaron's message. It gave T.J. a flicker of hope that the painting would work, and *that* he hated. He'd be a fool to believe it for a second. "Don't get your hopes up, Miss Hattie." He looked down at her, spoke gently to not upset her. "Bringing the painting here won't make any difference. I'll be a Seascape prisoner forever."

Miss Hattie twisted her lips, clearly disagreeing. "Something unusual is going on here, but I'm sure it's only temporary."

"Nine months is stretching the bounds of temporary," T.J. countered. She'd said before she had no earthly idea why he couldn't leave, and he believed her. The situation was frustrating for him and clearly perplexing to her. From her jerky movements, she didn't much care for feeling perplexed.

They started back toward the house. The path was speckled with patches of ice, and he gently clasped her arm to help support her. "I just wish I understood what was happening to me." A spark of fear threatened him. The wind had died down but the mist still clung to the shore. "I don't feel crazy." He shoved his free hand into his coat pocket. "Am I crazy?" Finally, he'd asked the question out loud.

"No, Tyler, of course not." She patted his forearm, linked with hers. "I wish I could explain this to you, but I'm afraid I don't understand it myself. Let's just hope that the painting works, mmm? We both feel it was spared from the fire for a reason. Maybe helping you now was the reason."

"I always believed that about the painting, Miss Hattie, but my gut's telling me I'm not the reason it didn't burn in Carolyn's wreck. I don't know how I know it, but I do. Still, I'm desperate. I've got to try this. What else is there left to try?"

"Once you believed in the magic of healing."

"I know. And I know that you think the healing magic I felt when painting *Seascape* will somehow help heal me now, but —"

"It is possible."

Was it? No. But Miss Hattie believed it, heart-and-soul. It'd been easier to send Bill to get the painting and prove her wrong than to argue with her. She was a nurturer down to her bones, pure and simple, but she was also Maine-stubborn.

Sidestepping a large stone, T.J. returned

34

to the path, feeling helpless and vulnerable. Both were feelings he'd had and hated before. He still hated them. "As soon as I prove it won't work, I'm going to burn the darn thing. I'm going to burn everything that has anything to do with my work."

"Tyler, no!" Miss Hattie gasped and squeezed his arm. "You can't squander your gift. It isn't —"

"It isn't a gift. Painting used to be . . . everything, but not anymore. Now, it's my curse."

"Tyler!" A strong, phantom wind gust furled the end of her scarf like a flag.

"It's true. My artistic ability has cost me everything that matters to me. Would a gift cost a man everything that matters?"

"It hasn't." They'd arrived at the road, at Main Street. Pausing, Miss Hattie looked up then down it, and, on seeing the way was clear, she crossed and started up the fir-lined drive to the house. "Your gift wasn't responsible for your losses, and neither were you."

"Then why can't I leave here? Why do I land on my backside every single time I try leaving?"

"I don't know." Leaves crunched under their feet. "Jimmy really needs to do some raking. Remind me to mention it to him when I phone him about Bill, mmm? I'd be lost without Jimmy helping me out around here, but I do so wish he'd find himself a good woman and settle down."

The swift subject switch had been intentional. She knew more than she was telling him. "How long has Seascape been an inn?"

"About twenty-six years. Why?"

"Twenty-six years. And I'm supposed to believe that I'm the only guest who has ever run into this kind of trouble."

"Tyler, you sound like Beaulah Favish. Are you going to start troubling the sheriff with nonsense of weird happenings here too?"

"I'm not like your nosy neighbor, and you know it. Have I told anyone about this?" People — including Batty Beaulah — would think he'd slipped over the edge.

"No. I doubt you'd even have told Bill Butler, if he hadn't come upon you prone during one of your failed attempts."

T.J. wouldn't have told Bill. Or anyone else. "Regardless, something weird is happening. You can't deny it."

Miss Hattie looked straight ahead and said not a word.

His heart rate quickened. She had her suspicions about exactly what that something weird was, all right. When Aaron had relayed the message from his father, she'd gotten the strangest, serene expression on her face. That worried T.J., and he prayed it didn't signal another matchmaking attempt in his immediate future. Though well-meaning, he was about sick of her match-making attempts. But he wasn't so sure matchmaking schemes had prompted that expression. "You aren't going to tell me a thing, are you?"

"I can't tell you what I don't know, dear." She patted his arm. "Things will work out as they're meant to. When one has little else, one must believe in fate."

"Fate." He sighed. Looked as if another attempt was inevitable, anyway. Irksome, but he'd nix it soon enough.

"You're listening but not hearing, Tyler. You'll come to understand. I will say, though, that soon there might well be burn-ing at Seascape. We agree on that. But, un-like you, I'll wager here and now that not a snippet of ash will be canvas."

What did she mean by that? T.J. looked up at the attic window. Something flickered, and his skin crawled. Surprised at his re-action, he blinked and checked again, but saw nothing. A trick of the light?

"Tyler?" Miss Hattie slid him one of her helping-things-along looks he definitely recognized as a pre-matchmaking signal. "I need for you to move into the main house."

Here it came. Opening the back door into the mud room, he paused. "Why?"

"The Carriage House needs a new roof. I intended to get it done this fall, but you so enjoy your privacy in its apartment, I didn't want to disturb you. Yet I can't wait any longer now. Winter is here." She stepped past him, shrugged out of her coat, then hung it on a peg on the wall. "Do you mind?"

"Not really." He minded a lot. He pegged his coat and toed off his muddy shoes, glad to be out of the biting wind and cold. "If the weather holds, I'll move this afternoon."

"I think Maggie Wright will arrive this afternoon and I hate to welcome a new guest while we're in turmoil. This morning, mmm? After breakfast — which might well be late if my muffins have burned."

He smiled. "They wouldn't dare."

She smiled back, then grew serious. "You know, Tyler, your situation sincerely troubles me. This is the first time in all my years at this house I've been uneasy. I sense you have reservations, but I truly have no idea what is happening to you." She stared up at the ceiling as if miffed and speaking to someone else entirely, then added, "And I don't much like it."

He didn't like it either. But what could he do about it that he hadn't already done?

The smell of blueberry muffins drifted on the air. His stomach growled and, without an answer, he followed Miss Hattie into the toasty, warm kitchen.

The phone rang.

She walked over to the wall, pulling her clip earring from her lobe, then lifted the receiver to her ear. "Hello."

Miss Hattie listened, smiled, then cupped her hand over the receiver and whispered to T.J., "Maggie Wright."

"Wonderful." The matchmaking queen *was* at it again.

"Just a moment, dear." She looked at T.J. "Go wash up, Tyler. Your help is on the way."

His *help?* Did she mean the painting? Or the woman?

CHAPTER 2

"I'm afraid I've brought the rain with me, only here it's sleet." Maggie watched Miss Hattie finger through the little ceramic boxes on the old, L-shaped registration desk in the entry hall of Seascape Inn.

The round, ample woman looked ageless, her soft white hair in a neat bun and her kind green eyes catching the light from the banker's lamp on the desk. With her floral dress, apron, and her rosy cheeks, she could have been Norman Rockwell's *Grandma* model.

"Well, we're glad to have it, dear. The plants and grounds need feeding too, mmm?" Looking distracted, the caretaker patted her pockets in time with the grandfather clock's steady ticks. "Ah, there it is."

Smiling, she fished the key out of her apron pocket, separated it from her handkerchief, then passed it to Maggie. "I expect it seems strange to you, but we live simply up here. Few locals lock doors, so keeping up with keys is more of a chore than it seems to folks from away."

"Nice. That you have that luxury. Definitely not a good idea in New Orleans." The registration book lay open before her. Both pages were full and Maggie quickly scanned the names. The inn was a popular one, judging from the number of guests. The pages dated back only to August. No opportunity right now to see if Carolyn had been here. Maggie would have to check later — hopefully, unobserved.

"I've put you in the Great White Room." Miss Hattie replaced the pen from the open registration book to its wooden holder. Being bumped back into proper rows, the little ceramic boxes clinked together. "Top of the stairs, first door on the right. It's one of the rooms with a phone, though I'm sorry to say that the thing works only when it wants." She replaced the lid on the third little box. A lighthouse had been hand-painted on it. "I've had the phone company out three times, but they can't find a thing wrong. Tried to tell those youngsters it has to be in the wiring, but they say it isn't. Anyway, if you need the phone and it's on the blink, you're welcome to use the one here or in the kitchen. Hope that won't be an inconvenience."

"None at all." Who would call her? These days, she rarely saw outsiders. "I'll just need to check on my mother every couple of days."

"Good." Miss Hattie dabbed at her temple with a white lacy hankie, then tucked it into her apron pocket. "The Great White Room has the turret and faces the ocean. Pretty window seats, if you're of a mind to do a little dreaming. From our chat earlier, I thought you'd like that."

Maggie smiled, showing her appreciation for the thoughtful gesture, though after the past two years, she wasn't honestly sure she knew how to dream anymore. "I'm fond of the water. It's . . . vast. Helps a person keep things in perspective, you know?" She slung her purse strap back over her shoulder, then picked up her tapestry-designed suitcase.

"Indeed I do know." Miss Hattie smiled back at her. "We all need our chance to dream."

An odd tingle shimmied through Maggie. As if she'd just heard something extremely significant and was being warned to pay attention to it. But that was silly, wasn't it? Miss Hattie was a sweetheart, only engaging in polite conversation to make a new guest feel welcome in her home.

42

Maggie tucked her briefcase under her arm, then lifted her makeup case, adding those items to her already considerable load. The stuff weighed a ton. She hoisted it, trying to get a firmer grasp. Her purse strap promptly slipped from her shoulder, dropping the purse onto the makeup case and threatening to knock the whole mess out of her arms.

Miss Hattie repositioned the strap and gave Maggie an apologetic look. "I'm really sorry Jimmy couldn't be here to help you take your things up to your room. You're loaded to the gills."

She walked Maggie through the entry, past the grandfather clock. Its chimes tinkled charmingly and reverberated through the entryway.

Pausing at the foot of the stairs, Miss Hattie sighed. "It's the storm. Jimmy's out rescuing stranded drivers. Course, the boy will be down with a cold come tomorrow, but he says he does what he has to do. I've already taken the chicken out to thaw so I can make him up a big pot of soup. He's orphaned, poor dear. Was even when his mother was alive, I'm sorry to have to say."

Jimmy. Ah, the mechanic from the shop she'd seen when driving through the village. That Miss Hattie worried over him was clear. Maggie liked that about her. "It's good of you to watch out for him."

"Wouldn't anyone?"

They wouldn't. But Miss Hattie's expression proved that possibility had never occurred to her and Maggie refused to shatter the woman's illusions. "I'd better get on upstairs before I scatter these things."

The lights flickered off, then came right back on.

"Just the storm, dear," Miss Hattie assured her. "I'll fix you a snack. The Blue Moon Cafe doesn't start serving dinner until five, and you look hungry now."

"Thank you, I am." A guardian angel in the flesh. "I was timid of veering too far off the highway, and I didn't see an open restaurant until I got to the village. Awful, but I have no sense of direction. I'd likely have ended up in Canada." Maggie smiled then started up the stairs.

The smell of lemon oil was pleasantly strong on the staircase and explained the mahogany paneled walls' polished gleam. Everything she'd seen appeared well-tended, with not a speck of dust in sight. Even the third stair's creak under her foot seemed homey and attuned, as if the house opened itself up and surrounded those in it in a safe and warm cocoon.

44

Midway up, two large portraits hung side by side in fine oak frames. A handsome man and a striking woman. Looking at the portrait of the woman, Maggie sensed her gentleness, her caring, and felt both deep down inside. It was a strange sensation. One alien to her last week, but one experienced twice lately. First, when viewing the painting of Seascape Inn at the gallery and, again now, looking at this woman's portrait. Feelings of peace and calm and serenity mirroring those she'd felt at the gallery flowed through her. How . . . odd. But, oh, how very welcome. The last two years had been worth everything they'd cost her, yet now that they were over she realized just how stressful they'd been. She really did need time to dream, as Miss Hattie had said, and time to heal. It seemed that this was the perfect place to do it. Already, she loved it here.

Prisms of light from the chandelier overhead pooled on the wooden stairs and reflected on the brass platelets attached to the paintings. Maggie paused to read them. *Cecelia Freeport* and *Collin Freeport*. Mmm, were they the village founders? Seascape's original owners? Miss Hattie's relatives?

No, Miss Hattie was the caretaker here. Not the owner. According to her, the owner was a judge in Atlanta. Maggie would have to ask about them.

Someone was watching her.

She glanced up to the second story landing. Empty. Not a soul in sight. She walked on up, feeling the slightest bit uneasy. Not frightened, by any means, just sort of aware. The sensation was a strong one, but not one that threatened.

The hallway was long and dark, as all the other doors leading to it were closed and very little natural light slanted in through the bank of mullion-style windows at the end. She walked over a white Berber rug, passed the plump-cushion window seats and the hand-carved bookcases flanking them. Miss Hattie respected books. The spines were straight and aligned perfectly in depth on the shelves. Maggie slowed her step to glance at a few titles. *Boats, Boatbuilding in the Twentieth Century, Tall Ships, The Atlantic, The Old Man and the Sea, One Man's Army: A Guide of World War II; Ghosts, Goblins, and Bumps in the Night; Voodoo, Coming Up Roses.* An eclectic mix.

Maggie walked on, then stopped outside the heavy door to the Great White Room and gave the door a knee-nudge. It didn't open. Leaning over, she put her makeup case down. Her purse fell off her shoulder and thudded to the floor. Par for the course.

Someone hit her in the back from behind.

Knocked forward, she dropped her suitcases and tumbled, scudding a good half-foot across the planks.

"Darn." A man towered over her, his arms as full as hers had been with hangered shirts, slacks, and a red-and-black-plaid coat. "I didn't see you."

T.J. MacGregor? Impossible! Stunned, Maggie just lay there. *It is him. What on earth is he doing here?*

Frowning, he shifted, adjusting his load. Hangers chinked together.

He didn't recognize her.

She'd known that if she ever saw him again, he wouldn't. They'd only seen each other once, at Carolyn's funeral. They hadn't spoken, and Maggie had being wearing the traditional black mourning veil. There was something positively galling in that the man had occupied so many of her thoughts, so much of her time in the past two years, and yet he didn't know her from Adam.

"Are you all right?" He shoved the hangers down from near his chin so he could look at her without dumping the armload of clothing onto her head.

"Yes." She cleared her throat. "I'm fine."

"In that case, would you get up? You're blocking the hall."

She gained her feet, hanging onto the doorknob, fearing her cheesy-knees wouldn't hold her. *Why is he here? Why hadn't Bill Butler warned me MacGregor would be here? Had he set me up?* "Charming."

"Hate to disillusion you, but charming, I'm not." He stepped around her. "We're the only two guests up here right now. Goes that way during the winter, after the last of the leaf-peepers bug out. Let's make a deal." He gave her a cold, hard look. "I'll stay out of your way, and you stay out of mine."

No apology? Arrogant jerk. What was wrong with the man? Did she look ready to attack him or something? He certainly had nothing to fear there. She grabbed the hem of her brown skirt, which had ridden indecently high on her thighs, and gave it a good jerk down to her knees.

The glimpse she'd gotten of him at the funeral had been obstructed by heavy coats and a sea of black umbrellas, and what she remembered most of all had been the slump of the man's shoulders. Here, with her view unobstructed, he wasn't at all what she'd expected from her memory. He stood much taller, about six-foot-two, lean and well-muscled, though broader. His coat back then *hadn't* had padded shoulders after all.

The man was supposed to look like an artist — intense and sensitive — not like a perfect-nosed, roughened lumberjack with huge hands. Doing intricate work on canvas had to be a hassle. His jeans were obscured by the clothing he carried, but his shirt was a typical, warm-looking L.L. Bean classic in a faded blue that really did wonderful things to his gray eyes, especially in the soft light. A shame he spoiled the effect with his killer glare. His hair was on the long side, jet black and wind-tossed, loosely curled at his nape and plastered to his head in front by the droplets of what likely once had been sleet. Unfortunately, that didn't do squat to diminish the impact of his face. It was interesting. Strong-boned and distinct, lived-in. Faces that looked as if their owners hadn't lived in them a while bored her. T.J. MacGregor had lived plenty in his and, from the telling signs on it, he'd laughed and suffered his fair share.

The devil deserved his due and she'd give it to him. He was dynamite-looking. Sinful that his TNT attitude, which she didn't like one bit, and the chip on his shoulder the size of Maine's granite cliffs, ruined him.

And those sins paled beside his worst: He

was a key player in Carolyn's death. Maggie knew it as well as she knew she stood in the upstairs hallway at Seascape Inn, staring at the man.

"Oh, I won't bother you," she assured him, and nodded to let him know she truly meant it. "I'm tired, wet, cold, and hungry. I don't want to be bothered myself. But even if I did, I'd find myself another victim. Frankly, I can't imagine anyone wanting to bother you."

"Frankly, good." He smiled but there wasn't any warmth in it. "Sounds perfect."

The tiny lines near his eyes crinkled and she cursed herself for noticing. The man was an egotistical, arrogant jerk. Tempted to tell him so, she yanked open the door to her room, then hauled her belongings inside. "Perfect," she snapped, then slammed the door shut.

Her hands were shaking. She was shaking all over.

What on earth is he doing here?

Miss Hattie definitely was at it again.

T.J. dumped the hangered clothes onto the bed in the Cove Room, wishing he could go right back to the Carriage House suite and hole up until the new arrival finished her visit and went home. The last thing he needed was another matchmaking experience. He had troubles enough and he darn well didn't have the extra energy to carry off being a jerk.

He was doing fine at it so far, though.

Guilt stabbed at his stomach. He grabbed up a few hangers and walked over to the closet. Maybe the new roof would be on in a day or so, and he could get back out to his suite, not that the Cove Room wasn't fine. Large and comfortable and cathedral-ceilinged, it had plenty of space for a man to move around in. Three windows overlooking the pond, gazebo, and Batty Beaulah's, provided decent light — and not first light, thank goodness, like the Great White Room. Forest green and brown-tone bedding and curtains and rugs spared him the lace and frills. Yeah, this room was okay. He could handle it for a few days, until the roof was done.

He walked past a Colonial washstand holding a cream-colored pitcher and bowl and looked at the windows. The panes were fogged. He rubbed the heel of his hand against the cold glass then looked out. Through a sleety haze and the stretch of tall firs, he could make out the village rooftops and the granite cliffs. A dull pain crept into his chest. Only in his mind could he go

51

there, beyond the boundary line. Beyond the misty shore.

At night, he'd lie in bed in the Carriage House and imagine himself walking down Main Street, visiting Miss Millie's Antique Shoppe in time for tea. At one time, her family had owned all of Sea Haven Village, Little Island — just offshore, which she'd donated to the villagers a couple years ago — and the land where Seascape eventually had been built. He could almost taste Miss Millie's drop-dead, melt-in-your-mouth chocolate chip cookies. They were the best. And Lucy Baker's cornbread. What he wouldn't give for a quick run over to the Blue Moon Cafe for a slab of Lucy's hot cornbread slathered with butter.

Heaving a sigh, he turned back to his chore. Something flickered in the mirror. The hair on his neck stood on end. He backed up a step, and looked to see what it had been. Sunlight reflecting?

But there was no sun. He glanced at the window. Still sleeting to beat the band out there.

Yet that was the feeling he'd gotten. That the flicker had been of some sheer, pure light. Strange . . .

"Get over it, T.J.," he muttered to himself. "You've knocked yourself out on the rocks one time too many. So now you're seeing strange lights. So what?" He grabbed a bunch of hangers and slammed them onto the closet rod. "These days, what around here *isn't* strange?"

He finished hanging up the clothes, then started on the suitcase he'd filled and carried over on the first trip, stuffing his underwear and sweats into the armoire on the east wall. Seeing a tiny crystal bowl filled with potpourri atop it, he sniffed. It smelled like the sea.

Until lately, he'd loved the smell of the sea.

With a little less enthusiasm for his task, he emptied out the forty or so travel magazines he'd accumulated in the last couple months and all the catalogues, then dumped them onto the desk, reminding himself to order a pair of gloves. From all signs, he was going to be stuck here awhile.

Bitterness burned strong inside him and that claustrophobic feeling had him banking down an anger that couldn't be healthy. He snatched up a dry pair of jeans and a shirt, then headed for the bathroom down the hall.

That woman hadn't noticed, but she wasn't the only one around here who was tired, hungry, and wet.

Another twinge of guilt stirred in his belly. He'd really been obnoxious to her. But he'd been determined to quickly disabuse her — and Miss Hattie — of any ideas about throwing the two of them together coming out of the gate. No doubt, he'd succeeded. The woman had looked at him as if he'd stunned her — which he likely had, knocking her sprawling on her rear — then as if she hated him.

A shame, in a way. She had terrific legs, and when she'd taken the tumble, he'd seen a lot of them.

The bathroom door was closed, but light seeped out from under it into the hall. Figured. He gave the door a hard rap.

"Yes?"

The woman. Who else? He grimaced and slumped against the jamb. "How long are you going to be in there?"

"I'm taking a bath." She sounded irritated at him interrupting.

Great. It could be hours. He sighed. "You're supposed to put out the sign." He looked at the bare nail meant to hold it, centered in the door.

"What is — Oh, I see it now. Sorry, I didn't know."

"Yeah, well, try not to homestead, huh? I'm wet, too — in case you didn't notice."

54

Why did she grate on his nerves?

Maybe because right now everything grated on his nerves. Man, he wished he could just go home. Coming back here had been a big mistake.

"Look, Mister . . . whoever-you-are. I have just as much right to this bathroom as you do. So cool your heels — and your mouth, okay? I'll be out in a few minutes."

He grinned. He didn't want to grin. In fact, he told himself he would not grin. But he couldn't help himself. His size tended to intimidate and it wasn't often a woman stood up to him. Obviously, he didn't worry this woman a gnat's worth.

Despite his resolve to hate Miss Hattie's latest hopeful on sight, he had to admit that he liked her style. "I'm tired of thinking of you as *that woman.* My name's T.J. Mac-Gregor. What's yours?"

"Maggie Wright," she said, then grumbled something nasty, he was sure, though he couldn't make it out through the door.

"Can we please do the honors another time? I'm a little busy at the moment."

Water splashed. And for some reason, he pictured her jerking her arm at him in a heated gesture. That had him grinning again. He bit it from his lips. "Sure, Maggie Wright. But if I catch cold because you parked it in the tub for an hour — relaxing while I'm out here freezing my buns off — it'll be on your head."

"Your buns can fend for themselves until I'm done, MacGregor. I've earned this. It's been a wicked day, and I'm not feeling very compassionate or gracious at the moment." Another splash, followed by a content sigh. "Frankly, I'm feeling very self-indulgent. So go away."

"I'll be sick as spit for a week." Aaron Butler would be proud of him, effecting one similar to his favorite phrase. And Miss Hattie would reprimand T.J. as if he, too, were only eleven years old.

"Sorry, fresh out of sympathy here. It all went to my aching arches. Blame the man who designed heels."

Her sympathy remark held a ring of truth that went beyond her feet. "A man might have designed them, but you chose to wear those heels."

"You're blowing our deal."

He was. Still, he intended to be obnoxious, right? She didn't have to know he was also curious. "Why are you here? Tourist season is over."

She hesitated along minute. "Go away, MacGregor. I'm sure there's a Thou-shalt-not-harass-a-woman-in-the-tub house rule around here — and if there wasn't, well, there is one now."

He grinned again, and positively hated that. "Leave it to a woman to make up the rules as she goes along. I, at least, made a deal with you."

More grumbling.

Shoving away from the wall, he dropped his clothes to the floor in front of the bathroom door, just to be contrary. He'd get her out of there. She was tired, wet, cold, and hungry, she'd said.

Ah, hungry . . .

Maggie's mouth watered.

The smell drifted under the door and filled the bathroom. Beans. Hot pastrami and cheese? Beans being a New Orleans staple, she knew she'd correctly identified them, but the rest of the scents were debatable. Whatever they were, they smelled darn good, and her growling stomach proved it.

The rap at the door sounded.

Expecting it, she didn't jump. Just toed the drain release so the water could start flowing out of the tub. "What now, Mac-Gregor?" she said, forcing a sharpness into her tone that her mother wouldn't have recognized.

"How'd you know it was me?"

His voice boomed through as if he stood on the rug next to her instead of on the other side of a closed door. "Who else around here nags the heck out of a woman while she's bathing?" Had he forgotten that they were the only guests at the inn?

"Miss Hattie sent you up some food. If you want it, you'd best be out here in ten seconds, or you'll be starving and hearing me tell you in minute, intricate detail just how delicious every single bite was."

She dried off with the white, fluffy towel, rubbing briskly. The man wanted a bath badly. Or to convince her he was a total, unredeemable jerk — which was exactly what she'd decided mid-bath, and why she considered it prudent to keep her connection to Carolyn to herself. So long as Maggie got to Bill Butler first and gained his agreement to not mention it, she'd be okay. "Are you threatening to eat food you know is mine?"

Maybe she could worm her way around MacGregor's attitude and into his life, where she could find out the truth. Shrugging on her pink, terry-cloth robe, she knotted the sash and gave it a firm tug. Provided the man didn't provoke her into killing him first.

"Not threatening, Maggie. Consider it a

friendly warning."

She jerked open the door, stepped over his heaped clothes, then snatched the plate from his hand. "Consider it wasted."

Lifting a pickle spear from the plate, she crunched down on it and walked away down the hall, back toward her room.

"Hey, this place is like a *steam* bath." MacGregor groused. "It'll be an hour before there's any hot water."

Maggie smiled and kept right on walking.

The grandfather clock chimed eight.

Maggie stepped onto the foot of the stairs. The smell of hot, yeasty bread filled the entry and her stomach growled, clearly still on Central Time. In caring for her mother, she'd kept to a six P.M. dinner schedule, and to Maggie's stomach, dinner was an hour late. Hopefully, the Blue Moon Cafe smelled half as good as Miss Hattie's inn.

"Ah, there you are, Maggie." Miss Hattie stepped from the kitchen into the gallery between the dining and living rooms. "I was about to send Tyler up with a message for you."

"Oh?" Had her mother called?

Miss Hattie tilted her head and let her gaze drift over Maggie, head to toe, her expression serene and sweet. "My, don't you look lovely. I adore pearls. Lovely. Doesn't she look lovely, Tyler?"

"Lovely." Smelling like winter pine, and sounding typically sarcastic, MacGregor breezed past her wearing gray wool slacks and a navy sweater. His scent lingered in his wake.

"Jimmy called a bit ago and said we're in for a wicked night. The weather isn't fit for man nor beast." Miss Hattie wiped her hands on a red-checked dishtowel. "You're welcome to have dinner here."

MacGregor paused at the dining room threshold. "At the risk of having Lucy Baker cut out my tongue, unless you're used to driving in heavy sleet, I highly recommend you stay put."

Whoever Lucy Baker was, Maggie liked her. "We don't get much sleet in New Orleans." Staying would give her a chance to work on MacGregor. "Thank you, Miss Hattie. I accept." Maggie walked into the dining room.

Already seated, MacGregor propped his elbow on the lace-clothed table, then rested his chin on his hand and stared at her.

Maggie stiffened, feeling like an ugly bug that just had slithered out from a crevice in the cliffs. If MacGregor weren't so bored, she bet he would stomp her.

60

What was wrong with him? She couldn't look that bad. Her dress was simple. A classic black sheath that fit like a good glove with only a single strand of pearls at her throat and ball earrings on her lobes adorning it. Definitely understated. She had swept her hair up because it'd gotten wet in the tub and she couldn't muster the energy to blow it dry. Little tendrils fell free from the knot at her crown and tickled her nape and her face, but there was nothing odd about the style. She'd no idea how Mainers dressed for dinner, so she'd played it safe — or so she'd thought.

She slid MacGregor a glare and a cool smile she hoped would slam his attitude into a deep freeze. "Miss Hattie, may I help?"

"Oh, no, thank you, dear. Dinner is ready. Just keep Tyler company while I bring it in." Looking angelic, the old woman smoothed her pristine apron over her tummy. "It's such a treat to cook for more than two again."

She turned, rounded the corner, then disappeared, heading toward the kitchen.

MacGregor stared at Maggie's every move. Holding off a grimace by the skin of her teeth, she slid onto a padded chair opposite him and swept the tablecloth back from her lap.

He didn't say a word. The grandfather clock in the entryway ticked softly, but in the silent stillness it echoed, thudding inside her head. The man was intentionally making her tense. Why? Regardless, she resented it. Suspecting him of involvement in Carolyn's accident had her tense enough — if it had been an accident. *Please* let it have been an accident because Maggie couldn't bring herself to even think that awful "M" word.

The Tiffany light above the table set his hair to gleaming blue-black, accentuated the slope of his perfect nose, and hid his eyes in shadows. "Why are you here?" she asked, though she hadn't meant to. The words just had tumbled out.

He unfolded his napkin then smoothed it over his knees. "I'm hungry."

Maggie mimicked the gesture. "I meant, here at the inn."

"I like it here."

She held off a sigh. "Are you always so sociable?"

"Pretty much." He slid his gaze over her face. "Especially when the matchmaking queen is hard at it."

Surprise streaked up Maggie's back. Just the thought of getting back into the dating scene after her two-year absence made her stomach knot. Returning to it with Mac-Gregor made her absolutely nauseous. "Not interested."

"Me, either."

"Good. Then maybe now you can be civil. I know it'll tax your good nature — providing you have one. I can't say I've seen so much as a hint of it."

"It left with the tourists." Something dark glinted in his eyes.

Unable to peg it, Maggie shifted on her chair. What had Carolyn seen in the man? True, so long as he kept his acid mouth shut, he was gorgeous. The things he did for a simple white shirt and navy cashmere sweater should come with *Unsuspecting Women Beware* warning labels. But the minute he opened his mouth, his attitude made the man insufferable.

Miss Hattie bustled back into the dining room, carrying an aromatic platter of roast beef surrounded by new potatoes and fresh carrots that smelled heavenly.

"Tyler, be a dear and pour Maggie some wine, mmm?"

"No, thank you. I don't drink." Seeing what alcohol had done to her father, and consequently to her mother, had made even an occasional glass of wine turn bitter on Maggie's tongue.

"I've a fresh pitcher of iced tea, if you'd like some. Lemon's already wedged." Miss Hattie put the platter onto the table. "Tyler, will you carve?"

"Sure."

"First get Maggie the tea, please. I'm a bit weary." She gave him a totally false sigh. "Oh, Maggie, go with him, dear — so you can see where I keep the glasses and such."

Though she'd rather walk barefoot on a bed of hot coals than into the kitchen with MacGregor, Maggie stood up and followed him.

It was a warm room with a homey, lived-in feeling, decorated in light oak with white lacy curtains at the windows and pretty ceramic canisters lining the white counter. A large bowl of porcelain bisque, yellow daffodils rested on the round, oak table, and a second bowl filled with red apples, bananas, and oranges rested on the counter edge. Before the corner fireplace sat a red rocker — obviously a favorite spot to rest, judging by the indentations in the checked cushions — and a toasty fire burned in the grate. Moisture seeped from the logs and the crackling blaze soothed her frayed nerves.

"Glasses are here." MacGregor opened the cabinet door next to the fridge, pulled out a tall, square-cut glass, then stuck it under the ice dispenser in the fridge door. "Crushed or cubes?"

"Cubes." Were his neck an option, her choice might have been different. "Please."

The ice plopped down and clinked into the glass. The fridge motor clicked on and whirred softly. "You can lighten up anytime, MacGregor. We've established I'm not after your body — or anything else."

"Remember our deal? You stay out of my way, and I'll stay out of yours."

The fire snapped and hissed. Crazy as it seemed, she had the feeling the fire was angry. Or maybe disappointed. She glanced through the screen at the gold and blue flames curling over the logs and, sensing nothing in the least strange, silently chided herself for letting her imagination run wild.

"I remember our deal." She leaned a hip against the cabinet, eased off her shoe then rubbed her sore arch against the top of her other foot and took the ice-filled glass he offered. "I don't understand why you're determined to be an obnoxious jerk." She stared up at him. "But then, it isn't mandatory I understand, is it?"

The phone rang. Then rang again.

Miss Hattie answered it. Her muffled voice carried through from the entryway into the kitchen.

"No, it isn't mandatory that you under-stand." T.J. stared back at Maggie, a muscle ticking in his jaw.

She schooled accusation from her expres-sion, forcing it bland. The man sent out confusing mixed signals. One minute, he wielded sarcasm as if it were a weapon. The next minute, he wore it as a shield. Which was it? One, the other, or both?

Time for an olive branch. "I really don't want anything from you, but I might be able to help. Something's obviously wrong. Won't you tell me what it is?"

T.J. grabbed the ironstone pitcher and filled her glass. What wasn't wrong would be an easier question to answer. Maggie wasn't after him — when he'd mentioned it, her reaction removed any doubts he might have had on that — so why couldn't he drop the anal act and treat her decently?

That he didn't know why irked him. That he suspected he didn't *want* to know why irked him more. Maybe she kind of, sort of, in an atypical, illogical way, appealed to him.

He grimaced. Of course she appealed to him. She was a beautiful woman and he'd been here without any woman for a long time. Of course, she appealed. And, of course, her appeal to him irked him. What man with a record for destroying women he loved wouldn't be irked at the first sign of attraction to another woman? Especially a woman he'd deliberately treated shabbily who still reached out a hand to help him?

"Everything's fine," he lied. "Lemon's in the fridge. Top shelf."

Miss Hattie came in, wearing her black coat. "I'm afraid you two will have to excuse me." She scooted around T.J. and retrieved a covered dish of something from the fridge. "Jimmy's gone and gotten himself sick, rescuing those stranded drivers. The boy is sneezing and hacking something awful already. I'm going over to see about him."

"I'm sorry to hear that, Miss Hattie." Maggie sounded sincere.

She no doubt was sincere. The thought of sharing a meal alone with him couldn't hold much appeal. T.J. looked at Miss Hattie. "Can't Lucy check on Jimmy? She's right next door, and you shouldn't be out in that mess. You'll get sick yourself."

"Bah, I never get sick. Too stubborn, most likely. Anyway, Jimmy needs some hot chicken soup." She hiked the bowl, balancing it on her hip. "Oh, I nearly forgot, Tyler. Vic was late with the mail today. You've got about a half-dozen catalogues and two travel magazines on the desk."

"Sounds like Vic's been to the Grange

dance again." T.J. grinned.

"Afraid so." Miss Hattie sighed indulgently. "The man is awfully hard on his feet. But, my, he loves to dance." She headed toward the back door. "Just leave the dishes. I'll see to them later."

"Be careful." Tyler frowned at her back, then returned to the dining room.

Miss Hattie dropped her voice to a whisper. "Maggie, dear, forgive Tyler. He's upset because he can't walk me over to Jimmy's. Be patient with him, mmm?"

Why couldn't he walk Miss Hattie over to Jimmy's? Maggie started to ask, but felt guilty about prying when she herself held a mountain of secrets. Instead, she nodded.

Seconds later the door closed behind Miss Hattie, and Maggie went back to eat dinner, certain it'd be the longest meal in her life. A shame really. With its attractive wainscoting, pretty pink-floral-on–navy-blue wallpaper that matched the pads on the chair seats, and its crown molding, the dining room was as charming as the rest of the house. A long, shiny buffet rested against the west wall, and three huge windows defined the south. Behind Maggie, French doors led to a veranda that she pictured laden in summer with hanging baskets brimming with marigolds, petunias, and impatiens.

T.J. sliced the roast. Though huge, his hands moved swiftly, deftly, and she suffered a totally unreasonable urge to see them busy doing his work. "When you aren't hassling women in the bath or sending them sprawling over tons of luggage in hallways, what do you do, MacGregor?"

"I did paint." He didn't meet her eyes.

Past tense. An odd chill whisked over her nape. "Paint?"

He motioned for her plate. "Paint."

She passed it over. Like pulling teeth. "What did you paint?"

"Miss Hattie claims I did a wicked job on her gazebo and greenhouse."

Why was he lying to her? "Greenhouse. That explains the fresh flowers everywhere. They're all yellow, too — even the porcelain ones on the kitchen table. Have you noticed that?"

He nodded. "She gripes about the expense — the woman's as frugal as only a Mainer can be — but she loves tending the flowers. She has a real touch with them." He filled her plate. "Lucy Baker says keeping fresh flowers is Hattie's duty." He lifted the meat fork. "And before you ask, no, I don't know what she meant by that."

Maggie accepted her plate back, then took a sip of tangy tea. "Who's Lucy Baker?" He'd mentioned her several times.

"She and her husband, Fred, run the Blue Moon Cafe. Fred's homegrown. Sits on the Planning and Zoning Commission."

T.J. was confusing her again. Maggie frowned. "Why are you smirking?"

"Fred took the commission seat because he hates tourists. They don't respect the land like locals do."

"I'm figuring that eventually you'll get around to explaining that smirk, Mac-Gregor. What does Fred hating tourists have to do with it?"

"He married one."

Maggie felt her lips curve. "Where's Lucy from?"

"Mississippi, but Fred calls her a pseudo-local. Her father was from here. He relocated in Mississippi with his job, but Lucy and her family came back here every summer."

"Sounds like a good family life. Refreshing, these days." A stab of envy slipped into Maggie's voice. Realizing she'd spoken aloud, and not wanting to be pressed to explain, she quickly added, "What's Lucy like?"

"She's a great cook, and she chews a mean

piece of gum." He paused to reach for the salt, sprinkled his potatoes, and then continued. "But she's a bit of a romantic."

"Ah." Maggie cut into her meat. The knife slid right through, promising it would be tender, and the smell of garlic had her mouth watering. "So she fell in love with Fred and stayed in Maine."

"Actually, she says she fell in love with Maine and married Fred to stay."

"Seriously?"

"No, just Lucy's sense of humor." He paused and cocked his head. "At least, I think it is. She seems nuts about Fred, but who knows? Appearances can be . . . deceptive. Especially in relationships."

"True." To outsiders, Maggie's parents had seemed the perfect couple, and nothing could have been further from the truth.

T.J. spooned a large serving of carrots onto his plate. "You never mentioned why you're here."

Dangerous Ground warnings flashed in her mind. She chewed slowly, then swallowed. She'd better stick as close as possible to the truth. "I needed a rest."

"From what?" Clearly surprised, he stabbed a hot-buttered carrot with his fork then raked it into his mouth.

"My mother was injured in an accident.

I've spent the last several years caring for her." Her hand shook. Had she been too specific?

He looked down at his plate. His voice lost its acidity, almost gentled. "Did she . . . recover?"

Strange. He seemed genuinely empathetic. Because of Carolyn? "Yes, she did."

Empathetic? Genuine? Impossible. Maggie took another bite of hot, succulent roast, warning herself to be careful here. This man was *not* what he seemed.

As soon as the thought formed in her mind, a whisper of heat crept over her skin as if verifying the thought. Again feeling watched, Maggie instinctively turned to look behind her. But, as on the stairs earlier, she saw no one. Nothing except the French doors, which were tightly closed.

"Something wrong?"

T.J.'s voice startled her. Maggie whipped back around in her chair and forced a smile to her lips. "No. No, everything is fine."

He watched her warily, and she tilted her head. "There's something . . . I don't know . . . special about this house. Do you feel it?"

He didn't answer. Just chewed his food and stared daggers at her.

What had she done wrong now? Well,

shoot. At this rate, they'd both die of old age before she got past his first line of defense. "Have you been here long?"

"Yes." He speared a potato.

And he didn't like it. So why didn't he leave? "Mmm." She sipped at her tea. The chilled glass was sweating, and droplets of moisture ran down it in rivulets to the tablecloth. "How long will you stay?"

"Until I leave."

Why did he sound upset? Evasive? "Miss Hattie mentioned magazines. Do you enjoy traveling?"

He polished off his last carrot, dabbed at his lips with his napkin, then stood up. "If you'll excuse me. This session of Twenty Questions is over." He lifted his plate, then went into the kitchen.

Maggie let out a frustrated sigh. Something wasn't right here. What it was, she didn't have a clue. But MacGregor reeked of being a man in trouble — and one peeved to the tips of his arrogant ears about something. The question was what. Did it have anything to do with Carolyn?

After finishing her meal alone, Maggie took her plate and the platter into the kitchen.

MacGregor stood at the sink scrubbing a blue enamel roasting pan, his arms submerged in hot, soapy water up to his elbows.

She set her plate onto the counter and, when he finished rinsing the pan, she grabbed a dishcloth and reached for it. "I'll dry."

He frowned, didn't utter so much as a whisper, but passed the pan.

She took it, her cool fingers brushing against his warm, wet ones. Their gazes locked. Emotions fumbled through Mac-Gregor's eyes. Hope. Bitterness. Then anger. His frown deepened. Before he could smart-off at her, she gave him her best, disgusted look. "I don't know how long you've been here, MacGregor, but your social skills could stand a little elbow grease."

"I'm not social." He plunged the lid into the suds. A wall of water splashed onto the counter.

"No kidding?" She cupped her hand and swiped the water back into the sink, then patted the counter dry with the cloth.

He scrubbed the pan lid until she thought the enamel would be worn clean through. An apple in the fruit bowl looked entirely too tempting. She grabbed it. Sidling up to MacGregor at the sink, she stole the stream of water he was using to rinse the pan, and washed off her apple. Lord, but it irked her to look at his shoulder. To see his face, she'd have to crane her neck. "Thanks."

"You always eat so much?"

She took a crunchy bite. It was sweet and firm — perfect. "Yes, I do."

He held out a clean plate, waiting for her to take it. "Better watch it. Your metabolism might shut down on you."

Droplets of water sprinkled steadily onto the floor. "You think I'm fat?"

"Not yet."

The man sounded about as interested as if he'd been discussing drippy weather. Good thing she wasn't in this for an ego boost. Her mother's flatter-than-a-flitter expression regarding stomachs took on a whole new meaning. "Hate to break it to you, MacGregor, but your sleeve is getting soaked."

"It'll dry." He reached into the sink and pulled out the plug. "Good night."

"Good night." So much for accomplishing anything tonight. She munched her disappointment, taking it out on the apple, still having no idea why the man was here.

T.J. turned out the dining room light, then just stood there in the darkness. Maggie Wright worried him. She was a beautiful woman who watched him like a hawk. It

75

wasn't an appreciative woman/man kind of look, though. More like she expected at any second he'd sprout a spare head.

He leaned back against the wall and let his fingertips drift over the smooth, wainscoted wood. Worse, he couldn't, shake the feeling that her seemingly innocent questions actually were pointed and razor-sharp. He told himself again that she'd just been making polite conversation with a stranger, but he didn't believe it. Though he knew he couldn't trust his instincts, he wished he could, because she sure didn't strike him as a woman on a resting vacation.

An odd tingling started in his toes.

It worked its way up his legs, crept through his stomach, then spread through his chest and up his neck, into his head. What in the world was happening to him now?

He tried to move and couldn't. Knowing only Maggie Wright would hear him, he tried to yell out, but he couldn't make a sound.

The grandfather clock ticked louder and louder until it pounded inside his head, blocking out all other sounds. The rhythm suddenly altered to a deep, melodic whisper. It wasn't a trick of the mind. He heard a whisper. A man's whisper. A message meant for him. A warning.

She's on a mission. On a mission. On a mission . . .

The whisper ceased.

The clock's ticks returned to normal, then softened, and the sounds of the house, of the sleet slanting against the roof and pinging against the windows, returned. And, as suddenly as it had started, the tingling inside his body stopped.

Shaky, T.J. dragged in a great gulp of air, but didn't risk trying to move. Instinctively he knew the room was empty. So who had whispered that message to warn him? Who . . . or what?

He was losing it. It couldn't have happened. It had to have been his imagination. Of course, it had been. Stress-induced. Not insane, but psychological — just as Bill Butler had said.

Footsteps sounded. Seconds later, Maggie walked down the gallery toward the stairs, humming and clearly not realizing T.J. stood there in the darkness.

She's on a mission.

Wary, T.J. followed her.

Midway up the stairs, she stopped and studied Cecelia Freeport's painting, touching the canvas with delicate fingertips, as if it were fragile glass she feared would shatter.

Carolyn crossed his mind. She and Maggie didn't resemble each other, or even stand or move alike. But the way Maggie touched Cecelia's painting bitterly reminded T.J. of the way Carolyn had caressed his painting of Seascape Inn. Man, had she given him grief over that painting.

Her guard down, Maggie let out a sigh that T.J. felt in his bones. Because he suffered the same malady, he recognized it instantly in her. The woman was in trouble.

But what kind of trouble? Was it the reason she'd come here? What was her mission?

When she walked on, he took to the stairs, pausing and touching Cecelia's painting as Maggie had. Warmed by the overhead light, the paint felt smooth, though the canvas beneath it added substance and texture. Paint reminded him a lot of skin.

A warm spark of heat ignited inside him. A flicker of healing, of peace. Only a flicker, but how he savored it. His eyes filmed over and he blinked hard. It'd been so long since he'd felt either.

"MacGregor!"

Startled, he jumped, jerked his hand away from the canvas and stared up the stairs to the landing. Empty. Ah, she'd found them. And she was indignant as all get out about

78

finding them.

Grinning, he rushed upstairs.

At the landing, he paused and deliberately slowed his pace to a swagger. "You bellowed, Miss Wright?"

Standing outside the door to her room, she snatched her underwear off the doorknob. "What do you think you're doing?"

He leaned a shoulder against the hallway wall and crossed his chest with his arms. "You mean you didn't want your underwear back?"

"Where did you get them?" She perched a hand on her hip. "Have you been in my room?"

"You left them in the bathroom."

Narrowing her eyes, she balled the fragile snippet of lace in her fist. "If you hadn't nagged and threatened me out of the bathroom, I wouldn't have forgotten them there." She marched back to him, her shoulders stiff enough to snap. "Was it really necessary to hang them on my doorknob?"

"No." He shrugged. "But I figured you'd take exception to me putting them in your room."

"You could've just left them in the bathroom."

He slid her his best innocent look. "You mean you weren't issuing me an invitation?"

Her face went apple-red and her shoulders hiked up a full three inches. "Fat chance."

"Mmm, then I highly recommend you be more careful about the signals you're sending."

Her jaw gaped. She sputtered. Sent him a glower he'd still be feeling in his grave. Then turned and stormed down the hall, back to her room.

Holding the doorknob in a death grip, she looked back at him. "You are one arrogant jerk, MacGregor. So arrogant it's hard to believe you can stuff all your arrogance inside your body."

"Thank you." He smiled.

"That wasn't a compliment."

"Sounded like one from here."

"A walking miracle," she muttered, convinced that was absolute truth. It *was* a miracle no one had killed him yet.

"Haven't you heard, Maggie? There are no miracles."

He stepped into his room and softly shut the door.

A pang of pity slid through her, head to heels.

What was that all about? The man deserved a lot of things, but pity sure didn't rank among them. Still, she would rather he'd yelled at her again than sounded so

disillusioned. He'd looked disillusioned, too.
And despairing. No.
   No, not despairing.
   He'd looked . . . haunted.

CHAPTER 3

"I still think we should put a pad on the rocks, Tyler." Huddled deep in her sturdy black coat, Miss Hattie slid him a worried look, her stiff collar hiked up around her ears.

"We can't risk it." Bill Butler sniffled, his nose buried in a forest-green muffler. "Anything straddling the boundary could extend it. We won't know if the painting worked or not."

"He's right." T.J. curled his fingers around the painting's frame, avoiding eye contact with the canvas he'd painted of Seascape Inn. He gripped it so hard that his red fingertips turned white.

"All right." Miss Hattie blinked, stuffed her hands deep into her pockets. "I agree it makes sense and it could have an effect. But, Tyler, you must believe in your heart that this is going to work. I would say that's vitally important."

He couldn't believe it. How could he? He hoped — good grief, how he hoped — it would work, but he didn't dare to believe it. Live with another failure? See another little piece of himself die? No, he didn't dare to believe. He'd lost too many of those he'd loved and far too much of himself already.

Still, Miss Hattie looked so worried. She needed the lie, and he couldn't stand the thought of disappointing her. "I'll believe it," he told her then quickly looked at Bill. She was too intuitive, and she'd told him a hundred times that his eyes mirrored his soul. Even if she couldn't see the truth, looking into her eyes and deliberately lying to her rankled — regardless that he'd done it for her own peace of mind.

Bill locked gazes with T.J. and gave him an encouraging nod. His gentle umber eyes shone support and approval. He knew the truth. He knew T.J. didn't dare to believe the painting would work. And his friend's silent message was that he understood and believed enough for both of them.

Swallowing hard, praying that friendship with him didn't somehow kill Bill, too, T.J. nodded back and stepped up to the invisible boundary line. Sweat trickled down his temples, rolled over his ribs. He dragged his foot through the coarse sand, drawing the line, then closed his eyes and focused hard, concentrating all of his energy on the healing he'd once received at Seascape Inn. The healing that had restored his ability to create the painting he now held in his hands. The painting Bill and Miss Hattie — and half the time he — hoped would act as a conduit to his subconscious to free him from Seascape.

Images flashed through his mind. Images of him arriving here, all those years ago. Images of him feeling that sense of peace and calm and serenity that Maggie Wright had been feeling, and T.J. had been envying, last night at dinner.

She'd been right, too. Seascape Inn *was* special. Very special.

Another image flashed. He saw himself crossing the line, walking into the village and waving to Jimmy, whose long, brown hair needed a trim. Though in a squat, changing a flat tire on Horace Johnson's dusty blue '53 GMC pick-up truck, Jimmy paused to wave back. His brown eyes never missed a thing — by necessity, T.J. supposed. Jimmy had always had to look out for himself. T.J. walked on, then paused again at Miss Millie's Antique Shoppe's big window. Sitting in her rocker, she sipped at a cup of steaming tea, enjoying the warmth from her Franklin stove. He smelled the wood burning, heard its friendly popping. Next door, Fred Baker was sweeping the porch of the Blue Moon Cafe, hiding the dirt behind a huge anchor propped against the wall, his gold nugget ring catching the sunlight and, across the street, the stuffy, social-climbing Lydia Johnson, who'd renamed herself Lily years ago because it sounded more regal to her, stood near the gas pumps at The Store, overdressed and all excited, telling the pastor about her and Horace's new Slurpee drink machine. "It's the height of modernization," she said, preening. T.J. shunned the urge to shake some sense into her. The woman wanted it all and was so busy running after it all that she didn't realize she already had everything worth having: her family's love.

Pulling the sights and sounds and smells of small-town life into his heart and holding them close, T.J. issued himself his standard pre-attempt reminder, then stepped across the line.

For a long moment, he stood there feeling as if he were dangling at the edge of some invisible, mystical precipice. Hope flared in his heart. The wind burned his eyes, but he was afraid to blink. If he moved, would he break the magical spell and fall?

His instincts screamed at him to run, but he couldn't move. Seemingly suspended in this mysterious place that was neither there nor here, he felt torn, at war with himself. Did he risk taking another step? Did he risk losing what could prove to be his only opportunity to run for his life?

He had to run!

As quickly as the thought properly formed, the temperature plummeted.

That veil of icy mist blanketed him.

Those hated fingers of cold applied debilitating pressure at the soft hollow of his shoulder. And his hope died.

"Nooo!" he screamed. *"Nooo!"*

What on earth were they doing out there?

Kneeling on the turret's window seat in her room, Maggie sank into the soft cushion pads and leaned closer to the glass. Bill and Miss Hattie stood watching MacGregor as if he were about to singlehandedly evoke the Second Coming.

Thank goodness she'd phoned Bill last night and asked him not to mention she and Carolyn had been related. It had taken some talking, but he'd finally agreed. Too, he'd imparted an interesting bit of information. MacGregor believed Carolyn had been an orphan. Technically, that had been true, but why hadn't she mentioned Maggie's parents or Maggie to him? She'd lived with the family from the time she'd been orphaned at twelve until she'd graduated high school.

Miss Hattie and Bill backed away from MacGregor. Why was he standing on the rocks holding the painting from Lakeview Gallery of Seascape Inn? Why was he drawing a line in the sand with his foot?

He closed his eyes and just stood there. Maggie clocked him on her watch. A minute, twenty-four seconds. Was he praying? Meditating? What?

He stepped over the line. Just stood there, still and stiff as a statue. Maggie glanced at Miss Hattie — definitely worried — and then at Bill. Hands clenched at his sides, he looked serious. Solemn. Scared.

MacGregor jerked. The painting flew through the air toward Bill as if MacGregor had tossed it. Bill caught it, and Maggie looked back at MacGregor just as he spun around. He glared back at the house, an expression of horror, then sheer terror, on his face, and he screamed: *"Nooo! Nooo!"*

Maggie gripped the window sash and squeezed. MacGregor was swinging his fists. What was he fighting? There was nothing there. And why were Miss Hattie and Bill just . . . standing there watching him? Not trying to calm him down? Not moving an inch toward him? Should Maggie go down there?

MacGregor slapped his left hand to his right shoulder, gripping and grimacing and bending and twisting, as if trying to release himself from some awful, wrenching hold. What was happening to him? Was he having some kind of seizure?

It couldn't be. Certainty slammed into her with the force of a sledge. Whatever was happening to him, Miss Hattie and Bill Butler had expected it. Miss Hattie's lack of alarm proved it. Bill's lack of assistance verified it.

MacGregor fell to the ground.

Maggie watched, horrified. She couldn't move.

Bill calmly walked over to MacGregor, circled the larger man from behind, wrapping his arms around MacGregor's ribs, then dragged him over the rocks back onto what must be the Seascape side of the line T.J. had marked. Gently, Bill lowered MacGregor back to the ground, released him, then backed away.

When Miss Hattie bent down, Bill retrieved the painting and checked it over. Looking for damage? Miss Hattie did the same thing to MacGregor, running her

88

hands over his scalp. Evidently she was satisfied that he wasn't seriously hurt because she reached beneath her coat and into her apron pocket, withdrew her hankie, then fluttered it over MacGregor's face.

Was he unconscious?

This was definitely strange. Shocking and strange. Something glinted on the window and Maggie shifted to see past it, her heart thumping hard in her chest. Frankly, this whole episode went beyond strange. It was weird. Dark and —

Oh, no. It couldn't be some kind of cult ritual. Miss Hattie? Bill? Involved in a cult? Not even MacGregor could be involved in a cult.

So what *was* going on?

MacGregor sat up, rubbed at the back of his head, and said something to Miss Hattie, who was fussing over him, plucking dry, dead grass from his coat and hair.

They talked back and forth, with Bill adding something intermittently, then Bill and Miss Hattie began walking back toward the house.

Miss Hattie glanced up at Maggie's window.

To avoid being seen, Maggie leaned back, away from the glass. But it wasn't her window Miss Hattie stared at as if she were highly peeved. It was the attic bedroom window — or maybe the room below it. But why would Miss Hattie be glowering at her own rooms?

When they walked under the porch roof below her own windows, Maggie could no longer see them. She darted her gaze back to MacGregor. Where had he gone?

He hadn't moved.

His shoulders slumped, knees bent, feet flat on the brown grass, he sat on the rocks, looking out through the sheer haze to the open sea.

Waves of despair washed through Maggie. Despair she somehow knew was his. He had been in physical pain during the course of whatever had been happening out there, but now that it was over, his pain hadn't subsided. It had strengthened and deepened, invaded his spirit and soul, and she felt it as if it were her own pain.

Stunned, weakened by its powerful force, she rested her forehead against the glass and fought letting the sympathetic tears blurring her eyes fall to her face. Maggie Wright *never* cried.

An unbidden thought spilled through her mind on a whisper. *Help him.*

On Saturday, Maggie witnessed the same scene again, minus Bill and Miss Hattie, who for reasons unknown to Maggie were absent.

On Sunday, shortly after Miss Hattie had left for church, Maggie watched MacGregor's third attempt. Watched him fail. Watched him then sit on the rocks and stare out to sea for over two hours. And again she suffered those same waves of despair. Heard that same muffled but calm and insistent voice whisper: *Help him.*

Maggie wanted to help him. It was frightening to watch him fall, and it sickened her that she had watched and hadn't lifted a finger much less rushed out to see if he was all right. She would have. She'd tried. But for some mystical reason, when *he* had fallen, *she* hadn't been able to move.

It was as if some unseen hand held her there on the cushions at the window, reducing her to doing no more than watching, waiting, holding her breath and gripping the window sash so tightly her arms ached to her elbows, until MacGregor sat up and she saw with her own two eyes that he was okay.

She denied it at first. But each time she witnessed his attempt and failure, the waves of despair in her grew stronger, hurt her deeper. Each time, the calm, steady whisper grew a little louder and clearer, a little more insistent — and a lot more frightening.

T.J. grabbed the bannister, started up the stairs, and saw Maggie, standing looking at Cecelia's portrait. He walked on, then stopped three steps below her.

"Who are they, MacGregor?"

Her question surprised him. She hadn't shown a sign of knowing him there. "The Freeports bought the land from the Stanfords and built this house in nineteen eighteen. Collin carved all those boats and fowl in the case in the living room. Talented man."

"I'll have to go look at them. Haven't made it down there yet." Maggie leaned back against the bannister. "What about her?"

MacGregor leaned back, too. His arm brushed against Maggie's shoulder. That she didn't move away pleased him. After yet another failure, the warmth of another person, even impersonal and seemingly innocent warmth, felt good. "Cecelia assisted the village doctor until he died. For years, she and Collin tried to find another doctor to come to the village, but they never did. The locals kept coming to Cecelia to treat them."

"Did she?"

"As much as possible, yes, she did."

"A healer." Maggie looked up at him and smiled. "I sensed she was special."

"She must have been." The urge to paint Maggie seeped through T.J.'s chest, into his arms, and set his fingers to itching to pick up a brush. Knowing the futility and frustration that attempt would bring, he buried the urge deep inside him, then folded his arms across his chest to hold it there. "They say the night Cecelia died, hundreds of villagers and people she'd helped came out into the bitter cold and held a candlelight vigil on the front lawn. Mothers with babies she'd brought into the world, those she'd healed and kept from prematurely departing it. Must have been something."

"Mmm, kind of makes you feel if you aren't as devoted to others as she was, you're just taking up space, doesn't it?" Maggie studied Cecelia's face, as if trying to figure out something. "What do you think it is, MacGregor? Do the rest of us lack some special gene or something?"

"Maybe." He shrugged. "Or maybe it's got to do with looking out rather than in."

She swiveled her gaze up to his. Her brow wrinkled. "Looking out what?"

"Outside ourselves. Cecelia definitely looked out."

"I don't get it."

He hadn't either for the first couple of months he'd studied the painting. Then as if a light bulb went on in his head, it seemed so simple and clear. He propped his socked foot against the spindle behind him. "It's like when you're going to paint something. You see it with your eyes, but you feel it with every fiber in you. It isn't until you feel it in here," he cupped his fingers and thumped them against his chest, "that you can paint something and do it justice. For Cecelia, healing was like that. She felt it in here."

"Empathy versus sympathy." Maggie nodded.

"Yeah." Quick, and a lot more intuitive than he'd given her credit for being.

Maggie smiled. "So how did you learn all this — about the house, and them?" She nodded toward the portraits. A shadow streaked across her chin.

"Miss Hattie. She's lived here most of her life. Loves this house and everyone in it."

"Sometimes I get the feeling she's reading my mind. Not like a psychic, or anything like that. I don't know. Like she somehow sees inside me."

"I've had that feeling, too." Why had he admitted that? It opened the door to all kinds of questions he didn't want asked because he'd have to refuse to answer them.

"It doesn't bother me, really. It's just sort of" — she shrugged — "oddly comforting. As if you're unconditionally accepted as you are and you don't have to explain anything." Maggie worried her lower lip with her teeth. "When you painted the gazebo, did you look outward?"

She knew. He felt his face flush. "Um, no."

"But you did when you worked on canvas."

It wasn't a question, more of a statement. He hesitated before answering, certain that if he had any sense, he'd shut this conversation down right now. "Yeah," he said. "Yeah, I did."

"You don't paint on canvas anymore, then?"

He looked away. "I haven't for some time."

"Why not?" She rubbed her forefinger down the bannister.

He stiffened. "I'd rather not talk about it."

"Sorry." She sounded as if she truly meant it. "I didn't mean to pry — and this isn't another session of Twenty Questions. I'm just curious."

"I'll bet you drove your mother nuts."

She grinned. "Just about."

He looked down at her coat. "Are you on your way out?"

She nodded. "I thought I'd walk down to the village and soak up some serenity."

Envy, hot and hard, slammed into him. "Enjoy it."

He stepped around her, then took the rest of the stairs two at a time. Would he ever again be able to say that — that he was going for a walk in the village?

"Hey, MacGregor."

"Yeah?" He paused and looked down at her.

"You're not half bad when you're civil."

He grunted. "Show your appreciation, then. Leave me some hot water."

The weak sun felt good on her back. There were no sidewalks in this part of the village, so Maggie stopped on the worn, dirt path paralleling the street and watched all the activity. Across the street, two African American boys rode their bikes bent-for-leather, speeding dangerously close to the entry of Landry's Landing.

A young woman with a red-and-white bandana circling her forehead like a sweat band rushed outside and cupped her hands at her mouth. "Aaron Butler! You and

96

George slow down before you kill somebody!"

The boys breezed right on, not slowing a bit. Maggie grinned.

A man stepped out of The Store, next door to Landry's. "Aaron, George, you heard Miss Landry! Slow it down!"

He was a plain man in his mid-forties, thin but not frail. His arms covered with dark hair, he propped his elbow atop a gas pump, then reached up and adjusted his green baseball cap. *Local Yokel* was embroidered above its bill.

Maggie walked on. Off to her distant right, she glimpsed a white picket fence. Headstones shone through the slats. A cemetery. Right in front of it sat a pristine little clapboard church with a tall, wooden steeple and a stained-glass window that looked pretty new. Looking at that window, feeling calm and restful again, Maggie made a vow. Come Monday, she would not watch MacGregor's attempt.

Whatever was happening with him had nothing to do with her and it shouldn't rob her of peace. Besides, she had her own agenda here. Carolyn.

Hooking a U-turn, Maggie headed back down the path, back toward the inn. She'd given MacGregor several opportunities to tell her about his troubles, but he'd elected not to do so. And, aside from the odd event that took place each morning on the shore, everything at the inn seemed the same as it had before she'd become aware of anything unusual occurring.

MacGregor acted like his habitual sarcastic and nagging self, though admittedly he had softened a bit on the civility front earlier today on the stairs. Miss Hattie continued being her usual angelic self. That woman really was a treasure. And Maggie's conscience pestered her constantly because she hadn't helped MacGregor. Seeing a stone, she nicked it with the tip of her sneaker. But she just might feel more guilty than pestered because a part of her wanted to help him. That made her disloyal to Carolyn, didn't it?

The post office's shadow slanted across the path. Maggie stepped into it and saw Vic Sampson through the window. Polishing the brass framing the glass fronts of the old-fashioned post office boxes that lined the wall, he glanced up and clearly recognized her from when he'd delivered mail to the inn. She'd never seen boxes with dial combinations before, though she'd heard of them. Quaint, but hadn't the postal system recalled them all? Mmm, how had Sea

Haven Village managed to keep theirs?

Vic shook the cloth in a greeting and mouthed, "Hi, Maggie."

Glad to see a familiar face, she lifted a hand and smiled back, then walked on. Maybe if she just had *tried* to help Mac-Gregor her conscience would stop badgering her. Turning her back on anyone in trouble reeked of indifference to their suffering, and wasn't indifference just the worst kind of insult? She'd always respected anyone who — right or wrong — loved or hated and fought for or against anything with the passion of their convictions. It was the bystanders, those who elected not to get involved, those who didn't care, that she'd held in disdain. She frowned. Now she was one of them.

The porch of the Blue Moon Cafe was freshly swept and empty of people. To the right of the front door, a blue moon had been painted on the green cinderblock wall. Like everything else this close to the sea and its salt, it had weathered and faded a little. The sheriff's car was parked in the lot.

Rounding a rough cedar staircase, Maggie nearly collided with a short, stooped woman who rushed to the cafe's door on thin, bird-like legs. Her coattail flapping behind her, she muttered something about a Mister

High Britches needing a reminder that she'd once been his teacher. She deserved a little respect and he was going to give it to her or she was going to blister his ears.

Maggie skirted a half-barrel of orange silk flowers, replacing those in the dirt that surely bloomed there in summer, and the biggest anchor she'd ever seen, rusted and propped against the wall with a little mound of dirt hidden behind it. She caught a whiff of fried chicken. If she weren't so troubled, she would've stopped in and had some. But she was troubled so, heavy-footed, she kept walking, silently reviling MacGregor. Even here, she couldn't get the man off her mind.

Near Fisherman's Co-Op, she saw a knot of men sitting on its slab slate porch, rocking and laughing around a wire-spool table. Behind it, around the cove on a little point, she saw a lighthouse. The mild wind carried the men's voices, and she heard snatches of stories they were swapping about fishing in the good old days. From the newspaper accounts she'd read, those days were ones preceding the fishing industry being thrust into crisis because of large government-funded boats and hi-tech electronic equipment. The big commercial fishermen had about fished out the Atlantic. Most of the fish caught here flirted with being listed as endangered species. Some already had been dubbed "commercially extinct."

Maggie hurt for the little guy. Many of them third- and fourth-generation fishermen who now were in dire straits, in danger of losing everything they owned.

At the foot of the inn's gravel driveway, she stepped between the rows of firs lining it and headed toward the house. MacGregor was a little guy, too. Not in stature but, like the little fisherman, he stood alone.

She stuffed her hands in her jacket pockets and blew out a heartfelt sigh that made fog of her breath. What if she forgot about Carolyn temporarily and tried to help Mac-Gregor? What could she actually do for him? She didn't even know what was happening out there on the rocks. Or where those strange whispers to her were coming from, though she strongly suspected they were no more than her conscience. What she did know was that watching him disturbed her, hurt her in ways she didn't understand, and that robbed her of the peace and serenity she'd needed and found here.

The last thing she needed in her life was more turmoil. And MacGregor pounded out vibes of having a truckload of it. Well, she had her fair share, too. That's how life worked, wasn't it?

He had his problems, and she had hers. She couldn't afford to be sidetracked by him and lose sight of her reason for being here — he might be a very large part of that reason. She still suspected him of being involved with Carolyn's death, though she had to be honest, with a lot less certainty than when she'd first arrived here. Mac-Gregor clearly was worried. She didn't see his hopelessness growing stronger, but when she watched him attempt and fail to cross that line, she sure felt it. *That* worried her. And it made her feel even more guilty. Still, her first loyalty was to Carolyn. Guilty or innocent of manipulation, Carolyn was family.

No, Maggie promised herself, on Monday she would not watch MacGregor's attempt. She wasn't being hard or cold or indifferent — she'd even warned him — she simply had no sympathy to spare.

First light streamed in through Maggie's windows. She opened her eyes, stretched, slid out from under the warm quilts, then padded over to the window seat and looked outside.

Dawn had come, but the sky remained a dull, weak gray, as if it struggled under November and prayed hard for an early spring. She'd left the window shade up to catch first light. Sounds carried in the quiet house, and she hadn't wanted to risk awakening MacGregor by setting an alarm.

It was Monday. She'd made a vow and she intended to keep it. She would *not* watch him. She'd be dressed and down in the village long before MacGregor turned over in his bed much less before he pulled his nasty morning ritual of rapping on the bathroom door and rushing her out.

Ten minutes later, she sneaked down the stairs like a thief, feeling as guilty as she had when at six years old she'd stolen that piece of bubble gum from 7-Eleven. She passed Cecelia's portrait and deliberately avoided looking at it. Still, knowing she'd passed it, Maggie felt guilt sink deeper into her and it weighed heavily on her conscience. Cecelia would have found a way to help MacGregor.

The third stair creaked.

Maggie's heart thundered. She stopped, darted her gaze back to the landing, expecting MacGregor to appear any second and look at her with those accusing gray eyes.

When he didn't, she breathed easier, rushed down the last of the steps, then on into the kitchen.

The smells were wonderful.

Miss Hattie took a pan of fresh blueberry muffins out of the oven and set them on the white counter, then closed the oven door. "My, but you're up with the chickens this morning."

Maggie's face went hot. More guilt poured acid into her stomach. "I saw a lighthouse on my walk yesterday. I wanted a closer look."

"Mmm." Miss Hattie pulled the mitt off her hand and set it aside. "Aren't you going to have breakfast first?" She reached into a cabinet and pulled out a pretty rose-pattern plate.

"Those do smell sinfully good," she said, watching Miss Hattie transfer the muffins from the pan to the plate, "but I'm anxious to get going."

"I see." Miss Hattie's green eyes sparkled. She took a white cloth from a stack on the counter, freshly laundered or brand new, from the looks of them. "Well, take a muffin or two with you to bribe Hatch for the full tour. He loves muffins."

"Hatch?" Maggie zipped up her blue and green parka. Her boots were in the mud room. Was she forgetting something important? No, no. She'd talked with her mother last night, and she'd been fine. A little more time to adjust . . .

"Hatch is the lighthouse keeper," Miss Hattie said, setting three muffins inside the cloth. She caught the corners, drew them up, then folded them over the muffins. "Well, he was. The lighthouse isn't functional anymore, of course. Coast Guard took over all of them a couple of years ago. Automated them."

The twist of Miss Hattie's lips clearly conveyed her opinion on that bit of progress. She opposed. "So Hatch was tossed out?"

"Oh my, no." She refilled the muffin pan from a large stainless bowl still half-full of batter. "The Judge would never sit still for that. He worked out a special deal with the Coast Guard about our lighthouse. Not sure how he did it, exactly, but he said something about humanitarian reasons." She slid the pan into the oven, then passed Maggie the cloth-wrapped muffins. "Hatch was born, raised, and has grown old in that lighthouse. Moving would've killed him, and that's fact. He can stay there, so long as the light isn't functional."

Maggie took the muffins. They felt warm against her palm. "I never thought of the Coast Guard as having a heart before, but clearly it does. That's comforting, isn't it?"

"I think so," Miss Hattie said, "and I

reckon Hatch does, too. Very wise man, Hatch."

Maggie walked toward the door to the mud room. "There's a lot of comforting things here, Miss Hattie." Maggie gestured with the muffins. "Thank you."

The white-haired angel patted her soiled apron and looked at Maggie through those sparkling emerald, too-seeing eyes. "We're all capable of comforting, dear. Sometimes it's the comfort that's hardest to give that brings the greatest rewards. Remember that, mmm?"

Feeling the warm whisper of heat warning her of something significant happening that she'd felt before, Maggie blinked, nodded, then blinked again. For some reason, she sensed approval. "I will," she said softly, then nearly knocked to her knees by guilt about MacGregor, she went out to the mud room and closed the door.

By the time she'd skirted the back corner of the house and stepped onto the flagstone walk, she'd changed her mind fifty times, torn between going on and going back and watching MacGregor.

She had to stop this. Brushing against an evergreen, she saw a bed of giant delphiniums that had lost the battle to winter. Their stems drooped and what remained of their dull and faded blossoms kissed the ground.

Tears formed in Maggie's eyes. Cursing herself as forty kinds of fool, she swore. "I will *not* feel guilty about this." She shouldn't. She'd come here for Carolyn and that's where Maggie's loyalty had to lie. MacGregor was part of that problem . . . maybe. His guilt about Carolyn could be the source of his troubles here.

What about the oddities?

Maggie plucked a leaf off her sleeve. She'd ignore them. The whispers, the despair, and even that flicker of interest she felt for Mac-Gregor she had no business feeling, lied and swore to herself she wasn't feeling and would give just about anything she owned not to be feeling — she'd ignore them all.

Someone was watching her.

At the side of the garage, she came to a dead stop. The feeling burned strong, nearly overwhelming her. She glanced toward the house, scanned the windows, and saw not a soul. Turned, looked across the sweeping lawn to the stretch of firs, let her gaze drift toward the pond, the gazebo, to the little stone wall between Seascape land and the next-door neighbor's. Again, no one. Nothing but the morning haze, the gentle wind rustling the leaves on the evergreens and shimmying the sticklike branches on those left winter-barren.

Help him.

That awful whisper! The hairs on Maggie's neck stood on end. She ran to the front corner of the house, stopped, and stared at the rocks at the boundary line.

"MacGregor."

Her chest muscles clenched. Her breath swooshed out. She couldn't move.

There he stood, as he had all the other times, holding the painting. So still. So very still.

Help him.

"Shut up. Go away," she pleaded. "Please."

Help him.

The peace she'd recaptured drained away. Why couldn't she move? "I can't help him! Don't you see that? I . . . can't!"

Help him, Maggie. The whisper grew stronger, clearer.

Fear streaked up her spine and spiked into the roof of her mouth. She tasted it on her tongue, felt it permeate her every pore. Heaven help her, the whisper hadn't come from her conscience. It hadn't come from her at all.

It had a man's voice.

"Who are you?" She darted her gaze, but didn't see any man anywhere. "How are you doing this?"

Miss Hattie's words flooded her mind. *Sometimes it's the comfort that's hardest to give that brings the greatest rewards.*

"Never mind. I — I don't care how you're doing it. Just stop. Just go away."

Help him.

Maggie cupped her hands over her ears to block out the voices. "Don't you hear me? I can't help him. I can't do it!"

This time is different.

"Who are you? Why are you doing this to me?"

He could die.

MacGregor fell.

"Nooo!" Maggie screamed. She ran, half-sliding, half-falling, down the sloping lawn toward the boundary line. Her feet pounded the ground, jarring her ankles, her knees, her teeth. Her heavy breaths fogged the, air and more than halfway there she realized that whatever had held her captive and had forbidden her to move had released her. Who — what — was it?

Her chest heaving, she dropped to her jeaned knees beside MacGregor. He was so pale! Surprised she still held them, she set the muffins aside on the ground. "Mac-Gregor?"

No answer.

She checked his throat for a pulse and found it steady. It beat hard against her fingertips. "MacGregor?"

No response.

He was still alive. Think, Maggie. Think! She cupped his cool face, pulled back his eyelids with her thumbs and looked at his eyes. They were rolled back in his head. He was unconscious.

What should she do? The voice said to help him. But how? She wasn't a healer! She didn't know what to do.

Frustrated, feeling inadequate, scared stiff to even think about what was happening here, she gritted her teeth, plunged her fingertips through his thick, black hair and glided them over his scalp. No bumps. Was that good?

Geez, had she lost her sense? Of course no bumps was good — unless there was internal swelling. "MacGregor?"

Still no answer.

He'd been out for so long! Much longer than the other times.

This time is different.

He could die.

"Oh, MacGregor. If you knew how lousy I was in a crisis, you'd come around."

In her mind, she saw Bill pulling Mac-Gregor back onto the Seascape side of the boundary line.

"Yes! Yes!" She scrambled to her feet. Shoved, tugged, and pulled until she'd lifted his shoulders and worked her arms around his middle. He was too big. She was too little. She couldn't stretch that far and still gain leverage with her feet. The rocks were so slick!

Fighting panic, she kept her grip, sat down and heaved, hauling his back up against her thighs. His head slammed against her chest. It stung and her jacket zipper cut deep into her skin. Bending her knees, she wedged her boots into hollows in the rocks, then lay back and pulled.

MacGregor moved with her!

Heartened, she scooted back on the dirt-covered rocks, bent her knees, found new footholds, and lay back again. And again, MacGregor scraped the dirt and moved with her.

Certain now that it hadn't been luck, that the method worked, Maggie repeated it again and again, inching closer to the line.

By the time her bottom slid over it, she was exhausted. A little farther, just a little farther, and MacGregor, too, would cross over. Her arms and legs ached, felt as heavy as lead and trembled, water-weak. Her muscles burned, and her backside hurt more than when at twelve she'd tried to impress Sam Grayson by sitting on the hood of her father's car, then lied to him about it. That day, her father had spanked her for the first and last time, and he'd put her on six weeks' restriction.

Carolyn had laughed.

Maggie had cried — and had sat gingerly for two full days. But she'd learned from the experience. Carolyn had told on her because she liked Sam and she wanted Maggie out of the way. That had been but the first of many of Carolyn's manipulations. And the last time that Carolyn, Maggie's father, or anyone else had seen Maggie cry. Not since that day had Maggie allowed herself the luxury of tears.

Finally — *dear heaven, finally!* — MacGregor's loafered feet crossed the line. Maggie twisted and tugged her way free of him, then gently lowered his head to the ground, scraping her knuckles raw on the gritty sand-covered rocks. He still hadn't come to. Why?

What else had Bill and Miss Hattie done?

The handkerchief.

Maggie grimaced, shoved back her sweat-drenched hair. Where was she supposed to get a blasted handkerchief?

The muffins!

A white cloth would just have to do. She rushed over, grabbed it, then ran back, unwrapping the fabric folds and stuffing the muffins into her jacket pockets. She shook the crumbs from the cloth. A script *S* had been sewn inside an oval at one corner. This wasn't a napkin. It was a hankie. A brand new hankie.

Shivering from all that implied, when combined with Miss Hattie's remarks about comforting, Maggie bent low over Mac-Gregor, as Miss Hattie had, then flapped the hankie back and forth near his face. "Come on, MacGregor. Wake up. Would you just wake up?"

His eyelids fluttered, then opened, and he stared up at her. When he focused, disappointment, then regret, flashed through his eyes, and his mouth twisted into a frown.

Maggie stuffed the hankie into her pocket and just looked at him, so relieved she wanted to cry and so choked up she knew if she tried to whisper a single word she'd bawl for hours.

"Oh, no." MacGregor squeezed his eyes shut.

Was he blacking out again? "Tyler?" She touched his shoulder. "Tyler, don't!"

He snapped his lids back. "Why you?"

What did she say to that? Deflated, she

frowned back at him. "Charming. How do you manage, MacGregor?" She dropped and sat down beside him, then pulled a muffin from her pocket and took a healthy bite. Her hand shook like a tree caught in a gale. With luck, he'd still be too preoccupied with himself to notice.

"Manage what?" He rolled to his side then sat up, swaying and looking a little woozy. He shook his head.

"Carting around so much arrogance that you're above saying thanks to a woman who's just saved your backside."

He frowned deeper at the smoothed dirt spread over the rock. "Frankly, I'm feeling like most of me is still on the trail."

He was fine. Out a lot longer than before, but fine. Her eyes burning, the back of her nose tingling, she grinned and pulled a second muffin from her pocket, then passed it to him. "Eat. It always makes me feel better."

He dusted his hand off on his jean-clad thigh, then took the muffin. The breeze ruffled his hair, the finer hair on his arm. "Thanks."

"See, it didn't hurt a bit." She took another bite. "You can stop worrying. I'm not going to bombard you with questions."

Relief, then suspicion played across his

face. "Right."

She polished off the last of her muffin. A crumb clung to the corner of her mouth. She licked at it. "Scout's honor."

"Uh huh." Sarcastic, but he visibly relaxed. "And just when were you a Scout?"

"Well, actually I wasn't." She pulled out the third muffin and broke it in half. "But that doesn't mean I'm not sincere."

He lifted his brows. "Oh, you look sincere, all right."

She gave him a good frown and held it so he wouldn't miss it. "Watch it, or I might change my mind and bombard you after all."

His look debated whether or not she was serious. Without a word, he chewed slowly, then swallowed his last bite and eyed the second half of the third muffin in her hand.

She passed it over, deliberately not meeting his gaze. "MacGregor?"

"Yeah?"

"Can I ask you one question?" She stared at his chin.

"Only one?"

Her heart thudded, and she lifted her gaze to his. "Yeah, only one."

He stared at her for a long time, the breeze playing with his hair, his gray eyes wary and indecisive. Finally, he heaved a sigh. "Okay."

Her heart rate shot up like a rocket on lift-off. He'd cracked open the door to his personal life. Now, she just had to stick her foot in it and hope he didn't slam it shut. She licked a crumb from her fingertip, then brushed the back of her hand over her mouth. "This isn't my question," she warned. "But when I ask it, you will answer, right?"

Stone-faced, he nodded.

Knowing from Bill that Carolyn never had mentioned Maggie to MacGregor, she pulled from her memory the single question she'd mulled over, pondered on, and worried about for two years, nearly unable to believe that in a matter of moments she'd know MacGregor's version of what had happened to Carolyn.

Then Maggie looked into his eyes.

She felt his dread, his desperation, his despair. Sensed his emptiness, his feelings of isolation and regret. So much regret.

But as clearly as she'd heard the whisper, she sensed his regret didn't stem from what he had done, but from something he hadn't done. Something he'd . . . caused.

The seeds of doubt she'd had niggle at her before about his involvement in Carolyn's possible non-accident/accident sprouted and bloomed. But could a man

116

capable of such intense emotions, a man who definitely had a conscience, be involved in such an awful thing — even indirectly?

Struggling as he was, if he turned out to be innocent, what would asking him if he had been involved do to him? She remembered her mother's reaction to being questioned about her injury. Her embarrassment and shame. It had nearly pushed her over the edge. With all MacGregor was dealing with already, would asking him push him over the edge?

Maggie couldn't do it. She couldn't risk confronting him with her suspicions. Not without proof. And, as of this moment, she didn't have any.

"Maggie?" He prompted her.

She swallowed hard and looked him straight in the eye. "Are you okay, Tyler?"

He opened his mouth, then shut it again without saying a word, and just stared into her eyes. He blinked rapidly several times. The wind had died down. What burned his eyes? Dust? Dirt? Tears?

He wished he could lie to her. But how did she know that? How did she know that he wouldn't do it? He lifted a hand and cupped her face. Cool, work-roughened, it quivered ever so slightly. Or was it her chin?

"Okay?" He let his fingertips drift across

her cheek, then down her jaw. "No, Maggie," he said softly. "I'm not okay."

CHAPTER 4

He didn't trust her.

She didn't trust him, either.

He didn't want to talk to her. She was on a mission. He didn't know *what* mission, but if he talked with her, he might find out.

She *had* helped him, and he needed to talk with someone. Miss Hattie was holding out on him, and Bill still thought this mess was all in T.J.'s mind.

It wasn't. But Maggie might think it was, too.

Then again, she might not.

T.J. struggled between the forces of mind and heart. Knees to knees, he sat facing Maggie on the rocks. For the first time in days, the sun broke fully through the barrier of dull, gray clouds and shone brilliantly. Warming temperatures melted the icelets of sleet, and drops glistened everywhere — on the dew-damp ground, the brown grass, the barren trees.

119

Maggie stuffed her hands into her jacket pockets. "Tyler, I'm not trying to butt in or anything, and I haven't forgotten our deal either. But I want you to know, well, if you need to talk, I'm here. And I'll even can the sass."

A red-headed, red-nosed, sassy woman bearing an olive branch. Should he grab it? His heart thudded *Yes, with both hands.* But his mind locked down on a firm and irrevocable, *No.* She'd swear he was a fruitcake.

Still, he didn't want to hurt her feelings. It couldn't have been easy for her to offer. He hadn't exactly endeared himself to her, playing Mr. Congeniality. "I don't want to talk, Maggie. I need to, but I'm just not sure I can."

"If it helps, I've watched you out here with the painting for days," she confessed, glancing at it, lying on the ground on the other side of the boundary line.

She'd watched? And said nothing? Hadn't taunted him, or hassled him for explanations?

She grunted. "You can stop gaping, Mac-Gregor. I'm curious, not crass. I figured if you wanted to talk, you would."

He almost smiled. Almost. He felt the skin near his eyes crinkle. "No, you're not crass.

But you are a hot-water hog. Do you know that I haven't had a warm — forget hot, we're talking warm — shower since you got here?"

"Subtle revenge." She wiggled her brows at him.

"Not so subtle." He guffawed. "Trust me."

She cleared her throat. "Notice I let you shift the subject, MacGregor. Remember that the next time your attitude threatens to take a chunk out of my hide."

He lowered his gaze to her knees. A damp spot circled her jeans at her kneecap, and sand and dirt clung to it. She was so little, and yet she'd dragged him. "I guess I came down pretty hard on you."

"I'd say so. You knocked me on my keister — literally."

"I meant verbally. That collision was an accident."

"Verbally, too." She swiped at her knee. Tiny flecks of mud and sand sprayed onto the ground and spattered on a patch of weedy grass.

He rubbed at his neck. Man, it was stiff. "I guess I should explain. I'm really not an arrogant jerk." He picked up a brown pebble and rolled it between his fingers and thumb. Amazing how much that remark had stung his ego.

"Right." A phantom wind gusted, raising goose bumps on her arms. Shivering, she stuffed her hands back into her pockets.

"Okay. Sometimes, I am," he confessed. "But honest to goodness, Maggie, if you'd fended off all the women I have here, you'd be arrogant, too. Miss Hattie is darn persistent."

"She's a doll and you know it."

He tossed the pebble down. It pinged against the rocks, then settled. "Did I say she wasn't?"

"No."

"Look, she's an angel, but she's also got a hard head and a will of iron. She's determined to hook me up."

Maggie smiled. "Just how many woman has she shoved your way?"

"Seventeen — not counting you." He frowned, perplexed and not liking it. "For some reason, she hasn't said much about you — yet. But I expect she's just lulling me into complacency so I'll let my guard down. Then she'll lower the boom on me."

"Seventeen? Geez, MacGregor."

"Exactly. See what I mean?"

"Yes, I do." Maggie frowned. "My mother pulled that on me all the time. Nearly drove me insane. No matter how many times I told her the last thing I wanted was a man in my life, she —" Maggie stopped mid-sentence and stared at him. "Just how long have you been here?"

Great. Here it came. He stiffened and swallowed hard. "In three days, it'll be nine months."

She sent him a prudent, sidelong look. "You sound disgusted."

"I am."

"Why?"

The time had come. He either turned back now, or spilled his guts. What difference did it make? If he didn't tell Maggie himself, she'd just ask Miss Hattie. "I can't leave."

Maggie's forehead wrinkled. She shoved her hair back behind her shoulder. "Can't? Like you can't cross that line you draw in the dirt?"

His throat muscles clenched. What if she thought he'd lost his mind? He didn't want to get involved with her. Didn't want what she thought to matter. But it did. She appealed to him. Her sass, her intuitiveness, her quick mind, her heart. She'd been watching him for days and said not a word. He'd treated her like an intruder and she'd helped him, anyway. "I draw that line where Seascape land's end. You've seen what happens to me whenever I try to step over it."

"That happens every time?"

He heard her shock, and a thread of fear. Why fear? "Every time."

She frowned. "Why do you think it's happening?"

He sighed. How many times had he wondered? "Honestly, Maggie? I don't even know *what's* happening, much less why it's happening. It just is."

That rattled her. Her hands shook and she blinked hard and fast. But just as quickly as he noted those reactions, she seemed to calm down. As if she'd pulled something from deep inside herself and had gotten a grip. Man, but he envied her that.

"It's a big world, Tyler," she said softly. "Lots of strange things happen in it."

Her words held a familiar ring. Then he pegged the reason. "You sound like Bill Butler."

"I should. He said those things to me at the gallery."

"The gallery?" She was from New Orleans. "Lakeview Gallery?"

She nodded. "I saw the painting there."

T.J.'s heart nearly stopped. "*That's* why you're here?"

She dropped her gaze to his chest and shrugged. "Sort of."

She wasn't being honest — not totally. He

124

couldn't blame her, though. Trying to explain what happened when looking at the painting was like trying to explain what love felt like. At least on this, he could help her out — and maybe redeem himself a little in her eyes.

"You looked at it and felt as if your troubles disappeared. They were like huge inkblots that shrank smaller and smaller until they shriveled up to nothing and just weren't there," he said. "You got this bubbly feeling deep in the pit of your stomach. It spread everywhere inside you. The bubbles burst. You could hear them — *Pop! Pop! Pop!* — and, when they stopped, you felt calm and serene and at peace.

"Somehow you knew that if you'd just come here, to the actual inn, then you'd heal. It lured you and, intoxicated by all you were feeling that was good, you couldn't resist its charm. You had to see, to know firsthand, if all those good feelings were possible to feel. Your mind warned you they weren't, that you were a fool to traipse up here on a peace pilgrimage, but your heart promised that if you could summon the courage and take the risk, then you'd find the truth and feel the feelings yourself. And so you came."

Her jaw hung loose. She stared at him,

awestruck.

"You felt as if the weight of the world you'd been carrying on your shoulders had grown feather-light. As if your heart had been set free. You didn't need to walk on the ground, you could float above it. You felt as if you could find answers here that would put you at ease for the rest of your life." He blinked, then blinked again, remembering so well, so vividly. "Is that why you're here, Maggie? Is that how you felt?"

"How," she stammered, and started again. "How did you know?"

"It doesn't matter." He couldn't tell her after all. "What troubled you so deeply?"

Lowering her gaze, she seemed to focus on the placket of his shirt. "It's not a pretty story."

"Ones that cause us that kind of turmoil never are."

She raked her lower lip with her teeth. "My mother fell down some stairs. I think my father pushed her. She denied it, and likely will until the day she dies."

Something dark twisted in T.J.'s stomach. "Did you confront him?"

"Couldn't." Maggie snatched a blade of dead grass up by the roots and dragged her fingertips down its length. "He took off the day it happened. We haven't seen or heard from him since."

"So you took care of your mother."

She nodded. "I'd moved to Baton Rouge after college and hired on as a marketing rep at Maison's. Shortly before the accident, I'd been promoted to Senior Account Executive."

"Pretty young for that, weren't you?" T.J. straightened one leg and propped his elbow on the other.

"Youngest in Maison's history." Her pride in that accomplishment was obvious. "Luckily, I had inherited money from my grandmother and had gotten lucky at investing it. So when Mom got hurt, I took an extended leave of absence, went home, and took care of her."

Maggie was modest, too. No one got lucky at investments these days. They either knew what they were doing or they became shark bait. "Only child?"

"Yes, I am."

"Me, too." She looked close to tears and he wanted to comfort her. He reached out and put his hand on her arm. It trembled. "Her fall wasn't your fault, Maggie."

She snapped her head up, looked at him, pain radiating from her eyes. "It was."

Man, did he recognize the hurt in her. "He abused her, you didn't. The blame

127

belongs at his front door."

She shook her head and looked out to sea. "You don't understand."

A gull cawed overhead. He glanced up at it, saw it swoop low over the ocean, then watched her emotions shift with the same ferocity that the waves thrashed against the rocks below them. "Explain it to me, then."

"I suspected it, MacGregor. For years, I thought he was hurting her. He'd do things to make her think she was going nuts, then belittle her and tell her she was crazy."

"What kind of things?"

Her shoulders hunched, her arms wrapped around her bent knees, Maggie rocked back and forth, tapping her toes in the dirt on each forward roll. "The first time I remember catching him, she was cooking this green bean casserole. The kind with mushroom soup and canned french-fried onions. She had everything out on the counter and was heating up the soup. She poured it over the beans, then reached for the can of onions. It was gone. She looked and looked, knowing it'd been there. She checked everything. Even went outside and dug through a weeks' worth of garbage, looking for that can.

"She came back into the kitchen and there it was — on the counter right where it had been before it'd gone missing. She looked devastated, MacGregor. Really weary and scared. So scared."

"Did she just miss seeing it the first time?"

Maggie sent him a level look. "The can was empty."

"Empty?"

She nodded. "Mom checked the casserole. No onions. It'd been a new can. By this time, she's shaking, muttering that they couldn't have just disappeared.

"Dad comes in, wanting to know what she's so upset about. Now she's nearly in tears. She's looking everywhere for the onions — even in the fridge. He's nagging at her, giving her a hard time.

"She starts crying. Goes to the sink and washes her hands so he doesn't see her tears, but he knows. Her shoulders are shaking. And while her back's turned, I see him pull a bowl out of the oven and dump the stuff in it into the casserole."

"The onions."

Maggie nodded. "The onions. Then he says, 'Christ, Elizabeth. What's wrong with you? The onions are already in there.'

"She's shocked, of course. Swore they hadn't been there a minute ago. And do you know what he does?"

T.J. shook his head that he didn't.

"He tells her that if she keeps this up, he's going to have her committed."

T.J.'s stomach soured. "Why?"

A tear rolled down Maggie's cheek. "Because he was an untrustworthy rotten man, MacGregor. Because he got his jollies hurting her. Because it made him feel powerful and strong and in control. He really had a thing for control."

"Did you tell her what you'd seen?"

"Yes." Maggie clamped her jaw and nodded. "I told him, too."

And she'd been terrified. Even now her fear trembled in her voice.

"I never caught him again, and Mom never admitted to further incidents, but I expect they happened. She told me it had been a game."

"Protecting you?"

"Yes. I think that's why he left. Because of me."

"You?" Surprised, T.J. failed to school his voice.

She blushed, embarrassed. "When I got the job at Maison's, I warned him that if he ever put a hand on her, or played mind games with her again, I'd kill him."

Instinctively, T.J. knew Maggie wasn't the type to make idle threats, and she certainly wasn't the kind to threaten a life without

130

serious provocation. But he understood her threatening her father in this situation, and that the threat had been sincere. Obviously her father had known it, too.

Another flicker of respect for her flamed to life inside T.J. Confronting her father had to be terrifying. He could've just as easily as not turned on her. Still, she'd done it. In the same situation, though T.J. couldn't know for sure what his reaction would be, he liked to think he'd do the same thing. "I'm surprised your mother didn't kick him out."

"No," Maggie said, looking sad. "She would never do that — which is exactly why I didn't just threaten to have him arrested. She'd never allow it, and he'd see to it that she didn't.

"One of the tragedies of abuse, Tyler. Abusers work on their victims' self-esteem until the victims think they deserve the abuse. It's their fault, see? Men like my father are very clever and very manipulative. They're twisted. But they're good at this stuff. And before the victims know what's happened to them, they end up like my mother. Where they'll put up with anything because they deserve nothing, and anything — even abuse — is better than being alone."

T.J. gave Maggie's arm a gentle squeeze. "I'm sorry you and your mother had to go through that."

"Me, too." She patted his hand and gave him a watery smile. "But at least it's over now. He's gone, and we survived. She's safe."

T.J. nodded. Why hadn't Maggie included herself? Wasn't she, too, safe? "So what happens now?"

"We pick up the pieces and go on."

"Back to Maison's?" He really shouldn't be asking. What she wanted to tell him was different. Quizzing her, he was butting in.

She shrugged, seemingly unoffended. "I don't know. I love marketing, and Maison's has been great to me. They refused my resignation and put me on an extended leave of absence so I could keep my benefits."

"Sounds like a good company."

She nodded. "Yes, but you know, Mac-Gregor, I've been thinking. What I was doing there, well, in the grand scheme of things, it didn't matter. I think I'd rather do something that matters."

He lifted his brows. "Solid marketing matters. It can make or break companies, and that makes or breaks the people working for the companies — and their families. Execs need straight-talking, bottom-line info to get to the public. They depend on marketing gurus like you to get it there efficiently."

"True." She rubbed at her shin. "Maybe I just need to be more selective about what I market, eh?"

He shrugged for show. "Sounds like a plan to me."

Looking a little wrung out but a lot more at ease, she gave him a nervous laugh. "Hey, I'm supposed to be the listener here, not the soul-barer."

"Works both ways." He smiled.

Looking dazed, she opened her mouth and her lips spread apart into a brilliant smile that had his heart flipping over in his chest.

"So are you going to tell me how you knew?"

"About the painting and how it made you feel?"

She nodded.

"Not just yet. But someday."

"Unfair, MacGregor."

"I'm prudent." He hauled himself to his feet and his knees cracked. "It's life that's unfair."

She let out a sigh she clearly meant for him to notice and stood up. "First you tell me there are no miracles, now you say life's not fair." She swatted at her damp bottom. "You're blowing all my fantasies here, MacGregor."

"Right."

"Yeah, right." She retrieved the painting then passed it to him. The serenity on her face had him aching. "But you'll pay for it. I'm kind of fond of my fantasies, you know. I don't take kindly to someone shooting them to smithereens."

He bet he would pay. "How?"

She gave him a wicked grin that lit her eyes from the bottoms, turned, and walked back toward the house. "Hot water, MacGregor," she yelled back at him. "Gallons and gallons of it."

He watched her go. The woman was as serious as a heart attack. And he'd croak before admitting it, but he thought he might just be developing a thing for sass.

"Hey, MacGregor." Maggie hiked off the garden path and cut across the lawn to the pond, her skirt swishing against the basket swinging from her hand then into her thighs. It felt good, being unencumbered by a coat and heavy clothing. Maine weather was nothing, if not changeable. From freezing last night to warm and toasty this afternoon.

Sitting on the ground and leaning back against a gnarled oak, MacGregor watched her walk toward him. He'd taken his jacket off. It lay in the dirt beside him. His soft, sand-colored shirt, too, did wonderful things to his eyes and, this time, he'd ditched the killer glare and he hadn't chiseled sarcasm into his lips to ruin them. Sweet progress, though she almost wished he had. He'd be a lot less appealing to her then.

"What are you doing out here?" He tossed a stone into the pond. It plopped down into the water, raised a little splash, then the smooth surface rippled.

"It's too pretty to stay inside so I'd have come outside anyway, but it so happens" — she spread out his jacket between two exposed roots, then sat down on it — "I'm a woman on a mission."

He paled.

"What's wrong?" What had she said? The man looked ready to faint.

He squinted at her, a hard glint in his eyes. "What kind of mission?"

"Oh, chill out, MacGregor. No questions heading your way from here." She shifted her bottom and got comfortable, then opened the basket. "Miss Hattie sent me with lunch."

"Lunch." He scraped his back against the tree to hide his relief.

Maggie nodded. "The kitchen's a disaster. She's making more soup for Jimmy, a snack for the roofers working on the Carriage House — isn't that hammering driving you nuts? — and she's whipping up a batch of muffins for Hatch. Vic's going to pick everything up and deliver it when he makes his rounds with the mail."

"So we're banned, huh?" MacGregor smiled.

"That's about the size of it." Maggie opened the basket, pulled out napkins and passed one to T.J. "But get your taste buds ready. They're in for a treat. We've got roast beef and Swiss on rye sandwiches, apple slices with some kind of dip I've not had before — but I snitched a taste and it's nothing short of heaven — some kind of chips that Miss Hattie says have the right kind of fat in them. Don't look at me — I don't have a clue what they are, and I thought it wisest not to ask. And strawberry pie for dessert. Whipped cream is optional."

"Sounds good, all right. I didn't realize I was hungry."

"I'll share, provided you're nice."

"Hey, I'm a walking paragon."

"Naw, you're not. You're a popsicle with a

growling gut. Comes from those cold showers."

He grinned. "I've been meaning to talk to you about that."

"Oh?" She passed a sandwich to him. Their fingers brushed and a pleasant little sizzle streaked up her arm.

"Just how long does subtle revenge last?"

She set out the bowl of apples, then tossed the lid back into the basket and pulled out the dip. "Depends. We'll see how you do during lunch."

"Blackmail, eh?"

"Yep." She grinned. "As you so often say, 'pure and simple.' "

His eyes twinkled. Her breath caught in her throat. She hadn't seen him without his mask before. Even when she'd told him about her mother, he'd buried his reactions. She liked this. She didn't want to like it, but she did.

"You're a hard woman, Maggie." He grabbed a piece of apple, dipped it into the bowl, then crunched down on it. "I guess, in the interest of thawing out, I'll behave."

"Glad to hear it." She nibbled at her sandwich. The mustard was hot and spicy. Her nose tingled. "MacGregor, can we talk about what's happening to you?"

"I thought you said no questions."

"I lied." She shrugged. "I'm curious, remember?"

"Why? This is my problem, not yours."

"Because it's strange." She finished the first half of her sandwich. The man had the most gorgeous nose. Hers was the slightest bit crooked, so she really noticed noses. His was perfect. Not too long, straight and smooth. Perfect. "You've got to admit what's happening to you is weird, MacGregor."

"My friends call me T.J."

She cocked her head. "You don't look like a T.J. to me. You look like a MacGregor."

"Kind of rough around the edges, eh?"

"Yes. And soft in the middle."

"Is that your subtle way of telling me I've got a gut?"

"No, that's my subtle way of warning you not to hog all the apples."

"I get a hog warning from the Hot-Water Head Hoggett?"

She hiked her chin and shrugged. "Hey, haven't you heard? Life is unfair."

"Touché." He finished his sandwich, scooped up a couple apples, then studied a thick slice. "I don't know what's happening to me. I told you that."

"Do you know why it's happening?"

"No. Maybe." He sighed. "I don't know."

He scooted away from the tree to reach the dip and looked at her. "You clean up pretty good."

"That almost sounds like a compliment. Better watch it, MacGregor, or I might start thinking you're interested in me. Mixed signals, you know."

He shifted the subject back to the topic at hand as if, of the two, the strange events were easier to discuss. "It might be guilt."

She nearly choked. When the coughing fit ended, she dabbed at her teary eyes and cleared her throat. "What are you feeling guilty about?"

"I came here once before. A long time ago."

"Really?" Her throat still tickling, she set her sandwich aside, filled two glasses with ice, then poured them full of iced tea from the thermos.

"It's a long story."

Ice clinked against the sides of the glass. As the tea splashed over the cubes, they popped and crackled. "I've got time."

"Okay, but remember you asked for it." He took the glass from her hand and leaned back against the tree, stretching out his long legs in front of him and crossing them at his ankles. "You know about me painting."

"Yes, I do. Tyler James, world-class artist.

You can talk straight, MacGregor."

He nodded. "I'd just landed my first international showing in Europe. Officially arrived in the art world. My folks wanted to fly over for the opening, but I talked them into flying to London and then taking a train. My dad was a bit of a workaholic and my mom loved to travel. It seemed like a good way to get him to slow down a little and for her to see some of the European countryside."

"Sounds like a good plan." Maggie swatted at an ant crawling on her ankle and began putting the food away.

"The train derailed."

She fumbled the basket lid. It slammed shut. "Were they . . . ?"

"They died."

"Oh, Tyler." She clasped his hand and held it tightly. "I'm so sorry."

He nodded, stone-faced. When she tried releasing his hand, he gripped hers tighter, refusing to let go. This was hard, painful for him. Relaxing her fingers, she curled them around the thick, blunt tips of his. "It wasn't your fault."

"Yes, it was. They never had been on a train and wouldn't have been on that one if I hadn't badgered them into it."

"They decided, though."

"Afterwards," he said as if he hadn't heard her, "I couldn't paint. Months went by and I was starting to panic. A photographer friend of mine, Meriam Richards, told me about Seascape Inn."

"That's how you knew." Maggie scooted closer, her thigh brushing his knee. "She showed you a photograph of Seascape and when you looked at it, you felt all the things I felt when I saw your painting."

He nodded. "Meriam told me she'd had photographer's block. She never said it, but I think she and her husband, Bryce, were having their problems. A shame. He's a good man, and they've got three kids. Anyway, she told me that she'd come up here, and when she'd left, she'd left healed. She swore Seascape held magic."

Maggie half-agreed with her. Though she hadn't yet decided if it was black or white magic. "So you came."

"Yeah, I did." He lowered their clasped hands to his thigh. It was as hard as the rocks on the shore.

"Did you heal?"

"I painted the painting of Seascape Inn." He dragged his thumb down her hand, fingertip to wrist, then back again. "After that, I went home and painted like a demon."

"So why did you say you aren't painting anymore?"

"Because I'm not. I haven't for two years."

Two years. The same length of time since Carolyn's accident. "How come?"

"My fiancée was killed in a car accident." He closed his eyes and lifted his chin. "My Seascape Inn painting was with her, Maggie." His voice shook and he looked at Maggie as if steeling himself for her condemnation. "It's my fault she's dead."

Maggie's thoughts spooled. Spots formed before her eyes. She took in three deep breaths and warned herself to calm down and not to jump to conclusions. "Like your parents' deaths were your fault?"

"More so. With them, I didn't know what to expect. But with my fiancée . . ." He let out a sigh laden with self-disgust. "Have you ever sensed something coming and ignored it?"

Surprise streaked up her backbone. She'd tried to ignore him, his despair, those ominous whispers. "Yes."

"So did I. That's why her death is my fault. I knew she was headed for trouble, and I didn't stop her."

Knowing Carolyn, he *couldn't* have stopped her. Once she'd made up her mind, she'd had tunnel vision until she'd gotten what she'd wanted. Was that all there was to MacGregor's involvement in her death? Was the guilt Maggie had sensed he'd caused only that he hadn't stopped Carolyn from self-destructing? "Maybe you weren't supposed to stop her. Maybe you were just supposed to try." Maggie rubbed his finger with the forefinger of her free hand. "Did you try?"

"Too late, but, yes, I did. She wouldn't listen." His Adam's apple bobbed and the veins in his neck bulged. "I — I really don't want to talk about that anymore."

It hurt him. Maggie could see that it did. But did it hurt because he'd loved Carolyn, or because she'd died? "All right."

"The bottom line is I couldn't paint again. Every time I picked up a brush, or even thought about picking up one, I remembered just how much my gift has cost me, you know? Everything and everyone I care about is dead — because of my gift."

"Tyler, that's not true."

"It is. My parents were coming to see my exhibit. Carolyn had my painting with her — she was obsessed with the thing, Maggie. They died. They all died."

She cupped her free hand over their linked ones. "So you came back here to see if you could again be healed."

"Yes." He loosened his tight jaw. "I don't want to paint — how could I want to paint?" He paused and dragged in a shuddered breath. "I need peace, Maggie. I just . . . need peace."

His torment reflected in every fiber of his expression. "I understand." She scooted closer still and rested her bent knee on his thigh. Her shadow spilled over his chest and slanted onto the root-roughened ground beyond him. "Do you think maybe it's because you feel guilty about these things that you can't leave here?"

"Yeah, I do. But it isn't all in my mind. Bill Butler thinks it is, but he's wrong. I'm not crazy."

"Of course, you aren't crazy. But you aren't guilty either, and yet you still feel guilty. Maybe that's what's happening to you. You think you can't go, so you just can't go. You feel guilty."

"I am guilty."

"Okay. I disagree, but I'm not going to argue the point with you." A little speckle of dip spotted his cheek. She reached up and thumbed it off.

"Maggie?" he whispered.

She looked at him, their hands clasped, her thumb still resting against his jaw.

"What would you think about us kissing?"

"Bad idea." She wanted to pull back, meant to pull back, but it was as if someone held a hand at the center of her back, refusing to let her. She stared into MacGregor's eyes. So dark. So intense. So many emotions flitting through their depths.

"Very bad idea." His pupils dilated and he focused on her mouth. "You wanna do it anyway?"

Her heart careened, nearly shattering in her chest. "Yeah," she whispered. "I guess I do."

"I have to taste you. Just once." He let go of her hand, cupped her face in his upturned palms, and leaned toward her.

"Just once." His lips were warm, soft, and as gentle as a summer breeze. She fisted her hands on his thigh, wanting to touch him, to let her fingers drift through his hair to see if it was as soft as it looked, to stir his heated, winter pine scent that conjured all manner of romantic fantasies in her mind, to feel his chest to see if his heart was beating as hard as her own. She wanted to do all those things, but she didn't do any of them. She couldn't. She had no right.

He pulled back and looked into her eyes, his own, solemn.

"MacGregor?"

No answer. He just looked at her.

He knew she felt torn about this. And he wasn't going to make it easy for her. In fact, he wasn't going to sway her decision either way. She shouldn't do it. It wasn't right. She wasn't playing straight with the man, and she wasn't any more sure he was playing straight with her. But he looked so good. Smelled and tasted and felt so good. And if she didn't get one really serious kiss from him, she'd die wondering what it would have been like. She didn't want to die wondering . . .

"Well, shoot, MacGregor." Sighing her resignation, she circled his neck with her arms, and kissed his lips.

CHAPTER 5

T.J. walked into the bathroom and saw her clothes puddled on the floor. Fresh ones lay on the countertop. He grimaced, picked up the little *Occupied* sign and rapped it against the inner door, separating the rest from the shower and tub. "Hey, Maggie. You forgot the sign again."

Water splashed. She gurgled and came up muttering. "Blast it, MacGregor, you scared the socks off me."

He arched a brow. "Bathe in your socks now, do you?"

"Go away. How'd you get in here? I know I locked that door."

"It's broken."

"Well, thanks so much for passing along that tidbit of information."

The corner of his mouth twitched at her sarcasm. Forget a gnat. He didn't worry her a mite's worth. He dropped down and sat on the step up to the tub room. "I've got an idea."

"Can it wait?" She lowered her voice to a mumble. "The man just can't *stand* the idea of letting me bathe in peace."

"Yeah, it could wait. But what's wrong with talking now? It's not as if I can see through walls or anything." But he sure could hear through the door. And she had no idea . . .

"So much for privacy." She elevated her voice. "All right, talk. But I'm warning you, so much as one fingerprint shows up on my underclothes out there and I'll be using your razor for more than shaving my legs."

"You're using my razor?" He glared at the door. "First you leave half my backside on the rocks, now you're bent on mutilating my face. Exactly what is your problem with my skin?"

She laughed.

The sound warmed him. "Ah, I get it. Just what infraction have I allegedly committed against you to prompt *this* subtle revenge?"

"No revenge," she assured him. "I left my own razor in my room."

"Well, thank heaven for small mercies." Now, she owed him. But he thought he'd just wait a while to tell her. Maybe until she was good and steamed.

"So what do you want to talk about?"

"I've been thinking," he told her. "Maybe you have a point about the boundary line."

"What do you mean?"

Splash. "Ah, geez."

He frowned. "Cut yourself?"

"Nicked. Is this a new blade? I hate new blades, MacGregor. The darn things are lethal weapons."

"It's new." He smiled, hoping she'd spare her shins a little skin. They were much too nice to be scabbed up. "What if this stuff isn't happening to me because I'm crossing the boundary, but because of where I'm crossing it?"

"Mmm. I never thought about that. Do you think location will make a difference?"

A pang of disappointment stung him. She thought this was all in his mind — just as Bill did. But could T.J. blame her? If this weren't happening to him, he'd think that, too. Sometimes he still thought it. "I don't know if it'll make any difference at all," he answered honestly. "Probably won't. But there's nothing else left to try."

He leaned back against the door. Stared at the streaks of shadows the light played on the ceiling. "I'm thinking to try crossing out by the pond. Up by the stone wall between here and Beaulah Favish's place."

149

"It couldn't hurt." She muttered as if she'd nicked herself again. "MacGregor, when you actually cross over, what do you feel?"

Should he tell her? Right now she just thought he was nuts. But if he told her about the episodes in detail, she'd be certain of it. He knew how crazy it sounded, but he wasn't crazy, and he knew that, too. She didn't. Whatever was happening here fit into the weird, strange, abnormal and unusual categories, but it *was* happening. It was real.

But if he didn't tell her, she'd just ask Miss Hattie, who might or might not tell her. Better it came from him. "First the temperature takes a nosedive." He studied his nails, disassociating from the things he felt when this happened, fearing if he didn't, Maggie would hear all the emotion in his voice and think him nuts *and* weak. "Then this mist comes up over me. I feel it everywhere, like a blanket. No. No, it's more like a second skin."

A thread of anxiousness stole into his voice. He paused to level it out, to further distance himself.

"What else?"

She sounded controlled, her tone not reflecting the strangeness of what he was telling her at all. Grateful for that, he went on. "Then it's like these icy-cold fingers grab me by the shoulder. I try to knock them loose, but I can't."

"That's what you're fighting, then?"

"Yeah." He stared at her clothes on the floor. Her sleeve was crumpled and twisted around the leg of her jeans. Her undergarments lay right on top. He shut his eyes. "Yeah, that's what I'm fighting."

"Then what?"

The water rippled, lapped against the sides of the garden tub. Her skin wet and rosy from the heat, her cheeks flushed, her eyes soft and slumberous.

"MacGregor?"

The image popped like a bubble. "Then I'm too weak to fight. I see spots, know I'm blacking out — and I know that there's nothing I can do to stop it." He swallowed an emotional knot from his throat. "Then I'm out."

"Sounds creepy."

It was. "Try experiencing it."

"No, thanks."

Something in her tone alerted his sixth sense. He stared at the wood grain in the door, wishing he could see her expressive eyes. "Maggie, have you been experiencing strange things here, too?"

She hesitated. "Um, no." The water pipes

groaned ominously and the room temperature seemed to suddenly drop. "Why do you ask?"

She'd lied. "Just curious." He leaned back, rested his head against the door and stared at the antique brass shell soap dish on the marble counter. Why had she lied?

"What happens to you then?"

"Nothing. Out's out, Maggie." He pivoted, leaned his weight fully against the door to scratch an itch in the middle of his shoulders. "The next thing I know, I'm waking up looking at angels."

"Angels?" She opened the door.

Not expecting it, T.J. crashed onto his back.

"Sorry." She looked down at him, her hair damp and swinging forward cupping her face.

He looked up her legs to the fluffy pink towel circling her middle. Droplets of water clung to her skin, between her clavicles, in the soft hollow of her throat. A lone trickle slid down her shoulder and onto her arm, and she smelled of lavender soap. He loved the smell of lavender soap as much as the smell of the sea.

"Tell me about the angels."

He sat up. "They're not your halo variety."

"Glad to hear it. You were starting to worry me."

Telling her about the boundary crossing should have her plenty worried already. Why didn't it? "These angels flap hankies, not wings."

"Ah, Miss Hattie."

"And you." He rolled his shoulder, bowed his spine, and worked a kink out of his back.

She smiled. "I don't think anyone's ever called me an angel before."

"No? Well, don't let it go to your head. I curse you plenty, too."

"You?" She drew in a sharp breath that was totally faked. "Well, what do you know? And here I had you pegged as a gentleman."

"Uh-huh. And I buy swampland by the parcel to build subdivisions on, too."

"Now, MacGregor" — she flipped at a curl clinging to his ear — "who these days other than a gentleman asks a woman for a kiss?"

He caught her finger and held it. "I've been meaning to talk with you about that."

"Oh?"

"Color me uninformed on the politically correct scene — I've been out of circulation for some time — but at least I asked you before I kissed you. You didn't ask me. Worse, you kissed me *and* cursed me." He cleared his throat. "Notice how chivalrous I was about that, Maggie. I'm needing to rack up some redemption points here."

"Intention noted."

He nodded. "Did you note, too, that I didn't hold it against you — your not asking me before you kissed me, I mean? I didn't. I kissed you back, anyway."

"Did you?" She pressed a fingertip to her temple and walked past him, then scooped up her clothes. "Gee, MacGregor, I can't say I did notice."

"You didn't?" He stood up and moved toward her. "How could you not notice?"

She looked up at him and shrugged, her eyes glinting mischief. The towel, knotted around her torso, lifted with each of her breaths. "I guess maybe it was one sorely-lacking kiss."

"You're lying, Maggie."

"Am I?" She feigned innocence.

"Yeah, you are." It was so transparent. Too transparent. She meant for him to realize it. "You know what I think?"

"No idea." Holding her clothes bundled near her stomach, she backed up a step, against the hallway door.

He stepped closer, hemmed her in, determined to see her eyes on this one. She didn't know it, but every emotion she even

154

thought about feeling shone clearly in her eyes. "I'm thinking it wasn't a sorely-lacking kiss. I'm thinking you want to kiss me again."

"Nope. Not me." She shook her head, setting her hair to swinging. "You're thinking wrong."

"No, I'm not. And I'm also thinking that you don't want a sweet and gentle kiss." He nodded to let her know he meant it.

Her little quiver had the knot at her breasts heaving. "Uh-uh."

"Uh-huh." He stepped closer still, until they touched chest to chest, thigh to thigh. Her clothes crushed between their stomachs, she moved her hands, hesitated as if uncertain what to do with them, then lowered them to her sides, palms flat against the door.

He lifted his hands to her shoulders. Her skin was creamy soft, so warm and tempting. "I'm thinking you want to feel passion, Maggie."

She hissed out a spurted breath that he thought might just be the sexiest sound he'd ever heard. "I don't," she said shakily. "I really, really don't."

Again, she'd lied. But this time he knew why. She didn't want to find him appealing any more than he wanted to be attracted to her. He let his fingertip trail down from her temple to her earlobe, traced the shell of her ear back to her lobe, then to the soft spot behind it. A second finger joined the first and skimmed down her long neck, over her pulse point to her slim shoulder, to the soft hollow at her throat that was still damp and moist and warm from her bath. "If passion is what you're needing to feel, I can —"

"No, MacGregor." Her voice softened to a pleading whisper. "I can't."

"But you want to."

She swallowed, her breaths rough and loud in the still, moist air hanging between them. "Yes."

He nearly collapsed from relief. This wasn't one-sided. Neither of them wanted anything between them, but they were both feeling something. He didn't like it, but he'd acknowledged it. So had she, though she hadn't yet acted on it. And that, she had to decide to do.

He locked their gazes, let his hand fall to his side, then slowly and deliberately backed up a step.

The bundle of clothes between them dropped to the floor. Ignoring them, she grasped his arm and squeezed. "Mac-Gregor?"

He paused, watching her inner struggle reflect in her eyes, and then the pressure from her fingers strengthened, urging him toward her. His heart thundering hard, his blood rushing through his veins, he took her into his arms and closed his mouth over her waiting lips.

She lifted her hands to his sides, glided them over him, ribs to waist, then gathered him close and drifted them down his spine. He'd been right. No gentle kiss, this. This kiss demanded, touching parts of him he thought had died. This kiss teased and tempted and promised more. And he wanted more. He wanted all it promised. He wanted her.

He had to stop. If he didn't stop — now — he'd be taking her to his room. He knew it. She knew it. And though he'd like nothing better, he also knew that the time wasn't right.

Fighting tremor upon tremor of protest, he lifted his head and stared into her unfocused eyes, knowing his own were every bit as desire-glazed, and brushed his fingertip over her lower lip. "I want to be with you, Maggie."

Bemused, she breathed in deeply three times, each breath lifting the towel's knot to brush against the heel of his hand. Each breath expelling warm heat that fanned over his chest. Each breath timing itself with the beats of his heart. "I can't."

"I know." He did. They both were caught in inner struggles, though hers he couldn't yet begin to understand. She'd told him too little.

She didn't move, stayed leaning against the door as if it were all that kept her upright. "I lied, Tyler."

Tyler, not MacGregor. Tyler meant serious trouble. His heart beat harder still.

"Your kiss wasn't lacking."

A pang of pure male pleasure rippled through his chest. "I know." And to show his appreciation at her being honest with him, he kissed her again. Longingly. Lovingly.

When he released her, the bathroom mirror had fogged solid and she didn't look any more steady on her feet than he felt. "I think" — he backed up, putting some distance between them — "we'd better find something else to do. Want to come with me to try my luck at the pond?"

She swallowed hard, clutching at the towel. Their contact had loosened the knot and it threatened to come undone. "Give me five minutes." Opening the door, she stepped out into the hall. "Ten max."

"Uh-huh. Meet you downstairs in ten."

Watching her pad down the hall, he smiled at her back. He'd been sharing the bathroom with the woman for a week. He'd give her an hour, and hope that was long enough.

Telling herself she hadn't been as affected by MacGregor's kiss as she had been, Maggie dressed quickly. Black slacks, a copper silk blouse that seemed to set her hair afire with golden glints, and a black jacket with copper lapels and patch pockets.

She dropped her brush back onto the vanity and stared at herself in the mirror. "What are you doing? Why are you letting him get to you?"

He was gorgeous. But she'd met gorgeous men before. He was a good listener, empathetic and nonjudgmental — and he was in trouble. Possibly weird trouble.

Feeling his despair and hearing those whispers, she feared she might be in weird trouble, too.

Her hand trembled. She shut her eyes. "Think calm. Think serene." Why that seemed to work, she didn't know. But she'd done this several times since she'd arrived here, and on each occasion it had worked.

When the tension coiling in her stomach unwound, she phoned her mother. Thankfully, the phone chose to work. Maybe hearing her mother's voice would get Maggie back on track and focused on her purpose for being here. She hoped it would.

MacGregor's lure was too strong. He appealed to her physically but, worse, he appealed emotionally. She sighed. The man appealed to her in every way a man could appeal to a woman. And that made him even more potentially dangerous.

Fifteen minutes later, she headed downstairs, her black high-top sneakers squeaking on the wooden stairs. On seeing Cecelia's portrait, she whispered, "I wouldn't mind a little help here — if you can spare it," then walked on, her hand gliding over the gleaming bannister.

At least her mother had sounded terrific. Taking a ceramics class. Imagine that. Maggie smiled, no less happy that the call had had the desired effect on her, too. She was focused. Intent. Determined. And she was confident that she could keep this attraction to MacGregor in perspective.

At the foot of the stairs, MacGregor stood waiting. He checked his watch and looked awfully pleased with himself.

"One hour — exactly."

Definitely smug. The third stair creaked under her feet. "Excuse me?"

"Nothing important."

Looking up at her, his gaze turned warm and appreciative. Her heart fluttered. And the serenity she'd spent the last hour gathering scattered like seeds tossed by the wind.

"Guess that means you're back to cutting me off, eh?"

"Excuse me?" Maggie stepped around a juniper that didn't look particularly enamored with the warmer weather then moved to MacGregor's side.

He slid a hand into his jacket pocket. "No hot water for the wicked."

Maggie grinned at him. He looked gorgeous in jeans, a steel blue shirt, and denim jacket. What the man did for clothes was sinful.

The pond was just ahead. Smelling the scents of spruce and fir and clean fresh air, she watched a gull flying high above them, toward the ocean. "There ought to be some penalty for cornering a woman in the bathroom and forcing her to admit things she'd certainly rather not."

"Forcing her?"

"Okay." Her cheeks flushed hot. "Coercing. Now bury the attitude."

"Every action causes a reaction, Maggie Wright." He clasped her waist then heaved her over a fallen tree blocking the path.

"One of these days, it'll be payback time for all those cold showers. And even coercing is stretching it."

"A gentleman wouldn't gloat."

"Ah, but we've already established that I'm no gentleman."

Clasping his shoulders, she waited until he stepped over the tree, then asked, "What kind of payback?"

"It'll be steep. You owe me for using my razor, too, remember?"

"Geez, MacGregor. Do you always keep score?"

"When I have an end result in mind, yep, sure do."

She let out a heated puff of breath. "You were going to tell me about this payback business."

He drew her to him, those beautiful gray flecks warming his eyes. "I was thinking of something like maybe me joining you in that garden tub."

A pang of longing, of yearning, streaked through her. One of guilt followed right on its heels. Part of her wanted it, wanted him. But another part of her, the part that harbored doubts about him with Carolyn, insisted Maggie had to be crazy to even consider getting more deeply involved with him. And yet, only through getting involved could she ever hope to learn the truth.

A Class-A dilemma if ever there was one.

"Don't fret, Maggie. If that happens, it'll be by mutual choice."

Fearing him right, the disclosure meant to reassure her only worried her more. He set her onto the leaf-strewn ground and then they walked on.

Near the wall, Maggie felt that spooky feeling again. The hairs lifted on her neck, and she snagged MacGregor's hand. "Tyler."

"What?"

Her use of his Christian name as much as her tone had alerted him. She sensed him stiffen. "Someone's watching us."

He nodded, relaxing. "Batty Beaulah Favish." He lifted his chin. "Three o'clock. Bent down between the second fir and the dead oak."

Maggie glanced over. The sun glinted on something shiny. She looked back at MacGregor to explain.

"Binoculars." He smiled. "Madam Bird-Watcher is actually a disguise. She's got a good heart, but she's one nosy lady."

The woman about Miss Hattie's age that Maggie had heard muttering outside the Blue Moon Cafe bolted through her mind. "Does she call someone Mister High

Britches?"

T.J. laughed. "Yeah, the sheriff. She used to be his teacher so that gives her a license to aggravate him to death." MacGregor stepped over a rock. "You've met her?"

"Nearly collided with her is more like it. When I walked down to the village the other afternoon."

"Blue Moon Cafe, right?"

"Yes."

"One of her favorite hunting grounds — for the sheriff."

Maggie nodded, feeling relieved. Maybe it had been Beaulah watching all those other times she'd had that feeling, too.

But many of those times, she'd been inside the inn.

And Beaulah Favish didn't have a man's voice, either. Her's had been tinny.

He stepped up to the boundary line. "Well, I'm ready."

"MacGregor, wait." Maggie clasped his arm, torn. If she brought this up, he could take it as if she were expecting him to fail. But if she didn't, she might not get him back over the line soon enough. That last warning — that he could die — weighed heavily on her mind.

A worried frown creased the skin between his brows. "What is it?"

She had no choice: "Not saying you will, but if you should happen to fall, there's no way I can drag you over that wall. In case you haven't noticed, you're a lot bigger than I am."

"Oh, I noticed." His gaze heated. "How about we move down there?" He pointed north of the gazebo, at the end of the wall.

"Better." She looked down at the leaf-strewn ground. "I hope you don't think —"

"I don't." He hiked a shoulder. "You dressed up. That told me you weren't planning on me failing. And I really do appreciate you considering all possibilities."

They walked on over, and it hit Maggie that MacGregor's hands were empty. "You forgot the painting."

He rubbed at his neck and looked away. "No, I didn't."

She opened her mouth to ask why he'd not brought it, but then realized she already knew why. If this new location failed to work alone, then he still had something left to try.

Poor Tyler. Reduced to pinning his hopes on variations of variations. Her heart aching for him, she gave him a nod to go on.

He dragged the tip of his boot in the sandy soil, then looked at her as if silently pleading for encouragement. "Believe you can do it, Tyler. Believe it like when you paint." She cupped her fingers and pressed them to her chest. "Feel it in here."

He dipped his chin, then turned his back to her. Her heart felt lodged in her throat. Her blood pounded in her temples, and she curled her hands into fists at her sides.

The tension grew unbearable. Maggie squeezed her eyes shut. She didn't trust him but, oh how she prayed this would work for him. She didn't see how it could work and, in her heart, she knew he didn't see how it could work either. Still, she prayed for a miracle.

This situation had to be psychological. It was the only thing that made sense. He'd felt guilty about his folks and couldn't paint. He'd come here, healed, then gone home.

Then he'd fallen in love with Carolyn. She'd gone gaga over his painting, gotten herself killed — with, or without intentional help — and again he'd felt guilty and couldn't paint. So he'd come back here. Only this time, things were different. He hadn't healed. Something inside him wouldn't let him heal.

What?

It had to be psychological. Had to be. What else *could* it be?

The temperature plummeted.

Maggie shivered, surprised. It'd been such a mild and warm afternoon. Maine weather notoriously changed quickly, but there'd been no clouds in the sky. There'd have to be clouds . . .

She tried and failed to open her eyes.

Tried to move, but stood statue still, as trapped as MacGregor.

A veil of mist curled around her feet. In her mind, she saw it swirl and swirl, steadily rising until it covered her toe to head and clung to her skin.

What in the world was happening?

Something cold slapped against her shoulder and snagged. As if someone held an ice cube pressed hard against her flesh. Instinctively, she tried to reach up to swat it away, but she still couldn't move.

The temperature.

The mist.

The icy fingers . . .

Oh no. No! It was happening to *her*! It was happening to her just as MacGregor had described it happening to him!

MacGregor screamed, *"Nooo!"*

Maggie snapped her eyes open. Saw him hit the ground.

"Ahhhhh!" A woman's high-pitched screech rent the air.

Maggie spun toward the sound, saw the

birdlike Beaulah running back toward her house and tried to yell out to her for help. Her throat muscles locked and all that escaped her throat was a tiny mewl.

Crying, only one thought raced through her mind, repeating over and again as if she stood tapping rewind then replay on the VCR.

It isn't psychological.

CHAPTER 6

"Maggie?" T.J. shook her shoulders. Her black jacket scrunched up in his hands. "Maggie?"

Her skin had turned the color of melted wax and her lips were as blue as those of the kids who'd swam in the ocean last summer, swearing the water wasn't too cold. "Maggie, answer me."

No response. Her eyes focused on something he couldn't see, something inside her mind. Panicking, he shouted. "Maggie, answer me!"

She let out a growl that rumbled through her throat, swung her fist at him as if he'd attacked her. A burning fear took root in his stomach. "Maggie, no. Maggie, it's me. It's MacGregor. Look at me, Maggie!"

She darted her gaze at him. Blinked, then blinked again. Midswing, she stilled. "Mac-Gregor?"

The wild look in her eyes slowly faded and

she groaned, threw herself at him, slamming hard against his chest. Her fingers dug into his skin at his sides and she pressed harder to him, as if she couldn't get close enough, as if she were doing her darndest to crawl inside him.

He circled her with his arms. "It's all right now, Maggie. It's all right."

Her knees collapsed. Taking her weight, he lifted her to him, buried her face at his chest, his chin at the crook of her shoulder. "Shhh," he whispered, stroking her hair with long tender sweeps. "Shhh, it's okay."

She burrowed deeper, shaking so hard he nearly lost his grip on her. What had happened to her? Maggie just didn't rattle easily.

"You didn't pass out." His bunched shirt muffled her words.

"No, I didn't. We're both okay," he reassured her, rubbing tiny circles on her back. Why he hadn't was as strange as everything else going on around here. But that would have to wait until she was calmer so it could be discussed.

He carried her back to the garden, back to the little white bench nestled under the firs and secluded by giant evergreens. "I'm going to put you down on the bench, Maggie."

"No!" She tightened her hold on him, then said more calmly, "No, not yet."

Whatever had happened to her had rattled her to the core. "Not yet," he promised. Telling her what he was about to do, hoping not to startle her, he sat down, moved her leg over his so she half-sat, half-lay in his lap, her head nestled to his shoulder. "Okay?"

She nodded, rubbing her cheek against his shoulder, her nose against his neck, her forehead bumping his chin.

"Okay. We'll just sit here for a while. That's all we'll do. Just sit here and listen to the crickets and the frogs down at the pond and enjoy the breeze. It's so gentle it feels almost like summer, doesn't it, Maggie?"

No answer.

"You don't have to talk. We'll just sit here and not worry about a thing. We'll think only happy thoughts and just sit here and soak up some serenity like you did when you walked down to the village. We'll be calm and peaceful and if we listen real close, we'll be able to hear the waves. And then we can watch the sky for a while. The clouds are pretty tonight. Soft and billowy, and the moon's full. It's a pretty moon, Maggie. And in between the clouds we can watch the stars. Maybe if we watch long enough we'll see a shooting star. I used to pretend to ride them when I was little. Did you ever pretend to ride a shooting star?"

Still no answer, but he kept talking, rambling on about everything and nothing. It was working. She wasn't shaking nearly so hard now. He dropped his voice lower, made it even gentler, just above a whisper. A soothing tone, his mother used to call it. He hoped it was. Because until he got Maggie soothed enough to talk to him, he wouldn't know what had happened to her. That gave his imagination a free rein to play out scenarios that had him sick inside.

How long they sat there, him talking, her shaking less and less, he didn't know. It could have been minutes or hours. Some time ago, her shudders had weakened to tremors and, for the last few minutes, her breaths had leveled out, slow and even, and she'd been so still he thought she might have dropped off to sleep.

"MacGregor?"

Her voice startled him. "You okay?"

She tilted her head and looked up at him. "It's not psychological."

His heart thudded a slow, hard beat that thumped in his temples.

"Did you hear me?"

He nodded, afraid to think, to know

she'd —

"I felt it, Tyler. All of it." She dragged in a breath. "It isn't in your mind."

He didn't know whether to laugh or cry. To feel relieved or terrified or outraged. It was real. He wasn't crazy. She'd felt it.

Oh no. . . . He pulled her closer, tightening his arms around her like a shield. *She'd felt it.*

"It's dark."

"Twilight," he lied. It had been dark for hours. The hard bench cut into T.J.'s back. His legs long since had gone numb. They should go back to the house, and they would, when he just could make himself let go of her.

She pulled back her shoulders and sat up on his knees. "Tyler, I really am okay. I freaked out on you, and I'm sorry. What happened . . . rattled me, but I've got a handle on it now."

Her collar was rumpled. He reached up and rubbed it straight, the backs of his fingers brushing against her warm neck. "You went through the same thing I go through? The temperature drop, the mist, the fingers of cold?"

She nodded. "All of it."

He rubbed her arm, a knot of regret in his

throat. Why had he let her get involved in this? "What do you think it is?"

"The truth?"

She tensed slightly, and uncertain if he'd felt or sensed it, he didn't mention it to her. A cloud scudded across the sky, blocking the moonlight, and her shadowy face grew blanketed by darkness.

"Yes, the truth." She'd lied to him before and he hoped to encourage her that this wasn't the time to do it again. "Whether or not we want it, there's a bond between us, Maggie, or this wouldn't be happening to us. I feel it, and I think you do, too. And I think we owe each other the truth, don't you?"

"I think it's something . . . mystical."

He'd thought it a hundred million times. But to hear it out loud, to actually hear the words spoken by someone who also had experienced it . . .

He swallowed hard. "Me, too." His voice had cracked, and being a woman with heart, Maggie pretended not to notice. He thought he might just love her for that kindness. "The question is what mystical is it?" He rolled his gaze skyward. "You know what I mean."

"That I don't know." She fingered the placket of his shirt, running her fingertips over the fabric between the third and fourth buttons. "But I don't think it means to harm either of us, sans scaring a decade or two off our lives."

"Why would you think it doesn't mean us harm? Maggie, it knocks me out."

"I know."

She kept rubbing his placket, her knuckles scraping against his chest. The friction felt good.

"But think about it, MacGregor. If it — whatever it is — can knock you out so easily, then couldn't it just as easily kill you? Or both of us?"

T.J. paused to mull that over. It made sense. She'd made an insightful observation that hadn't occurred to him. He was totally helpless against this mystical entity. He couldn't defend himself in any way. So if the entity's objective had been to harm, T.J. would have been dead months ago.

"There's another reason I don't think it means to hurt you." Her voice suffered a catch and she wrapped her arms around his neck and rubbed her nose against his neck.

Whatever this reason was, it worried her and she wanted warmth and reassurance before disclosing it. He understood that. Spoken, the words were heard. They were acknowledged real by the speaker. Thoughts could be fanciful, but words were meant or they went unsaid. "Why?"

She swallowed, grabbed a steadying breath and blew it out against his skin. "Because it talked to me, Tyler. I heard it. Whether from inside my head or with my ears, I don't know. But . . ."

He frowned into the darkness. It was pitch black. He couldn't even make out her silhouette. "But what?"

"It knew my name. And it talked to me in a man's voice."

A shiver streaked up his backbone. The mystical entity was a he? When T.J. had heard it, it'd had his voice. It had been it, hadn't it? And not T.J.'s conscience. He just couldn't be certain. "What did it — he — tell you?"

"Help him."

"Help him? Help him how? Help him do what?"

"He didn't mean to help him — if it was a him. It could be anything."

The entity wasn't a he, then? "Who did he — it — mean for you to help?"

She hugged T.J. tighter, and her voice shook. "You."

"No." T.J. clenched his jaw until it felt ready to crack.

"But —" Maggie interrupted.

"No!" He sighed. "I'm sorry I shouted, but, no. No." It was the fear. The worry and the hate for whatever was doing this. Why did it have to extend this nightmare to Maggie? Wasn't T.J.'s enduring it enough?

T.J. grimaced. Why didn't he have enough sense to see the mistake he was making with her in handling this? Maggie was stubborn. If he put his foot down, she'd just stomp it and do as she pleased. He had to appeal to her softer side, to use logic and tenderness and compassion, to get her to stay out of this.

"Maggie, look." He lifted her hand and held it in both of his. Tiny and fragile and yet strong and capable. She'd dragged him. A knot of tenderness lodged in his throat. "I don't want you to get caught up in this. You see what it's done to me."

She expelled a frustrated sigh and looked away.

"It's just too . . . bizarre. It's *my* problem." He gave her hand a gentle squeeze, rubbed the back of it, knuckles to wrist, with his thumb.

She wasn't backing off so much as an iota. He had to keep trying. "What are we talking about here? Mystical. Some entity with a man's voice — or one capable of adopting a man's voice." What did that mean —

specifically?

"I agree we don't know what it is, Mac-Gregor, but that doesn't change the fact *that* it is. And it doesn't —"

"Listen. Shhh, Maggie, listen to me. This isn't your problem, honey. It's mine. And I want you out of it. If you go now, maybe — just maybe — it'll turn you loose." His muscles coiled into tight knots, and regret seeped through him like a spill soaks through carpet. Hatred spread with it. And guilt. Always guilt. "Don't you see?"

"I see plenty."

"Oh, Maggie, you don't." He hugged her tightly and propped his chin on the crown of her head. "I didn't want to care about you. I tried not to care about you. But —"

"No, Tyler. Don't." She leaned back, pressed her palms flat against his chest. "Don't —"

"How do I stop? I'm flesh and blood, not stone. I needed you and you were there for me."

She scooted off his lap, stood before him, her hands fisted at her sides. "Don't do it. It'll only end up hurting us both."

Slowly, he stood up and looked down at her. "I care, Maggie. What you did got to me. You've gotten to me. I didn't want you to. Heaven knows, I'd never want to risk hurting another woman. But you've crawled down deep inside me, anyway, and I won't pretend you didn't because you don't want to be there. And I won't lie to you because the truth makes us both uncomfortable."

"It isn't that."

"It *is* that." He huffed a sigh of sheer frustration. "I can't let you just stroll into the middle of this as if it's no big deal. You could be hurt. True, I agree, if this entity wanted us dead, we would be. But I think the thing is playing with us, Maggie. To it, it's play. To us — to me — it's torture. I've been at this for nine months. I know what I'm saying here."

"MacGregor, let me —"

"I can't!"

She grabbed his arms and squeezed. "Will you shut up and let me say what I have to say?"

He stilled. The leaves on the fir above their heads rustled in the breeze and the moonlight dappled her skin with light and shadows.

"I know what you're feeling, Tyler, and it's got a lot more to do with having lost your parents and Carolyn and a fear of losing me than is healthy for either of us — even though you don't love me and all you're really feeling is a good dose of lust and a little gratitude." She gentled her voice, lifted her hand from his arm to his face and stroked his jaw. "I *do* see."

His beard's light stubble being grazed by her hand created friction that heated his skin. He let her see the truth in his eyes, his pain and his fear. "I've loved and lost too many people already, Maggie. I can't say I love you. I don't. But I owe you, and I care about you. I can't be the reason I lose you, too."

She sighed. "What I'm trying to tell you is that I don't think we have a choice."

He clamped his jaw shut. "Oh, yes. We do," he gritted out from between his teeth. "There's always a choice, and I've made this one."

He turned away from her and strode toward the gazebo. He'd killed Carolyn because he'd ignored the signs and let things go too far. He'd done what was most comfortable for him, so he wouldn't upset her. But, by gosh, he would not stand by, feed his own needs and desires, and kill Maggie, too. He wouldn't do it. He couldn't, not and survive.

Maggie gave him a good half-hour to come to terms with their situation. Denial, much as she would love it, wasn't an option.

She leaned back on the bench and looked up through the brittle, twisted leaves at the sky. Clouds drifted, moving ever on, uninterrupted, unencumbered and, lord, but did she envy them. It was quiet, dark and cold, and why, with all this weirdness surrounding her she wasn't scared stiff, beating a hasty retreat, and exiting Seascape, she couldn't imagine. But the truth was she felt at peace here. It'd been a long, long time since she'd felt at peace, and she'd put up with a lot to keep it. But that she'd put up with a mystical entity struck her as nothing short of baffling. How could she explain it to MacGregor when she didn't understand it herself?

MacGregor. She sighed.

She'd lied to him, not told him her relationship to Carolyn, and now she couldn't tell him the truth. He'd throw up a defense blockade that guided missiles couldn't break through. And he'd admitted he cared about her. That made her feel guiltier still — toward him, and toward Carolyn. Well, more toward her mother than Carolyn really. It was her mother's promise and family duty that had gotten Maggie into this, not Carolyn herself. Maggie had tried and tried to be a good pseudo-sister to Carolyn, but she'd failed a long time ago, and Carolyn had given her no alternative but to accept it.

Maggie stood up. MacGregor'd had long enough to realize they were unwilling actors in this entity's little drama. They would play the parts given them because that was all they could do. Obviously, this mystical force held the strings like a puppet-master, and she and MacGregor were simply manipulated puppets.

Manipulated? Maggie stopped. *Master.*

"Master manipulator." Shock stormed through her. "Carolyn?"

CHAPTER 7

No. No! "Absurd." Maggie gave herself a serious mental shake. "Carolyn is dead."

Is she? Maggie's own voice whispered inside her head. *The body in the wreck burned beyond recognition. Are you sure it was her?*

Licking at her lips, she watched a leaf caught by the wind tumble across the ground. "It was her. The dental records proved it was her."

What if she switched them? What if she substituted someone else's records for her own? She could have done it. When it's suited her, she's exchanged things before, and you know it.

"No," Maggie insisted. "When MacGregor tries crossing the line, there's no one there. If Carolyn were alive and doing this, he'd see her. Bill and Miss Hattie would have seen her. I would have seen her. No, Carolyn's dead. She's dead, and that's that."

You're right, of course. You all would have seen her — if she were alive. But dead is a relative term, mmm? And, by your own admission, you're dealing with something mystical here . . .

Maggie shivered, shunning the direction her thoughts were taking her. Carolyn couldn't be a ghost. Maggie couldn't even be thinking ghosts! That went beyond mystical. Heck, it went beyond absurd!

She took off toward the gazebo at a good clip. Dead, dry leaves crackled and crunched under her feet, and the hard sounds and jarring steps felt good. "No, there's a reasonable explanation for this. One that has nothing to do with anything mystical. I overreacted. Panicked. It has to be something logical and reasonable."

Like what?

Maggie stepped over a dead branch. "Like . . . MacGregor feels guilty and, until he resolves those guilt feelings, he can't leave. I empathize strongly with him — because of Mom's situation. Guilt and parents are strong common ground between me and MacGregor. It's part of the bond. The other part is that we're attracted to each other. I hate — boy, do I hate — admitting that. But it's true. And my attraction to him makes my empathy for him

184

stronger. So strong that when he was crossing the line, I felt everything he'd described to me just as he'd described it to me."

The wind gusted, tossing her hair. She swept it back from her face and walked on across the grounds. "Because I felt everything so strongly, and saw it so vividly, I panicked and misinterpreted it as real. And, on conveying it all to MacGregor, because he's attracted to me — and because he feels he owes me for being there to help him out when he needed me — well, he wants to protect me."

It made sense. It was logical. Reasonable. And non-mystical.

She slowed to a stroll, feeling much more at ease now that she'd reasoned it all out. And she had reasoned it out. There was no *mystical* in the mystical events occurring here. It was emotions. As simple and complex and as awful as that.

Now, all she had to do was to explain it to MacGregor. And she would . . .

Just as soon as she figured out the part about the man's voice and whispers.

And just as soon as she figured out why when MacGregor had crossed the line and she'd experienced his symptoms, he hadn't passed out.

Ahead, she saw him. Sitting on the little

bench just on the Seascape side of the property between it and Beaulah Favish's place. Moonlight streaked over the bench, casting slatted shadows on the rocky ground.

She walked over. He must have heard her footsteps because he slumped forward. His elbows on his knees, his head bowed to his hands, he sighed as if resigned, then hauled himself to his feet and shoved his hands deep into his slacks pockets.

Stopping beside the bench, she waited for him to acknowledge her. When it became obvious he had no intention of doing so, she frowned. "MacGregor?"

No answer.

"MacGregor, please don't shut me out. I'm in this, too, and I'm scared."

He lifted his chin and looked out over an island of evergreen shrubs.

"You can't ignore me. I won't go away." For pity's sake. Why wouldn't he at least look at her? "I listened to you, now I want you to listen to me."

Still no acknowledgment.

Well, he couldn't block his ears. "Though I bless you for wanting to, you can't protect me from whatever we're fighting."

Not so much as a grunt, but at least he hadn't walked off from her. She let her head loll back, crossed her arms over her chest. "I'm not sure what's real and what isn't anymore. One minute I can explain almost everything away. The next, I can't explain any of it, and I know in my heart that something mystical is at work here."

He looked at her then, and she nearly cried. Torment etched deep into his handsome face.

"The way I see it is that if all of this is explainable, Tyler, then we've got to work together to explain it."

"And if it's not?"

She swallowed bitter fear. "Then whatever it is, it's got us both now, and the only hope we've got is each other."

"No." He looked down at her. "I've thought about this, and I've got a solution. You have to leave. Now. Tonight."

Her heart ricocheted as if it were the ball being swatted on a Ping-Pong table. "I can't."

"Yes, you can."

She'd give anything not to have to tell him this but, it appeared, she'd have no choice. "No, Tyler. It's not that simple. I can't leave and that's all there is to it."

"It *is* that simple. You pack your clothes, you get into your car, and you drive away from here."

She put her hand on his arm. "I won't leave."

"You have to, Maggie. Before you get into the same situation I'm in. Before you want to leave and can't."

"You don't understand. It's already too late. I *can't* leave."

"Why not?"

She couldn't hold his gaze. She tried, but she just couldn't do it. "Because to help you wasn't all the whisper told me."

He didn't ask. She figured he would, but he didn't. She glanced up, saw his wooden expression then looked back down at his chest. He wasn't going to ask, just to wait and accept what she elected to disclose.

She'd give more than anything, she'd give nearly everything she owned not to have to tell him, but he needed to know. About this, if not about Carolyn, Maggie had to trust him. He deserved the truth and she couldn't justify keeping it from it. "I pulled you back over the line that day because the voice warned me. I'm not proud of this, Mac-Gregor, but I had no intention of watching you that day. I was headed over to visit with Hatch at the lighthouse. But then I heard the whisper, and it said that this crossing attempt was different from the others. And it was. You were out much longer than any other time before then. Much, much longer."

"What else?"

Not a word about her turning her back on him. She'd have felt better if he'd reamed her ears, yelling.

"I asked you what else, Maggie."

He knew. How did he know? Her mouth went dry. Her throat muscles quivered and her heart hurt. "It said you could . . . die." His expression didn't change. She hadn't stunned him. "Did you —"

"Better me than both of us. I want you to go."

Protecting her. Still. Knowing his own life was at risk. "I won't do it."

"Yes, you will, honey."

She glared at him. "I won't."

"All right. All right, I can't force you to leave — though I wish I could get you to see that it's the smartest thing you could do. But I swear if you stay, Maggie, you'll stay away from me. It's not much, but it's all I can do without your cooperation."

He meant it. There was no doubt whatsoever in her mind. And, man, did it hurt. "You lied, MacGregor." Tears blurred her eyes. "You said you cared about me. If you cared —"

"I do care!" He raked his hands through

189

his hair. "Blast it, don't you see that's why I want you to leave?"

"If you cared," she went on as if he hadn't interrupted, "then you'd never force me to face this alone. You wouldn't do that to me."

He looked down at her. Didn't say anything. Didn't move. Then surprise flickered in his eyes and he lifted a hand to her face, touched a finger to a tear sliding down her cheek. "Oh, Maggie."

She stepped close to him, wrapped her arms around his sides and rested her head against his chest. He had appeared *in* control, but he wasn't. His heart beat hard and fast against her face. "Don't make me go through this without you, Tyler. Please. I'm not that strong."

"What have I gotten you into?"

Slowly, he pulled his hands from his pockets and circled them around her. He was trembling, or was it her? It didn't matter. They'd be safe together. Somehow she just knew they would. And her mother and Carolyn, well, they would just have to understand. For now, alone, Maggie had stood all she could stand. When this resolved, then she'd worry about keeping her promise. For now, she needed him. She'd seen to her mother's needs and, for years, she'd attempted to see to Carolyn's. For the

first time in her adult life, Maggie had needs
that she couldn't see to herself. Was it so
wrong for her to seek help? Hadn't she
earned a turn at leaning on someone else?
On having someone to share her fears with?

S banked down a flood of resentment
at always having to be the strong one. The
em-fixer. The . . . healer.

swallowed hard. The healer. Like Ce-
. "You didn't do anything, MacGregor.
d."

e held her closer, and she gave his sides
queeze to thank him. She'd half-expected
it even pushed he'd walk away from her,
nd she was grateful he hadn't.

"All right." He let out a resigned sigh that
heaved his chest. "Explainable or mystical,
we'll face it together."

The moon grew brilliantly bright. The hint
of a smile touching her lips, she dipped her
chin, leaned back, and saw his shoes. Surprised, she blinked then blinked again.
Could she actually be seeing what she
thought she was seeing?

The little ridge of soil from his previous
attempt to cross the boundary line hugged
his heels.

MacGregor stood on Beaulah's land!

Fighting the glare of the bright sun, Maggie

squinted up at MacGregor. "Just humor me."

Last night, she couldn't act on this. She'd needed time to think, to consider the implications for both of them, to have daylight to be sure as certain she saw what she thought she'd seen.

"No. Not until you tell me what the experiment is all about."

She tugged at his arm, led him back across the grounds to the little bench by the stone wall between Seascape and Beaulah's. Maggie didn't want to explain, to risk getting his hopes up then shattering them. What if she'd made a mistake? She could have been wrong. What if it'd been a trick of the moonlight? Of the *entity?* Wishful thinking? Or something else entirely? "MacGregor, you'd set a saint to swearing."

He stopped beside the bench. "If you'd just tell me why you're doing this, I wouldn't be frustrated to the point of —"

"Okay!" She grimaced at him. "Okay. I'll make a deal with you. You're into deals, right?"

"Depends."

"You'll like this one," she promised. "You do what I tell you — no questions asked — and you'll never have to take cold showers here again."

He slid her a wary look. "You're really hauling out the heavy artillery here."

She was. "It's important."

He rotated his jaw, rubbed at it with his hand and watched her for a long minute, then lowered his hand to his side. "Okay, I'll do it."

"Thank you!" She slapped her hair away from her face, walked over and sighted the boundary line, looking down the little stone wall for a gauge, then dragged the toe of her sneaker in the cool dirt. She didn't dare to so much as glance at MacGregor. Her heart was already threatening to pound right out of her chest, and he surely had figured out at least her main intent already.

She turned back to face him, shaking the loose dirt from her shoe, shored up her courage, hoping he'd put his faith in her, then lifted her gaze.

Slowly, giving him time to adjust, she steeled herself for his rejection, and held out her hand. "Come here."

He let out a sigh of sheer frustration. "Haven't we tempted fate enough lately?"

"No questions. You promised."

"Maggie, I don't want to try this again until we get a better grip on what we're dealing with here."

"Think hot showers, MacGregor. Long,

steamy hot showers."

"Honey, this is more important —"

"Darn it, man, would you just do it?"

He frowned at her for yelling at him, slapped his hand against hers so hard her palm stung, then stepped over the line.

CHAPTER 8

MacGregor didn't black out.

He just stood there, his hand clasped with hers, blinking. Maggie waited. Counted in her head to ten, then twenty, then sixty.

Nothing happened.

He hadn't flinched so much as a muscle. "You okay?"

"I think so," he whispered.

"No temperature drop?" she whispered back. Why were they whispering?

"No."

"No misty veil?" She hadn't moved, either. She was afraid to move. Afraid anything sudden would make something happen. Awaken the slumbering beast.

"No."

Her heart started throbbing, knocking against her chest wall. "No icy fingers?"

"No, nothing." Tears shimmered in his eyes and he squeezed her hand hard. "Maggie, I'm free!"

He laughed straight from the heart, caught her up in his arms and covered her face with rapid, tiny kisses wherever his lips happened to touch.

"Tyler, I'm so pleased." She cupped his face in her hands and gave him a firm peck on the lips, then settled in and did the job right.

The taste of his happiness had her giddy and, when she broke the kiss and he set her onto the ground, she slid her hand down his arm, captured his hand, then lifted it to her cheek, not yet ready to end the celebration. It hadn't been a mistake. Thank goodness, it hadn't been a mistake.

"How did you know?"

She smiled up at him. "Last night, when we were out here and we hugged, I looked down and I thought we were standing on Beaulah's land. I couldn't be sure, but I was nearly certain."

"And you didn't tell me?" He dropped his arm, freeing his hand.

"I didn't want to give you false hope. I wasn't sure — Tyler, what's wrong with you?" He turned ashen. "Tyler?"

He bent, twisted, gasped, reaching for his shoulder, pain twisting his face.

Maggie grabbed his arm. "Tyler!"

Bent double, sweat beading on his forehead and trickling down his face from his temple, he held onto her arm as if it were a lifeline and sucked in great gulps of air.

Maggie gaped at him. He hadn't passed out. He looked weaker than water, but he was conscious — and upright.

"Oh, no." He stared down at the dirt, then squeezed his eyes shut. "No!"

"Tyler, what in the world is it? What's happening to you?"

His heavy breathing hiking and dropping his shoulders, he glared into her eyes, his own wide and round with shock. "I can cross, Maggie. But — But only while I'm touching you."

T.J. sat at the kitchen table, about as confused as he'd ever been in his life — and more outraged than he'd been since realizing he again couldn't paint.

The kicker was, where did he target that outrage? In whose — or what's — direction? On whose head? And what was happening here now?

Things had been complicated enough before Maggie had come along. Now they were — he sighed, propped his elbows on the table, braced his chin on his hand and stared into his coffee mug — worse. Much worse.

She was a woman on a mission. One to help him. One that warned he could die. One that dragged her into the middle of this mystical mess and him into an even deeper panic.

The fire crackled and moisture hissed from the logs. He watched the flames curl around them. He didn't love her. He'd never let himself love anyone again. But he did care about her, and he didn't want her hurt. Was that so wrong?

She'd said he suffered from a good dose of lust and a little gratitude. Well, she was right. But he felt more for her, too, and he'd be a fool to deny it. He didn't want the feelings. He sure didn't need them. But they were there.

He sipped from the mug and watched steam rise and twine over the top of it. The hot coffee burned going down his throat. She should've left. She still should leave. And she should stop holding out info on him. He'd had it with her holding out on him. And she'd held out plenty. Like what the man's voice had whispered. Like seeing T.J. standing on Beaulah's land. Like her telling him she hadn't been experiencing anything strange here . . .

The coffee smelled good, yet turned bitter on his tongue. He cared for her. But he sure couldn't trust her. He set the mug back down on the table. The firm *thunk* set the salt and pepper shakers knocking together.

She breezed into the kitchen looking like a breath of spring and sunshine, and headed straight for the fridge. "Hi, MacGregor. I wondered where you were."

He leaned back and lifted his cup. "The possibilities are limited. Not many locales to choose from." This was getting bad. Even he heard the frustration in his tone.

She leaned over to get something out of the fridge and her jade slacks stretched tight over her bottom. His chest tightened, reminding him just how long it'd been since he'd been with a woman. He sighed again. Deeper.

"Just caught the weather report in the parlor. Can you believe it? Ice a couple days ago and today the high's sixty." She straightened up, holding a slice of cheese and a can of grape juice. "If you're interested, the low's forty-five."

"I'm not. Weather here changes fast and frequently. So long as it isn't going to rain, who cares?"

Unwrapping the cheese slice, she sat down across the table from him then popped back the flip tab on the juice. Air swooshed out of the can. "Sorry to slay your fantasy, dragon. It's gonna rain tomorrow."

He grumbled under his breath then took another sip of coffee and watched Maggie lick a drop of juice from her thumb.

"What's wrong with a little rain?" She tore a sliver off the cheese slice and nibbled at it.

"Roofers can't work in it."

She shrugged and propped her foot on his chair rung. "Don't you like your room here?"

"I like my privacy better." He frowned.

She paused, holding the can midair. "I hate to be critical on such a gorgeous day, MacGregor, but in case you haven't noticed, your attitude is rearing its nasty head."

It was. He needed to be thinking about their situation and on how to get this stubborn woman out of here, and all he could think about was holding her in his arms on the bench outside and in the bathroom upstairs, of how good she'd smelled and felt and tasted, of how good she smelled right now. And of how much he wanted to take her upstairs to bed.

"Where's Miss Hattie?" Maggie polished off the cheese and eyed the blueberry pie on the counter next to the fruit bowl.

"Gone to the village. She always does her shopping on Tuesdays."

"I saw her leave the greenhouse earlier with a huge bunch of flowers."

He nodded. "She goes by the cemetery on her way to the store."

"Ah. Her husband?"

"She never married. She was supposed to, but he died. They were both very young."

"How tragic." Maggie lowered her gaze. "She must have loved him very much — to have never married."

"All her world."

Maggie smoothed a hand down her side. "Have you ever wondered what it'd be like to love someone that much? Or to know that someone loved you that much?"

A twinge of the old betrayal burned in his stomach. He clenched his muscles and stared into the fire. "I thought I knew, but I didn't."

"I'm sorry, I forgot about your fiancée." Maggie's cheeks flushed. "Leave it to me to put my foot, calf, and thigh in my mouth."

"You didn't." A muscle in his cheek twitched. "Things weren't as I thought they were between my fiancée and me. I thought we wanted the same things. But we didn't." He gave Maggie a ghost of a smile. "Funny, but even now that's hard to admit."

"Life has a way of doing that, doesn't it? Turning the tables on us, I mean." Maggie poured herself a glass of milk, splashing a drop onto the counter, then set the carton back into the fridge. "Every time I think I have my life about like I want it," she grabbed a dish cloth and swiped at the spot, "something happens to screw things up."

Looking thoughtful, she carried the glass back to the table and sat down. "I've about concluded my destiny in life is to learn patience." She grinned. "I guess it's good that I never expected to find a love as strong as Miss Hattie's was for her guy. So far, I'm flunking on a grand scale."

T.J. seriously doubted Maggie ever in her life had flunked at anything important. Still, what did he know? He couldn't trust his judgment about others — or himself. Not after what had happened with Carolyn. "I think the kind of love Miss Hattie felt must be very . . . rare. The kind only the luckiest people find — and then only once."

He motioned toward the pie. "She said to tell you to help yourself, by the way. I warned her that you had an insatiable appetite and she'd likely come home to an empty plate."

"Terrific." Ignoring his commentary, Maggie scooted back her chair. It scraped against the floor. "Want a slice?"

"No, thanks." The fire in the grate snapped

and a shower of sparks went up the chimney. It kept the chill out of the room, but it also set up a potent, domestic scene. T.J. wished it didn't. Maggie at the counter, slicing pie, the silver server clinking against the pie tin. Her sliding a sliver onto a plate with the tip of her finger, then licking crust crumbs off her fingertip. Him sitting at the table, watching her every move, noticing little things about her. The way her nose turned slightly askew and, with her movements, the way her dainty gold bracelet slid up and down from her forearm to her wrist.

He wanted to paint her. Laughing. Her head tossed back, her lips parted, her eyes sparkling. The way she'd looked when he had crossed the boundary and hadn't passed out. He wanted to paint her.

"This is *soooo* good." Maggie glanced at him. "MacGregor, you don't know what you're missing."

He didn't. But, man, could he imagine.

She closed her eyes, her expression enraptured. "Mmm, wonderful."

The twinge turned to yearning, dove deeper still, and his throat went thick. He wanted to paint her, but he also wanted her. All of her. Her sass, her temper, her revenge of using his razor and stealing all the hot water — even her appetite. And he wanted her kisses and hugs. He loved the way she held him. How she turned to him when she was afraid, and admitted so easily to him that she was scared. A person had to be very self-confident to admit fear.

She lied. Do you want her lies, too?

No, he didn't want her lies. He hated her lies. In an offbeat way, he understood why Miss Hattie had to hold out on him. Strange events happening at the inn couldn't do business any good, and the judge wouldn't appreciate the negative notoriety. Miss Hattie could end up out of a job and out of a home. But Maggie lying to him, he couldn't understand. Why would she?

"You might not have exaggerated." She turned and grinned at him.

He followed her pointed finger to the pie tin. "I can't believe you've stood there and eaten nearly half the thing." He grunted. "You're going to be sick."

"Naw. I've got a strong constitution." She took another bite, raked it off the fork with her teeth. "But even if I do get sick, it's worth it. This is the best blueberry pie I've had in my life."

He folded his arms over his chest and leaned back on his chair. "Yeah, and tomorrow you'll be griping that your jeans are too tight."

She waved her fork at him. "There's that attitude again."

She finished up and rinsed her plate at the sink, humming.

The woman hummed? Hummed, as if she hadn't a care in the world while he sat here worried sick and dying from yearning?

He got up and refilled his coffee cup. There was no justice in anything anymore. Not much sense, either.

"Oh, geez." She turned her back to the counter and leaned against the cabinet. "Now you've got the snarl." She let her gaze drift to the ceiling. "The attitude and the snarl." She clicked her tongue to the roof of her mouth. "Things are not looking good here."

He set down his mug and leaned his hip against the cabinet, facing her. "I want you to leave."

"No, you want me to be safe." She let out a little sigh. "There's a difference, Mac-Gregor."

"Okay, you're right. I want you to be safe."

She stepped closer and lifted her hand to his waist. "It hasn't occurred to you yet, has it?"

He hated her tone. It was the same one she habitually used for dropping bomb-shells. He really didn't need another bomb exploding right now.

"This entity, whatever it is, is mystical." She softened her voice as if to make that declaration easier for him to accept. "There's nowhere to go."

The phone rang.

Maggie answered it and smiled. "Hi, Miss Hattie."

She paused, listened, then wrapped the spiral cord around her finger. "Tyler told me. I loved it. Ate almost half." She laughed. "Did you put cinnamon in it?"

T.J. stared at her open-mouthed, doing his best to refrain from snatching the phone out of her hand and slinging it across the room. How could the woman be standing there discussing pie ingredients not ten seconds after telling him there was no place to go where she'd be safe?

He wanted to choke her. To shout some sense into her. He wanted to kiss her until she was dizzy, put her and her things into her car, and drive away with her. But he *hadn't* thought about it. Even if they could leave, *where* could they go? When pursued by an entity with mystical powers, there was no place to hide . . .

"Sure," she said. "I'll be happy to run it over. Be there —"

She stopped midsentence and laughed out

loud. The sound had him aching.

"It's the least I can do. Mmm? Yes, I love apples. Oooh, cobbler sounds great. Gee, I don't think I've heard of anyone putting that in cobbler before. I definitely want to try it."

She'd weigh a ton by the time she reached forty. But, he let his gaze drift down her slim body, she was perfect now. Petite, but not boyishly slim. Slender, but softly curved and very feminine. He'd loved her hair down and loose, but he loved it in a French braid, too.

"Miss Millie's. All right. Yes, I saw it the other day. Near the post office, right?"

Enough. Enough. Uncle! T.J. walked up behind her, wrapped his arms around her stomach, then bent down and planted a kiss on her neck. It tasted sweet, and he laid a trail of kisses along it, from right behind her ear down to her shoulder. She smelled like spring. He loved spring. Sighing, he slid his hands from her ribs to the waist on her jade blouse. The silk felt soft, her body smooth, and its heat seeped through the fabric and warmed his palms.

"I'll, um, tell him." Her face flushed. "See you." Maggie hung up the phone.

Finally. With a hand at her shoulder, T.J. urged her to turn toward him, anticipation burning deep inside him.

She looked like the cat that had swallowed the canary — and its cage.

"I, um" — she cleared her throat — "have a message for you from Miss Hattie."

"Oh?" He didn't like the sound of this — or Maggie's smirk.

"Uh-huh." Again with the throat clearing. "She says Lydia Johnson at The Store says to tell you that she's sending the razor blades you asked for on the phone this morning, but she can't send the 'personal items' because she promised the pastor she wouldn't sell them to anyone who wasn't married."

"What!"

"She, meaning Lydia, also said that she called Jacky Landry over at Landry's Landing cuz, being a pseudo-hippie, Jacky will sell anything to anyone except for bait — won't cut in on Bill Butler's turf — but Jacky doesn't have the brand you wanted. Anyway, Lydia said not to worry. She's added them to the shopping list on the bulletin board over at the Blue Moon Cafe and Jimmy Goodson will pick them up for you on his next trip over to Boothbay Harbor — which is on Friday — and she hopes that in light of all the dreadful diseases one can catch from immoral behavior, you'll refrain until he gets back."

"On the bulletin board?" T.J. shouted. "For —"

"And, Lydia says she's awfully sorry about this inconvenience, but the pastor's already in a snit because Horace insists on putting a keg full of crushed ice and canned beer by the front door of The Store on weekends, and he's not too happy about Jimmy's swimsuit calendar, hanging in his garage, either. She just couldn't risk upsetting the pastor anymore. He'd be long-winded sure as certain come Sunday, and it absolutely mortifies her when Horace dozes off during services. The man's a fine mayor, but his attention span on Sunday mornings runs a wee bit on the short side and he could wake the dead with his snores."

T.J.'s face had to be purple. The veins in his neck felt ready to explode.

Maggie swallowed a belly laugh, but it danced in her eyes.

"Is that it?" If she didn't laugh soon the woman would blow a gasket.

She clenched her teeth. "I'm to run into the village to bring a book to Miss Millie for their Historical Society meeting. Miss Hattie's going to make me an apple cobbler tomorrow for the favor. And she doesn't use cinnamon in her blueberry pie, but she does add a dash of nutmeg." Maggie leaned back against the wall and tapped her lips. "I think that's it."

"Go ahead, then."

"What?"

"Laugh. Get it out before it chokes you to death."

She did. She laughed until tears streamed down her face. "Oh, MacGregor, isn't it a riot? Proves what they say about small towns. If it's happening, everyone knows it." She laughed some more.

"Uh-huh." He folded his arms over his chest. "Done yet?"

"Yeah." She swatted at her eyes with one hand, and held her side with the other, as if putting pressure on a stitch.

"Good." He gave her a smile that even he felt was more akin to a snarl. "Two small points that might be of minor interest."

She blinked. "What?"

"One. Just who do you think everyone in the village — including Miss Hattie — figures will be my partner, regardless of whether or not I can refrain until Jimmy gets back from Boothbay Harbor with the goods?"

The smile lurking at the corners of her mouth faded. "I — we —" She sputtered. "We haven't even discussed that. Geez, it's on the bulletin board, MacGregor! Everyone in the world around here goes to the Blue Moon!"

Finally hit her. "And, two, I didn't call Lydia Johnson at The Store this morning and place an order for razor blades, 'personal items,' or anything else. The phone's been out of order since last night. Remember? You tried calling your mother."

"I did!" She frowned. "But . . . then, who — ?"

"Or what?" He frowned with her.

Her eyes stretched wide. "Our mystical entity?" She shot him a look of total disbelief. "Don't you think that's stretching it —"

"Who else?" He shrugged. "We know it can effect a man's voice."

"Great." Maggie grumbled and sighed. "Great. Just what I need. A man with an attitude and a mystical entity with a warped sense of humor." She flung up her hand and walked toward the gallery. "Boy, I love it here."

When Maggie came back downstairs with *Tall Ships* tucked under her arm, MacGregor was sitting in the rocker beside the fire, his foot tapping the floor on every forward rock, his expression grimmer than her mother's stories of the Reaper.

"I'll be back in a bit." She zipped up her brown jacket. The stiffer suede patches rubbed at her elbows.

He looked at her, almost accusingly.

"Look, MacGregor, would you just spit it out and let's get it over with?"

"What?"

"Whatever burr is under your saddle now."

He looked into the fire. "Go on. Miss Millie's waiting."

"She'll have to wait a few minutes longer then." Maggie leaned forward, braced a hand on each of the rocker's arms. "I have the feeling I know what's eating at you, and I'm telling you that it isn't my fault."

He glared at her, nearly nose to nose.

"You're ticked because you can only cross the boundary while we're touching."

"We don't know that for a fact. Just because it happened once —"

"No, *we* don't know it," she interrupted. "But *you* do."

He clamped his jaw.

"I know you made another attempt this morning," she confessed. "I saw you and Miss Hattie down at the bench from up-stairs."

He didn't say a word. Wouldn't look at her. Why was she beating herself to death over this? She hadn't asked for any of this to happen. And if she had her rathers, none of it *would* be happening.

It was the frustration. He was a proud man. After his family experiences, being vulnerable to anything made the blow to his ego that much stronger. He needed Maggie and that pegged the problem. MacGregor didn't want to need anyone.

She pecked a kiss to his temple. "I'm sorry, MacGregor. I really am. But it isn't my fault and it isn't fair for you to punish me for something that's out of my control."

That he didn't respond didn't surprise her. It disappointed her, but it didn't surprise her. Maggie left, closing the mud room door.

All the way around the corner of the garage, she pouted a little herself. Hearing hammering, she waved to the two men putting new shingles on the Carriage House roof. They looked to be about half-done. If the weather held, it wouldn't be long before MacGregor could move back into his suite there and have his privacy.

A little ache settled over her heart, and she swore that she'd left her good sense back in New Orleans. Getting more and more deeply involved with him — heart and all — which after seeing what heart-to-heart relationships had done with her parents she'd sworn she'd never do. Sneaking around like a thief in the night, checking the Registration Book and finding Carolyn never had made it to Seascape, though she had reserved a Carriage House room — the same Carriage House room MacGregor had occupied for the last nine months. Finding no evidence proving the man in any way involved in Carolyn's possible non-accident/ accident, and half-suspecting him guilty as sin anyway — even though every bone in her body swore he could never hurt any woman — not after losing his mother and Carolyn as he had. Contending with the sorry sense of humor of some mystical entity without so much as a grunt of protest when she should be scared stiff. And loving MacGregor's kisses. Geez, she hadn't just left her sense at home. She'd left her sanity!

True, she didn't feel insane. She felt calm and at peace. Serene. And, she might as well admit it — if only to herself — on the brink of falling in love.

That alone proved she'd stacked up a brick short. That alone should have her lunging headlong beyond scared stiff and firmly entrenched in mortified.

So why didn't it?

How she wished she had a clue.

The sounds of the waves lapping against the rocks enticed her closer to the shore. At the boundary line, her stomach fluttered and she hesitated for a mere twinkling. Giving herself a good mental shake, she stepped over the line.

The temperature cooled.

It didn't plummet, but it dropped enough to chill her through her jacket and raise goose pimples on her arms.

That veil of mist curled at her feet, swirled and swirled, but it didn't rise higher, and the icy fingers pressed lightly against her neck. Not debilitating, but dizzying.

Her stomach lurched a level deeper with the onset of each event, and she gasped. "Tyler!" The sense of peace she'd felt drained out of her body. "Tyler!"

He didn't answer but, as quickly as it all started, the sensations stopped. Maggie spun around and looked back toward the house. Slowly, her panic ebbed, but the sense of peace didn't return.

Strange. A moment ago . . .

A moment ago, she'd been on the other side of the line. On Seascape lands.

Her heart skipped a solid beat. She gulped in a deep breath, then stepped back over onto Seascape. The peace still didn't return. "MacGregor," she whispered, knowing he couldn't hear her. "Something weird is happening here . . ."

An image of him filled her mind, and a deep glow of contentment spread through her heart.

The peace was back.

It couldn't be. But it was. The serenity and calm and peace — the security she sensed when they were together — all of it had come back. She'd associated all those good feelings with the house — with Seascape itself. But — but somehow, those things had shifted . . . to MacGregor!

Her heart thudded wildly. Frightened, feeling more vulnerable than she'd ever felt in her life, and more resentful, she shunned the truth, afraid MacGregor had been right. She'd waited too long to leave.

She didn't *want* those feelings attached to him. Falling for MacGregor was crazy. Something she didn't understand. Something her mother never would understand. She'd always been devoted to and doted on Carolyn. She'd never forgive Maggie for this. Never.

And Maggie couldn't help doubting that she'd ever forgive herself.

What was she going to do?

Her ears started ringing. She shook her head, trying to clear them, but the ringing

216

only grew louder . . . then changed to that awful whisper.

Stay away from him.

CHAPTER 9

The woman, darn her, was right.

T.J. snatched up a small stone and hummed it into the ocean. It wasn't fair, or just, for him to be angry with her because he couldn't cross the boundary without her. But was that really what had him angry? Or was it knowing she loved driving him crazy like this?

He could just see her. Looking down her sleek nose, snubbing his dependency on her as no more than her due. Flashing him that oh-so-cool and distant half-smile that made him want to punch holes in walls because it degraded him into feeling inferior, then freezing him with that icy blue gaze that held far too many mysteries to interpret whatever emotion, if any, lay behind it. Yeah, he could just see her. Loving every minute of his misery.

Maggie? This is Maggie?

His pricking conscience had him shaking

his head to clear away cobwebs of confusion. No, not Maggie. Carolyn. Maggie wouldn't — *hadn't yet* — done any of those things to him. When he'd treated her like dirt, she'd reached out and helped him. She'd dragged him . . .

Why had he confused them? Apart from both being women, the two were nothing alike. He chewed at his lip. Maybe because he had cared for both of them and hadn't wanted to care for either of them? Maybe. But the comparison still struck him as odd. They didn't belong on the same side of the planet.

Carolyn, svelte and blonde and never a hair out of place, had chilled like a quarter moon in winter. Cool and distant. More mysterious shadow than sleek, shining sickle. She invited a man's gaze yet forbade his touch.

Maggie, vibrant and passionate and full of flaming-red sass, burned hot like the summer sun. Searing. Relentless. Far too brilliant not to lure, and far too blinding not to leave a man scorched and sizzling. A heat-hazed rim secreted the source of her flame, but a man could never be so far away from Maggie to not feel her warmth.

He let his gaze drop down below the tree line to the angry waves thrashing against

219

the rocks and swamping the beach. If he had to cross the boundary with someone, why not with Bill, or someone safe like Miss Hattie? Why Maggie? Why someone he could hurt — or kill?

He refused to need her. He'd never need any woman.

Or be needed by any woman.

That sobering truth fueled the resentment that had become as much a part of him as the enamel on his teeth, and left him snarling, then hollow.

The roar of the ocean and the soothing scent of its spray drained his anger. He lifted his face to the mist-laden wind, feeling it cut across his skin, hearing it moaning through the pines. A gull squalled, sounding lonely. T.J. empathized, and accepted the truth winging through his heart. Pure and simple, he missed Maggie.

The woman was an enigma. One minute he thought her brave, the next, a fool. She should leave here — that certainty sank down to the marrow of his bones. Leaving might not do any good but, then again, it might. She *should* at least try.

An empty ache arrowed down his center and spread. Shunning it, he tensed his muscles, clenched his jaw, fisted his hands. He wanted her to leave. He really did.

A phantom wind stirred and whipped, whistling in his ears.

All right, all right. That was a lie. *Part* of him wanted her to leave. But, Gosh forgive him, part of him wanted her to stay. The selfish part who couldn't see him making it through another exiled day without seeing her face and hearing her laugh.

He stared at the top of the lighthouse. A strong sense of urgency attacked him and the hairs on his neck stood on end.

Jerking back, he looked through the dull gray haze toward the Co-Op. No sign of Bill, Leslie, or their boys — or of anyone else. Toward Seascape, a sliver of weak sun broke through the heavy clouds and glinted on the attic window. A raccoon raced across the widow's walk, clearly looking for mischief — or running away from it. T.J. frowned. Odd, it was midafternoon. Raccoons are nocturnal — and they rarely race anywhere. Still, nothing evidenced a physical sign of distress anywhere.

The sense of urgency intensified . . . and attached itself to Maggie.

Not pausing to puzzle it out, T.J. hurried over the jagged rocks to the slick stone path, then headed down to the road at a breakneck clip. When his feet hit the paved street, he gained speed, reached the sloping lawn in a dead run. Then he saw her. Stumbling toward the house, she looked as if she'd seen a ghost.

His heart tripping over its own beat, his sweat-soaked shirt clinging to his body, he ran over to her. "Maggie?" Her face was pale, her eyes as blank as a zombie's. "You okay?"

"Fine." Stiff-spined as a sea urchin, she kept walking. Didn't look at him. Didn't blink.

"You don't look okay," he said, falling into step beside her. "You look upset."

"I don't want to talk about it, Tyler."

Tyler not *MacGregor*. This was serious. A confirming rush of impossibly warm air blew over the back of his neck. More chilled by it than by any frigid cold, he shuddered. "All right." A strong gust of wind threatened to knock him back. He shifted against it, stuffed his hands in his pockets, and looked up toward the house. Something had rattled Maggie deeply, but unlike before she had no intention of turning to him with it. Why? What had changed?

Bereft, he cut around the corner of the house then twisted the knob on the mud room door. It creaked open. Maggie breezed past him without slowing down. If he hadn't opened the door, he had the distinct feeling she was so preoccupied she would have walked right into it. She hooked her coat on a peg, then went on into the house and headed for the stairs.

T.J. followed her. When he passed Cecelia's portrait, he whispered, "If you're feeling the least inclined, a little insight here would be majorly helpful."

Upstairs, at the shadowy landing, he nearly collided with Maggie. She'd been to her room. Shoeless, she clutched her pink robe balled at her stomach. Her pale face now bleached a milk-white that had him feeling sickly. *What the heck had happened to her?* "Headed for the bath?"

"Yeah." She didn't stop walking.

Hating her deadpan tone, he stepped aside, off the edge of the white rug, and hugged the wall to let her pass him. "I've noticed something about you. Whenever you get upset, you take to water like a duck."

"I'll be out later." She walked right by, stepped inside and gave him a look so sincere it curdled his stomach. "Hopefully before the turn of the century."

The door closed and T.J. frowned at the nail centered in it. She'd seemed almost . . . hopeless.

Though no open windows or doors or central heat register provided a source,

223

again he felt that confirming rush of impossibly warm air breeze over his neck. The entity?

The water pipes groaned, filling the tub. When she turned the tap off and he heard splashing, he opened the outer door. She hadn't thought to turn on the light but she'd shut the inner door that separated the dressing room from the one housing the tub and shower. He flicked on the switch. A rosy glow flooded the dressing room, lifted from the pink-tinge streaking through the tan marble vanity. Pausing at the step up to the tub room, he listened at the door.

No muttering. That was a good sign, wasn't it?

Had he lost his mind? When irked, Maggie muttered. Furious, she shot visual daggers at him, raised the roof with her sass, and muttered. Terrified, as at the bench when she'd felt what he'd felt on crossing the boundary, she'd clammed up.

Clamming up was definitely a bad sign.

He lifted his hand to knock, but didn't do it. He was invading her privacy. Yet she *had* forgotten to put out the sign . . .

At war with himself, he touched his fingertips to the smooth wood. The defeated slump in her shoulders, the absence of fire in her gaze, and her ghostly pallor had him imagining all kinds of awful things. If she'd just talk to him, reassure him that she was all right. Darn it, he was worried about her.

He pressed his hand flat against the cool door. "Maggie?"

Water sloshed. "Geez, MacGregor. Are you going to interrupt every bath I take in this house?"

"Maybe." Oddly relieved by her cranky tone, he sat down on the step and stared at the brass light fixture above the mirror that stretched wall to wall. "What's wrong?"

"I don't want to talk about it," she said, then grumbled, "I already told the man that once, didn't I?"

"Okay, but that just leaves my mind wide open to all sorts of wild imaginings." It did. He hadn't exaggerated a bit. And those imaginings *had* to be worse than anything that had happened to her in the village. "Did someone give you a hard time about the 'personal items?'"

"No one mentioned them. But Miss Millie, bless her heart, blushed until I thought she'd have a stroke." Maggie sighed. "I intended to go to the Blue Moon and erase them off the bulletin board, but the sheriff's car was out front and Batty Beaulah had him cornered on the porch — having a field day, nagging at the man. The cafe was crowded, too, so I figured maybe when it wasn't so busy would be a better time."

He studied his nails, a smile curling at his lip. Beaulah had zip to do with it. "Embarrassed, huh?"

"Yeah." More grumbles. "Why does he do that? Dang, but I hate it when he does that."

She loved it, pure and simple. He propped his forearm on his bent knee, one foot on the step, the other on the floor. Smelling mint, he spotted an open box of green dental floss near the sink. "You realize I'm going to sit here until you tell me what's up, so you might as well —"

The door opened, surprising him. He looked over his shoulder, back at her.

Her shoulders hunched beneath her fluffy pink bathrobe, she stared at him, her eyes bright with unshed tears. Without a word, she bent down and kissed him.

Her lips were warm and tender, if not quite steady, and her hand at his shoulder trembled. He tasted her fear, her regret, and her longing. Their combined power shook him to his soul.

She straightened back up, let her fingertips drift down his face to his chin, then leaned against the doorjamb and crossed her arms over her chest. Was she shutting him out or locking herself in, distancing herself from him emotionally?

"That was for me. Because I needed it and it was my turn to get what I needed." She lifted her chin. "But it can't happen anymore, Tyler. In fact, nothing can happen anymore — and it shouldn't have happened, anyway."

What in the world was she talking about? "Could you put this in English, please?"

"I care about you." Her chin quivered. "I didn't want to. I even knew I was crazy to let it happen, and I swore to myself a hundred times that I would put a stop to it." Her expression crumbled and she bunched bits of her robe in her hands. "I did try. I really did. But it didn't work." She drew in a shuddery breath. "It just didn't work."

She cared. And she knew he cared. And he knew what happened to women he cared about, but still couldn't make himself *not* care.

Heaven help them both.

Guilt swarmed in his stomach like angry bees. From the step, he looked up at her. "Maggie, I know this bond of ours hits us both pretty close to the bone, but —"

"It hits a lot deeper than that." She shoved away from the door jamb, then pulled herself up straight and smoothed her rumpled robe over her thigh. "But it's finished as of now. It — it has to be. From here on out, I have to stay away from you, Tyler. I — I have to."

She'd been hesitant and she hadn't liked issuing the edict — her shaky tone made that clear. But there was more to this than that. She didn't just fear caring about him, she feared something deeper. Something not at the village. Something . . . mystical?

Squelching the urge to shout the truth out of her, he frowned. "What happened to you?" How had he gotten himself into this quagmire? "Did our entity pull something?"

She lifted then lowered her gaze from the ceiling to him, a glimmer of sass fringing her tone. "You're going to nag me until I tell you, aren't you?"

"Darn right, I am." Nag, beg, whatever it took.

"Okay. I'll save us both some heartburn, but I want to go on record that I really *hate* being nagged."

Didn't everyone? "Noted," he said, preparing for another installment of her not-so-subtle revenge.

Lowering her pointed finger, she looked him straight in the eye. "When I crossed the boundary alone, I felt what you feel." She rubbed her arms as if her bones were cold and she feared they'd never again feel warm. "Not as strong as you feel it — I didn't pass out or anything, but I got dizzy, and I felt so . . . desolate."

A knot of fear exploded in his stomach. "You've got to leave here. Now. Please, Maggie." It was too late for that. He knew it. Yet if she went and he stayed, maybe the entity would be satisfied. Maybe —

"There's nowhere to go!" She pressed her hands to her temples, shook off some frustration by ruffling her hair. "How many times do we have to go through this, Mac-Gregor? Ten? Twenty? Two hundred?"

He forced himself to calm down and think. There had to be more to this than what she'd told him. She'd felt the symptoms at the bench and then she'd turned to him for comfort and solace. Now she was turning away from him. Why? There *had* to be more . . . "You heard another whisper, didn't you?"

She didn't answer, just stared at him.

"Maggie, blast it, woman, tell me the truth."

"Yes."

His heart nearly stopped. *Please, please don't let it be that she could die, too. Please!* "What did it say?"

Her voice cracked and her chin trembled.

Her eyes looked too big for her face, too small to hold all her fears. "To stay away from you."

T.J. stilled. That didn't make sense. It had told her to help him. Warned her. Now it'd done a one-eighty and told her to stay away? "Honey" — he softened his voice — "are you sure it wasn't your conscience?"

"I'm sure." She looked devastated. "It's told me the same thing, but it has my voice. This message had the man's whisper."

She'd been afraid of facing this entity alone, but she'd chosen to do it, and clearly there was no way he could sway her decision. T.J. knew it. Just as he knew she'd made that decision to protect him.

He stood up, so humbled and rattled his knees felt weak. He wanted to hold her, to reassure her, but he couldn't. Against this entity, they were helpless. How could they fight an adversary without knowing even its form?

They couldn't. That was the bottom line. But if she stayed away from him, her odds of staying safe had to be better. Yet just the prospect of her being distant with him had his chest feeling as tight as his throat. "Thanks for trusting me enough to tell me, Maggie. That, um, means a lot to me." She meant a lot to him. More than even he had realized, until now. He gave her arm a gentle squeeze, and kept all he would have told her, if he'd had the right, locked inside him. "I think we'd better listen to it."

Her eyes wide and glossy, she nodded her agreement.

And because he needed it, as she'd needed it earlier, he kissed her. This time — give him the strength — goodbye.

Maggie stared out the kitchen window. Bleak and dreary. Again.

"Well, I can see my banana pudding doesn't rank nearly so high as my blueberry pie or apple cobbler." Seated in her rocker, Miss Hattie kept her gaze on the knitting in her lap, the needles quietly clacking with her stitches.

"I'm sorry." Maggie looked down at the untouched bowl of pudding before her on the table. The whipped cream had melted into the crumbled vanilla wafers. "I just don't have much of an appetite these days."

Pausing to tune the old-fashioned radio behind her, Miss Hattie stopped the dial on a Big-Band-era station. Strains of soft blues filled the kitchen. "Ah, that's better." She picked up her knitting and her lips moved, as if she counted stitches, then she resumed rocking. "I've also noticed Tyler's appetite's declined. I have to say, dear, that it appears you two have been avoiding each other this past week. Is there a connection?"

Boy, was there. Maggie sighed and rubbed her cheek against her upper arm. "I'm afraid I've done the dumbest thing I've ever in my life done — and there have been some real lulus."

"Anyone who's lived has suffered their share of lulus, I'd say." She kept rocking, kept counting her stitches. The chair creaked five times, then she added, "It might help to talk about it."

Tempted, Maggie hesitated. Because she'd always had to stand on her own, she'd learned young to be a decent judge of character and something in Miss Hattie did invite trust, but Maggie should handle her problems alone. She always had. And wasn't it just an awful weakness to not meet personal challenges head-on, under your own steam? Besides, she'd leaned once on MacGregor, and look at the misery that had gotten her. Who needed another week of lonely suffering?

"I don't want to intrude, dear." Miss Hattie tucked her knitting down into a little black bag embroidered with yellow flowers on the floor beside her rocker. The metal needles clanked. "But a fresh eye never hurts."

"I shouldn't worry you with it." Maggie grimaced. "I got myself into this and, somehow, I've got to get myself out." She gave Miss Hattie a heartfelt look laced with all her doubts. "It'll take a miracle."

Rosy-faced from the warmth of the fire burning in the grate, Miss Hattie dabbed at her temple with her hankie then pressed it back into her blue sweater pocket. "Just offering food for thought — not directing you in your affairs, by any means — but there are times when we all need to lean on others."

"I appreciate the advice." Tempted, Maggie fingered her spoon, tapping its bowl to the table. No. If she failed, better she had only herself to blame. "But I think I should try to work through this myself."

"I know what you mean. I'm independent, too, when I can get by with it." She fell quiet for a long moment, then clicked her tongue to the roof of her mouth. "I've lived in this house all but one year of my life. Have I mentioned that?"

"No, ma'am, I don't think you have." Relieved at the topic shift, Maggie curled her foot up under her on the chair. The smell of the wood burning, the gold flames licking at the screen, the fridge motor purring, calmed her tattered nerves.

"My father was the gardener here and my mother cared for the house, as I do now." Her voice dropped lower, softened and grew more melodic. "I've seen a lot of miracles happen inside these walls. And I'm hoping" — she paused and slid her gaze to the ceiling as if speaking to someone else entirely — "for another one. One for you and Tyler."

Maggie's heart sank. "Tyler doesn't believe in miracles." Why did that bother her so much? She couldn't exactly claim to be a staunch advocate herself.

"I know." Rocking gently, her comfy old chair creaked. "I'd say that means you have to believe enough for both of you."

The refrigerator's icemaker dumped ice, and the trickle of water refilling the trays blended with the calm crackles of the fire. The homey sounds conspired, and Maggie grew wistful. "I'd like to believe in miracles, but I'm not sure I do. Not anymore." After the way her father had treated her mother, how could she believe in miracles? How could she believe in relationships?

"Mmm. I know you and Tyler care deeply for each other, Maggie — just as I know that, since you were a child, you've been weighed down with responsibilities that shouldn't have been yours. Children need the chance to dream. You're no longer a child, of course, but you still need to learn to dream, dear, and to believe in life's magic."

How did Miss Hattie know that — about her responsibilities and her childhood? "Magic?" What magic? If she didn't respect Miss Hattie so much and know her heart was well-meaning, Maggie would have snorted. "Life isn't Pollyannaville, Miss Hattie. I've wished it were a million times, but it's not."

"What is it, then?"

Maggie lifted then lowered her brows and pursed her lips. "It's accepting that the good guys don't always win. Sometimes the bad guys get off scot-free. And it's conceding to the truth."

"Which is?"

Maggie's voice quavered. "That sometimes the best we can hope for is just to absorb our lumps and survive."

"Of course you know best, dear." Miss Hattie slid her a gentle smile. "But I've come to old age with the opinion that most things in life are profoundly affected by a person's attitude. It's pretty much what you make it. Life might not be Pollyannaville, but it doesn't have to be Hades, either — unless you deem it so."

Generous-natured, she hadn't said it, but the implication lay as thick as a sheet of ice between them. "Like I've made it between me and Tyler this past week?"

"Only you and Tyler can answer that. Though if you'll allow an outsider her objective opinion, it's clear as a sunny day that being distant with each other has you both upset and unhappy."

Maggie was upset and unhappy. She missed him. But Tyler? Fat chance. More than likely, he was relieved. Probably plotting out another virtual vacation from his travel magazines and not giving her a penny's worth of thought.

Yet he had said he cared about her. He could be missing her a little. Maybe. She was all he had here, aside from Miss Hattie and, on occasion, Bill Butler and his son, Aaron. The man worked hard for a living and didn't have much spare time, and the boy was fond of MacGregor, but he was a boy.

Considering their breach from his perspective rather than from her own, after nine months of exile, no doubt he *did* miss her. He'd have missed a toothache. A knot lodged in Maggie's throat, and she lowered her gaze. "I didn't realize we were both so . . ."

"Transparent?"

Miserable had been her first thought. But transparent fit, too, and it seemed a lot less confidence-draining to admit. She nodded.

"Don't worry, dear." Miss Hattie chuckled softly. "To most people, it wouldn't be obvious."

Deserting her spoon-tapping, Maggie propped her arm on the table, then fingered the petal of a porcelain bisque daffodil on the centerpiece. "Then why is it so obvious to you?"

"Because I've experienced what the two of you are going through now." Miss Hattie let her gaze drift and glide along the ceiling. "The road to love is rougher than our rock-bound coast. But, oh my, what a spectacular road to travel."

Maggie smiled. "Tyler told me about your fiancé."

Grabbing the poker, Miss Hattie stirred the fire, then lifted a log from the wood box and plopped it onto the grate. Sparks spewed up the chimney, flashed midair, then sizzled out. "Ah, he was a fine man. Field-promoted during the war, you know." She closed the screen, then sat back down in her rocker. "A fine man."

"I'm sure he was," Maggie said, "or you wouldn't have loved him so much."

"True," Miss Hattie said, her tone matter-of-fact. "But that's in the past now, and you and Tyler are not."

She lifted her hands to her rocker's arms. "You know, dear, this is the second time in my life that I've watched Tyler suffer. I'd so hoped that you . . ." She fell quiet and her expression clouded.

"What?" Maggie urged, curious at what Miss Hattie had hoped.

Her gentle face turned serious, as solemn as if she'd said far more than she intended and regretted now that she couldn't pull the words back inside and keep them unspoken.

"I'd hoped you'd have the courage to help him."

Courage? An odd choice of words, unless . . . Surprise streaked up Maggie's spine and the flower petal stabbed into the tip of her finger. "You know, don't you?" Stiffening, she swallowed hard. "About the mystical entity?"

"Mystical entity?" Miss Hattie smiled, appearing totally at ease. "My goodness but that's an uppity name for it."

"Well, what do you call it?" Maggie frowned. "Tyler and I have no clue."

"Most people call it love, dear."

"Love?" Maggie nearly choked. "Good grief, Miss Hattie, I don't *love* MacGregor."

Seemingly unaffected by Maggie's shout, Miss Hattie lowered the radio's volume then resumed rocking. "Oh?" She studied Maggie through those too-seeing, emerald eyes.

"No. Why, that would be absurd." Maggie fidgeted on her chair, restless and agitated. Didn't she know about the entity after all, then? "I mean, he seems like a good man and he's certainly attractive, but love? Oh, no. That'd be absurd."

"Why?"

Maggie had to think a moment. Good grief! Because of Carolyn, of course. "He's too temperamental," she lied. She couldn't tell Miss Hattie about Carolyn.

"True, but he has been under an awful lot of pressure, dear. That's worth remembering." She stopped rocking. "Tyler fears he harms everything he cares about, which is why he's so, er, temperamental, when it comes to you."

Was he? Maggie felt rotten. Lying to Miss Hattie. Letting herself have feelings for a man who might be involved in Carolyn's death. How much lower could she sink? "I care about him," she confessed, "and I've tried to help him. But I don't love him."

239

She could never let herself love *any* man — most especially not MacGregor.

"You know best, dear."

What she knew was that if she told Miss Hattie about the entity, about it warning her to help MacGregor, then warning her to stay away from him, Miss Hattie would lock her inside a padded room and surround her with men in little white jackets who study inkblots and ask embarrassing, probing questions about mothers.

"Carolyn hurt Tyler very deeply," Miss Hattie said softly, her gentle eyes filled with concern. "He fears you because you can hurt him even more."

She knew about Carolyn! Maggie's heart nearly stopped. "I — I, um, don't think so. He was engaged to her. He meant to spend the rest of his life with her."

"Yes, I know." Miss Hattie's gaze leveled. "But he didn't love her."

"He did," Maggie countered, her voice carrying her conviction. "MacGregor wouldn't marry a woman he didn't love. He's not that kind of man."

"True."

Confused, Maggie frowned and straightened back in her chair. "But you just said —"

"He *thought* he loved her."

240

He might have. Him alone, having lost his parents, thinking Carolyn alone, too, after having lost hers. Maggie picked up her spoon and stirred the crumbled wafers soaked with melted whipped cream into the pudding. The banana scent enticed her, and she took a nibble, then a bite. Hadn't MacGregor told her this same thing? That he'd thought he'd loved Carolyn but . . . no. No, he'd said he'd thought *she'd* loved *him* but that she hadn't. Big difference.

Maggie looked at Miss Hattie. "I lied to him." She dropped her spoon. It splattered pudding onto the table and landed with a dull *thunk. Why had she said that? She hadn't meant to say that!*

Miss Hattie didn't bat an eye. "I know, dear. And I suspect he does, too, though of course he doesn't know your reasons."

Heat gushed up to her face. Not eager to meet Miss Hattie's gaze, Maggie dabbed the corner of her napkin at the pudding splotches. "Do you know them?"

"Your mother and I had a nice, long chat about it — and about her ceramics class. She's loving every second of it."

Maggie squeezed her eyes shut and rubbed her forehead. Great. Just great. Now Bill *and* Miss Hattie knew the truth about why she'd come here. She should just take

241

out an ad in the *Portland Press Herald* and call it a done deal. "Are you going to tell Tyler?"

"Not unless he specifically asks me. But if I might give you a bit of advice —"

"I know. I should tell him." Maggie sighed and slumped over the table. "But I can't. Not now. I waited too long."

Miss Hattie sent her a sympathetic look, her eyes bright. "You know best, I'm sure. But remember that love is too precious to be squandered on half-truths and deceptions, dear. It's like quicksilver. It can be snatched away as quickly as it's given." Her gentle nod set her white hair to shimmering in firelight. "Don't let it slip through your fingers, mmm?"

Love again. Why was she insisting that Maggie loved the man? "I agree in theory, just not in this case. I really don't love Tyler, Miss Hattie. I, care about him, but I don't love him."

"Really?" She arched her brows and retrieved her knitting from the little black bag beside her rocker, then situated the shiny green needles in her hands.

"Really." Maggie didn't . . . did she?

Of course not. She'd never love *any* man — and that was that.

"Well, as I said, I'm sure you know best.

But for a woman who doesn't love a man, you sure are willing to go to extraordinary lengths to protect him."

"I'm not and you know it." Certainly her mother had dispelled that illusion. "I'm trying to find out if he had anything to do with Carolyn's death."

"He didn't."

The woman sounded just like Bill Butler. The idea of MacGregor being involved was *not* that far a stretch. Maggie grimaced and lowered her voice. "The Portland police report says no other car was involved in the accident, and there were no signs that anyone had tampered with Carolyn's car. They did a very thorough investigation and found nothing unusual."

"Then why do you feel suspicious?"

"Because, to me, something *extremely* unusual happened."

"What?" Curiosity glinted in her eyes.

"There was a painting in the car with Carolyn. The car exploded and she burned beyond recognition, but that painting wasn't touched." Maggie leaned closer, dropped her voice a notch lower. "The police in New Orleans insist Carolyn stole that painting from the gallery. But if it'd been in the car at the time of the accident, then it would have been destroyed like everything else.

Since it wasn't, that's got to mean that someone put it into the wreckage *after* the accident. And that means someone else had to be there."

"You suspect Tyler?" Miss Hattie guffawed, then stilled and stared up at the ceiling as if listening to something Maggie couldn't hear.

The little hairs on Maggie's neck prickled. Did Miss Hattie hear the entity's whispers, too?

"Oh my."

Her heart skipped a beat. "What is it?"

"Nothing, dear." Miss Hattie lowered her gaze to meet Maggie's, worry creasing her aged brow. "Nothing at all."

This nothing was definitely something. Miss Hattie fairly reeked of it. Maggie licked at her lips. "Miss Hattie, is there anything . . . unusual going on here?"

"At Seascape?" The worry disappeared and her laughter tinkled through the fire-warmed kitchen.

Stiffening, Maggie nodded, not at all reassured.

"Why, things here are just as they've always been, dear."

Maggie let out a nervous little laugh, then started to express her relief, but stopped short. *As they've always been?*

■ ■ ■ ■

It had been the longest, the most miserable, of all his miserable months of weeks here. Maggie avoiding him at every turn. Him knowing she avoided him to protect him and worrying that nothing he could do would protect either of them. Him fearing that this entity — whatever it was — would play with them until it tired, then do only heaven knew what to them. And, T.J. finally accepted it, him knowing that more than his next breath, he needed to talk with Maggie. To just be close to her.

She'd gotten to him.

How had it happened? Why hadn't he seen it coming and stopped it?

Heck, he *had* seen it coming. He just hadn't realized his heart had been at risk. Had he mistaken serious attraction for a good dose of lust because the woman had stunned him?

He stared at his bedroom ceiling and pondered on it. Maybe. Her reaching out to him when he'd deliberately been acting like a jerk toward her had stunned him. But maybe she'd gotten to him because when she'd said she wasn't interested in him he'd known she'd been telling the truth and he'd let his guard down. Or maybe — just maybe — she pulled off this coup because, before he'd recovered and raised his guard back into place, she'd crept inside him and seeped soul-deep. At this point, what difference did *how* or *why* make? It had happened, pure and simple.

Unlocking his bent arms from behind his head, he rolled out of bed, then crossed the creak-ridden floor to the window and looked outside. Gloomy and gray. He sighed. Again.

She'd taken this last warning to stay away from him seriously. Not once had she forgotten to hang out the *Occupied* sign on the bathroom door's nail. Not once had she snitched his razor. He frowned and tapped the heel of his fisted hand against the window sash. He'd nearly slit his throat because he'd expected a dull blade and instead had gotten one that hadn't been touched. And not once had she ventured down to the boundary line to watch him attempt — and fail — to cross it without her.

That might just hurt most of all.

He paced the length of his room, the woven rug muffling his footsteps. Man, it felt stifling in here.

Back at the window, he jerked it open. Pine-tinged fresh air gushed in and he breathed in deep, filling his lungs. Still, he felt ready to suffocate. Almost as if the house had shrunk in on him and he couldn't get enough oxygen into the room.

Claustrophobia? With his head hanging out a window? With crisp air blowing against his face, tugging at his eyelids, and slicking back his hair?

It wasn't logical. But then what around here *was* logical anymore? Maybe if he went outside . . .

Fifteen minutes later, he'd combed the lawn, the garden, stood on the Seascape cliffs, climbed down the stone path to the little strand of beach then back up again, and he *still* felt smothered. Stopping on the jagged rocks, he stared out onto the foamy, white-capped sea. Even its roar howling in his ears, its cold and misty salt spray gathering on his skin, didn't soothe him this time. Seascape grounds just weren't big enough. He had to get away from here or he'd lose his mind. But there was only one way to do that.

Maggie.

And, man, but it appalled him to have to humiliate himself and ask her for help. To have to accept her pity — especially considering the odds ranked about a hundred percent that she'd turn him down cold.

Maybe not. A man's voice sounded in T.J.'s

head. *Ask her.*

Was it T.J.'s own voice? The entity's?

Does it matter?

Did it?

All she can say is no . . .

No.

No way.

Uh-uh, absolutely, positively, unequivocally, no way. Miss Hattie *had* to be wrong. That's all there was to it.

Maggie sighed, shrugged, then grimaced. Sitting alone on the bench, she stared out on the wind-rippled pond. Without the sun's brilliant glint, the water looked murky, dense and dark and almost threatening. Of course, Miss Hattie had been wrong. Maggie had been at the *in love* brink, but she hadn't taken the plunge. She didn't love MacGregor. Spit, most of the time, she didn't even like him.

But there was something . . . special about him.

The way he talked? Slow and reassuring, as soothing as the ocean's gentle roar. The way he looked? Gorgeous, but his lure went much deeper than that. She appreciated his easy moves — what woman wouldn't? They were relaxed, his carriage proud but not boastful. And he did have a perfect nose.

Because he was so big? She did like that. His size and strength tugged hard at her feminine cords, but neither would appeal so much if he weren't gentle and vulnerable — which he hated — and open in admitting his flaws. Heck, he even admitted them when they weren't valid — like with his parents.

She wrapped her arms around her bent knees and dipped her face against the sharp wind. Men weren't often that comfortable with their masculinity, or in their skin. Nor did the prospect of deceit typically trouble their consciences so much. Her father's certainly hadn't been. But MacGregor was . . . sensitive where her father had been calculating, keeping score and making sure he stayed one up on her mother. Of course, an artist had to be sensitive to paint, so that had come as no great surprise. But his sensitivity carrying over into other aspects of his life *had* surprised her. Oh, he was a nagging pain in the gluteus maximus, with an attitude and a killer snarl as fierce and disarming as his killer smile. True, but under the bluster, that sensitivity was there. When he held her, she sensed it so strongly it stunned her. The way he made her feel stunned her, too. Sighing, she hugged her knees tighter. She wasn't sure she was crazy about feeling stunned, but she did really like the way he held her. And the way he hassled her. She even liked the way he drove her up the wall when she was in the tub.

Oh-oh. She pulled up a dead blade of grass and slid it between her forefinger and thumb. *Serious trouble brewing here. Very serious trouble.* She liked too much about the man, especially his huge hands and the way he skimmed them over her back . . . She positively hated loving that. And, aside from his lethal kisses, she just might hate loving their through-the-bathroom-door conversations most of all.

Sighing deeper, she tossed the grass blade onto the stony ground and watched the wind catch it and send it tumbling toward the big oak down by the water. Poor grass. It was as out of control of its destiny as she seemed of her own. She didn't love Mac-Gregor, no. But she sure did miss him.

"Maggie?"

She jerked, turned and saw him standing not three feet behind her, wearing a gray shirt and jeans and a black cashmere sweater that made him look as dark and dangerous and as alluring as the *Seascape* painting. Her heart started a slow, hard beat. "You've got to stop sneaking up on me, MacGregor. You're stunting my growth and I'm determined to reach five-eight."

His eyes twinkled. "Hate to break it to you, but I think your growing years have passed."

She feigned a sigh. "There you go again, blowing my fantasies."

"Old habits die hard."

They did. And sometimes, without a whimper. Depressing, that.

"How about if I make it up to you?" He shrugged. "I have shattered a lot of your fantasies."

He'd generated a lot of them, too. Especially in the past week. "How?"

He flipped his sweater over his shoulder and held it with a careless thumb. "I could tell you that you look fantastic in burnt umber."

"Burnt umber?"

"Brown." He smiled. "Burnt umber is a paint color."

"Ah."

"Sorry. Like everyone else, artists notice things in the familiar — even when they can't work." He cocked his head, lowered his lids to half-mast and gave her a killer smile that wilted her knees. "Or, I could take you to the Blue Moon Cafe for dinner."

Oh, how she wished he could. "We can't

risk that" — a wave of regret washed through her — "so I'll take the fantastic compliment."

The wind stilled. She returned her gaze to the slick pond. A bug lit on its surface and tiny circles expanded to large ones, rippling out. For some reason, the old saying about casting your bread upon the water came to mind. Silly really. "You shouldn't even be here talking with me. What if our entity gets ticked?"

"I'll risk it."

The wind started up again. Shivering off a chill, she looked over the slope of her shoulder, back at him. The breeze had his shirt and sweater blown snug over his chest, molding his shoulders, and his wind-tossed hair kissing his forehead. Blades of brown grass clung to his shoes.

She envied it all. Everything touching him. And she was angry with herself because she did. Even now, after a solid week of stern lectures and heart-to-heart talks with herself about accepting her feelings for him but limiting expressing them to her mission here, she got one look at him and envied even the wind because it could touch him and she couldn't.

I'll risk it. How easily those brave words had tripped off his tongue. And, oh, what she'd give for just an ounce of his courage.

But he could afford courage. He had far less to lose. *His* self-respect wasn't in jeopardy. "You don't know the consequences. Why are you willing to risk it, MacGregor?"

"Because."

"Well" — she smacked her lips — "that explains that."

He frowned.

"Wait, I know." She lifted a pointed finger. "You have faith everything will work out okay."

"You *are* kidding." He snorted. "Faith? With my track record?"

Pollyandying, he wasn't. She forced her expression to become passive. "Why, then?"

"Because I'm feeling . . . landlocked." He sighed and looked skyward at the heavy, gray clouds scudding across the sky. "Because if I don't get away from here and see other people and do something semi-normal, I think I'll go crazy." He lowered his gaze to her. "Because I've missed —"

"Shattering my fantasies?" she interrupted, unwilling to test her resistance if he should say he'd missed her. "And because you can't go without me?" *Coward! Coward!*

He blinked twice, shuttering the longing from his eyes. "Yes." His jaw tightened.

"Please, Maggie."

Please, Maggie. Take the risk. Jump off the bridge. Act like a fool, knowing you're acting like a fool to *please Maggie*.

Inside, she sighed. She wanted to do this for him, but she wanted to do it for her, too, because despite her family responsibilities and obligations she wanted to be with him. Foolish move or sorry judgment factored into the equation, she still wanted to be with him. But did she want it more than she feared crossing the entity? It *had* played a joke on them with the drugstore order, yet what if they angered it? Would it still joke? Or would it grow deadly serious?

Lacing her fingers together, she studied them. No, she couldn't risk defiance. Wanting to help and to protect him, wanting to be with him, even wanting his rendition of what had happened to Carolyn, Maggie just couldn't risk defiance. But curious — half-obsessed, actually — she did want the truth. And maybe at the moment MacGregor was vulnerable enough to give it to her.

What signs had he ignored, in his own words, that had caused Carolyn's death? Ninety-nine point nine percent of the time, Maggie felt convinced MacGregor couldn't have been involved, not even remotely or indirectly. But there remained that shadow of doubt and, if only she'd been honest with him from the start, she could just ask him. But she hadn't been honest. And if she told him the truth now, he'd hate her. She didn't want MacGregor to hate her . . .

"Maggie," he said, sounding irritated. "Countries have settled wars in less time than it's taking you to decide on dinner."

Arrogant man. Asking for a favor and sounding irked. No, that didn't feel right. Irked, yes, but not at her slow decision. That he'd had to ask her. That she'd forced him to admit his vulnerability, to forfeit his pride. Why had she done that? Tables turned, she'd have hated it. Clearly, he had, too.

Wanting to apologize, she looked into his eyes. Hunger that gnawed soul-deep reflected there. He didn't just want this, he *needed* it.

Her heartstrings suffered a fierce tug. What should she do? She reached deep for the courage to resist him — one of them had to remain responsible and aware of the possible consequences of crossing the entity. he opened her mouth to refuse him, but a tom wind suddenly tore through the Its keening grew shrill, ear-piercing, steeled herself to hear that ominous

Take him.

She shut her mouth without uttering a sound. Had it been the man's whisper? Her own wishful thinking?

She didn't know.

She didn't *want* to know.

Shunning thought, she stood up and clasped MacGregor's outstretched hand.

He closed his thick fingers around her slender ones, gave them a gentle squeeze, and smiled. "Thank you, Maggie."

Her heart lighter than it had been for a week, she saw the cut on the underside of his chin and conjured a little audacity-laced lip. "What happened to you, MacGregor? Looks as if you nearly slit your throat."

He cocked a brow at her. "I expected a sassy redhead had been using my razor." He fingered the cut with his free hand. "She hadn't."

"Let me get this straight. You wrongly assume I've been on a revenge binge — while I've truly been a virtuous paradigm — and nearly slit your throat."

"A virtuous paradigm? You?"

She ignored him and went on. "And t^h inaccurate assumption on your p^a somehow *my* fault?"

"That's about how I see it."

He would. She stepped closer.

breasts rose a hair's width from his chest. "Now, why doesn't this bit of twisted male logic surprise me?"

He dipped his chin, his eyes twinkling those beautiful gray flecks that stole her sense. "Guilty conscience?"

That suggestion she hadn't expected. "I should feel guilty because I *didn't* use your razor?"

"No." He wrapped an arm around her shoulder and pulled her close. Her hips bumped against his warm thighs. "Because you know how much I've missed you and you haven't admitted that you've missed me."

She nuzzled him, resisting the urge to purr at the soft feel of his sweater against her face, deeply inhaled his scent, and loved it. Pine, sea, and warm man. Could it get any better than this? "You're definitely suffering from Inflated Ego Syndrome, MacGregor. That, or possibly Acute Arrogant Jerkism."

"Tacky, honey. Surprising coming from you. You called me a gentleman."

"I was suffering delusions." She sniffed.

"You weren't."

"So if not either of those, what is your affliction?"

"I'm not sure yet, but it's specifically attributable to you."

"I'm one busy lady."

"Just admit you missed me, Maggie. I won't gloat, I promise."

What were his promises worth? "Now, why would I do that?"

"Because it's true." He hooked a determined thumb under her chin and lifted it. "Don't bother denying it. You've missed me, Maggie." His lips hovering over hers, he dropped his voice to a seductive whisper. "Every bit as much as I've missed you. Maybe more."

"Arrogant. And the attitude."

"Yeah." He pecked a kiss to her forehead, lingering a second too long to qualify as chaste. "But not acute." She cocked her head and he added the unasked answer. "Honest, and no snarl."

A smile curved the corner of her lip. "Still racking up redemption points?"

"All I can get. I figure I've got a way to go."

He didn't. But she didn't tell him so. Mainly because the battle between loyalty and desire raging inside her demanded all her attention. His heated breath fanning her face had her senses snapping to, on alert. She shut her eyes, trying to soothe them, angry, resentful. Yearning. Just once. Just once couldn't her needs come first? Just once?

Yes. The whisper — definitely the whisper. *Now, Maggie. You have the chance now. Seize it with both hands and hold tight. Dream. Feel the magic.*

Miss Hattie's remark reverberated in Maggie's mind. *I've seen lots of miracles inside these walls. I'm hoping for another one, one for you and Tyler.*

A miracle? No, Maggie didn't dare to hope for a miracle. In their situation, a forever after kind of miracle was impossible.

"I haven't thanked you," MacGregor said.

She blinked. "For what?"

"Hot water."

"No, you haven't." She smiled and looked up at him. "But that wasn't a gift. We made a deal, remember?"

"I remember. But you didn't welsh on it."

"I don't do that." She grunted. "And you don't thank someone for not cheating you, MacGregor."

"You do if you're trying your darnedest to get yourself kissed."

Her breath swooshed out on a sexy little puff. "Is that what you're doing here?"

He nodded.

"Oh."

"Just oh?" A muscle in his jaw twitched.

259

"Does that mean I get my kiss?"

"Yes." She swallowed. "I guess it does."

His eyes filled with tenderness, and he slid his hands up her back to her shoulders. "Thank you, anyway, Maggie, for not welshing. You're restoring my faith in womankind." He pressed his lips to hers, urged her mouth open, then slipped his tongue inside.

Her, a liar, restoring his faith? She wanted to stop him, to tell him she didn't deserve his faith, but his tongue rubbing gently with hers, his hands kneading her sides, his lips so eagerly mating with hers, she couldn't stop him. She couldn't think. But, oh, could she feel. And the things this man made her feel . . .

It's like quicksilver. Don't let it slip through your fingers.

No, that was love. This wasn't love. This was . . . wonderful, but it wasn't love.

I'd hoped you'd have the courage . . .

Courage? Yes, enough courage for today. If only just for today. Maggie stretched higher, onto her tiptoes, wrapped her arms around MacGregor's shoulders, then broke their kiss long enough to rub their noses. "I've missed you, too, MacGregor. I really have."

His pleasure at her honesty shone in his eyes, and she did what she'd ached to do, what she'd dreamed of doing every night for the past week. She kissed T.J. Mac-Gregor unstintingly, greedily. For the first time, taking all he cared to give.

Chapter 10

"Finally." T.J. clasped hands with Maggie at the boundary line. "I was beginning to think we'd never get out here."

"Oh, chill out, MacGregor. So my timing was off a little. It's not as if being punctual is critical, and I'm supposed to be on a resting vacation, remember?"

"Forty-five minutes — over and above the additional fifty minutes I'd allotted because I happen to know you — is a little more than not being punctual. It's being late."

She gave him a level look. "Too bad you didn't use the time to work on improving your disposition."

He returned the look with one of his own. "Sorry, too busy cooling my heels. I'll just add this to the list."

Cocking her head, she looked up at him. "What list?"

"The one of your debts."

"What debts?" The collar on her royal

blue blouse was stuck half-in, half-out of her jacket. She tugged at it. "I don't have any debts."

"Using my razor." He ticked off items on his fingers. "Clipping coupons and ads out of my travel magazines. Promising to save me a little hot water then using it all anyway." He swatted at an insect buzzing his neck. "Those are just a few."

"I didn't steal all the hot water."

"You did. Three times, so far."

Flustered and giving up on getting her shirt collar straightened, she jammed it down inside her jacket. "Is it my fault that the inn needs a bigger hot water tank?"

"It is when I'm still working at racking up redemption points."

"Oh, I see what this is all about." She let out a grunt. "You're stacking the deck so you can use it against me, aren't you?"

Quick on the uptake, as usual. He smiled to himself and feigned an innocence he didn't dream for a second would fool her. "Would a gentleman do that?"

"You would." She sidled up against him and drifted an errant fingertip down the slope of his nose, her tone turning whiskey-husky. "So tell me, MacGregor, what exactly do you plan to do with these redemption points, once you acquire them."

"I'm shooting for a rendezvous with you in the bathroom's garden tub." A pang of longing slithered through him. "After that, well, it depends."

Her cheeks flushed. "I . . . see."

She lowered her lids, but too late. He glimpsed a flash of longing in her eyes, a flicker of curiosity. "Looks like you might be beginning to." She wanted an explanation of that *it depends* but she'd cut out her tongue before asking for it. "Question is, what's your opinion about that rendezvous?"

Silence.

"Opposed to baths?"

Still, no answer.

"Cleanliness is a noble aspiration, isn't it?" Her pulse throbbed in her neck. She'd cut loose on him any second. Anticipation burned deeply, exciting him. When Maggie got fired up, few could match her spirit. That's when he most wanted to paint her, rosy-skinned, eyes shining, nostrils flaring ever so softly. Breathtaking. Fantasy-making . . .

Still no answer.

He wouldn't let her get away with it. Not this time. "Running, Maggie? Does the prospect of sharing a bathtub with me terrify you that much?"

"No. Nothing about you terrifies me, MacGregor. I'm just not sure it'd be in my best interest to do it, that's all."

"Your best interest?"

She looked down at the ground, then back up at him. "Look, I don't know what I think about it, and don't nag at me, because that's the truth."

If her words got any stiffer they'd crack. "I asked what you think about it, not what you intend to do about it." She should at least be able to commit to thoughts — if she would.

"Quit pushing, will you?" She gave him a frown that made her stiff voice seem smooth and easy. "I just told you not to nag. Didn't I tell you not to nag? You know I hate it."

But she didn't hate him. "I'm not nagging. You're running."

"I'm not." She glared at him.

Cranky, but cute. "You are." She was, which proved the woman a lot wiser than he, because if he had half an ounce of sense he'd be running like demons pushed hard at his heels.

"Okay, okay. I want you." She jerked her hand free of his. "There. The big secret's out. I said it. Satisfied?"

It was one of the hardest things he'd had to do. He wanted to shout the news from

Seascape's widow's walk, wanted to scoop her into his arms and kiss her until her knees gave out. Instead, he masked his expression and, forcing a blasé tone shrugged. "I knew it." He had, of course. She thought he'd meant to taunt her into confessing a weakness. But, pure and simple, he'd just needed for her to give him the words. He stood on shaky ground in this non-relationship relationship and he'd needed a little reassurance. He also needed his head examined for allowing there to be a relationship.

"I knew it?" she mimicked him. "Has anyone ever told you that you are a Class-A, arrogant jerk, MacGregor?"

He dragged a fingertip down his jaw. "I believe you've mentioned it several times now."

"Well, consider it mentioned again."

Man, but she fired his blood. The hint of a grin tugged at his lip and, to keep her from seeing it, he pressed a kiss to her temple, reaching for the proverbial laurel leaf, then breathed against her temper-warmed skin. "Maggie, honey."

"What?" She nearly spat the word out.

"Would you tell me again — without yelling?"

"Ah, geez, MacGregor."

She stiffened, clearly to resist him. To heighten temptation, he lifted his arms and circled her shoulders. "Please."

With a resigned groan, she pulled away and looked him straight in the eye. "I want you, MacGregor. In fact, I'm sick with wanting you." Agitated, she swiped her hair back from her face. "Heck, maybe I'm just plain sick."

No danger of getting an overinflated ego around her. That was for sure. "Charming, honey."

"Glad you approve. I've been studying with a master."

Absorbing her angry words without comment, T.J. looked up at the sky. Swirling, gray clouds took on a yellowish cast and slanted strange hues into rain-laden ones, and even stranger shadows spilled onto the ground. She didn't mean it. It was fear talking. She wanted him, and she feared wanting him or anyone else because she'd seen what wanting her father had done to her mother. Maggie feared control, not T.J. MacGregor. She'd proven that often enough. And, if they survived all this, maybe he'd have the chance to prove he was nothing like her father. Maybe.

"So are we going to do this crossing, or what?"

He gave her a frown because it was expected, though he had to work at not hugging and kissing her and giving her soothing, reassuring words that would help ease her fears and hopefully his own. Would he endanger her simply by caring for her? "Ready when you are."

She reached out and grabbed his hand. She was shaking. "Let's do it, then."

T.J. nodded, his stomach flip-flopping as ferociously as the ends of her wind-whipped hair. Detecting a glint of light, he visually followed it. "Wait."

"What is it now?"

He sighed. "Batty Beaulah's at four o'clock — near the crooked oak — with her binoculars."

"Ah, I see her. Is that George and Aaron Butler with her?"

"Yeah." Hearing chirping, T.J. looked over to a branch about five yards south. A squirrel and a raccoon were engaged in a territorial Mexican standoff.

"What's Aaron holding?"

"His dad's antique spy glass." T.J. grimaced, hoping the animals didn't start battling. From the looks of them, neither was willing to compromise an inch. Was the little squirrel nuts? The raccoon would kill it. "Aaron hangs on to Beaulah's every word.

Thinking some of her 'wild tales' about Seascape might be true fascinates him."

"Mmm. He breaks that glass and Bill's apt to fascinate him with a truth or two."

"More likely, Leslie. She's the disciplinarian in the family. Bill's too tender. His poet's soul, Leslie says." The squirrel, showing a spurt of sense, leaped to another tree then scurried down its trunk to the ground. "They look happy, don't they?"

Maggie sounded wistful, as if remembering her own childhood and finding her memories less pleasant than the ones Aaron and George were currently making. T.J. hated that. "Yeah, they do."

"That's how it should be for kids. Happy. No worries. No response —" She stopped suddenly and cut herself off. "Sorry." She slid her glance past him to the pond, clearly embarrassed by the longing in her tone. "You ready?"

Ready to hold her? Yes. Ready to make love with her? Most definitely. Ready to love her? No, it was far too risky. Ready to cross the line? "Not really."

"Why not?"

He forked his fingers at his temple and dragged them over his skull. "I don't want to kiss the dust in front of an audience."

Maggie clicked her tongue to the roof of

her mouth. A weak shadow streaked over her chin. "Geez, have a little faith, Mac-Gregor. If you expect failure, that's certainly what you're going to get."

"Easy for you to say, Hoggett. You haven't flunked at this for nine months."

"No, I haven't." She laced their fingers and pressed their palms. "But we have succeeded a —"

"We succeeded together," he interjected. "And that worked once. Who's to say it'll work again?" His doubt crept into his voice, and he hated it. Hated it for being there, and for knowing Maggie would hear it, too.

"Me." She hiked her chin and genuine anger burned in her eyes. "I say it."

"Well." He waved offhandedly. "Now that we've established you're on the job, hey, that sets any questions about this to rest, doesn't it?"

"Yep. That's about how I see it."

Tossing his own words back at him. Figured. He frowned. "I was being sarcastic."

"Really? And here I thought you were expressing unconditional faith in me." She shook her head. "From where I stand, that bath is looking very doubtful."

Beautiful liar. That bath was all but *fait accompli*. "Knock it off, Maggie. This is serious."

"Ah, geez." She sighed and slapped at her hip. "Here we go with the snarl and the attitude again. You know, MacGregor, you require an awful lot of work."

Where in the world was she going with this? Wherever it was, he hoped it lasted long enough for Beaulah and Bill's kids to take off. "Oh?"

"Yeah, but I don't mind. Seriously."

She wanted him to ask why. Just to be contrary, he didn't.

"Don't you want to know why?"

Disappointed. He heard it in her tone. So she who hates it, nags. What the heck. In for a penny, in for a pound — though he knew he'd regret it. "Okay, why?"

"Because you've got good hands and cute buns," she slid him a wicked smile, "for a former popsicle."

"That's *paragon,* not popsicle."

"The spit it is." She snorted. "You're trying to weasel your way into my good graces because you're maxed out on subtle revenge."

Subtle revenge had zip to do with it. Lust, now, was a different matter. "You have good graces?"

"You're not going to do it, MacGregor. I'm not going to get ticked." She crooked a

271

slender finger at him. "I've got your number."

She did. But it'd been worth a shot. "So you expect me to have a little faith, huh?" He snapped his fingers. "Just like that?"

"Just like that." She snapped her fingers back at him, then turned to look him in the eye. "What have you got to lose?"

"A lot." Though the truth wouldn't take a laundry list, he clamped his jaw shut to refrain from being more specific.

"A lot." She pressed a fingertip to her lip. "Well, that narrows things down."

Blast, but he hated it when she pushed. More so because she pushed without actually outright insisting. Just guilted him into telling her what she wanted to know. Why'd he let her do that? "When you only have a little left and you lose anything at all, it's a lot, Maggie."

The smirk curling her lip faded and her gaze grew solemn. "Yes, I know." She stepped up to the line and lifted their clasped hands to her cheek, as if somehow shielding him. "Now, you've delayed with this nonsensical conversation long enough, MacGregor. I'll be deducting two redemption points for this infraction, by the way. Trying to slip me a mickey." She sniffed. "Batty Beaulah and the Butler boys have gone, so you can quit stalling and we can get this show on the road."

She had his number, all right. And here he thought he'd been so clever. Heat surging up his neck, he dragged the tip of his shoe down the line in the sand, then glanced at her.

Why had she closed her eyes? Was she praying? "Maggie?"

She looked at him, but didn't smile. Her eyes were glistening — not with tears, but with some secret known only to her. "Believe, Tyler," she whispered. "Just . . . believe."

The woman could have asked for the moon and stars and he'd have considered her wanting less than her asking him to risk the little he had left to lose. He wanted to be honest, to refuse her outright, but that secret shining in her eyes bore confidence and, because he sorely lacked it himself, he wanted — he needed — to trust it in her. "All right. Just this once, I'll dare to believe."

"You swear?"

Feeling that tender hitch he felt every time he recalled her dragging him, he crossed his heart with his fingertip and smiled. "It's the best I can do. I wasn't a Scout."

She laughed. "I'll take it — but only if

you promise to toss salt over your shoulder as soon as we get back to the house."

"Salt?"

"Forget it." She rolled her gaze. "Family joke."

"Well, it's lacking."

"So was the family." As if only realizing she'd spoken aloud, she attempted a quick recovery. "Charming, MacGregor. Totally charming. And I'm taking notes." She gave his arm a yank. "Come on."

Sassy, head to heel, and a zero intimidation factor. Loving that, he twisted the wrist of their linked hands, then laced their fingers together. They stepped over the line, then stopped. Feeling nothing at all odd, he looked at Maggie. "Anything happening?"

A long second crept by, then she answered. "Nothing." She sounded relieved.

"Good." *Understatement of the millennium.* His throat as dry as a dust pit, he swallowed hard. "Me, neither."

"Ease up on the death grip, MacGregor. You're about to crack my bones." Maggie winced. "I won't forget and let go."

"Sorry." He loosened his hold on her hand, rubbed at the white marks he'd left imprinted with his thumb, and stepped onto the worn path beside the sand-dusted road that led into the village.

As quickly as they'd come, the claustro-phobic feelings disappeared. Amazing. Had they been naturally or psychologically induced? He caught the fleshy part of his inner cheek between his teeth. Or maybe . . . entity-induced?

Regardless, they were gone now and, breathing easier, he squinted against a glare reflecting off a pothole puddle. The sun was shining. That hit him like a sledge. When had the clouds disappeared? "This is the first time in a week the sun's been out."

"Nice, isn't it?" Maggie stretched her step to match his, her expression tight and worried, and in direct conflict with her light tone.

"What's wrong?" Was she feeling effects of crossing, after all?

"You're not serious." She slid him an incredulous look. "What *isn't* wrong?"

"Look, I agree it sounds like a stupid question, but it really isn't — unless . . ." His stomach knotted. "It told you to come, didn't it?"

She looked out over the water, avoiding his gaze.

"Maggie," he growled from deep in his throat.

"I'm not sure."

She hadn't done this for him, or because

she'd missed him. The entity had intervened. Again. Disappointment shafted through T.J. like a sharp arrow.

"I heard a whisper, but I can't honestly say whose it was, MacGregor." She side-stepped a large rock, took to the more level dirt path, then focused on the sheriff's car. Rolling down Main Street, it headed toward the Blue Moon Cafe. "You know, this whole thing scares me in a way. Not in a boogey-man kind of way, because I don't think the entity means to hurt us so long as we don't cross it."

"Good grief, Maggie. If this didn't scare you, I'd be worried about you. It's bizarre."

"You're worried anyway." Passing an oak, she plucked off a dead leaf. "What I mean is that this whole situation scares me because I feel as if it's . . . life-altering."

A shiver shot up his spine and a warm wind crawled over the back of his neck. She was right. He sensed it. Tasted its bitterness on his tongue. She crumbled the leaf in her free hand. It crackled and crunched.

"Life-altering," he said, "can be good or bad."

"I know." She sighed and tossed the crumbled leaf onto the ground, then wiped the dust from her hand against her thigh. "That's why I tried to leave here."

Surprise followed the shiver, bolted up his backbone, then stung the roof of his mouth. "Tried? As in tried and failed?"

She nodded. "Three days ago."

Why hadn't she told him? Had she planned on leaving without even saying good-bye? "Car trouble?"

"No." She looked away, stared at the big, rusty anchor leaning against the wall of the Blue Moon Cafe. "Closet trouble." Underneath the outside staircase leading to a rooftop dining area, she paused and looked up at him. "I went to get my suitcase so I could pack. But when I tried taking it out of the closet, the door slammed shut and wouldn't open."

The closet didn't have locks. No doubt she knew that, too. "How'd you get out?" He stopped walking and joined her under the stairs. When she responded, he wanted to see her face. The experience had to have rattled her and to accurately gauge how much he needed to see her eyes.

"I finally figured out it wasn't me our entity objected to leaving the closet. It was my suitcase." She pulled a blade of dead grass off his sleeve. "It was sending me a message, Tyler."

"It's not going to let you leave."

"Right." The pulse point at her throat

throbbed. "No more so than it's going to let you leave."

He frowned down at her. "Yet, together, we have left."

"And now you see why I'm worried. Why did it let us go? Do you have any idea?"

"No." Unfortunately, that was the truth. But he suspected that, for some unknown reason, the entity wanted them together.

She stepped closer, away from the cobwebbed underside of the stairs. "Would you hate me if I admitted that in a way I'm glad it wouldn't let me go? I know I shouldn't admit it. You've got an awful track record, what with dashing the hopes of seventeen possibles Miss Hattie's offered up to you, but, well, would you hate me?"

His heart nearly burst. "No, Maggie, I wouldn't hate you." Did she mean she wanted to be with him? It sounded as if she did but, unsure of her answer, he didn't dare to ask. "And those mismatched possibles have nothing to do with you."

Her cheeks flushed. The sun shone brilliantly, dappling her in the slatted shade of the step rungs. "I don't mind if you don't like me, MacGregor. I just don't want you to hate me, you know?"

She would mind, the beautiful little liar. He caught up her hand in his, saw marks in her palm from where she'd fisted her hand and dug in her nails. "Would you hate me if I admitted that part of me — a very selfish part — is relieved that you can't go? I'm the one with the awful track record, and I know it." His mother. Carolyn. Seventeen mismatches. He gripped Maggie's upper arm with his free hand and rubbed it shoulder to elbow, sliding his hand up then down her smooth sleeve, stirring her sweet scent and praying for the right words. "I want you to be safe, but I don't want to be here without you."

"Me, too." Her face burned brighter red. "Despite all the weirdness, for some goofy reason, I'm at peace here. It's been a long time since I've had that luxury, and I don't have to tell you how needing peace gnaws at your mind."

"No, you don't." Had a peace pilgrimage been her mission here, then?

"Tyler, I — I —"

"Me, too." Sensing they both needed it, he closed the circle of his arms around her slender shoulders and kissed her lips.

It touched him in a way no woman's kiss had ever touched him. No eager kiss, this. No passion or desire evidenced, just unity. An expression with lips and gentle hands and tender pressings of bodies of all the things they couldn't, wouldn't, give each other with words. Reassurance that what was happening to them might be insane, but they were not. Recognition of their bond, of how much courage it'd taken her to get past her father's ill treatment and let herself be vulnerable enough to admit to them both that she wanted to be with T.J., of how much courage it'd taken him to get past what had happened to the other women in his life and trust that it wouldn't also happen to Maggie.

She kissed him back, tenderly, almost shyly, without the heat or desperation or fear she'd shown him before, sighing softly against his mouth, the vibrations from it coursing through her chest to his. This kiss acknowledged the gentler, more fragile, side of their feelings. The side that realized them caring for each other was forbidden, yet carried an awareness that, though they should not care for each other and there would be stiff consequences to pay for the privilege, they cared anyway, hopeful that whatever recompense demanded would be worth the price of them being together now — at least, for a time.

He let his hand glide down to her forearm. Giving her cool hand a light squeeze, he raised his head, dizzy from all the emotions churning from what to others would appear as a chaste kiss, then pulled her out from under the open staircase and into the sunlight.

A tear slid down her cheek.

A knot slid up into his throat.

She looked up at him, her eyes turbulent. "I — I —"

She cared. "I know, honey."

They stared at each other fearful, in awe, then Maggie swallowed hard, and they walked on.

In comfortable silence, they passed Miss Millie's Antique Shoppe, City Hall — which also housed the post office — then paused at the wooden-steepled church. T.J. frowned up at the window, high in the steep eave. "When did they put in that stained-glass window?"

Maggie shrugged. "I don't know."

"I'll bet the pastor's happy." T.J. felt amazingly happy himself, though he knew it foolish with everything going on here. "He's wanted one for a long time."

"Well then, I'm glad he's gotten it." Maggie looked toward the cemetery. "Isn't that Miss Hattie?"

"Where?"

"Over there, in the graveyard."

A flash of something yellow caught his

281

eye, and T.J. looked past the squat, white-picket fence. Such a different atmosphere from the above-ground tombs in New Orleans. Bending over, Miss Hattie put yellow flowers on the graves. "She does that every Tuesday, on her way to The Store. I told you that before, though, didn't I?"

"Yes, you did. But I'd forgotten." Maggie swung their clasped hands. "Whose graves does she visit?"

"I'm not sure." He freed his hand, let it wind up her arm, then slipped his arm around her shoulders. "We'll ask Lucy at the Blue Moon. She'll know."

Maggie arched a brow and curled her arm at his waist, inching her fingers up under the hem of his jacket. "We'll erase that note off the bulletin board, too — unless Jimmy's delivered your goods and some kind soul's taken pity on us and already erased it."

She wanted to touch him. To feel him rather than his clothes. Was it another unconscious touch, or an intentional one? Intentional, he hoped, but those were darn rare. "Are you going to start hassling me about that, too? I've heard enough from Vic, Hatch, and Bill."

"Really? What are they saying?"

"Trust me. You don't want to know."

She gave him a look that agreed he was likely right. "Tell me about the note instead, then."

"It's still there. I know it'll break your point-deducting heart, but don't blame me. Blame Miss Hattie." T.J. slid Maggie a mock warning frown he had to work at — her fingers were kneading at his waist, and her touch felt really good. "She gave Jimmy strict orders. Bed rest for his cold. So he hasn't yet made it over to Boothbay Harbor."

"Ah, geez." Maggie let out a frustrated huff and promptly stumbled on a loose stone, then righted herself by leaning on him. "If it's been up there a week, everyone in the village has seen it."

"Maggie. Everyone in Sea Haven Village saw it, or heard about it, within an hour."

Aaron and George rolled down the street on their bikes. Jacky Landry rode with them. She squealed and yelled out, "Hey, look, Aaron! I did it — no hands!"

T.J. smiled. Some people never grew up, the lucky stiffs. "It's too early for dinner, but how about a piece of pie?"

"Sounds good." Maggie grinned. "All this walking has given me an appetite."

"Right." T.J. grunted. "You've always got an appetite." He pulled her closer to his side and eased his arm down around her waist. "A shame it's for food instead of me."

She slid him a consoling grin. "You have your appeal, too."

His heart lurched. Of course, she thought it, but he never imagined she'd admit it. "Does that mean I can look forward to you attacking me at some time in the future with the same zeal you attack Miss Hattie's blueberry pie?"

"Maybe." She laughed, deep and throaty. "Depends on how much I get chewed out today for *not* using your razor."

He smiled. "If that's the deal, we can forget all about the razor. What's a little slit throat between friends?"

She tweaked his chin. "You're so easy, MacGregor."

"I'm not." Why was he doing this? He knew what happened to women he cared about, and yet he was encouraging this relationship with Maggie. Had he lost his mind? He looked away.

No, not his mind. His sense maybe, and his control definitely. He wanted her. More than wanted her. And that scared the breath out of him. But did it scare him enough to put a stop to this?

That question, he couldn't honestly answer.

■ ■ ■ ■

Though smaller than most efficiency apartments, the Blue Moon Cafe clearly served as the village hub. It bustled with sounds of people, clanking silverware, music, and a menagerie of welcoming, homey scents. Cornbread dominated.

Maggie walked in, holding MacGregor's hand. They wound through a maze of red vinyl-seated chairs and wooden tables, on past the jukebox which belted out a Willie Nelson tune that had the nets hanging on the walls vibrating. The corks and sea shells and starfish inside the nets clunked together.

Tyler led her down alongside the long, wooden bar. Marred and scuffed and worn smooth in spots, it had been well-used.

"Hey, T.J." Smacking on chewing gum, a tall, slender woman about thirty-five with a distinct Southern accent and golden red hair, gave him a welcome home smile.

"Lucy." He nodded. "Have you met Maggie Wright?"

Wearing jeans and a University of Maine sweatshirt, Lucy stepped over and offered her hand — one holding a red bar rag. She grinned, tucked the end of the cloth into the back pocket of her jeans, then shook

Maggie's hand. "Nice to meet you."

The infamous Lucy Baker. "You, too. I've heard wonderful things about your cooking."

Lucy waved off the compliment and dropped her voice to a conspiratorial whisper. "I've got these Yanks fooled into thinking it's good but, as cooks go, I ain't a patch on my mama's apron."

Maggie cocked her head. "I thought you'd always lived here." Ah, she remembered too late. Lucy's father had been local. They'd visited.

Lucy laughed. "Only in the summers. My folks homesteaded in Mississippi. You can be gone for a hundred years, but you never lose that Mississippi twang. Nice asset, I think. Anyway, I fell in love with Maine and wanted to stay so I married me a local." Her eyes twinkled sheer mischief. "But don't tell Fred. He thinks I fell for him."

T.J. pulled out a chair and rolled Maggie a subtle "I told you so" look.

He had. Maggie sat down. And, like him, she couldn't tell for certain whether Lucy teased or was serious on the "Maine for Fred, or Fred for Maine" remark. "Don't worry," Maggie assured the woman. "Your secret's safe with me — providing your blueberry pie is half as good as Miss Hattie's."

Lucy laughed, slid the silver-knobbed salt shaker over near the pepper and gave the table a swipe with the cloth. "Sweetie, nobody makes better blueberry pie than Miss Hattie. But," Lucy whispered, "I use her recipe."

MacGregor sat down across from Maggie and rested their clasped hands atop the table. "Lucy is the reason everyone calls Miss Hattie 'Miss Hattie' instead of 'Miss Stillman.' Hatch started it, right, Lucy?"

"Sure did. I kept forgetting that 'Miss' and, to keep my mama from blistering my backside for it, Hatch, bless his heart, started calling her Miss Hattie to help remind me. It caught on, spread to Miss Millie, and it's been that way ever since."

"You know," Maggie said, "I've wondered why everyone addresses her by her Christian name — Miss Millie, too — when that's not typically done here like it is at home."

"Maggie's from New Orleans," MacGregor told Lucy.

"I know. Same as you." She stared at their clasped hands and a knowing quirk curled her coral-tinted lip. "You two meet each other down there at home, then?"

"No," Maggie said. "We met at Seascape."

"Oh, really?" Lucy's eyes danced excitedly. "Well, my-my, isn't that interesting?"

Maggie shrugged. What was interesting about two people living in a metropolitan area not meeting there? Not wanting to hurt Lucy's feelings, she just smiled.

"We'd both like pie and coffee," MacGregor said, then winked at Lucy. "Better make Maggie's a slab. She's got an appetite."

"Geez, MacGregor."

"You do."

"Well, you don't have to announce it."

Lucy laughed and patted Maggie on the shoulder. "Don't fret, Sweetie. A woman needs a good appetite up here to survive the elements." She pointedly swiveled her gaze to Fred, making it apparent she wasn't talking about weather.

"She'll have no trouble, then." MacGregor grinned.

Maggie squeezed the dickens out of his hand, trying to shush him, and watched Lucy stroll over to the bar and nod to the short, graying man behind it. He had an intelligent look to him — not book-smart, but world-wise, people-smart — and a gold-nugget ring on his pinkie finger winked in the light from the Budweiser beer clock on the wall behind him.

"Give me two coffees, darlin'," Lucy said. She picked up a black marker, moved over to the infamous bulletin board on the wall beneath the clock, then scribbled something down, looking very pleased with herself.

The door opened and two men walked in. Lucy greeted the one with thinning, brown hair who stood nearly as tall as MacGregor, and wore a police uniform and a weary face. "Hey, Leroy. The coast is clear. Ease yourself on down."

"Thanks, Lucy." He slid onto a stool at the bar and settled in. "What we got today?"

"Blueberry and cherry." Her gum cracked. "Name your poison, Sweetie."

"Cherry. Big hunk." He set his hat on the empty stool beside him. "Lord, but it's been a wicked day. Those kids from Boston have been driving me nuts with their three-wheelers over at Pumpkin Cove."

Lucy put a cup of coffee down in front of the man. "These the same bunch the paper said wrecked all the flowerbeds over at Indian Point yesterday?"

"The same." He grimaced. "Tore up everything in a five-mile radius."

"Why didn't you arrest them?"

"Not a witness in sight." He took a swig from his cup. "Those kids don't have a lick of sense, Lucy. One more call and I'm tossing 'em into the tank even if I have to trump up charges to get 'em off the streets. Maybe if their folks have to drive over to bail 'em out, they'll get mad enough to do something about this."

"Sheriff Cobb," MacGregor whispered to Maggie.

"I figured," she whispered back, then looked at the second man. He was a good deal younger than the first — early twenties, not wildly attractive, but nice-looking. Better than nice if he'd get his long brown hair a decent trim — and very interested, it appeared, in the young lady who looked a lot like Lucy waiting on a table in the far corner. His nose was red, his eyes watery, and his grease-smeared jeans needed a good wash in a bad way but, from the way he carried himself, Maggie bet those jeans had been spotless before the man had gone to work this morning.

He spotted MacGregor and walked over, grinning. "Good to see you off Seascape, T.J. It's been a while."

"Yes, it has." The men shook hands. "Maggie, this is Jimmy Goodson."

The mechanic who often helped Miss Hattie at the inn — and who ran shopping trips for the villagers to Boothbay Harbor. Her cheeks went hot. "Hi, Jimmy. It's good to see you up and around." Maybe he'd gotten that shopping list off the board, anyway.

"Excuse me?" His forehead wrinkled.

"I thought Miss Hattie had you on bed rest for your cold."

He rolled his gaze ceiling-ward. "She does, which is why I've got to get back home — before she catches me and blisters my ears."

He looked pleased at the prospect. Ah, Miss Hattie had told her that Jimmy was an orphan. Clearly, she'd adopted him. "I'll bet she would." Maggie unfolded her napkin and spread it over her lap — not an easy feat, one-handed.

"I need a word with you, T.J." Jimmy blushed. "Private-like."

Maggie looked at MacGregor, and her eyes stretched wide. They couldn't break contact, he'd pass out. What should she do?

Lucy set the coffee and pie onto the table, looking at Jimmy. "Miss Hattie's just left the cemetery for The Store, Sweetie. You'd best haul it back home pretty quick."

He nodded. " 'Preciate it."

MacGregor rubbed Maggie's thumb reassuringly. "Go ahead, Jimmy. You can talk openly in front of Maggie."

"It's, um, kind of delicate, T.J." The young man's face turned beet-red. "No offense, Maggie."

"I know about the note on the bulletin board, Jimmy."

"I took it down." Jimmy looked straight at MacGregor, turned his back to Maggie, then dropped his voice to a whisper and passed MacGregor a small box. "Next time you need something, um, personal, just call me direct."

MacGregor slid the box into his pocket and turned as red as Jimmy. And if the heat radiating from her face was a solid indicator, so had Maggie.

"Thanks," MacGregor said. "I'll do that."

"No problem." Jimmy cleared his throat. "I didn't figure you'd want your personal business spread all over the village."

Maggie grimaced. Geez, who was left that *didn't* know? Why couldn't the floor open up and swallow her? MacGregor recovered quickly and now looked amused, blast his hide. She resisted an urge to give his thigh a solid whack.

"Jimmy!" Lucy shouted from the front window. "Miss Hattie's coming across the parking lot. Move it!"

Jimmy took off like a streak of lightning, hurtled over the bar, then vanished into the kitchen.

Fred slapped at the bar and grinned at

the sheriff. "When he wants to, that boy can move."

Leroy lifted his coffee cup to his mouth and grinned through the steam. "Miss Hattie inspires him."

"How's the pie?" Lucy glanced down at their plates and frowned. "You haven't touched it."

"We've been talking with Jimmy." MacGregor snatched up his fork. "Lucy, Maggie was wondering whose graves Miss Hattie puts the flowers on. Do you know?"

" 'Course, Sweetie. The Freeports." She smacked her gum. "Gosh love her heart, she never misses a Tuesday, rain or shine." Lucy glanced over to Maggie. "Hattie Stillman don't forget those in her care — dead or alive."

Cecelia and Collin Freeport. Seascape's original owners. "She's an angel." Maggie took a healthy bite of pie. How could someone dead be in Miss Hattie's care?

"Durn near." Lucy grinned. "Well, as close as a body can get to being an angel without being dead." She leaned over an empty chair. "Maggie, me and Fred's been having this little debate for a couple years about this very thing. Do you think angels can be dead people, or can they only be nonhuman spiritual beings?"

T.J. tensed and squeezed her fingers in a death-lock, warning that this was a hot family debate. She looked over at Lucy. "I'd say that depends."

"On what?" Lucy swatted at T.J.'s shoulder. "Would you quit interfering with your warning looks and just let the woman speak her piece?"

"Sorry." He looked anything but.

"It's all right." Lucy returned her gaze to Maggie, her eyes glittering. "So what's it depend on?"

Maggie gave her an angel's smile. "God's will."

Lucy laughed out loud. "Oh, Maggie, that's choice. About the smartest answer anyone's ever given us. Shoot, me or Fred could hardly disagree, now could we? And yet you haven't sided with either one of us."

"Well, you *could* disagree," Maggie said softly, knowing it wouldn't happen.

"I don't think so, Sweetie." Lucy gave her gum a good crack. "I'm a *Mainiac,* but I ain't a fool. When Fred asked me to marry him, I told him I would if he promised me two things. One, we neither one ever dispute God's will. And, two, we never mess with IRS — at least not without solid proof and a big stick."

"Sounds like a good plan, doesn't it, Mac-

Gregor?"

He nodded, lips pursed.

"T.J." Lucy looked at him, her eyes shining. "You've got a real winner here."

Maggie opened her mouth to object to the insinuation that she belonged to MacGregor, but he squeezed the fool out of her hand until it tingled, his gaze never leaving Lucy's, and assured her silence by saying, "She's special, all right. I'm a lucky man."

The phone rang.

Lucy glanced up at the Budweiser clock and her grin faded. "Three-thirty. Beer bells. The sheriff's already having a bad day." She stretched over to the end of the bar and lifted the phone receiver from its cradle. "Blue Moon."

She listened for a second then rolled her gaze heavenward as if praying for patience. "I've been busy, Beaulah. Um, the sheriff?" Lucy gazed over at him.

Sheriff Cobb frantically waved both hands, gesturing and silently moving his lips. *I'm not here.*

Lucy frowned at him.

The sheriff slid off his stool, reached back for his coffee cup, then nearly ran out the front door.

A smile dancing in her eyes, Lucy snapped her gum. "Sorry, Beaulah, you just missed him. He left in a bit of a hurry today."

Big, burly Sheriff Cobb running from tiny, birdlike Beaulah — a woman nearly twice his age. Maggie grinned at MacGregor.

He grinned back.

"I'll tell him, Sweetie. T.J. MacGregor" — Lucy looked at MacGregor — "is busting the cliffs with his head and ruining the topography because a ghost is after him over at Seascape and won't let him leave there. Uh-huh. Sure enough, Beaulah. I'll pass that vital info along to Sheriff Cobb right away."

Lucy hung up the phone. "Dang, I'm standing here looking at you, T.J."

He shrugged and smiled.

She gave the phone a soulful look. "Poor woman's losing it, bless her heart."

A ghost? Maggie avoided his gaze, knowing he was avoiding hers, too. *A ghost?* Her stomach furled in on itself. *Impossible. Ridiculous. Absurd.*

The sheriff cracked open the door and peeked inside. "You off the phone yet, Lucy?"

"Yeah, Sweetie, sure enough. Come on back inside. I'll even get you a second hunk of pie for sparing my soul. Can't abide lying. Never could."

Looking guilty as sin, Leroy shuffled

across the floor, then slid back onto his bar stool. "Near miss. That woman makes me crazy." He flushed. "Sorry, Lucy."

She waved off his cussing. "No problem, Sweetie. Beaulah has a way of making us all forget ourselves. A shame she's got no kids to look after her and keep her busy."

Maggie polished off the last of her pie. A ghost? No, her and MacGregor's entity couldn't be a ghost. She'd considered it could be a multitude of paranormal things, but never a ghost. That was *too* frightening. A ghost would be totally and completely absurd. Oh she hoped it would. She swallowed hard, stiffened. Of course it would. Wouldn't it?

Risking a glance at MacGregor, she saw the same question she'd just asked herself reflected in his eyes.

"Are those chocolate-chip cookies I smell, Miss Millie?" Maggie walked over to the petite, delicately boned widow about Miss Hattie's age sitting in her chair beside her Franklin stove. The hem of her simple, forest-green dress brushed against the floor with her every rock.

She sipped from a delicate, china cup, then smiled up at Maggie and T.J. "They sure are. Hattie dropped by a while ago and said you children were eating your way through the village today, so I thought I'd whip up a batch." She gave her short-cropped, violet-tinged hair a pat, then waved them to sit down on a rosewood settee opposite her. "Tea's already steeped, too. You pour, Maggie."

As they sat down across from her, she glanced at their clasped hands then gave them a crooked smile. "Tyler, it's good to see you here."

"Feels good to be here, too, Miss Millie. You been feeling okay?"

Maggie poured the tea one-handed, then passed a cup to MacGregor. Did Miss Millie know he was landlocked at Seascape? She could. She and Miss Hattie had been friends since birth — that Maggie had learned when she'd brought the book here for the Historical Society's tea — and they talked on the phone every day.

While MacGregor and Miss Millie chatted, Maggie looked around the cluttered shop. No counter. The business conducted here was settled at a beautiful, old oak roll-top desk by the light from a Victorian lamp with a violet fringe shade.

"Maggie, help yourself to some cookies, dear."

Maggie smiled and lifted one from the

plate. "They smell wonderful." The table beneath the plate was gorgeous. Beveled glass and wood trim that encased a collection of cut crystal figurines worth a small fortune. "You have a lot of lovely things here."

"Thank you, dear." Her gentle blue eyes twinkled.

"What smells so good?" MacGregor asked. "Aside from these drop-dead, melt-in-your-mouth cookies."

"Potpourri." Miss Millie motioned toward the back wall. "In fact," she stood up, "come with me, Maggie, and we'll make you a sachet."

"Oh, you don't have to —"

"I want to. A little thank you for bringing the book to the tea for me."

Maggie swallowed. Did she dare to let go of MacGregor's hand? She looked at him for guidance.

He nodded and whispered, "Let's try it."

Well, at least the man was sitting down. He wouldn't crack his head on the rocks. Imagine Beaulah saying he was ruining the topography. What about the man's skull? She released his fingers then waited a long moment. "Anything?"

"No," he said uncertainly, slowly. Then more sure of himself, he added, "I feel fine."

"Then why are you frowning?"

"This is baffling me. I just don't get the pattern."

"Me, either." She started to touch his face, but pulled back. "Sure you're okay?"

He shrugged. "Fine."

"Maggie?" Miss Millie called out from the back of the shop. "Come choose your colors and scent, dear."

Feeling torn, Maggie. hesitated.

"Go on." MacGregor nodded toward the rear of the store. "I really am okay."

Maggie wound past a sleigh bed, then threaded her way through the maze of expensive clutter to the back of the store. Wide-mouth glass jars lined the wall on two wooden shelves, and bolts of colorful tulle and fine lace stood on end in a dowel-stick bin.

"We need one color lace and one of the netting." Miss Millie sat down at a work table. "And your fragrance, of course."

Maggie fingered the fine netting in rich jewel-tone colors. The dark teal really appealed, but so did the royal blue. "Teal tulle," she said. "And ivory lace."

"That'll be pretty." Miss Millie smiled. "Can you bring the bolts over here?"

"Sure." Maggie put the two bolts on the worktable. It was a well-crafted piece of furniture with heavy, dark wood and claw feet. The surface gleam showed not a scratch. For a worktable that seemed impossible, but this clearly wasn't a typical worktable. It'd been pampered and well-tended. "Very attractive table."

Miss Millie looked pleased by the compliment. "Thank you, dear. My husband, Lance, made it for me a few years before he died. I had it in my kitchen, but I spend more time here than there, so I had Hatch and Vic and Jimmy move it over here where I can enjoy it."

She cut an eight-inch square of tulle, then one of the lovely antique lace. "Vic oils it for me twice a year. A good man, Vic."

Maggie returned the bolts of fabric to the bin. "I think he has a crush on Miss Hattie. At least, when he comes by to deliver the mail, he seems flustered around her."

"Guilt's what's got him flustered." Miss Millie pulled a spool of deep teal satin ribbon from the shelf, then unwound a length of it.

MacGregor came up behind Maggie and put a possessive hand on her shoulder. "Why should Vic feel guilty?"

"Why, he's loved Hattie for years." Miss Millie snipped the ribbon then returned the spool to the shelf, the soft fabric of her dress

301

swishing at her calves. "He and her soldier were best friends, you know. It still upsets me so that he had to die before he could marry Hattie. She was crazy about that man."

"She still is." MacGregor polished off the last of a cookie.

Miss Millie nodded her agreement, sad-faced at her friend's misfortune. "Have you chosen your potpourri, Maggie?"

"Not yet." Maggie walked over and sniffed at the jars, one by one. Why had MacGregor avoided talking about the possibility of their entity being a ghost? Likely for the same reason she had. It was a ridiculous idea. Ghosts weren't real. Paranormal events were possible, though she still hadn't ruled out psychological in this case — despite the whisper insisting this wasn't psychological because that whisper could have been psychological, too. But not ghosts.

A strong whiff of Winter Rose had her threatening to sneeze. She twitched her nose and read the label on the jar next to it. Seashore Secrets. Mmm, wonderful. Inhaling it, she grew dreamy, almost dazed, and visions of MacGregor filled her mind. Visions of them walking along the cliffs hand-in-hand. Of them bathing together in the big garden tub. Of them lying together in the Great White Room's blue-coverlet-draped bed.

Knowing she shouldn't, she pulled the jar off the shelf and brought it to Miss Millie. Her hands weren't quite steady and her body temperature had definitely spiked at least ten degrees. Of all men, why did it have to be MacGregor who made her feel all these wondrous things?

Miss Millie sprinkled the potpourri onto the tulle, pulled up the corners of it, and of the lace beneath it, then secured it with hands far too deft for their many blue veins by tying the satiny ribbon into a pretty bow. "There you are, my dear." She passed it to Maggie.

"It's lovely." Maggie smiled. "Thank you."

Miss Millie gave her a crooked grin, then winked. "I'll make you another on your wedding day."

Maggie laughed and stepped closer to MacGregor. He glided his arm around her waist, and she felt more at ease. "I'm afraid that could be awhile."

"Oh?"

"I've no intention of ever marrying."

"Oh my," Miss Millie blinked then shifted her focus to MacGregor.

"Me, either," he answered before she could ask.

"I see." She stared down at MacGregor's arm circling Maggie's waist.

"We'd better get going," he said, shifting his feet. "I promised we'd go for a walk before dinner."

"Burn off some calories." Maggie nodded, not liking Miss Millie's look a bit. It was that same too-seeing one Miss Hattie gave her all too often. The women were the best of friends, and Miss Millie had Miss Hattie's "they're in love" look in her eye. "Thanks again for the sachet."

Millie watched them leave the shop then walk on down the street toward the church. When they stepped from her sight, she lifted the phone receiver from its cradle on the old rolltop desk, then quickly dialed.

Lucy answered on the third ring. "Blue Moon."

"Afternoon, Lucy. It's me, Millie." She wound the phone cord around her fingertip. "Put me down for five dollars on Maggie and Tyler."

"Sure thing. What day?"

"Mmm." Millie looked at her wedding band. A widow for years, she still hadn't been able to bring herself to take it off. As long as she wore it, a part of Lance remained with her. It glittered in the sunlight streaming in through the window. "What day did

Jimmy Goodson pick?"

Lucy chuckled. "December twenty-fifth."

"A Christmas wedding?" Millie worried her lip. *Just as Hattie's was to have been.* "I'll take the twenty-fifth, too. Four o'clock. No, make that two."

"Jimmy's already got two o'clock. How about two-fifteen?"

Mmm, Millie considered it. Were they in Pennsylvania, there wouldn't be a need to pause. There, weddings are always on the clock's upsweep — the half-hour and funerals on the hour. But here . . . "No, I need two o'clock." Same as Hattie's. "I'll split with the boy. I'm not greedy."

"Yes, ma'am." Lucy dropped her voice. "Can you believe Lydia Johnson is betting that they won't marry at all?"

"Oh my." Millie frowned. "This isn't good news. Lydia is a bother I simply can't abide, but she's got a good nose for smelling love in the air."

"Rarely misses." Lucy agreed. " 'Course, Jimmy wins the bets more often than not. Mmm, I guess this one could go either way, couldn't it?"

"It seems so." Millie glanced out the window. What was Aaron Butler doing with that spyglass? Bill had waited nearly a year for Millie to find the perfect one for him and, if the boy broke it, he'd pitch a fit. "Does Hattie know about Lydia's bet?" Hattie would be devastated if another Christmas wedding failed to come to pass. Especially if it were Tyler and Maggie's. Hattie had been so excited about them . . .

"I don't know. She was in earlier today, checking on Jimmy, but I can't say for sure whether or not she got a look at the bulletin board."

"Well, I'd best phone her straight away." Millie sighed, wishing she could avoid the task. But if her best friend faced possible heartbreak, she just had to prepare her as best she could. "This doesn't look good at all, I fear. Not good at all."

CHAPTER 11

"Tyler, I don't feel well."

T.J. looked at Maggie. In the bright sunlight, her skin paled to a pasty pallor and her forehead felt clammy cold. He looked around but there wasn't movement on the street or so much as a bench this close to the cemetery. A horn tooted and Jimmy waved as he passed them, heading on down Main Street in his old truck. Obviously, he'd eluded Miss Hattie. "Let's go sit in the church for a while."

"But I wanted to see whose graves —"

"Later, honey. They aren't going anywhere." Was it the entity making her sick? If so, why? They were on a harmless walk. Together, which seemed to be what the entity wanted. And T.J. himself felt fine. "What do you think is wrong?"

"Too much sugar, most likely."

Could it be that simple? He led her up the wide, wooden steps, taking more of her weight. A distinct possibility with the pie and the cookies. But she'd eaten more sweets before — half a pie, once — and not been bothered. "Too much sugar? You, of the cast-iron constitution?"

"Shut up." She leaned against him.

Feeling her shaking, he led her through the big wooden door, then into the last row pew. "Charming, honey."

Deathly pale, she collapsed down onto it and sprawled. "I feel . . . awful."

Pastor Brown came in behind them. He paused and tilted back his head, admiring the window. His close-cropped beard gleamed blue-black in the sunlight streaking in through the stained glass. T.J. liked the young pastor. He was single, which meant he suffered the same malady here T.J. suffered. Half the women in the village were after him, the other half were trying to hook him up with a favorite niece, a daughter, or a cousin's child. Pastor fended them off pretty well.

He was a bit progressive for the anti-progressive village, although on most issues they seemed to have found a workable balance. On drinking and such, Pastor was too stiff-lipped for the locals, and that likely would remain a bone of contention for a long time to come. No small part of the workable balance was due to Pastor's excellent rapport with Andrew Carnegie, the son of Mayor Horace and the snobby, social-climbing Lydia Johnson. Lydia wanted the boy to be a lawyer and shoved it down his throat. Horace didn't, but he knew that a man who opposes his wife is a man who enjoys precious little peace. Pastor talked to Andrew Carnegie often, telling him he could be whatever he wanted to be — not in front of Lydia, of course. She'd cut him off at the collection plate. But Horace knew of the good deed and, being of the opinion that one good turn deserves another, he smoothed the pastor's path, listening to his progressive ideas with a kind ear — before promptly forgetting them.

The pastor walked over and stopped beside them. "Glad to see you two here — and that you've reconsidered on that shopping list."

"Maggie's sick," T.J. said, in no mood for lectures.

She pressed a hand to his forearm. "Tyler, I need some water."

"Tyler" not "MacGregor." T.J. shot the pastor a worried look.

His expression turned concerned. "I'll get it."

T.J. stroked her hair back from her face

until Pastor Brown returned with a full paper-cone cup. Taking it, T.J. pressed the edge to her lips. "Drink, Maggie." His voice shook and his hand trembled, none too steady.

She sipped at it. Then sipped again. "Thank you."

"Are you all right?" Her color was coming back, but she looked weak. Really weak. Had she started to suffer the boundary-crossing symptoms? They had been holding hands at the time she'd gotten sick, but that didn't mean much, since they'd let go of each other at Miss Millie's and they'd both been fine. Nothing was consistent anymore.

"Much better."

"Good." The pastor smiled. "I've got to run over to see Hatch. If you think of it when you're ready to leave, lock the door. Still some tourists roaming around and the sheriff's had a wicked day with those kids from Boston. Sure made a mess over at Indian Point, I hear. No sense tempting them here. Churches are easy targets for mischief these days."

T.J. didn't remind the pastor that *they* were tourists, nodded that he would lock up, and watched Brown leave.

"Can't do that in New Orleans." Maggie mumbled and took another sip of the water.

Her hand trembled atop T.J.'s on the cone-shaped paper cup.

"New Orleans is a little bigger than Sea Haven Village, honey." She looked almost normal again, thank goodness. "What happened to you?"

"I guess I overdosed on sugar. Until I decided to go into the cemetery to see the Freeports' graves, I felt fine. It's kind of weird, but as soon as I decided, *wham,* major sugar crash."

More likely timing, rather than any decision, spurred the sugar crash — unless for some reason, the entity didn't want her to see those graves. Could that be what had prompted this? What difference could seeing a few graves make about anything?

No, it had to be the sugar.

She licked at her lips. "Quit staring at me, MacGregor. I'm really okay."

What if she wasn't? How could he check it out? See if there was an entity connection? He couldn't do much without Maggie — including leave Seascape. That presented an obstacle he'd have to think on for a while. "Could it be that you overdosed on worrying, too?"

"It's possible," she agreed.

Highly probable, he figured. Feeling guilty about his no small part in that, he grimaced.

"Are we going to talk about it, or continue to pretend we didn't hear what Beaulah said through Lucy?"

Maggie scooped her hair up off her neck then leaned against the pew and closed her eyes. "I'd kind of prefer to pretend."

"Me, too. But we should discuss it. Do you think our entity is a ghost?"

Her eyelids snapped open and she stared at him. Without a word, she set her empty cup onto the wooden seat beside her then rotated her head against the back of the pew and looked at him. "That would be absurd."

"Yeah, it would." T.J. blinked then captured her hand in his. "About as absurd as me blacking out every time I try to leave Seascape alone."

"That could be psychological, anyway."

"And you feeling the same symptoms?" He stared at her hand, at her slender fingers, twining with his. "Could that be psychological, too?"

She worried her lip with her teeth. "Yes, it could. Empathy, because of our bond."

Her honesty surprised him. The woman was still keeping secrets. He didn't know what about really, he just sensed she was holding back. Could be his faulty judgment acting haywire again, but he didn't think so.

"Well, at least we've learned that once we

do leave Seascape, we don't have to constantly touch."

Didn't she like touching him? Peeved, he frowned. "Too bad, that."

She gave him a slow smile that tugged at his heartstrings. "Yeah, it is."

She liked touching him, after all. Pleased, warmed inside, he sat up straight, looked around the church, and let that news settle in. It sat well on his shoulders, if a little heavy. Would he end up hurting her? Being responsible for something awful happening to her, too?

The wooden pews were worn smooth from years of use and the rugged cross hanging above the altar gleamed, bathed in flickers of rainbow-colored light from the stained-glass window. It bore Collin Freeport's special mark. Had to be his work. He'd been a talented carver.

"It's so still here." Maggie sighed, clearly feeling better and relaxing. "I like that."

T.J. liked it, too. He let his mind wander, refusing to let it focus on their troubles. Maggie laced their fingers together more firmly, holding the fragrant sachet in her free hand. He lifted it and drew in its scent. It smelled like the sea and Maggie. Fresh, clean, alluring — sunshine and spring. Soothing smells. Pressing their palms together, he sat in the quiet, content just to be beside her. Content just to hold her hand and watch her look at the ceiling and stare at the rugged cross with that faraway look in her eye. When she drifted away from him like that, where did she go? Maybe one day, he'd drift with her. But until then, he took solace in knowing she'd come back.

"I love this church," she whispered softly. Snuggling closer to T.J., she rested her head against his shoulder. "I won't ever get married, of course, but if I did, it'd be in this church."

She'd marry. And envy for the man she'd make her husband slammed through T.J.'s heart like a prison cell door slams on a life-sentenced convict. "Why here?"

She didn't answer right away, and he didn't push, knowing instinctively that she hadn't yet worked through this and pinpointed her reasons.

Her voice softened to a mere, whisper. "I think, because it feels like love in here."

It did. But this kind of talk cut too close to the bone. It reeked of all the nevers he wouldn't share with Maggie because neither of them were free to marry. All the memories they wouldn't have. The joys and sorrows of a shared life they'd miss. Emptiness stole into his chest and flooded his soul.

"Probably just the heat."

"Charming, MacGregor."

"Thanks."

She frowned at him, fire blazing in her eyes.

"I think I see subtle revenge on my horizon."

She lowered her lids and let her gaze drift to his mouth. "Maybe you can head it off."

Sounded promising. "How would I go about doing that?"

"You could start by explaining why you let Lucy think we were a couple."

He hiked a brow. "Riled about that, are you?"

"Miffed."

"If you think about it, you'll thank me for it."

"I have thought about it, and I'm not thanking you."

He pulled the box from his pocket. "Remember these?"

"Put those away. Geez, MacGregor, you're in church, for pity's sake."

He leaned to the side and put the box back into his jacket pocket.

"What do they have to do with this, anyway?"

"I figured you'd rather everyone thought we have a very special relationship than they thought you sleep with men when you're not even a couple."

He heard her swallow. "Good point." She nuzzled closer. "Thank you."

"I'll take the three points you charged me, three more for doubting I had a good reason, and the bath."

"Five points — and that's my best offer . . . for now."

"Accepted." She hadn't tossed the tub into the realm of impossibility. She was weakening. Yep, the bath was all but a *fait accompli.* He smiled above her head.

"Wait a second. There's a provision."

"Now, why doesn't that surprise me? More making up the rules as we go — just like with the kiss."

"Provided" — she lifted her head and looked into his eyes — "you apologize."

"For protecting your reputation?" Weird logic. A thank you, now a demand for an apology? Women. Sometimes they just didn't make a snip of sense.

"To avoid subtle revenge."

Ah, now he had it. She wanted a kiss. He studied her lips and they parted. His heart flipped over in his chest. "I'd like that. Subtle revenge isn't all it's cracked up to be."

"Me, too."

He dipped his chin and, lips to lips, smiled, then kissed her lightly. "There."

"Uh-uh. A sincere apology, MacGregor." She cupped his head and pulled him back to her, then kissed him firmly, thoroughly, deeply.

A little groan escaped the back of her throat, vibrated against his hand. Knowing he'd earned it, he shuddered in sheer pleasure and thought he might just love this church, too.

For the first time in over two years, aside from the glimmer on the Seascape stairs, he felt a small measure of peace.

The Blue Moon Cafe had been busy this afternoon, but tonight it hummed. Nearly all of the thirty seats inside were occupied and the clattering of forks and animated conversations made for a cheerful welcome.

Pastor Brown sat at a table near the bar, his black hair and beard slicked down, his winning smile absent. The man Maggie had seen at The Store wearing the Local Yokel baseball cap sat across from the pastor, looking worried and rubbing at his neck. Right next to them, at a table for four snug to the bar, sat Bill Butler and a very pretty woman dressed in royal blue who Maggie figured had to be his wife, Leslie. All four of them talked simultaneously.

Maggie homed in on the voice of the Local Yokel. "I can't see any harm in having a keg with cold drinks by the door on weekends, Pastor. Folks get thirsty, and even Jesus drank wine."

"You're missing the point, Horace."

"I can't see that I am. Just as I can't see that Jimmy's calendar hurts a soul. It's not hanging outside in public view."

"It's hanging. That's the problem." Pastor Brown leaned forward to drive home his point.

T.J. gripped Maggie's shoulder and whispered close to her ear. "Looks to me as if Bill would welcome a diversion."

MacGregor's subtle scent had her throat thick and her wishing they could be alone, though she knew darn well they shouldn't. Bill did look rather grim-faced, and supposing she should be grateful for the reprieve, Maggie nodded and began the walk over to his table.

Bill looked up and saw them. Relief flooded his face. "Hey, you guys come join us. Be warned, though. Leslie's in a foul mood."

"Bill!" She swatted at his arm, gave him a solid frown, then grinned at Maggie. "The foul mood welcomes you, Maggie."

MacGregor held out a chair and Maggie sat down, glad she'd already "informally" met Leslie via phone. "I'd be in a foul mood, too, if I'd lost my backside at auction."

Cocking his head toward Maggie, Mac-Gregor told Leslie, "She's been griping for hours about the big boats depleting the stock and making life tough on the small fishermen."

Both Bill and Leslie looked pleased that Maggie had concerned herself with their plight. "Sinful, isn't it?" Bill asked.

"It is." MacGregor motioned, and Lucy came over with two iced teas. "I'll have whatever you cooked — and cornbread."

"Me, too," Maggie added, thinking that what was sinful was the way MacGregor enraged her senses. Why was she so intimately aware of everything about the man?

"Coming right up."

The phone rang.

Lucy grabbed the receiver and wedged it to her ear with her shoulder. "Blue Moon."

She listened for a scant second, then rolled her gaze, cupped her hand over the mouthpiece, and looked at Maggie. "Sweetie, will you hold this for me? It's Beaulah reporting another Seascape oddity sighting, bless her heart, and I just don't

319

have time to mess with her right now." Lucy thrust the receiver toward Maggie. "Just say 'Uh-huh' every now and again. Don't worry. You wouldn't be able to get a word in edgewise if you wanted to."

Maggie tucked the phone to her ear.

MacGregor grinned and squeezed her hand beneath the table. When mischief twinkled in his eyes, he was gorgeous. When it didn't, he was still gorgeous. She inwardly sighed. Carolyn or no, Maggie was in big trouble when it came to this man. It seemed he grew more dear, more important to her with each passing moment. Did looking at her do to him what looking at him did to her?

Their gazes locked and he smiled. She smiled back, heavy-limbed, and mentally drifted, mesmerized.

MacGregor poked her in the ribs. "Say uh-huh, darling."

Darling? Her heart skipped a full beat, and she mumbled into the receiver, lost in thoughts of him too rich to not indulge in. "Uh-huh."

Leslie and Bill were talking. On some level Maggie heard them, but she just couldn't focus on anything other than MacGregor and the heat in his eyes.

Again, he cued her. "Uh-huh."

She blinked, then blinked again, forcing herself to snap to and pick up on her surroundings. How had he done that to her? Beaulah was still raving, her tinny voice grating at Maggie's ears even more than usual, considering where her thoughts had been only moments before. She slid her gaze to Bill. Why did he look amused? Leslie seemed genuinely upset. The phone buzzed a dial tone in her ear. When had Beaulah hung up? And what else had Maggie missed while lost in lust?

She passed the receiver to MacGregor, who stretched and put it back onto its cradle on the bar. While leaning close, he whispered in her ear. "Leslie thinks she's not accepted by the fishermen because she's a black woman." He nuzzled Maggie's earlobe with the tip of his nose. "Bill's challenged her to take over the auctioning of their catch and she wants your opinion on whether or not she should take the risk and do it."

Maggie swallowed hard. Her opinion was that the man in the chair beside her was a furnace — and clearly not as affected by looking at her as she was by looking at him. She patted his thigh, offering her thanks for him catching her up on the conversation, or to hide her disappointment — she didn't dare to ponder which — then looked at Leslie. "Someone's got to blaze the trail. Why not you?"

"I could lose everything we've got." Leslie looked excited, and scared half to death.

Boy, could Maggie empathize with that feeling. Stroking MacGregor's thumb with hers, she looked Leslie straight in the eye. "I think if your heart and mind agree that something is right, you owe it to yourself to at least give it a try."

Leslie lifted her gaze to the wall behind Maggie's head, absorbing the advice. Bill winked at her. MacGregor gave her hand the most delicious squeeze. She could get used to him. So used to him. So easily.

"Nothing comes with guarantees," Leslie told Bill. "I'll do it." She pivoted her gaze to Maggie and it grew soulful. "Though the fishermen accepting me as one of them likely never will happen. Tight, closed-ranks, you know?"

Bill clasped her hand, lifted it to his lips, and gazed at her through a husband's adoring eyes. "They'll love you."

Just like me.

Bill didn't say the words, but Maggie sure felt them. Oh, but to have a man look at you that way. To show such belief and support. Such . . . love.

Leslie pecked a kiss to her husband's brow, then pushed back her chair, her eyes glistening. "We should go home and . . . check on the kids."

"Yeah, we should." Bill nodded and stood up. "You guys enjoy your meal."

From MacGregor's tender expression, he realized, too, that Leslie and Bill were feeling tender and wanted some privacy, and it didn't escape her notice that the pang of envy she felt that they could have that privacy while Maggie and MacGregor couldn't reflected in MacGregor's eyes.

Lucy brought out platters of coleslaw, fried cod, and beans. Then she made a second trip from the kitchen and set a paper-lined red plastic basket of cornbread wedges down on the center of the table.

MacGregor grabbed one, firmly pressed his thigh to Maggie's, then released her hand and slathered the steaming cornbread with butter. The corner of his lip curled.

Maggie frowned. "Why does Leslie feeling unaccepted amuse you?"

"I wondered how long it'd be before you asked."

"Your attitude doesn't usually extend to being heartless."

"Maybe you're corrupting me." Mac-Gregor grinned, not looking at all offended.

323

She'd misread this situation. "Okay, her feeling unaccepted doesn't amuse you."

"No, it doesn't."

"Well, what does then?" She cut into a wedge of cornbread. Steam spilled out over her fingertips and she blew on them to cool them down.

"It's her being so far off-base. Her acceptance has nothing do with her being black or a woman."

"Really?" Maggie wiped the butter sheen off her finger onto her napkin.

"Really." MacGregor sipped at his drink. The chilled glass sweated. "Fishermen are a special breed. They hang tough no matter what. They respect their families, their boats — they're sacred. But the sea . . . Ah, the sea, sweet Maggie, is like a seductive mistress. If Leslie wants to belong, then she has to do to them what the sea has done."

Maggie nearly choked. "You mean she has to seduce them and become a mistress to the fishermen?"

"Not hardly!" MacGregor dabbed at his mouth, chuckling, then leaned closer. "I was speaking poetically, Maggie. Doing it poorly, too. Leslie has to earn their respect and her place among them, just as the sea did. That's what I meant."

"I'm glad to hear it." Maggie didn't bother

to hide her relief. "Oh, wait. I get it. She needs to see things in the familiar."

"Exactly." MacGregor rewarded her with a heart-stopping smile. "You worry too much."

Maggie planted an icy chill in her tone. "Some things are worth worrying over, Mac-Gregor."

"True." He sipped from his glass then set it back down to the table and met her gaze, not a trace of humor left in his eyes. "But some things just are, Maggie, and, sooner or later, you've got to accept them."

Like us.

He hadn't said it, but he hadn't needed to. The words hung between them, no less clear because they'd gone unspoken.

Maggie looked away, slid a half-full bottle of ketchup across the table. It clanked against the salt and pepper shakers. He was no more talking about Leslie than about his work. He was talking about them and their relationship, and the awful man was letting her know he'd recognized her pang of envy for Leslie and Bill and their privacy, too. "Why doesn't Bill just tell her?"

MacGregor grunted. "Because he's not crazy."

"Why would —"

"Think subtle revenge, Maggie." Mac-

Gregor interrupted. "A man telling a woman how she feels is bound to earn him tons of it."

He had a point. Still . . .

MacGregor smiled at her over a forkful of cod. "Besides, when Leslie figures it out for herself, she'll be happier about it, anyway."

And so, too, would Maggie. Again unspoken, but not unheard.

MacGregor laughed. "Don't look so forlorn, sweetheart. Nothing will happen between us that you don't want to happen."

It would. It already had in her heart and her mind. Unable to meet his eyes, fearing he'd see that truth in them, Maggie looked past his shoulder, let her gaze drift to the wall, to the infamous bulletin board, hanging under the Budweiser clock. A shiver raced up her spine. Jimmy had taken the racy request off the shopping list. So why were her and MacGregor's names on it now? And what was that scribbled beside them? She squinted to see more clearly. *Dec. 25th, 2 p.m. — Millie $5, Jimmy $20, Lydia "No Way" $17.52.*

Maggie stared at the board. Miss Hattie had explained that when Jimmy went to pick up auto parts in Boothbay Harbor or New Harbor, he also ran errands for the villagers who posted their lists on the board.

But why were their names there? What did the names, the money, and Lydia Johnson's "No Way" mean?

The night air was clear and cold. Though T.J. didn't look forward to being confined at Seascape again, he didn't linger on the walk back to the inn. Maggie seemed fine, but she was shivering, huddled beneath the crook of his arm and in her jacket, and he feared whatever had made her feel bad earlier might come back again.

He opened the mud room door and Maggie scooted past him. "Boy, a cup of hot coffee sounds good, doesn't it, MacGregor?"

He closed the door, slid out of his jacket, then pegged it on a hook beside Maggie's. "Yeah, it does."

Miss Hattie evidently had gone on up to bed, so they had the first two floors of the house to themselves. He was glad of it, though he darn well shouldn't be, but he wasn't ready for their day together to end.

Minutes later, they settled down on the salon sofa holding steaming coffee mugs. The room was comfortable, inviting, and small enough to be intimate without seeming crowded. A television was near the far wall, in a corner, and a white fireplace centered on that wall. Floral paintings, brass sconces, and a gold-leaf branch centered between two windows lined the white walls. And two wing-back chairs covered in soft damask not only looked comfortable, but sat comfortably. He liked this room. Always had. But even more so now, being here with Maggie and them not at odds.

She dropped her shoes on the eggshell carpeting and curled her feet up under her. "You know, I love these Mainers' wit. Dry, but hilarious. And they seem to know instinctively what's really important."

"They do." T.J. stretched out his legs and crossed them at his ankles. His thigh brushed against Maggie's knee. "And they're as opinionated as heart attacks on matters of consequence to them."

"Aren't we all?" Maggie sipped from her cup, a smile tugging at her lips. "Do you think Leslie will do better than Bill at representing their catch at auction?"

"Bill thinks so, or he wouldn't have suggested it. He's a shrewd businessman."

"I asked what *you* thought."

T.J. shrugged. "Maybe. It depends on if she sees what's really there, or what she expects to be there."

"I suppose so." She stared across the room at the blank television screen, looking thoughtful, as if she wondered if she, too, saw what was really there or what she expected.

"I sat in on a few council meetings here. Spirited affairs."

"That spirit is part of their passion, Mac-Gregor. People should be impassioned."

More than a little curious, he looked directly at her. "What impassions you?"

She glanced down into her cup and studied its contents. "A lot more than when I first came here."

She didn't sound happy about that. "Would I happen to be included?"

"Yeah, you would. But I'm fighting it." Maggie lifted her knee atop his thigh. How could she not fight it? Keeping the truth about Carolyn away from him? "We don't really know that much about each other." Even to her, that sounded lame. She knew a lot about MacGregor from their talks, from their time together, from their bond. And, right or wrong, blessing or curse, she especially knew how he made her feel.

"I know everything I need to know about you, Maggie." He dropped his voice, soft and intimate.

Her heart welcomed that intimacy, but her mind refuted the joy of feeling so connected to him. She'd lied. How could she feel connected with him with lies between them?

She set her coffee cup down on the oak table at her elbow. "You don't, MacGregor. You really don't."

"I do." He reached over and set his cup beside hers. The handles kissed and clanked, bumping together. Rearing back, he lifted his hand and twirled a lock of her hair between his forefinger and thumb. "I know how you make me feel."

"That's about you, not me." Why did he have to smell so good, to have such warm and gentle hands? And why was she shaking so hard?

"I know how much I love your smile." He let a fingertip drift over her lower lip. "And the way you unconsciously touch me." He caressed her with his gaze. "I wouldn't mind at all if those touches became conscious ones, Maggie."

Enough courage for today.

She stared at him for a long, breathless moment, then lifted her hand to his face, traced his features slowly, deliberately. His beautiful nose. His hypnotic eyes. The curve of his jaw, his forehead, his brow. He gave her a slow blink that had his dark lashes sweeping his cheeks, the tender skin beneath his eyes crinkling. His lips, always enticing, now lured her. Oh, how she loved his lips.

The shape, the feel . . .

She wanted to kiss him. That wanting spread heat through her chest that turned to need, spread on to her middle, then settled low in her belly. A little puff of breath escaped from between her parted lips and fanned over his face, as gentle as a lover's whisper. She dipped her chin and fused their mouths. He curled his arms around her back, pulled her closer to him, and let out a telling little groan that might just be the sexiest sound ever heard by womankind. That same lure and tug she'd experienced at Lakeview Gallery on looking at the Seascape painting, experienced here on looking at Cecelia's portrait, that same sense of security and connectedness — of belonging — she'd felt on linking hands with MacGregor to cross the boundary line flooded through her again and warmed the doubts and fears from her heart. Maggie nearly melted.

MacGregor broke their kiss and let out a shuddered breath. He rubbed their noses and hugged her tight, then looked at her, his eyes desire-glazed, his voice thick and husky. "If I could paint, I'd want more than anything else in the world to paint you."

A knot of bittersweet tears lodged in her throat. "You'll paint again, MacGregor."

"I don't think I can — even if I could."

"One day you will, Tyler. I believe it."

"Maggie, I swear you almost make me believe in miracles — maybe even in the legend."

She purred and stroked his chin, loving the sound of his voice, the dreamy feelings inspired by his kisses. "What legend?"

He leaned back. "You don't know about Seascape's legend?"

His surprise had a smile threatening her lips. "No."

"It'll cost you. Legends are worth at least ten points."

"Ah, sweet redemption." She let a fingertip wander over the curve of his lip. "I'm feeling gregariously good natured at the moment. I'll give you seven."

"Nine." He caught the tip of her finger between his teeth and gently raked it.

"Seven." She said on an indrawn breath. "I'm feeling good natured, not generous."

"Deal. Let's get a refill" — he nodded toward their coffee cups — "then I'll tell it to you — upstairs."

A flutter ruffled her stomach. "Upstairs?"

"There's only one place to tell the Seascape legend, Maggie."

She swallowed hard. "The widow's walk?" she asked hopefully, half-squinting.

"The turret."

Oh, dear. "The, um, one in my room?" Of course it was the one in her room. It was the only turret in the house.

He nodded.

She paused, knowing full well that they were discussing far more than the relaying of a legend here. They were discussing making love. Her chest muscles constricted and her hand shook. Did she want to make love with MacGregor?

He stood up and she let her gaze drift down him, head to heel. She did. With all her heart and soul.

He doesn't know the truth. Can you do this with lies between you?

The whisper. She squeezed her eyes shut. *I need him. As much as he needs me.*

A warm heat breezed across her face and she felt eased, soothed, encouraged. Definitely the entity, not her conscience. Whether or not it was a ghost, she'd no idea. But about her and MacGregor making love, it was pleased. In fact —

"Honey, I haven't asked you to forfeit your life in the electric chair, only to hear the legend."

Liar. She lifted her chin. MacGregor had asked for a lot more than her life. He'd asked for her honor.

Courage.

Maggie silently responded. *Enough for today.* The entity was pleased and, more importantly, so was she. "This better be a good legend, MacGregor. Seven points is nothing to sneeze at."

He grabbed their cups. "It's good enough for ten — and the bath."

She cast him a doubtful look.

"Would I mess with a woman overly fond of subtle revenge?"

Would he? Wishing she knew, Maggie stood up.

Chapter 12

T.J. closed his eyes inside the Great White Room and absorbed the quiet. So much emotion had been felt in this room. He sensed it. Its intensity and its magnificent force. Was that the reason so many guests experienced healing here? Sensations of serenity and calm? Of acceptance and peace?

The Great White Room once had been Cecelia and Collin Freeport's private domain. The room where they shared their secrets, their joys, their worries, and their love. Their son and daughter had been conceived here and, T.J. smiled, he could almost imagine them sitting here, debating and deciding everyday issues during their children's growing years. Miss Hattie had told him stories of their son's request to move upstairs to the attic room so that he might strut his independence safely in his struggle to grow from boy to man, stories of their daughter falling in love and marrying and moving away. Here, most likely, they'd consoled each other on Mary Elizabeth's wedding day, knowing that she'd still be a woman when next she came to Seascape, but never again would she be their little girl. Likely it had been here that they had celebrated the joys of becoming grandparents to Mary Elizabeth's son, Jonathan Nelson, the Atlanta judge who now owned Seascape, and that they'd comforted each other when their own son had left Seascape for the Army, then again when the hearse carrying his body had driven past the turret window down Main Street to the cemetery for his burial.

All of that happened years before T.J. had come here, of course. But the emotions felt in this room hadn't stopped with Collin and Cecelia's passing. Or with those of their children. T.J. himself had seen Miss Hattie in this room more than once. All these long years later, when absent of guests, Miss Hattie still sat alone in here for hours. Though he'd never considered intruding and asking, he felt sure she'd been thinking about her soldier, Collin and Cecelia's son, and the lives theirs would have been had he not been field-promoted in the Army, not been sent to fight a war, not had died while saving the life of another.

Some sadness, but mostly joy and love had flowed in this room. T.J. liked to think that some of it remained. It was possible. If when we make a sound, it carries on and on, then the love we feel surely carries on and on, as well. Love is much stronger than sound.

"Penny for your thoughts." Maggie's hushed whisper slid over him like heated honey.

He reveled in it. "I was thinking that this room is big enough to echo." True, though she couldn't possibly realize he meant to echo the emotions felt and not the words spoken within its tall, paneled walls.

"I think the rugs and furniture absorb the sound, so it doesn't. But if it were empty, it might."

Stripped bare of furnishings, this room could never be empty. It'd taken him nine months of enforced exposure to understand that. Maggie would see it much quicker. Sitting on the plush, blue-cushioned window seat inside the turret, knees-to-knees with Maggie, T.J. smiled. Her subtle perfume filled the intimate space, reminding him again of soft summer breezes, of fresh air and spring, and of the sea. Always the sea. As tempting and alluring as Bill at his poetic best had described it.

She'd taken off her shoes and left them on the round woven rug in front of the window seats. The little tulip lamp beside the bed lifted a blue-tinged light from the coverlet and pooled on the floor, leaving her shoes in shadows. Comfortable, at ease, together and, finally, alone. He sighed contentedly and let his gaze drift past the window to the star-studded sky. A man could want for little more than sharing a quiet moment of peace with a beautiful woman in a room where so much love had been shared.

"You were going to tell me the legend."

"In a second. I'm soaking up some of your serenity." Amazing, but true. It'd been so long since he'd felt at peace and, until he'd sat down here and let all his anger and frustration seep away, he'd glimpsed serenity only once here on this lengthy visit — on the stairs, and then only a brief flicker.

He lowered his gaze to the ocean. Absorbing moonbeams, it sparkled like a thousand diamonds reflecting light. Romantic, intimate, and mysterious. Perfect for telling Maggie the legend.

She shifted around, leaned back against the narrow wall, and put her feet in his lap. "Okay, you're serene enough."

"Maggie."

"Seriously, MacGregor. Five more minutes and you'll be snoring."

He chuckled. She was likely right.

"So what's this legend that's worth ten points and a bath that you sold for seven without one?"

"Care to renegotiate?"

"Welshing, are we?"

"No."

"Trying to play weasel, then." She feigned a sigh. "The deal's been made, sweetheart. Now let's hear it."

She'd used an endearment, talking to him. His heart skipped a full beat and that tender hitch her dragging him conjured knotted in his chest. That was the first time ever she'd used an endearment when talking to him. He glanced down, watched her rub the arch of her left foot with the instep of her right. He moved her right foot onto his thigh, then rubbed the left for her. "You know Cecelia had *the touch* for healing."

"Right there. Oh, that feels good." Maggie grunted. "You told me she was a nurse and midwife."

"Right." He rubbed harder, working his fingers down her arch to her heel, then up to her instep. "Well, the legend goes that Cecelia and Collin were nearly newlyweds when they first came here. The Stanfords owned all the village land and the villagers had been trying to buy some for years."

"Stanfords. Wasn't that Miss Millie's name — before she married Lance Thomas?"

"Yes, it was. It was her family." T.J. let his hand drift up, under the hem of her slacks to her warm calf, and worked the knots from its muscle. Her skin felt whisper soft, silky smooth. Had she used his razor? That she might have had warm heat pooling in his belly. "When Stanford — the old man — saw how much in love Cecelia and Collin were, and how much they loved it here, he agreed to sell them this property."

"Ah, so they bought it and built —"

"Not yet. It was too expensive. They couldn't afford both the land and the house."

Maggie closed her eyes and rubbed her toes against his stomach. "So how'd they end up with it, then?"

"Collin took a leap of faith. A big one. He told Mr. Stanford that he was risking everything to buy the land because Cecelia loved it and —"

"He loved Cecelia." Maggie pointed to her other foot. "It's feeling neglected."

T.J. switched feet and began massaging the neglected one, grinning inside. "Right, because he loved her."

"Have you ever loved anyone that much — to take a leap of faith for them that might cost you everything?"

Wasn't that what he was doing here right now with her? Or was it? "I'm not sure." He gave her the only answer he could. "Have you?"

"Not, yet. Well, maybe almost." She shifted as if uneasy. "Get back to the legend that's costing me seven points."

She was teetering on loving him, if she didn't. And that had warm satisfaction mingling with cold, hard fear in his stomach. He agreed. The legend was much, much safer to discuss. "Well, Collin bought the land, and a couple months later he inherited a fortune — totally unexpectedly — and that's when he and Cecelia built Seascape."

Maggie smiled. "They were very happy here. I felt it the moment I walked in, though I didn't know then it was them, of course. I remember walking up the stairs for the first time and feeling as if I'd stepped into a warm cocoon where I'd always be safe. Then the entity started . . ."

He didn't want to talk about the entity. He wanted to enjoy this serenity for as long as possible. Reality would intrude soon enough. "They *were* very happy here, to

341

hear Miss Hattie tell it. And if it has anything to do with Seascape, she knows about it."

"So why doesn't she know what's happening to you here?"

"Because that's about me, not about Seascape."

"Mmm, a fine line there, but I won't disagree. I see the difference." Maggie worked a kink out of her neck, rotating it. "Did Cecelia and Collin have a lot of children?"

"Only two. Their son died, but their daughter, Mary Elizabeth, is the mother of the man who owns Seascape now."

"Jonathan Nelson — the Atlanta judge."

T.J. stopped rubbing. "Have you heard this story before?"

"No, he called to check on Miss Hattie yesterday and we chatted for a minute or two. Very nice man, though when I was talking to him, I kept getting the feeling he was lonely."

"Probably your imagination. I'm sure he's very well adjusted." T.J. pressed circles on her arch.

"You can be well adjusted and still be lonely, MacGregor."

"Okay, you're right. Don't get into a snit. I wasn't thinking it through."

o what's the legend?"

Mary Elizabeth grew up and went to college. She fell in love there, married, and drifted off to live her own life. Cecelia and Collin stayed here and grew old together: her with her healing, and him with his carving."

Maggie frowned and shifted on the cushions. "This is one sorely-lacking legend, MacGregor. No offense, but where's the magic?"

"You don't see any magic in a man and woman loving each other through an entire lifetime?"

"Well, yes, of course. But — but . . . you know what I mean."

He did. "It's coming, honey. Patience." He set her foot down and let his hand rest on her thigh. "Collin got cancer."

"Geez, MacGregor." Maggie sat straight up. "That's magic?"

"It —"

"It better get a whole lot sweeter than this, or you're never gonna see the inside of that tub with me in it."

Not a mite's worth of intimidation. Shoot, not an atom's worth. "That Cecelia kept Collin alive far longer than modern medicine deemed possible *was* magic." T.J. clasped their hands and laced their fingers

together. "Some of the villagers suspe
Cecelia resorted to dabbling in her Ha
grandmother's habit."

"Which was?"

"Voodoo."

Maggie drew in a sharp breath, and her eyes stretched wide. "I saw a book on that — out in the landing bookshelves." She scooted closer, swung one foot down to the floor. "MacGregor, you don't think our entity —"

"No, I don't. There wasn't any proof, Maggie. That was just gossip, and we know all about gossip, don't we? Remember the personal shopping list?"

"Yeah." Maggie frowned. "Then that's it? That's the legend?"

"I'm getting to it. Lord, woman, you're trying my patience. This is supposed to be a romantic tale."

"Romantic, eh?" She grinned, looking anything but repentant. "Well, you should've told me. I didn't know you were getting romantic on me."

"It doesn't seem likely I'll be able to with all your interruptions."

"Keep your attitude from taking a chunk out of my hide. I can't read your mind, you know. But now that you've told me, I promise I'll be an absolute angel." She crossed her heart with her forefinger, looking all too pleased with herself for his liking but, he had to admit, extremely angelic.

Still, his ego took a severe stomping. He was losing his touch. Since when had he had to *tell* a woman he was being romantic? "Remember me telling you about Cecelia dying and how the villagers held a candlelight vigil on the front lawn?"

"Yes." Maggie stroked the back of his hand with her fingertips.

Did she realize she was doing it? Or was this yet another unconscious touch? "Well, Mary Elizabeth was with her mother and, until the day she died, she swore that at the moment Cecelia passed away, Collin's ghost came down out of nowhere and carried Cecelia's spirit away."

Maggie went statue still. "You're kidding."

"No, I'm not. And there's more."

"Seriously?"

"Seriously." T.J. nodded to reinforce his words. "Jonathan, Mary Elizabeth's son, can't bear to part with Seascape but he can't bring himself to live here, either."

"Why not? You'd think that with his mother experiencing what she had here, he'd want to be here — unless . . . Is Collin haunting Seascape? Is he our entity?"

"No, our entity has nothing to do with

this, Maggie. You've got a one-track mind
— and you aren't being very cooperative —
or very angelic."

"Sorry."

She wasn't sorry. The sweet little liar.
"Jonathan won't sell Seascape or live in it
because of what *he* saw here."

"Are you saying he saw something, too?"
She frowned and her fingers gripped his
hand hard. "You know, I wouldn't buy any
of this for a second if it had happened
anywhere else. But strange things *do* happen here, and we both know it."

"Yeah, well, living those strange things has
a way of dispelling doubt."

"So what did Jonathan see?"

"The legend." Seeing her perplexed look,
he explained. "On the anniversary of his
grandmother's death, he saw her spirit lying
in her bed. Collin came and lifted her into
his arms — just as Jonathan had heard at
his mother's knee that it had happened all
those years ago."

"Good grief! Everyone in the village must
have thought he was nuts."

"They didn't know about it. They still
don't know about it. One of those rare
incidents where everyone in a small town
doesn't know everything about everyone in
that town."

"Well, that's hard to believe. There's quite a network around here. How did Jonathan manage to keep it quiet?"

"He only spoke of it once — to Miss Hattie — and he described it as the most awesome experience of his life."

"I guess he did. Seeing two spirits like that, well, it's not the kind of thing you experience every day."

"No, Maggie. Not the ghosts. Lots of people see ghosts and that didn't impress Jonathan at all. It was the *love* between them that struck him as awesome. It had transcended time. They'd gone on, yet their love had remained."

She stilled, blinked, and then blinked again. "Jonathan witnessed personified love."

"Exactly." Why was she staring at him so strangely? As if she, too, were witnessing something she never dreamed or thought or considered she would.

Maggie sighed. "It must have changed him forever."

A shiver slid up T.J.'s backbone. What had Maggie said? That she feared what was happening to them with the entity because she sensed those experiences life-altering. *Changed forever. Life-altering.* "I expect it did. It would change me forever." Was that what was supposed to happen here? Change? For him and Maggie to alter their lives? Maybe the entity wasn't playing games with them after all. Maybe its purpose was much more noble. Maybe —

"What does he say about the experience now that he's an adult? Does he see it differently now than he did then?"

"He doesn't discuss it — ever. But he returns here once a year on the anniversary date, stays overnight, then he goes home."

"What does Miss Hattie say, then?"

"That Cecelia's healing magic lingers in the house. That theirs was the kind of magic that lives on forever and gifts with miracles those who believe in it."

"Love," Maggie said. "Her love for him, and his for her. That's what kept Collin alive, wasn't it? That's the magic."

"Yes." He smiled. "Or so says Miss Hattie."

"She never lies."

"No, she doesn't — not intentionally."

Maggie sighed wistfully. "There it is again, MacGregor. That rare kind of love like Miss Hattie had for her soldier."

"Yeah, though I think Cecelia and Collin had it first." T.J. leaned back against the wall. "Seems to happen a lot around here."

Maggie scooted around and fitted herself

between T.J.'s thighs, then leaned back against his chest. "It's not fair, you know? I've never even seen love like that and it floats around here, touching people, left and right." She grunted. "Where's the justice? The best I find is Sam Grayson — and he dumped me for a kiss and an all-day sucker."

T.J. smiled above her head and twined his arms around her. Grayson. Sam Grayson. Why did that name ring a bell? He'd definitely heard it — somewhere. "Was this recently?"

"Yeah. I was twelve." Grinning, she rubbed her cheek against his shirt.

"Mmm, was the sucker grape?"

She rested her hands atop his. They were clasped together at her middle, just under her ribs. "What's the difference?"

"Grape is irresistible, honey. A guy just can't hold out against grape."

She grunted. "Or against a Judas kiss." She tapped a forefinger to his shoulder. "You realize that if you take Grayson's side in this, subtle revenge is inevitable."

"I figured it likely." T.J. smiled again. "Who was the Judas?"

"Supposedly, my best friend." Maggie sighed. "She dated him all through high school just to spite me."

And that betrayal had hurt Maggie deeply. "Pretty vindictive behavior for a friend." He inhaled her shampoo. Coconut. Enticing. "Maybe she just liked the guy."

"She didn't. He got zits in tenth grade. She hated zits — hated anything that rated less than perfect — but she stuck with him because she knew I was still crazy about him."

"First love?" T.J. stroked her silky hair, jealous, pure and simple.

"*Only* love." Maggie snuggled closer, pressing her side fully against him, shoulder to hip. "My dad didn't exactly inspire enthusiasm for even the prospect of loving someone."

Or instill much trust in it either, T.J. imagined. "I guess it's pretty normal that you'd figure all guys were like him."

"Aren't they?"

"No, and you know it."

"I do. Sam Grayson wasn't."

"Why was he so special?" Maybe a little insight would help T.J.'s cause.

"He believed in me."

He waited for her to go on, but she didn't. When it became apparent she wasn't going to, he frowned. "That's it?"

"Someone believing in you is nothing to sneeze at, MacGregor. You had it with your parents, but I didn't. My mother was too self-absorbed trying to survive living with and loving my father, and he was too busy making her miserable to worry about me." She ground her teeth as if sorry she'd lost her temper and disclosed that. "When you've never had it, belief in you is more than enough. It's . . . special."

"I expect it is." He rubbed her shoulder. "I'm sorry I didn't understand."

"How could you?" She sighed. "I'm sorry. I didn't mean to sound nasty. It's just that unless you experience that firsthand, you really can't understand it."

"Still, all men aren't like your father. Sam Grayson wasn't, and I'm not either."

"True. But, as you so eloquently put it, old habits are hard to break. It's like I know it in my head, but my heart just isn't convinced."

"Well" — he ran his fingers through her hair, loving the feel of it against his palm — "if you want my opinion, Sam Grayson was a fool."

"He was, wasn't he?" Maggie looked up at him. "You're not just saying this to save yourself a stint of subtle revenge, are you?"

"No, I'm not."

She smiled. "As it turned out, things happened for the best. Sam Grayson turned into a jerk. At the senior prom, he got wasted on vodka and drove his motorcycle into the school swimming pool and had to be fished out. Wrecked everything, including the turf on the football field. Cut donuts in it until it was as messed up as if circus elephants had trampled it for a week. His parents were mortified. Judas dumped him, and I refused to take him back."

T.J. returned her smile. "I'm glad he turned into a jerk."

"Me, too. Lots easier on the ego, you know?"

He did. In the end, hadn't his friends finally come forth with their true feelings about Carolyn? Hadn't knowing their opinions eased his mind about his own? He touched a thumb to Maggie's cheek, dragged it over the bone and down her jaw to her chin. "I'd have stuck with you."

Her eyes hid in the shadows. "Even over an irresistible grape all-day sucker?"

"Yeah," he said. "Even over grape."

"Sometimes, MacGregor, you say just the right things." She gave him a sweet smile and fingered the placket of his shirt, sliding from button to button. "May I ask you something — about Carolyn?"

He nodded. Maggie's hand moved steadily and the second button on his shirt came undone. Had it been intentional? Did he dare to hope so?

"Why did you say that it's your fault she died?"

This was important to her. Maggie's shaky voice proved it. T.J. licked at his lips, wanting her to know the truth but not wanting to risk seeing condemnation of him in her eyes. "It started the night we got engaged. She wanted the painting I did of Seascape as an engagement present."

"How come?"

"She was obsessed with it and had been for months — though I didn't see that at the time."

"Did you give it to her?"

"I couldn't. I'd already donated it to the gallery." The memories of all the anger and discontent he'd felt then threatened him again now. "But I offered to paint her another one like it."

"She stole it — from the gallery."

Surprise streaked up his spine. How did Maggie know about the theft? They'd kept it out of the paper to protect the gallery. "Yes, she did." Had Miss Hattie talked with her about Carolyn? "That's when I realized it wasn't me Carolyn loved and wanted. It was the painting. I was a means to an end for her. No more."

Maggie pressed her palm flat against his chest, as if to absorb the pain she knew that realization had brought him. "I'm sorry, Tyler." She pressed her head against his shoulder, pecked a kiss against his neck, then stilled.

Tyler. Not MacGregor. She was emotional. And so was he. He hadn't meant to tell her that, but he didn't regret now that he had. "Anyway, I recognized with the theft that she was obsessed. I knew she was leaving, that she wasn't rational. And I didn't stop her."

"You tried. You told me you did."

"I did. I went to her apartment, but I got there too late. She'd already gone. I — I didn't know where to look . . ."

Maggie lifted her head and looked up at him. "It wouldn't have mattered. You could have found her, but you couldn't have stopped her. She wouldn't have listened, much less let you."

"I tell myself that, but I can't be sure." He dragged his lower lip between his teeth. "I just can't be sure, Maggie."

"And so it's that uncertainty that makes you feel responsible for her death."

He nodded.

"And that makes you blame your art."

"If I hadn't painted the blasted thing,

she'd never have been obsessed with it enough to steal it. I *knew* it had magic. That's what makes me guilty. I *knew* it and I foolishly wanted to share that magic with everyone else. That's why I donated it to the gallery stipulating that it could never be sold."

"Sharing is a good thing, not a bad one. Why should that make you feel guilty?"

"We both know how strong the magic in that painting is. It brought you here. It brought me back here. For all her bravado, Carolyn was weak, Maggie. She didn't stand a chance at resisting the painting's lure."

"Whoa, right there. The painting lures, true, but it does *not* strip a person of free will, Tyler. I know that firsthand because I felt it. Maybe your reaction is stronger to it because you created the painting, but for me it lured, and yet I knew the entire time that if I didn't want to come here, there'd be no coercion or force insisting I did. I had a choice. Carolyn had a choice, too. And the point is that she stole the painting. She made the decision to steal it, and then she followed through on it. You have to put the responsibility for this at her front door. That's truly where it belongs, and deep down in your heart you know it."

"You're doing it again."

"What?"

"Throwing my own words back at me."

She shrugged. "No need to reinvent the wheel when you have one that rolls just fine." With a little sigh, she lowered her head back to his chest and snuggled closer.

At that moment, he thought he might just love her. He wanted her — oh, how he wanted her. But he might just love her, too.

"I saw all your painting gear in the mud room."

"Miss Hattie's encouraging me to give it another try."

"She's about as subtle as mud, isn't she?"

"Yeah." He smiled. "But she's special."

"She is." Maggie rubbed circles on his stomach. "Maybe you should give it another try."

"You know how I feel about my art, Maggie."

"Yes, darling, I do. And that's why I think you should try."

Darling. First *sweetheart* and now *darling*. Never had Maggie ever called him anything other than MacGregor or Tyler, and that, only when she was very intense. He liked this *darling*. In fact, he liked it a lot.

She stroked his chest soothingly. "It takes a lot of energy to carry around all that anger and bitterness."

"Wouldn't you be bitter?"

"Yes, I would." She looked up at him. "But I'd also know that it was destroying me, and I'd have to try to work past it or to live with knowing I'd given up. I don't want you to give up, Tyler. Regret costs too much, and the price is just too steep to live with for a whole lifetime."

Moonlight slanted in the window, across her face. Her eyes glossed over with tears. A thick knot of raw emotion threatened to explode in his chest and he hugged her tightly, forcing himself to remain gentle. "I'll think about it," he whispered. "That's all I can promise."

She smiled so tenderly he ached.

"Fair enough." Stretching, she toed off his shoes, then swept them with her bare foot off the cushion.

One at a time, they *thunked* onto the wooden floor. Feeling the heat of her body through her silk blouse, he lifted a brow.

"Scratching my arch," she said, lying to him, and letting him see it.

He nodded and she leaned into him, curling on her side against his chest. He looped his arms around her biceps and rested his hands on the swell of her hip. Her bare toes inched up under the hem of his slacks then down at the top of his sock, setting his heart to pounding beneath her hand. She wanted to touch him, skin to skin. Surprise faded to pleasure. He smiled, dipped his chin and pressed his cheek flat against her sweet-smelling crown.

Upon realizing he had no intention of calling her down on the lie, Maggie relaxed. Her body contoured to his, hip to shoulder, and she expelled a contented sigh. They settled in, her half-sitting, half-lying across him, staring out the window at the moonlit night, her left arm wrapped around his waist, her right one crooked and her hand resting over his heart. Quiet, content, and, suddenly again at peace, T.J. let his hand drift up and down her silk-clad back, his mind drift outside, beyond the misty shore.

Long minutes later, Maggie whispered softly, "MacGregor."

"Mmm?"

She arched her neck and looked up at him, her eyes wide and soulful, her voice thick with promise. "I'd have stuck with you, too."

His heart lurched. He smoothed her hair back from her face, then dipped his chin and tilted hers into the moonlight, determined to see her eyes. "Why?"

"Because."

So much emotion there. So much, he

couldn't absorb it all. His chest went tight, his throat thick, and his hand on her face began to tremble. He had to know. He'd be crazy to ask — he was crazy for even thinking it, but . . . but he had to know. "Do you love me, Maggie?"

Her eyes went misty then doe soft and, long before she answered, he heard her swallow hard. "I don't think I'm capable of loving anyone." Regret seeped through her voice and drove into his heart like a sharp, piercing stake. "But I really . . . care." She blinked then stared up at him wide-eyed, her lips parted, her breath coming in short, rasped puffs. "I do, MacGregor. I really do . . . care about you."

Vulnerable. Her father. Opening herself up to caring was so hard. And yet she'd done it . . . for him. A tumbled jangle of senses and nerves, T.J. stilled to absorb the magnitude of her gesture, suffered the shocks of being given such a costly and precious treasure. His heart swelled, his eyes burned, the back of his nose tingled and, wanting to crush her in his embrace, he tightened his hold on her chin ever so gently, sensing her fragility, her fear of rejection. He'd asked her the wrong question, of course. Though she thought she'd loved Sam, she'd never loved a man, or been loved by one, or been in love with one. How would she recognize it? Maybe with that, T.J. could help her. Help himself.

He fought the urge to just tell her and have it done. But not only she was feeling vulnerable. She was afraid. "If you could love, and you could choose, would you choose to love me?" Why was he pushing her? He knew the muddle her father had made of her emotions. He knew the risks his loving her would bring to her, as well. But he wanted her so —

Her lids dropped closed. A little shudder rippled through her. Her jaw lifted and her lips sealed together. A breathless moment passed, then another. She tensed, forcibly broke the seal, then opened her eyes and met his gaze. "I think I might."

His heart nearly stopped. *I think I might.* The words echoed off the walls of his mind, slid down his windpipe, then rattled in his lungs. They pumped through the chambers of his heart, rousing emotions he'd thought dead and buried, then raced through his veins.. The tender hitch he'd felt on her dragging him over the rocks, on seeing that tear slide down her cheek when he'd kissed her under the cobwebbed steps outside the Blue Moon Cafe, intensified, and more than anything he longed to tell her how much

she meant to him. "You know I want you."
Want? Want? Crave. I crave you, Maggie.

He tried, but couldn't make himself give her the words. They both feared them, he realized. But he could show her. Body and soul, he ached to show her. "Maggie," he choked past a lump of emotion in his throat. "Let me make love with you."

She shivered and stretched, looping her arms around his neck. "Yes."

"Without regrets later?" He swallowed hard, let his thumb caress her creamy cheek. "I don't want regrets between us, Maggie. Our bond is too . . . special." He'd die a thousand deaths each time he saw regret in her, too. Nothing was worth that.

She slid over the cushion, then stood up and looked back at him, her silk blouse creased from where it had been crushed between them, her pulse pounding at her throat. "No regrets, Tyler."

His heart ricocheting off his ribs, he stared at her bare toes and gave her yet another chance to change her mind, scared dry-mouthed that she would, and that she wouldn't. "This is what you want, too?"

She nodded.

A niggling fear her nod didn't nullify grew full-blown. "This has nothing to do with the entity, right? I mean, it didn't tell you to —"

"No, it didn't tell me to do this." She smiled and let her appreciation for him shine in her eyes. "Is it that hard for you to believe that a healthy woman would find you attractive, MacGregor?"

"Not really. I mean, I haven't had —" Well, heck. Now he was coming off as a conceited jerk. Man, he hadn't been this nervous since he'd hit puberty. *Life-altering.* This was. *Changed forever.* They were. *Believe, Tyler. Believe.*

She laughed. "I know what you mean."

He gave her a sheepish grin. "I just thought that you might feel differently. You don't, um, react to me as other women do."

She laced her arms over her stomach, akimbo. "I hope not."

He bit a smile from his lips, gave in to the urge to tease her. "Some of those reactions are darn nice, Maggie Wright."

"And some of them, no doubt, are responsible for that attitude of yours. I adore you, MacGregor" — she walked the three steps to him and, chest to chest, lifted her hands then curled them around his sides — "but your attitude just has to go."

Sweetheart. Darling. I think I might. She *adored* him? This room *definitely* held magic.

They might just stay in it forever. "I kind of like the attitude. Subtle revenge isn't so hot, but I'm developing a real liking for avoiding it."

She worried her lip with her teeth. "Then avoid it right now, mmm?"

Believe, Tyler. Believe.

Trembling inside, T.J. scooped her up into his arms, then walked with her over to the high four-poster bed.

The woman in his arms came across as sassy, nipping at his neck, but she was every bit as nervous as he. Her heart raced like a rabbit's against his ribs. He lowered her onto the bed then pressed her shoulder back against the pillow. Her hair spilled over her eyes and, one knee near her hip, one foot on the floor, he threaded his fingers through the silky strands, smoothed it back from her face, stirring her intoxicating scent. Soft light from the lamp spilled over her cheek, and he saw it blush rosy. "I'm sure about this, Maggie. I want you to know that. I mean, this isn't just sex." What was it? What could he tell her to make her understand? He couldn't love her. He didn't dare to love her because his love could kill her. How could he explain? "It's . . . more."

She nodded and looked up at him. No words passed her lips, but she lifted a fingertip and touched it to his nose, let it drift down its slope, then settle over his mouth.

Needing reassurance, he nipped at her fingertip. "Are you sure?"

Maggie didn't smile. Deep down inside, a part of her wanted to, but she couldn't do it. Words once spoken flashed through her mind, declared war within her. And the battle raged. *When you only have a little left and you lose anything at all, it's a lot, Maggie.* How right he'd been. How very right he'd been. She had so little left to lose! *It's like quicksilver. Don't let it slip through your fingers.* No, no she wouldn't. She couldn't. If not that rare love like Cecelia and Collin's, like Miss Hattie and her soldier's, if not love at all, then whatever these feelings for MacGregor inside her were, she wanted to share them with him. "I'm not sure about anything. Not anymore," she said, giving him the only answer she could.

Was she going to change her mind? He stilled, stared at her, his breath trapped somewhere between his throat and lungs, knowing if she stopped now he couldn't blame her, he wouldn't blame her, but he'd regret. Man, but would he regret. Them stopping was the sensible thing to do. Already the emotions stirred between them

364

raged too powerfully. They both should be sensible. Should . . . but would he regret?

The wait for her decision ended. Possible regret died.

A lifetime later, he kissed her with a new tenderness, his hand cupping her jaw and looked at her, unsmiling. "I believe in you, Maggie."

Her heart already full, overflowed, and tears swam in her eyes. A *lot of miracles have happened inside these walls. Miracles . . . Miracles . . . Miracles . . .*

Life-altering.

He *believed.*

Far too emotional to speak, she nodded.

Curling her close, he buried her face to his chest and sighed contentedly. "Honey?"

Satiated, limbs heavy, eyelids drooping, she mumbled, "No regrets, darling."

"No regrets."

Maggie awakened during the night. MacGregor's arm lay over her chest, their thighs and calves were tangled with the sheets. Did she love him? If for a second she believed she *could* love, she would say she did love MacGregor. But it'd take a miracle for her to believe.

Her heart heavy, she looked into his sleeping face. Relaxed and at ease, he was even more gorgeous to her. A flow of tenderness washed through her, and more guilt settled in its wake.

She'd shared her body and part of her heart with this man, but not all of her. She hadn't let him into her soul. She'd wanted to, but she hadn't been able to do it. Lies by omission were still lies. And her lies stood between them like a concrete wall.

Their lovemaking had been wonderful — a perfect blend of laughter and intense, sensual delight — but it had suffered from the slight of her holding back. She didn't regret making love with him, but for the first time in her life she understood the costs of those barriers that sealing off a part of herself while making love with a man who meant so much to her entailed. For a moment — one very brief, very shining moment — she'd let down her guard, let him touch that innermost part of her, and she'd glimpsed what their lovemaking could be like. But her guilt had intruded and that perfect unity of body and spirit had disappeared in a flash. She hated it. And she prayed that someday she'd have the courage to tell him the truth. That he wouldn't hate her for it. That she'd again have the chance to make love with him, holding nothing back. From that glimpse, she knew it would be the most magnificent, fulfilling experience of her life.

She eased free of him, then at the foot of the bed into her robe. He still slept, his breathing slow and even. She left the room and softly shut the door.

On the stairs, she sent Cecelia's portrait a forlorn look. *How I envy the love you and Collin shared. And how I resent that I'll never know the contentment that comes with that rare kind of love. I think I could have loved MacGregor that way. But as soon as I tell him I've lied . . . No, no, I can't tell him, can I? Not now, not ever.*

The third stair creaked and Maggie stiffened. Someone was watching her. Instinctively, she looked back up to the landing, expecting to see MacGregor. She didn't. Though she did sense more than see — something. A flash of pure light . . .

The entity? Her heart rate accelerated. "What do you want?" she whispered.

She waited and waited, expectant, but heard no response and saw nothing more.

Giving up, she went on down the stairs, crossed the gallery to the ticks of the grandfather clock, then padded on to the kitchen. At the refrigerator, as she reached for the carton of milk, an urge to get outside hit her with the force of a thunderbolt. The entity . . .

In the mud room, she grabbed her coat from a peg and slipped it on, then went outside.

Come to the cliffs, Maggie.

Trembling head to toe, she wrapped her coat more tightly around her. The night air was cold and crisp, but clear and not biting. The frigid cold came from within.

She walked around the side of the house and glanced over to the Carriage House, silhouetted and shadowed by the moon. The roofers would be done any day now. Would MacGregor move back over there? What would things be like between them now that they'd taken their relationship to intimacy? Would he still value his privacy most? Or would he forfeit it to be with her? Did she want him to forfeit it?

She'd never been in this position before with a lover. What did she expect? What did he expect from her? How did she behave?

One more reason she shouldn't have done it. She grimaced. No. No. She stepped across the road and climbed the stony walk to the cliffs. She'd promised MacGregor no regrets.

The blustery wind chilled her face, slicked her hair back against her head. It wasn't making love with him she regretted. It was that she'd done it when she'd had no right to do it.

So why had she?

The ocean roared and the strong wind cut through her. She'd lost her head. Otherwise she'd never have managed to tamp down an entire lifetime of memories of her parents' situation or to forget all about Carolyn.

Lust? Passion? Good old-fashioned desire? That just didn't feel right. She'd wanted to make love with MacGregor. She'd felt all those things for him, if she were honest. But she'd felt more, too. A lot more. She had before they'd made love, while they'd made love, and she still felt them all now, afterward. So there had to be more to this than just lust, passion, and desire. But what?

It couldn't be love. Not with their histories. If it were love, then Maggie would have trusted him enough to have told him the truth about Carolyn, to have let him into her soul.

And risked losing him? Isn't that why you haven't told him, Maggie. You're afraid he'll leave you?

The man's whisper. She closed her eyes and confessed the truth she'd hidden even from herself. "Yes, I'm afraid of losing him." Tears welled in her eyes. "He *matters* to me. I didn't want him to. I fought it. But he does. He matters. Is that so wrong? So awful wrong?"

"Maggie?"

She spun around and saw MacGregor. His coat was unbuttoned and flapping in the wind. He'd forgotten his shirt.

Worry creased the tender skin beneath his eyes. "You okay, honey?"

Her heart wrenched. The time had come for the truth. Give her the strength. "No, MacGregor. I'm not okay."

He stepped closer, lifted a hand to her chin and cupped it in his palm. "Tell me you're not sorry, Maggie. Please. Can you just tell me that?"

She looked him straight in the eye. "I'm not sorry. Not at all."

He dragged her to him, wrapped his arms around her, and held her tight. His heart pounded against her chest, thudding wildly. "What's wrong, baby?"

A wall of fog lay just offshore, headed inland. She eased her hand under his coat to his bare skin. Content. Warm. Safe. Could she tell him the truth, after all? What if he turned away from her? She'd never again feel as she felt this moment. Never again for the rest of her life.

"Maggie, please. Don't shut me out." He whispered against her ear. "I'm having a hard time here with you. I didn't want to care about you, but I do. A lot, Maggie. And that scares the fire out of me. You scare the fire out of me."

The doubts about him being involved in Carolyn's death had steadily grown in Maggie — until now. Now, they'd twisted on her. Could the man who had loved her with such gentleness, the man who held her now with such tenderness and care, have been involved? She wasn't so sure he could. "I care about you, too, MacGregor. So much. And I'm scared of caring at all for anyone, but especially for you."

The fog rolled ashore, obscuring everything around them. It swirled up to their waists then to Maggie's shoulders. She shivered and stepped away, feeling the cold mist settle on her face. "I have to tell you something," she said. "Something I should have told you a long time ago."

An Arctic blast of cold air cut through her like a knife and cold fingers pressed gently against her mouth, blocking her words. Blinking rapidly, Maggie looked back over her shoulder. A man stood there. He looked both aged and ageless, not threatening, but intent and determined. Curly golden brown hair, kind eyes and, through the mist and fog, she saw he wore some kind of old-fashioned clothes: a dark green suit with shiny buttons.

He looked into her eyes, and lowered his hand from her mouth.

"Tyler?"

"Yes, honey?"

From his tone, she knew he didn't see the man. "N— nothing."

"Maggie, I just want you to know that whatever this something is . . ." MacGregor talked on.

Maggie heard only a mumbled drone. The strange man behind her commanded her full attention, and it was his voice that she heard clearly.

Look not beneath the veil, Maggie.

His lips hadn't moved. She responded telepathically. *What veil? Who are you? Are you our entity?*

My name is Tony. Don't be afraid. I'm not here to hurt you, only to bring you a warning.

Maggie blinked hard. *To look not beneath the veil.*

Yes. It's not yet time.

My goodness. She swallowed hard. *You're a ghost!*

He smiled, and the truth slammed through her with the force of a sledge. Her knees went weak and spots formed before her eyes. This couldn't be happening. It couldn't be happening!

CHAPTER 13

"Honey, what's wrong?"

"Um, nothing." Maggie glanced at Mac-Gregor. He'd been right here and yet he hadn't heard or seen anything. Should she tell him about Tony? MacGregor would swear she'd lost her mind. Maybe she had lost her mind. Insanity would be a lot easier to explain than — Good grief. Was she actually saying she hoped she'd gone insane?

"Maggie, what is it?" He grasped her left arm. "You've gone so pale."

"I'm just . . . tired." She darted her gaze back to Tony.

He was gone.

Had he ever been there? Maybe she *had* lost her mind.

Get a grip, Maggie.

Not the whisper. Her conscience, thank heaven. Get a grip. Right. Right. Maybe the man had been a villager caught on the cliffs by the fog. It had rolled in very quickly. Oh, she liked that idea much, much better than insanity or . . . or the other. Of course, that had to be it. It stood up to reason, made sense, and sounded logical and believable. He had to have been just a villager. And MacGregor had been so worried about her — he'd come after her in such a hurry he'd forgotten his shirt, hadn't he? — that he just hadn't seen the man.

He talked without his lips moving, Maggie.

Her conscience. Definitely her conscience. Whose side was it on? Had it conjured the man?

Good grief. Now she talked to *and* answered herself. Well, was it any wonder? A ghost! For pity's sake. If she had any sense she'd just faint. She'd never escaped her troubles that way before, but well, if this oddity didn't warrant a good faint, she sure as spit didn't know what would warrant one.

And as much as she would like to ignore the possibility of . . . the other, there was a preponderance of evidence she couldn't explain away. Hadn't MacGregor said Aaron Butler hung onto Batty Beaulah's every word, fascinated that her tales about Seascape might be true? Hadn't Beaulah told Lucy that a ghost kept MacGregor landlocked here? Hadn't Maggie herself seen Aaron on his bike down in the village and asked him if he'd ever heard any weird stories about Seascape, and hadn't he spent ten minutes relaying Beaulah's stories and ended with a shiver-inducing: *Oh, yeah, Miss Wright, Seascape and all the land around it is haunted. And that's the truth.*

She hadn't believed him then. MacGregor warned her Aaron was a good kid but he was also the home-of-the-whopper story-teller of Sea Haven Village. Could that be true and at the same time Aaron and Batty Beaulah also be right about the haunting? If Maggie had seen what she thought she'd seen, then they were right. Question was, had she seen what she thought she'd seen?

Maggie worried her lip. The heavy fog made it so difficult to tell. She could barely see MacGregor and yet she stood less than two feet away from him.

Tony had stepped back, much farther away than two feet. Maybe he truly had been just a well-meaning villager out for a late night stroll and MacGregor hadn't seen him because of the fog — and, for the same reason, when he'd talked, she hadn't seen his lips move. Fog and mist certainly could distort perception.

At best, the hypothesis rated unlikely. Tony had known her name. But then so had Lucy and Miss Millie. Gossip traveled fast around here, and the shopping list tidbit had been juicy. Heck, after the bulletin board incident, there likely wasn't a soul in the village over the age of twelve who hadn't heard her name. With that second posting — whatever it was for — her name remained posted even now.

Furthermore, ghost or man — Oh, how she prayed he'd been a man — his voice belonged to someone. Mist and fog and that little bit of distance didn't distort sound. MacGregor hadn't heard the man, but Maggie sure had. And according to him, his name was Tony.

Had he claimed himself Collin, she'd really have something to worry about here. But he hadn't. So there was a strong possibility that this was a totally explainable occurrence and entirely non-entity related. It certainly couldn't hurt to ask Miss Hattie if she knew of a Tony. That shouldn't have the dear angel worrying and wanting to lock Maggie in a padded room with the white-jacketed inkblot studiers who ask too many questions about mothers.

"Maggie, where are you?" Holding her by both arms, MacGregor increased the pressure of his fingers. "You seem so far away. I hate it when you drift off like that and leave me in the dust."

She looked up and saw that worry chiseled into his expression. "I'm sorry, I'm just so . . . confused."

He circled her shoulder and pulled her close to his side. "Just please don't cry, Maggie. I can take anything but tears."

"I don't cry."

He stared at her strangely, started to say something, then stopped and clearly said something entirely different. "We'll sort through all this, but we don't have to do it right this second. Sooner or later, we'll get a firm grip on everything, okay? So long as you don't regret what happened between us, there's no reason to panic."

For the sake of her sanity, she hoped they resolved this matter sooner. "I don't regret it. Didn't I tell you that already? I know I did."

"Lord, but I love a feisty woman." He grinned. "Let's go back inside, mmm? You're trembling."

"I'm cold." She was. She shook like a leaf caught in an infamous Maine nor'easter. But it had nothing to do with the icy wind. This cold was internal. "Tyler, something has occurred to me and I want to talk about it." Heading back to the inn, she stepped onto the stone path and followed it on down to the street.

Seeing nothing but fog and darkness, they crossed over to Seascape's lawn and Maggie huddled closer to MacGregor's side. "When we're together and not angry with each other, it's usually sunny. But when we aren't — like that week the entity told me to stay away from you — or when we're at odds, then the weather turns foul." She paused at the back door to the inn. "Have you noticed that?"

When they were inside and putting their coats on the pegs, he answered. "From our earlier discussions, I think I know where you're going with this, but I don't believe Mother Nature is our entity, Maggie. Maine weather just changes like this. It's normal here."

In the gallery, the clock ticked steadily. Maggie focused on the sound and climbed the stairs. "Okay, I agree the weather here can spike both ends of a thermometer in a single day, but you have to agree that when we stick together this entity seems, I don't know, more content."

"That, I've noticed. It doesn't hassle us as much. When we're at odds, it lets us know it's ticked."

She stopped on the landing. "Any idea why?"

" 'Fraid not. You?"

"None whatsoever — aside from the obvious."

"It wants us together."

She nodded.

"That's about how I see it, too."

Standing at the top of the stairs in the dusky hallway, MacGregor looked as uncertain as she felt about where to go from here. He lifted his brows in silent question, asking her preference. Not knowing the proper protocol for lovers sharing a house these days — or any days, for that matter — she paused. At least about this she should just talk straight to the man. "Tyler, I —" Her throat muscles locked tight.

His expression turned solemn. "I want to be with you, Maggie."

The weight on her shoulders lifted and, oddly, her muscles relaxed as if massaged. "Me, too."

Feeling that warm, sourceless breeze blow across her skin, she sensed approval, clasped their hands, then walked back to her room.

The shades were up at the turret windows. Pale moonlight beamed into the room and slanted across the floor. Maggie didn't pause to turn on the lamp, just stopped beside the rumpled bed and took off her robe, then slid between the sheets, nude and shivering.

MacGregor was still undressing, and she cursed the darkness keeping secrets of him from her. Could his body really be sculpted as perfectly as it had felt to her hands?

He lay down beside her, then pulled the sheet and coverlet up over them. "Come snuggle me, Maggie. I forgot my shirt and I'm freezing."

"I noticed." Boy, had she. The man was walking temptation. Even from her side of the bed, she felt his heat, but since she wanted a good snuggle herself, she didn't mention his warmth, just slid over, rolled onto her side, and into his arms. She rested her head against his shoulder. "MacGregor, can I ask you something, mmm, personal?"

"Anything."

She pecked a kiss to his neck to thank him for that openness, and that earned her a gentle squeeze. "You won't take it wrong?"

"I can't say for sure, since I don't know what *it* is."

"Well, it could be taken as an ego stab — but I don't mean it that way."

"This would be easier if you'd just define *it*." He stroked her hair, scalp to ends.

"It's about when we made love."

"Finally, a little praise. No offense, Maggie, but you do leave a guy feeling wounded by not telling him whether or not you're pleased."

Spit. How could she ask him after that remark?

"Um, you're not saying anything." He swallowed hard. "This is about praise, isn't it?" His voice reeked an uncertainty that tugged at her heartstrings.

"Not exactly." He went stiff as a board, and she gave his chest a soothing pat. "I think I'd better try to explain, after all."

"That would be . . . appropriate."

Inwardly, she sighed. His tone couldn't be any more formal if he were participating in a UN diplomatic debate. "You were wonderful —"

"Of course." He expelled a long breath she bet he hadn't realized he'd held.

"Arrogant jerk."

"That's not praise, sweetheart."

"Really? You usually think it is."

"This isn't usual."

She propped her chin on his chest and looked him in the eye. "You really were wonderful . . . physically."

His cocky expression turned to a glare.

"Don't even think about snarling, Mac-Gregor. I said it was wonderful. That's praise."

"You said, *physically.* That's a qualifier. One that deals a man's ego a pretty hard blow, in case you didn't know."

"I knew you'd take this wrong. I just knew it."

"I'm still trying to determine what *this* is. How can I take it wrong when I don't what it is? And you can't toss in a qualifier on something like that and not —"

"Okay, here it is," she interrupted, her face hot with a good mix of temper and embarrassment. He wasn't making this easy for her, darn him. "When we made love, did it feel . . . right to you?"

Right? T.J. held off a grimace by a nail's width. She sounded worried. What was she getting at? She had been satisfied. He'd seen to it. "What do you mean, *right?*"

She twirled the hair on his chest. "You know what I mean."

"I don't." He looked down into her upturned face, not sure he wanted to know. He'd been too needy for a stellar performance, but she had been satisfied. Evidently, though, only physically. He sighed.

"I'm asking if you were . . . Never mind. Forget I brought it up." She looked away.

Forget it? How could he *forget it?* "It had been a long time for both of us," he whispered softly. "It was too fast, Maggie, but I wanted you so —"

"Then it *didn't* feel right to you."

"I didn't say that." Oh, shoot, she meant emotionally. Did the woman have a hotline to his soul? She couldn't. He had to be reading more into this than was there.

"You didn't say it, but you felt it, Tyler. I know you did."

"Because you felt it, too?" His heart nearly stopped.

Blinking hard and fast, she nodded.

Not only a hotline, it appeared, but a personal 800 number. "It wasn't that I didn't want you. I did. I still do." More than was safe or wise for either of them. "You mean . . . a lot to me."

"Then what was wrong? Did I do something —"

"No, you were perfect." From her tone, she wanted reassurance. He stroked the length of her back with tender, long sweeps of his hand and decided to ask her. "Do you really want the truth?"

"Yes."

She hadn't hesitated. He pressed a kiss to her temple to let her know that pleased him. "I think I've done something unforgivable, honey. Something so bad I can't believe I let it happen. And, I think, it's got me unintentionally holding back." He shuddered.

"Nothing can be that awful, MacGregor."

"It can. Knowing what I know, it's criminal and cruel that I think so much of you and yet I did this anyway, Maggie. What kind of person am I to do that?"

Maggie winced. He sounded so sincere, so troubled. "What have you done?"

"I think I've fallen in love with you."

Stunned, she went totally still. She couldn't, she *wouldn't* believe it. He was sincere, but he was wrong. He'd see that soon enough and, if she dared to believe it, then when he realized he'd been mistaken, she'd be hurt. "Tyler, you haven't," she reassured him, forcing a lightness into her voice that she sure didn't feel.

Why did knowing he didn't love her hurt? She should be happy. Elated. Delighted. She was the woman who didn't even like him most of the time. Instead, as Miss Hattie would say, Maggie felt depressed to the gills. "It's just lust. You've been alone here for a long, long time. When you have no woman around, any woman appeals."

"That's not true."

The seventeen mismatches. "Trust me, Tyler. Take lust, toss in a soft spot of caring because you're tenderhearted — I dragged you over the cliffs, and I didn't bombard you with uncomfortable questions — and you've got it. It's not love."

"Do you really think so?"

The hope in his voice crushed her. "I'm sure of it," she insisted, swallowing a knot of sudden tears that had lodged in her throat.

"I hope you're right."

"I am." Oh no, she was going to cry. Why in the world should she even want to cry? This wasn't a long-term thing with them. She'd known that going in. So why did she expect the rules to change in the middle of the game? Why did she want them to change? He could hurt her, and she knew it. He wasn't like her father now. But surely her father had changed *after* her mother had fallen in love with him, too. Otherwise, she'd never have taken the plunge.

T.J. sighed, as if letting go of the worry. "Maggie?"

"Mmm?"

"There's a little problem."

"What?"

"If it were lust, then when we made love, wouldn't that end it?"

"Maybe. I don't know." No lie there. She hadn't a clue. "Maybe it's been so long that you're just not satisfied yet."

"Are you?"

"No, but it's been a while for me, too." Thank goodness for darkness. Her face had to be fire-engine red. The heat coming off it likely would scorch him, but at least he wouldn't see her flaming face, too.

"I'm not satisfied — neither of us are — and that's my point." He urged her onto her back with a hand to her shoulder, then raised up on his bent elbow and draped his leg across hers. "If it were lust, I wouldn't be here telling myself that I shouldn't be here. I'd be having sex with you, slaking the lust, and not thinking about my feelings because I'd know that tomorrow I'd have no feelings and this thing between us would be over." He dropped his voice. "But it won't be over, Maggie. Not tomorrow, or the day after, or the day after that. And I'm not lying here thinking of slaking lust and having sex. I'm thinking of how much I want to make love with you because I want to give you all of me, and I'm fighting it because I'm afraid of what will happen to you if I do. I'm afraid I'll lose you, and I'm afraid of what will happen to me if I lose you. There won't be anything left inside me."

"I'm not Carolyn." Maggie blinked hard to keep the tears burning her eyes at bay. She would *not* cry. She'd never cry. Her father had loved her tears. Carolyn had loved them. But Maggie had stopped them then, and she'd stop them now.

"No, you're not Carolyn." He stared down at her, his eyes riddled with torment. "You mean more. I can't explain that. Please, don't ask me to because I can't. I don't know what it is, but I know it's . . . more."

He thought he loved her. But he didn't.

Miss Hattie's words. About him and Carolyn. He hadn't loved Carolyn, Maggie now agreed. But he didn't love her, either. He just thought he did. And why that devastated her when it should relieve her, she didn't dare to think about.

Though it seemed redundant, her heart insisted she tell him again. Maybe, just maybe in doing so, she could convince herself, as well. She reached up and cupped his hand on her face. "It's not love, Tyler. It's the caring that's confusing you. It's our bond. And it's because you're a healthy, virile, and very physical man who's abstained for a long time. When you're in lust, you satisfy it, and it's over. But when you care, well, the tender feelings linger. Yet that's still not love."

"You seem so sure."

"I am." He couldn't possibly love her. What in the world would entice him to love her? Of course, she was sure. And, oh, how it hurt to be right.

"Maybe we just need time for everything to settle."

They did. She grabbed onto the thought as if it were a lifeline. Because as much as he needed it, she needed it more. "Exactly," she said. "We've both been under a lot of emotional strain. We came here as wrecks, MacGregor. Then the entity cranked up his antics, and we realized we share a strong bond. All that rolled together, and it has our true feelings for each other muddled."

He settled back onto his pillow beside her then stared at the ceiling. "Maybe you're right. Maybe we're just clinging so hard because we're out of control."

Missing his warmth, feeling disconnected from him and hating it, she agreed. "That's about the way I see it."

The temperature in the room plummeted.

Shivering, Maggie scooted even closer to MacGregor, chest to chest, stomach to ribs, thigh to thigh, to steal some more of his heat. She buried her head at the crook of his shoulder and neck and inhaled deeply. "Feel better now that you're off the hook?"

"Yeah, I do." He slid his arm over her, then sighed. "But I think our entity is op-posing."

So did she. It had turned frigid in here. Had her longing, and her voice thick and husky. "Are we going to do anything about it?"

She'd thought it, but she hadn't meant to say it. *Tony, are you interfering here? If so, get out. This is private, and voyeurs aren't welcome.*

He laughed.

Maggie heard it — and just as quickly, she denied that she'd heard it. Denied she'd prompted that laughter, and then that she'd heard it. She absolutely, positively refused to believe in ghosts. It'd be absurd.

"Not just yet." MacGregor tightened his hold on her as if to ensure she didn't misunderstand and think he didn't want her. "We both need to sort out some things first — so it'll be right." He pecked a kiss to her forehead. "I want it to be right between us, Maggie. That's important to me."

He knew. Her heart sank. Before he could confront her, she'd confess what she should have confessed when he'd openly admitted to holding back. She'd taken the coward's way out, simply acknowledging something hadn't been quite as it should have been. "I held back, too, Tyler. I didn't mean to do it, it just . . . happened."

The lies between them lay heavy on her soul, but as long as they resided there, she couldn't make love with MacGregor again.

As things stood, she couldn't let him know all of her, and to let him know any less made a mockery of . . . whatever this was she felt for him and he felt for her. She should have realized that before and hadn't. But she did realize it now.

The temptation to tell him everything burned in her throat, in her heart. She fought it, knowing that in telling him the truth now, after withholding it for so long and through so much, she never again would know any of him. She *would* lose him.

And tonight she'd only worsened the problem. She'd added another row of bricks to the wall between them. Now she not only withheld information about Carolyn, but also about Tony.

Had he been real? Was she losing her mind?

That she didn't know terrified her.

"Maggie, honey, you're shaking."

Her throat tight, she whispered, "Hold me, Tyler. Would you just please hold me for a while?"

He closed his arms around her and whispered against her hair. "This is the second time you've told me that you're not telling me everything. I'm curious, okay? And I'm only human. I want to know what this is all about."

"Not now, please." She squeezed his side. "Please."

"All right. Not now." His sigh ruffled her hand and breezed warmth over her face. "But soon."

Maggie awakened snuggled to MacGregor's chest. The smell of the sea clung to his skin and she inhaled deeply, so relieved that he'd come back with her and stayed with her through the night. She hadn't wanted to be alone, she'd feared being alone, and she thought MacGregor just might have known it, though she'd no idea how he could have. Without him there holding her, she'd have paced the floor all night, worrying herself sick about this Tony business. Instead, MacGregor had held her and, feeling safe and warm and content, she'd stopped shaking and had fallen asleep in his arms. And, bless him, on her awakening, he'd still been holding her.

Though she hated to leave the haven of his arms, had the most awful feeling that if she did she'd never again feel them around her, she had to do it. She had to ask Miss Hattie about Tony — without MacGregor being around to hear it. She had to know if Tony had been real — *Good grief, am I seriously considering this?* — or a ghost.

■ ■ ■ ■

As Maggie passed the grandfather clock on her way to the kitchen, it chimed nine. She smelled apples and cinnamon and her stomach stopped fluttering.

When she stepped into the kitchen, Miss Hattie stood at the stove, humming along with the radio and pulling a coffee cake out of the oven. "Morning." Maggie got a glass out of the cabinet then at the fridge filled it with cold water. Her throat felt as if a camel had parked in it. Did she have a fever?

A *fever.*

Yes! With a fever she could have delusions. Tony could have been a delusion!

"Morning, dear." Miss Hattie glanced up at Maggie and her smile faded to worry. "Oh, my. Are you feeling poorly?"

Heat surged to Maggie's face. Did Miss Hattie know MacGregor had slept in Maggie's room last night? That he was still up there sleeping? Oh, please, *please,* let it be a raging fever. "I think I'm sick." She took a big gulp of water. "I think I might have a fever."

Miss Hattie came around the end of the counter and slapped a blue-veined hand to Maggie's forehead. "Why you're as cool as

393

a cucumber, dear. Though you do look a bit peaked."

No fever. No delusions. Darn. "I didn't get much sleep." That was true enough.

"Well, why don't you go on back up and rest some more. It's awfully messy outside this morning. Been sleeting since dawn."

She *didn't* know MacGregor was in Maggie's room. Maggie leaned against the wall beside the fridge and watched Miss Hattie step back around the counter then lift a knife to her coffee cake. "Do you recall me asking if anything unusual happened around here?"

"Of course, dear." Miss Hattie ran the knife's edge around the smooth edge of the pan, then turned the pan upside down on a pretty flowered plate.

Maggie had the feeling the angelic woman was avoiding her eyes. "Well, something strange might be happening." She had to be delicate here. What if Tony *was* just a villager? If she came across as though he were definitely a ghost, she'd look like an idiot.

"Strange?" Miss Hattie paused, holding the knife midair, and looked up at Maggie. "What might that be?"

She debated for a long second. Plan A. She'd tell Miss Hattie everything, and see how she responded. She knew about Mac-

Gregor's boundary-crossing attempts and didn't think he was nuts. But she did think those episodes were psychologically rooted, induced by his troubles. Still, she could be trusted. Maggie long ago had concluded that. She opened her mouth to begin relaying the oddities, but her throat suddenly went bone dry. She paused to sip from her glass.

Look not beneath the veil, Maggie. It's not yet time.

The man's whisper. *Tony's* whisper.

Maggie's hand shook, threatening to slosh the water right out of her glass. He obviously didn't want her telling Miss Hattie anything. What would he do if she did it anyway?

Because Maggie didn't know the answer to that, she switched to Plan B. "Do you know a man named Tony?"

Miss Hattie dropped the metal pan. It clanged on the tile counter, then vibrated on and on. She pressed a finger to it to stop the noise.

A knock sounded at the mud room door.

Maggie looked over and saw a sleet-dappled Vic through the foggy glass pane.

Miss Hattie looked immensely relieved to see him. "Ah, he's early with the mail today."

If her jerky gestures and edgy manner

were a fair indicator, she *was* relieved to see him right that moment. The timing of the interruption permitting her to avoid answering Maggie's question couldn't have been more perfect had it been choreographed. *Tony, are you doing this intentionally? What's wrong with Plan B?*

He didn't answer.

Maybe he couldn't answer because he didn't exist.

Miss Hattie rubbed her hands dry on her dishcloth then tossed it onto the counter. "Why don't you go on back to bed for a while, dear."

Knowing she wouldn't hear another word on the matter of Tony, Maggie nodded, mentally searching for Plan C. "I think I will."

"That's a good idea," Miss Hattie said, looking definitely upset. "Rest and you'll feel better. I'm sure of it." She headed toward the mud room door to let Vic in.

Of course! Maggie set the glass in the sink, left the kitchen then rushed up the stairs. *Vic!*

MacGregor was still asleep. Stretched out on his side, he held the twisted, blue coverlet scrunched up near his chin. Vulnerable. Tender. But strong and gentle and caring.

Maggie sighed. He was a good man.

And she'd lied to him repeatedly and suspected him of unforgivable crimes that paled to those her father had committed.

Guilt swarmed her and tasted so bitter. MacGregor had been busy earning redemption points, but she was the one who needed to earn them. She had to do what she could to make up for her suspicions and doubts, for all the wrongs she'd done him. But first, she *had* to resolve this Tony thing so she knew she hadn't totally lost her mind, only her good judgment and sense.

She dressed quickly, tugging on jeans and a sweatshirt, then jostled his shoulder. "MacGregor?"

He didn't stir. He didn't even flinch.

"Tyler, wake up." She jostled him again, harder. "It's important."

"I'm awake." He snaked an arm around her and pulled her down on top of him. "Oh, but I love an impatient woman."

"No." Maggie ordered him. "Quit, dang it, and get your buns out of that bed."

"Get out?" He faked a perfectly transparent frown, belied by the twinkle dancing in his eyes. "What, you mean you didn't wake me up to make love?"

Phony jerk. But a darling one, and far too gorgeous for his own good — or hers. "No,

I didn't." Her face burned hot for the second time already that morning.

"Are you saying that making love with me isn't important?"

"Blast it, MacGregor, get sex off your brain. This is serious."

"We don't have sex. And I take our love-making — very, very different from having sex, Maggie — extremely serious."

She squeezed her eyes shut. "Will you shut up and listen to me?"

"I think I'd rather kiss you."

"MacGregor, you're trying my patience here."

"I can tell." He laughed at her, ran a hand down her back and cupped her buttock in his huge hand. "You'll come out ahead by just giving me my kiss. I can be very persistent when the occasion arises, and you might —"

"You *might* not be dead by dark, Mac-Gregor, but only if you knock it off now." She glared daggers into his eyes. "I said this is serious, darn it!"

His expression immediately turned solemn. "What?"

She backed off the bed then stepped away. "I should've told you this last night, but we, um, got —"

"Last night?" He let out a sigh strong

enough to power windmills. "Woman, are you always going to hold out on me?" He sat up and stared at her. "What is it this time?" A muscle in his jaw ticked.

"Would you chill?" She wrung her hands. "You're making me nervous."

"I've never rattled you."

He'd *always* rattled her. But she kind of liked him thinking he hadn't. "True, you haven't, and this is no time to start."

"Well?"

He looked about as approachable as a ticked-off Doberman guarding his turf. She licked at her lips. How in the world could she explain seeing a ghost and not expect the man to think she was crazy — despite all the weird occurrences here. She'd *seen,* actually *seen,* a ghost — maybe. "I wasn't holding out on you. I saw something last night, and it shook me up. When we got back here, I intended to tell you about it, but then you brought up the legend and us making love, and well, I got sidetracked and the whole thing kind of got pushed right out of my head."

He smiled, clearly liking the thought of that. "Understandable."

"That arrogant attitude of yours is shining through, MacGregor, and I swear we don't have time for it."

"Okay. I'll gloat later at making you forget yourself. What's this crisis all about? What did you see?"

"A man. When we were out on the cliffs."

"Before I came out there?"

"No." This was the touchy part. "You were there. He said his name was Tony."

"You talked to him while I was there?"

He didn't believe her. Not surprised, but oh-so-disappointed, she nodded.

"I didn't see anyone, Maggie."

"I know." She paced from the side of the bed to the turret room rug then paced it again, rubbing at her temple, which had unwisely chosen this very moment to begin throbbing. "Get dressed, darling. We've got to talk with Vic before he leaves, and he's already here."

"Vic?" MacGregor tossed back the covers, rolled out of bed, then reached for his slacks.

"What's Vic got to do with this?" Mac-Gregor grabbed his shirt, tugged it on then started working on the buttons. When she didn't answer, he paused and stared at her. "Maggie? Honey, what's wrong?"

"Nothing." She answered too quickly, and her voice squeaked at least an octave too high. Heat surged up her neck and flooded her face. Seeing his insistence for truth coming, she answered before he could

400

express it. "I, um, hadn't seen you, um . . ."

"Maggie, are you embarrassed?" He sounded incredulous. "Honey, we just spent the night together. I've got your fingerprints on every inch of my body. You can't possibly be embarrassed."

"Shut up, MacGregor:" She glared at him. "Seeing you is . . . different."

He smiled, looking extremely pleased with her. "Oh."

"Don't you dare get smart-mouthed. I really don't need that this morning and, I'm warning you, any lip and I'll subtle revenge your backside for at least the next thirty years — provided you don't provoke me into killing you before then."

He didn't look worried at all by the threat. In fact, he looked kind of delighted by it. Ah, geez. Her mind really had taken a flying leap. He *liked* getting out of subtle revenge.

"Let me get this straight." He cocked his head. "I'm supposed to be upset that you find my body appealing?"

"No, but . . ." Well, shoot. Now, no matter what she said, she lost. How did she get herself into these situations with him? She rubbed at her throbbing temple. "Will you just get dressed, MacGregor?"

"I am dressed." He shrugged and slid her a wicked smile that had her heart fluttering.

So much for recovering even a shred of dignity. "Well, it's about time."

"Let's discuss it later. Right now, tell me about Vic and this man from last night."

She blew out a deep breath. "The man said his name was Tony. I'd never seen him before, but I figured Miss Hattie might know him. So I went downstairs a while ago and asked her about him."

"What did she say?"

"Nothing. But she'd been holding this pan, and when I mentioned Tony's name, she dropped it. The question clearly upset her, Tyler. Unfortunately, before she could answer it, or refuse to answer it, Vic came in."

"So she didn't say she knew this Tony, or that she didn't."

"Right. No confirmation or denial." Maggie frowned. "But once before, when I asked her if strange things went on here, she laughed and said that things were just as they'd always been."

"Ambiguous as all get-out." He finger-combed his hair.

"Exactly." Maggie passed him her brush off the dresser. "Your hair's standing on end." When he took the brush, she added. "Anyway, it's clear she has no intention of answering me, so I have to ask about Tony elsewhere. I figured who better than Vic. He knows everyone around."

"Clever." MacGregor's eyes shined appreciatively. "Vic's delivered the mail here since Maine was a baby state. If there's a Tony in the village, he'll know it."

"Exactly."

MacGregor swept her brush through his hair then put it back on the dresser. "Do you think this Tony is our entity?"

She lowered her gaze, afraid if he thought she'd lost her mind it'd show in his eyes. Shaky enough without seeing that this morning — *Why couldn't I have a fever?* — she wisely avoided the risk. "I don't know. Maybe. Or he might just have been a villager."

"It was awfully foggy." T.J. glanced at the window. "Sleeting like the dickens out there."

"It wasn't sleeting, it was misting. Don't spare me, Tyler."

"I meant now. But last night it was misty, and the fog was thick. I could just not have seen him."

"And hearing him? Could you just not have heard him, too?"

Sam Grayson flitted through T.J.'s mind. T.J. blinked then blinked again. He should have figured this out sooner. "I get it now, honey." He hugged her to him, his insides like jelly. She stood rigid enough to snap, her hands at her sides as if she didn't trust his embrace. Likely, she didn't, and the fault for that rested squarely on his shoulders. "You didn't tell me because you were afraid I wouldn't believe you."

She stiffened even more. "If you didn't, I wouldn't blame you."

"Yes, you would. Situations reversed, I'd blame you, too. But we've got a bond, Maggie, and you need to remember that." Sam Grayson's belief in her had been all important to Maggie. That bore remembering, too. T.J. cupped her face in his hands and looked directly into her eyes. "I promise to always believe you, Maggie. Always. No matter what. You just have to trust me, honey."

Trust him? Maggie couldn't trust him — or any man. But she didn't dare to risk talking about it. She didn't deserve his trust. And right now, she was closer than she'd been in a dozen years to crying. Oh, but she needed a bath to calm down. But that, too, would have to wait. Just as savoring the sincerity in MacGregor's promise would have to wait. "Come on." Maggie moved away. "Vic's bound to be done with his coffee by now. We'll miss him."

"We'll catch him." MacGregor caught her by the arm and pulled her back to him. "First things first."

He gave her his best killer smile. "Good morning, honey," he whispered, then kissed her lips.

Oh, she could get used to this. So used to this. So used to him . . .

Vic! She pulled back, faking frustration with a deep sigh and false bravado. "Geez, MacGregor. I'm telling you we've got a solid lead on our entity and you're acting as if it's no big deal."

"Not so, sweetheart." He rubbed her shoulder. "Vic's been in this village seventy years. He isn't going anywhere that we can't get to him in a few minutes."

"But —"

"Shhh, a man's got to keep his priorities straight." He slid his hand under the hem of her sweatshirt and up to her bare skin. "And, right now, loving you is mine."

Every muscle in her body seemed to contract at once. "I, um, thought we were going to sort out some things first."

He let his hand drift up her spine, the look in his eyes heated. "I have."

She wasn't ready to hear this. She knew it. "And?"

"It's stopped sleeting and the sun's out,

405

Maggie."

A glance at the window proved that true. "So?" Hadn't he said the weather wasn't connected to them?

"Our entity wants us together."

"That's no reason —"

"Shhh." MacGregor pressed a silencing finger to her lips. "It's not. But I want us together, too." He caressed her with his gaze. "I want to make love with you, Maggie. I need to make love with you — without holding back."

She needed him, too. So much so that she trembled with it. But she couldn't give in to it. After they'd made love last night there'd been fog. It hadn't felt right for all the reasons they'd already explored, and it still wouldn't be right now because none of those reasons had been dealt with and eliminated. Well, keeping Tony a secret from MacGregor had been eliminated, but Carolyn remained between them.

"MacGregor, it isn't that I don't want you. You know I do. And I'm glad you've sorted through all this, but I need more time." She forced herself to meet his gaze. "I don't want it not to feel right between us again, either. In my heart, I know it isn't supposed to be that way — not for us. And that it was . . ." Her voice trailed.

"Hurts you," he finished for her. "I'm sorry, honey. I was being selfish."

"No." She looked up at him. "I kind of like knowing you want me, MacGregor. It's just . . ." She borrowed a part of Tony's warning. "It's not yet time."

"When it's right, you let me know, mmm? I'll be waiting."

The promise shining in his eyes had her heart aching. "You'll be first on the list. I swear it."

T.J. stepped beside Maggie onto the road in front of Seascape Inn. Patches of ice clung to low dips in the spackled road where sleet pits had pounded into the light dusting of wet sand. Weeds and brown grass lining the sides of the surface crept onto its edges, and Seascape's rarely used mailbox had melting sickles of ice dripping into the dirt and puddling at its base. "Vic's probably headed toward the lighthouse. After Seascape, Hatch is next on the route."

They hurried past Fisherman's Co-Op. Leslie's minivan wasn't parked out front. Skirting around the wooden pier, they disturbed a squirrel who, indignant as Hades, chattered angrily at them then ran on into the woods above the high-tide line. "Watch your step, Maggie. The ice is slick."

She nodded and they went on, heading toward the narrow point at Land's End where the lighthouse stood silhouetted against the sky. On T.J.'s first visit here, it had still been operational. He missed the light. It'd always struck him as a welcoming beacon, guiding the fishermen home.

The path's slope steepened and, sure of his step, T.J. glanced up to the sky. It had clouded over, dull and gray, casting an odd pallor on the winter foliage and the ground, and the horizon had muddied, looking nearly black. "We're in for more storms."

Maggie scanned the sky, frowned, then lowered her gaze to Land's End. The wind shifted, tugging at her hair. "Look." She pointed, her nose and cheeks red from the suddenly frigid air. "There's Vic. He's coming this way."

A few minutes later, Vic stepped up to them, his fur-lined cap riding low on his ears, his breath fogging in the cold air. "Morning."

"Morning." T.J. shook Vic's gloved hand and reminded himself again to order a pair of gloves from one of his catalogues.

They dispensed with the courtesies, chatted for a few moments, then T.J. glanced at Maggie. She gave him the nod. "Vic, we need to ask you about something."

He blinked, his eyes watery as he faced the wind. "If this is about the condoms, T.J. — sorry to be indelicate, Maggie, but that's the tidiest word I know for 'em — I've been the soul of discretion. Ain't mentioned 'em to nobody."

Maggie's face went red for the third time that day, and it wasn't yet noon. "It's not about that, Vic."

"Oh." He cleared his throat and hitched up the mailbag on his shoulder, looking sorry indeed that he'd raised the matter. "Well, what is it, then?"

"Do you know a man named Tony?"

Vic narrowed his gaze and clacked his teeth together three times, clearly pondering. "I'm friendly by nature, but I ain't usually so accommodating as to answer questions about locals for folks from away, but if T.J. here will personally vouch for you, young lady, then well, that'll be good enough for me, and I'll answer your question."

T.J. nodded. "She's trustworthy, Vic."

Maggie's expression crumbled and she looked as guilty as sin. About what, T.J. hadn't a clue. He pretended he hadn't noticed, hoping Vic wouldn't either. She still hadn't revealed her mission here. Maybe it wasn't simply to rest, as T.J. had deduced. But what else could it be? Miss Hattie had told him all about Maggie and how she'd cared for her mother. Pretty much what Maggie herself had told him, though she'd been much more modest about it. That had put his mind to rest on the mission business. A woman who put her life on hold to care for another, well, she wasn't apt to be the kind of woman to be doing anything sneaky or underhanded — or so he'd thought, until seeing that guilt in her expression.

"Figured you would vouch for her, T.J. Miss Hattie ain't ever wrong about folks." Vic rubbed his clean-shaven jaw. "Only Tony I ever heard of anywhere around Sea Haven was Anthony Freeport. Some of his close friends called him Tony, including me. From the time we were sprouts, we were about as close as friends can get. We were quite a team, me and him and Hatch. But, other than him, I can't place a soul in these parts who goes by the name."

Maggie let out a sigh of relief that had T.J. grating his teeth.

She looked up at him, her eyes sparkling. "He *was* a villager."

Feeling as if he'd been kicked in the stomach by a mule, T.J. tried to interrupt. "Maggie —"

"Vic, I'm so glad we asked you. I need to

410

find Tony. Do you know where he lives now? Or maybe where he works?"

"I know where he is right this second." Vic's expression turned grim, deepening the lines in his face to creases. "Near the church. In the cemetery."

Oh, shoot! Anthony. Tony. T.J. grimaced. Why hadn't he put this together before now? True, he'd rarely heard the man referred to as Anthony. Everyone in the village and at Seascape just called him Miss Hattie's soldier. Still . . .

Maggie frowned. "Is Tony the grounds-keeper at the cemetery?"

Grumbling something under his breath, Vic rubbed at his neck and darted a covert plea for help T.J.'s way. "Er, not exactly."

"Well, what does he do there?"

"Maggie," T.J. cut in. "Vic's trying to tell you that Anthony Freeport is buried in the cemetery. He's dead."

CHAPTER 14

Maggie's knees threatened to collapse. She locked them.

"Tony died back during World War II." Vic tucked a protruding letter back down into his mailbag.

"Are you all right?" MacGregor curled an arm around her waist.

She leaned against him. "I'm fine," she lied. On the cliff, Tony had been wearing an old-fashioned green suit with shiny buttons. It could have been an Army uniform. Schooling her voice, she looked at Vic. "You knew Tony well."

"Since we were sprouts." He repeated his earlier remark, then slid MacGregor a look that asked if Maggie were slow to keep up. "Tony was my best friend."

An Army uniform! Shock streaked through Maggie like a thousand-volt power surge. She failed to keep it from her voice. "Anthony Freeport was Miss Hattie's soldier, wasn't he?"

Vic grabbed the bill of his cap and tugged it down as if to hide his eyes. Whether burning because of wind or remembrance, they were glossy. "Yep. Tony was the love of Miss Hattie's life then, just as he is now."

Maggie turned to MacGregor. "Tyler —"

"I know, honey." He didn't look at all surprised.

Why wasn't he surprised?

"Tony was special," Vic said. "Loved Hattie more than life itself. He swore nothing would ever separate them — not even death. Promised her that the day he left for duty. I drove 'em over to Bangor to the station, and I heard it with my own ears." Vic's expression grew melancholy. "Tony was a fine man. A fine man. He deserved Miss Hattie."

Miss Millie had been right. Vic loved Miss Hattie, but he'd loved Tony, too. And because he had, he'd condemned both himself and Miss Hattie to spending their lives alone.

A flash of Miss Hattie at the cemetery putting yellow flowers on the grave came to mind. It was Tony's grave she visited every Tuesday. And — oh, that had to be it! That had to be the reason Maggie had gotten ill so suddenly at the cemetery.

She and MacGregor had been about to see whose graves Miss Hattie had put the yellow flowers on. Tony hadn't wanted Maggie to see his headstone because then she'd have known his name. And it wasn't yet time. But . . . why?

MacGregor agreed with Vic. "Tony must have been special. He was well loved."

Incredibly sad, Maggie fought tears. What had gotten into her today with this urge to cry business? Well, she had to admit that Tony and Miss Hattie and Vic's situation was worth a good cry. Vic, worshiping Miss Hattie from afar, being a good friend to her. Miss Hattie, tending Tony's grave nearly half a century after his death, regretting the life they didn't get the chance to build together, knowing he'd loved her so much he'd vowed even death wouldn't separate them. How very, very sad. And how very rare and special indeed their love had been.

Maggie blinked hard, her heart heavy. The vow. Had that been what Tony had wanted her to know before learning his identity? That he had made that vow? That it was why he remained at Seascape as an entity?

MacGregor's deep voice claimed her attention. "Have there been reports of strange things going on at the inn?"

Vic's face went as pale as the winter magnolias.

MacGregor's hand tightened at Maggie's waist and he stiffened. "You know about the blackouts, too?"

Grim-faced, Vic nodded.

"Good grief, is there anything going on around here that everyone doesn't know?"

"If there is, I ain't figured it, T.J."

Once again, proof that life in a small town was like living in a goldfish bowl. The upside was knowing who you're swimming with. The downside, everyone knows when you sink, swim, float, or skinny-dip. Maggie licked at her lips. "Are there any *other* strange things happening at Seascape?"

"Only according to Batty Beaulah." The old man scoffed. "That woman drives the sheriff slap crazy with her senseless ravings — and by Aaron, of course. Repeats every word Beaulah says, that one. Not that anybody pays either of 'em no never mind — 'specially not Beaulah."

"Why not?" MacGregor asked.

"Because everyone in the village knows she's put out with Miss Hattie and Miss Millie."

"I didn't know it."

"Well, I can't rightly say you would've noticed, keeping yourself locked up in the

415

Carriage House, T.J." The wind caught Vic's cap. He tugged it back down over his ears. "Miss Millie don't invite Beaulah or Lily to the Historical Society meetings because Miss Hattie can't abide Beaulah's being nosy, and Miss Millie can't abide Lily's up-pity ways."

"Lily?" MacGregor relaxed, loosening his death grip on Maggie's waist.

"Lydia Johnson — the mayor's wife. Her real name's Lily, but she thinks Lydia is more regal so she renamed herself that right after her and Horace got married." Vic frowned. "Would've swore I'd told you that before."

"You had. I just forgot it for a second." T.J. toed a stone on the path. "My mind's been kind of . . . occupied with other things."

Vic shrugged. "Sometimes us old-timers forget, too, though when we do, Lily sure does take offense. And Beaulah, well, she don't take the slight of being excluded on the chin so well, either. Takes off to Little Island every time they have a meeting." He shrugged again. "Poor woman thinks no-body knows where she's going, or why. 'Course, don't nobody tell her no different. Folks need their secrets, Hatch says. Wise man, Hatch."

Maggie frowned. Batty Beaulah was a lot more sane than she was given credit for being. She hadn't been wrong in her report to Lucy on MacGregor, only her timing of that report had been wrong. "Where does she go?"

Vic slid Maggie a reprimanding look. "Sorry, but I ain't one to carry tales, young lady. If you're wanting to know the answer to that, then you'll have to be asking Beaulah yourself." He hitched up his bag, adjusting its strap on his shoulder. "I'd better be getting back to my route. Don't want to run late today. There's a dance at the Grange tonight and a band from Camden is playing." He nodded. "T.J."

Maggie stood at MacGregor's side and watched Vic head down the sandy path, back toward the village. When he was out of earshot, they started over the cliffs. The roof of Fisherman's Co-Op steepled up above the craggy rocks straight ahead.

"He's an amusing walking contradiction, isn't he?" Maggie laced her fingers with MacGregor's. "Telling us so much then clamming up as he did."

MacGregor sighed. "His heart's in the right place."

"Yes, it is." Her nose tingled, numb from the cold. Those heavy, black clouds were moving closer to shore at a good clip. She admired Vic a lot. Being so loyal to Tony and to Miss Hattie.

"So do you think Anthony Freeport is our entity?"

Maggie thought long and hard. "I think there's a strong possibility. My instincts say he is, but I need to see Anthony Freeport to know for sure."

"Honey, I doubt Sheriff Cobb will seek permission to exhume Anthony's body based on us telling him we think he's causing us some paranormal challenges over at Seascape."

Maggie imagined the big, burly sheriff's expression on hearing that request, and in her mind she saw him grabbing his coffee cup and hightailing it out the Blue Moon Cafe's door to hide from them as he'd hidden from Beaulah. She grinned at MacGregor. "I doubt he would. But I was thinking of something a little less blatant — and a lot less disturbing."

"Oh?"

"Photographs." Maggie touched her free hand to MacGregor's arm. "If Miss Hattie will let me see a photo of Anthony, then I'll know if he's the same man — or ghost — I saw on the cliffs."

MacGregor frowned. "She might refuse."

"True. She's very protective of Seascape, and it wouldn't be good news for the inn for something like this to get out." Maggie looked up at him. "But then again, she might not refuse. Nothing ventured, nothing gained. We've got to give it a try."

"Maggie! T.J.! Wait!"

A very excited Leslie Butler raced over from her minivan and intercepted Maggie and MacGregor on Main Street, right in front of Fisherman's Co-Op.

Out of breath, her chest heaved, tugging at the buttons of her brown print suit. "I just got back from my first auction representing Bill's catch."

T.J. smiled. Obviously, from her excitement, things had gone well. "How'd you do?" He asked the expected question, anyway.

"The guys were less than enthused to see me there, but I turned an increased profit — an extra twelve dollars and seventy-two cents."

Maggie laughed aloud, her eyes sparkling as much as Leslie's. "That's wonderful!"

"It was . . . exhilarating!" Leslie nodded. "Of course, the fishermen snickered — though they did no better themselves."

"They snickered? Really?" Maggie cocked

her head, clearly surprised at that.

"I snubbed them." Leslie shrugged a slim shoulder. "But twelve seventy-two is twelve seventy-two. Buys a couple gallons of milk. And that milk will be in *our* fridge, not theirs."

"That's terrific." T.J. shook Leslie's hand. "You should be really proud of yourself."

"Thanks. You know, I really am. Maybe it's not humble or modest, but it is the truth. I didn't think I had the guts to try. But Maggie got me to thinking. And failing was the worst that could happen. So I figured I might just get lucky and fail my way to success. It was worth a shot, and I'm really, really glad I took it." She swallowed a little laugh. "You'll have to come with me some time. Auctions really get the blood pumping, you know?"

"We'd like that." Maggie answered for both of them.

"Well, I've got to run tell Bill." She grinned ear to ear. "I can't wait to see his face when I tell him the news." She squeezed Maggie's hand, whispered a heart-felt thanks and then rushed back toward the Co-Op.

When Leslie reached the door, Maggie turned to MacGregor. "Okay, what is it?"

"She's found her niche here and doesn't

yet know it."

"Maybe." Maggie stared off into the clouds. They somehow had her feeling oppressed, as if they were heavy and closing in on her. "I'd find that easier to believe if the fishermen hadn't snickered —"

"Honey, I'll bet you fifty dollars right now that they were snickering at the buyers, not at Leslie."

Maggie frowned. "Why would you say that?"

"She got the price up. The fishermen are bound to be pleased by that."

"Makes sense." Maggie looked up at him, a little frown creasing her brow. "I wonder why she took it that the snickers were meant for her?"

"Leslie's no different from the rest of us. She sees things in the familiar."

"Huh?"

"She saw what she expected to see."

The words stung Maggie as if they were darts and she were a board they were penetrating to warn her of their significance. But why were they important? How did they relate to her and her situation? They did relate. She sensed it. But how?

Unable to answer that, she tightened her grip on MacGregor's hand and they walked on, back toward Seascape. Way too much time lately she'd spent wondering about things. Not the least of which was why she felt more and more comfortable with Mac-Gregor while keeping secrets from him. She couldn't fathom that — except . . .

At Carolyn's funeral and here at Seascape, had Maggie been like Leslie? Had she only seen in MacGregor exactly what she'd expected to see?

The wind whistled. Its pitch heightened to a piercing shriek — then turned to that awful whisper.

No trust.

The words repeated and echoed in her mind again and again. *No trust. No trust. No trust.*

Maggie stiffened, tried and failed to shut them out. And then the truth hit her with the force of a knockout punch. Leslie was just like *them!* Not just her. But *them.* Her *and* MacGregor.

That *had* to be why it hadn't felt right when they'd made love. They'd both admitted to holding back part of themselves. For different reasons, they'd both lacked *trust!*

The wind stilled. Nothing moved, and there were no sounds. Total and complete silence surrounded them, then a gentle breeze began to blow. It strengthened, then gusted and grew fierce, spraying up sand that stung Maggie's forearms and face. Frightened, she shut her eyes and buried her face against MacGregor's chest.

"Close your eyes, Maggie. It'll pass in a moment."

He sounded calm, and she blessed him for that. Her eyes were closed already — and she kept them closed.

It might have been seconds or minutes, but the wind calmed as quickly as it had started. Uneasy, not certain what to expect, she opened her eyes to slits, then snapped them wide open. The dark clouds which had hovered over the shore, had felt so oppressive and heavy and as if they were bearing down on her, had blown farther out to sea. Now they hung harmlessly just above the horizon. Ashore the sun shone brilliantly, bathing her and MacGregor in warm sunshine that heated her cold skin and dispelled her fear.

Despite MacGregor's insistence that the weather was completely unconnected to their entity, Maggie believed in her heart that Tony was their entity and he was giving her a sign. The oppression and clouds signaled his impatience at her slow awareness and grasp of what he wanted her to know and understand. And the sun signaled his approval and pleasure that she'd made those recognitions and the realization about trust. She'd pleased him — not that she'd mention it to MacGregor.

Whether or not it pleased her, she hadn't yet decided. Realizing something significant required one to act on it. Actions were life-altering. And though she'd sensed from the start that the oddities here were harbingers of something life-altering, she wasn't at all sure she had the strength to alter her life. Or the courage.

"Are you sure you don't have a photo of Tony, Miss Hattie?"

"Who, dear?" Miss Hattie rocked in her rocker and avoided Maggie's glance.

"Anthony. I meant Anthony."

T.J. heard the hope in Maggie's voice, and he'd no doubt that Miss Hattie had heard it, too. Her soft eyes had veiled with worry and her hands, holding the green metal knitting needles, trembled.

"I'm sorry, but I don't." She rocked faster than the tempo of the music playing softly on the radio. "Jonathan took all of the family's personal effects with him down to Atlanta."

Maggie frowned at that disclosure. So did T.J. Miss Hattie had loved the man all her life and she expected them to believe she had kept not a single photograph of him? She wasn't being honest, yet she had a penchant against lying. So maybe this was a half-truth?

"Maggie, I think you're just tired. If you don't mind me saying so, after two years of nursing your mother, you need to relax. Enjoy yourself and don't worry about such matters. They truly are best left dead and buried, dear." The old woman's eyes burned with concern and care. "You need to learn —"

"To dream." Maggie nodded. "I know, Miss Hattie." Maggie stood up and paced alongside the table over to the counter, then back again. "I'd like to do that. Really, I would. But I'm caught up in a little bit of a nightmare here and, until I reason it all out so it makes sense, I just can't focus on dreams. This is driving me crazy."

"It's not — if you'll allow this old woman her opinion." Miss Hattie softened her voice. "*You* are driving yourself crazy, dear." Dropping her needles into the little flowered bag beside her chair, Miss Hattie then stood up and went to Maggie.

She clasped Maggie's hands in her generous, blue-veined ones, her eyes shining wisdom, her voice as gentle as that of a loving mother. "You need to heal, child. You need to trust your heart. If you can believe in nothing else, believe in it and all it holds dear." She gave Maggie's hands a firm squeeze, then let go of them and turned to MacGregor.

"I've got to go get ready for a special Historical Society meeting. I hope you children don't mind, but as soon it stopped sleeting this morning and the sun came out, I phoned and arranged for Aaron to ferry you over to the island for a picnic."

"A picnic?" T.J. looked out the window and frowned. "Miss Hattie, the sleet's stopped, but it's as cold as all get-out outside. Maggie and I nearly froze on our way back from our, er, walk."

She lifted a dismissing hand. "Nonsense, Tyler. It's as warm as a midsummer's day out there." Gazing at the ceiling, she paused only a second, then lowered her gaze to MacGregor. "Some things you might want to take along on your picnic are in the mud room." She smiled, then left the kitchen, humming.

Doubt riddling her eyes, Maggie looked at MacGregor and shrugged.

He opened the window, stuck his arm outside, then pulled it back in and darted a worried gaze at Maggie. "Warm as a mid-summer's day — just as she said."

Maggie plopped down onto a chair and slumped over the table. "I dunno, Mac-Gregor. Maybe Miss Hattie's right. I came up here worn to a frazzle, and right now I feel like a ball of knotted wires — all hot ones, loose ends snapping and throwing sparks." She pushed her hair back from her face. "Maybe this Tony and Anthony business of them being the same person is a coincidence. Maybe I just imagined him out there on the cliffs. Maybe none of what's happened has been real, only tricks of my exhausted mind."

T.J. stared at her. And he kept on staring at her until she looked at him. "Do you believe any of that?"

She didn't answer.

She didn't have to. He saw in her eyes the doubt and fear that she had slipped into insanity, in the defeated slump of her shoulders. They'd both be more comfortable thinking none of the events here really had happened, but Maggie doubting her sanity was to him worse than the prospect of accepting they were dealing with a ghost. "Darn it, Maggie, do you believe it?"

Her chin quivered. "No."

"Good," T.J. said, inwardly sighing relief. "I don't either."

"But you were there on the cliff and you

427

didn't see him — or hear him."

Poor Maggie. Man, but he hated to see her fighting herself like this. "True. But I know what I feel." He cupped his fingers over his heart. "In here, I know the truth."

Her expression crumbled. "Me, too."

Upset, Maggie ate or bathed, and because he didn't want her alone while she stood on such shaky ground, he deliberately lightened his tone. "Now that that's settled, do you want something to eat before we boat over to the isle?"

"Why not?"

A valiant effort to pull herself together. To reward her, he smiled. "I make a mean grilled cheese. Sound okay?"

"Perfect."

Bless him, he was trying so hard to get her soothed. Feeling tender and bruised, Maggie watched him pull out the bread from the box on the counter, the cheese and butter from the fridge, and a griddle from the drawer under the stove's oven. His movements weren't clipped or jerky, just economic and deft — especially for a man his size. That economy never failed to surprise her and, again, the urge to see him paint shuffled through her. "MacGregor?"

He put a piece of buttered bread onto the heated griddle. It sizzled. "Yeah?"

"Have you given any more thought to painting?"

He nodded. "As a matter of fact, I have." He glanced over at her, looking a little sheepish. "I figure you were right about that, Maggie. I should at least try."

Like Leslie had tried. She'd succeeded, and maybe — just maybe — MacGregor would succeed, too. Maggie gave him her best smile. "I'm glad."

"Yeah." He snorted. "Well, we'll see how it goes."

Hearing in his voice his doubt that it would go well, Maggie fell quiet. His heart and mind didn't really agree on him painting again and that worried her. When it came to his art, he hauled around a lot of unjust emotional baggage, but that it was unjust didn't make the baggage any less heavy for him to carry. He needed complete faith in himself or there was no way he could possibly succeed.

A snatch of conversation from one of her and Miss Hattie's talks came back and replayed in her mind.

Tyler doesn't believe in miracles.

You have to believe enough for both of you . . .

Maggie couldn't. She'd tried to help him. She certainly owed him for her nasty suspicions, and she was attempting to make it up to him. But she couldn't believe enough for both of them, and that was the simple truth. She couldn't do it because she didn't believe in miracles, either.

Propping her elbow on the table, she dragged her finger over its top, tracing the grain in the wood. She wasn't looking forward to this picnic. What she needed was a little distance from MacGregor to grant herself a lot of perspective. Around him, her feelings got all muddled up with her logic and, considering their circumstances, that had to be a big mistake. If she hadn't left her sense at home in New Orleans, she'd have drawn that conclusion a long time ago. Perspective. Yes, that's exactly what she needed. Perspective.

Tell the truth, Maggie. If not to me or Tyler, then at least to yourself.

The whisper. Instinctively, she looked ceiling-ward as Miss Hattie had, but of course saw nothing but the brilliant white plaster.

The truth!

She started shaking, darted her gaze to MacGregor. The egg turner in his hand, he stared down at the griddle, whistling along with the radio. Obviously, he hadn't heard anything. Her mouth went bone dry.

Maggie, the truth!

All right! She answered telepathically, as she had on the cliff. *All right. I want to be with him too much, and that scares the socks off me, okay? That's the truth.*

It'll do for now.

Tony — if you are Tony —

I am.

Well, you're really being pushy here, and I don't much appreciate it. I don't like nagging. I've never liked nagging. Why are you making me tell you things that I just plain don't want to tell you? I don't like it.

The whisper grew to a clear voice. One tinged with sadness. *You don't have to like it, Maggie. You do have to accept the truth. I'm never going to let you lie to yourself again like you did with Sam Grayson.*

Sam Grayson? I didn't lie to myself about him.

You told yourself you hated him.

She had. *He hurt me, Tony.* Maggie stared at the porcelain daffodils, wishing she could shrink down and curl up inside one of the petals. *I didn't mean it, and I knew I didn't. I was just hurt.*

Pain is a part of life, but it's not a license to lie. And you're lying to yourself about Tyler now just as you lied to yourself about Sam then. It's time you faced that truth, Maggie.

It's time you stopped running.

I'm not!

Right.

Sarcasm. Couldn't she even get a ghost without an attitude? A man was bad enough.

He laughed.

Maggie frowned. *Okay, maybe I am running. But, geez, Tony, I know how men are about things. Are you forgetting about my father? What do you expect from me? That I just forget all the lessons I learned there?*

Are you like Carolyn?

No! But what's she got to do with —

Then why do you insist Tyler is like your father?

Maggie grimaced, hoping Tony would see it — wherever he was. *Don't be absurd. Mac-Gregor is nothing like my father. I see where you're headed here, but you're mistaken. They're both men but nothing alike, just as Carolyn and I are different. But the lessons are the same, Tony.*

Are they?

Were they? Was she doing the same thing with MacGregor about the lessons as she had about Carolyn? No. She couldn't be. *You're wrong, Tony. Look, why don't you go pick on MacGregor? You're supposed to be his entity. I just kind of stumbled into this mess.*

No, you didn't. I brought you here.

432

Surprise shafted up Maggie's spine. *What?* She looked over at MacGregor. Still cooking. Still humming. Still blissfully unaware, blast him.

The lure at Lakeview Gallery — when you looked at the Seascape painting. You felt it?

That was you?

Nice touch, eh?

And was that you on the staircase, too — with Cecelia's portrait?

No, sorry. Can't take credit for that one, though it's been me you've sensed watching you.

Good grief! Are you telling me there's more than one ghost in this house? Her heart nearly exploded in her chest.

Calm down, will you? I haven't told you there are any ghosts in this house.

Well, if you're not a ghost, then what the heck are you?

What's the difference? That isn't the question at hand, Maggie. The question is . . . what are you?

She blinked, then blinked again. *Last check I was sane and human, but I'd be scared to bet on either anymore.*

He laughed. *You're sane and human, Maggie. Never doubt it.*

Tacky, Tony. And I sure can put a lot of stock in your conclusions. I'm sitting here having a

433

telepathic conversation with a ghost who doesn't know — or won't admit he's a ghost — worried sick about my sanity because I don't believe in ghosts, and you're laughing and reassuring me that this is oh-so-common? Geez, I can't figure why I'd even think something was odd here. She frowned, deeper. *And, while we're on the subject of you, you're as arrogant as MacGregor.*

Thank you.

That wasn't a compliment.

Sounded like one to me.

I definitely see where you've been influencing him.

He's a man. Not so easy for him to discern my voice from his own conscience. Tyler and I have had a lot of conversations since he came here. I've been worried about him.

But you're not worried anymore.

We're not out of the woods yet. But we're on the right path. I'm . . . hopeful.

MacGregor put a plate down near her elbow. "Here you are." Then he sat down beside her and stopped humming. "You look peeved."

"I am."

"Why?" He shook the folds from his napkin then dropped it onto his lap.

"Because Tony's got his warped sense of humor and *your* attitude."

434

MacGregor frowned. "What?"

Maggie sighed and shoved back her chair. She'd had it with both of them. "Just get your paint gear ready in time for the picnic, MacGregor."

"Maggie, I said I'd try painting again, but I didn't say that I'd try today."

She leaned toward him, her thighs bumping against the edge of the table. "Today, darling," she whispered the warning. "Or you'll be old and gray before you ever so much as touch a drop of hot water again."

"You can't do that." MacGregor narrowed his eyes. "We made a deal."

"Extraordinary circumstances call for extraordinary measures."

"You're welshing."

"Yeah, I'm welshing." She pecked a kiss to the tip of his nose, straightened up, grabbed the sandwich off her plate, then turned and walked out of the kitchen.

"Where are you going?" He shouted to her, now in the gallery.

"To take a bath." She stopped and glared back at him. "And don't you even think about interrupting me, MacGregor. You'll lose fifty redemption points and you will *never* get that bath — and that's a promise."

The fifteen-minute boat ride went quickly,

435

and Aaron dropped T.J. and Maggie off at a dilapidated wooden pier on Little Island. "Don't be late getting back here," T.J. told the boy.

"No, sir. Five o'clock sharp." He grinned. "I'll be here, sure as spit."

T.J. nodded, his paint gear in one hand, the picnic basket Miss Hattie had prepared in the other. Aaron sped away, his boat leaving a wake that broke the whitecaps.

A sinking feeling hit T.J. in the stomach, and he looked at Maggie. If her expression proved an accurate gauge, the woman was still ticked to the gills. What had happened to her in the kitchen? Tony had a warped sense of humor and T.J.'s attitude she'd said, but what the heck had she meant by that?

Whatever it was, it had to be bad. She'd stayed in the tub two hours.

Maggie at his side, they walked down the pier in silence, and he looked around the isle. A rocky face, not too big, sandy and lush with winter foliage. Pretty in its natural state.

"I can see why Beaulah comes here." Maggie stepped over a patch of wild lilies that had fallen to winter weather. "It's got a serene feel to it, doesn't it?"

Finally, a civil word. "Yeah, it does. There's

a clearing over there — four o'clock, by that big oak."

She looked to where he'd semi-pointed with the basket, nodded, then headed in that direction. "Does anyone live out here?"

"No. There aren't any utility services. Until a couple years ago, the island belonged to Miss Millie. She donated it to the villagers."

"Mmm, not to the village, but the villagers. Interesting."

She was interesting. A beautiful bundle of contradictions that he adored. T.J. stepped around a sharp-edged rock. "That way the Planning and Zoning Commission can't do anything out here, like build. The villagers have to vote and approve any change."

"So only locals are supposed to be out here."

"Yeah."

"Well, how come Miss Hattie sent us, do you think?"

"I'm not sure. According to Hatch, the whole reason Miss Millie donated the island was because the villagers were complaining that Sea Haven Village was getting *'too touristical'*."

Maggie spread a red-and-white-checked quilt out on the ground, just beyond the oak's gnarled roots. "Mmm. The locals and tourists — it's kind of a love-hate relationship, isn't it?"

"Yes, it is." T.J. set down the picnic basket then his paint gear. "Maine depends heavily on tourism. The locals know they need those dollars — they're a big chunk of the economic base — but at the same time, they know that tourists don't hold the same respect as the locals for the land and resources."

Maggie chuckled. "Maybe they should put a sign beside the 'Welcome to Maine' sign. One that says 'Send Money But Stay Home.' "

T.J. laughed and sat down on the blanket. "Hatch would love that."

"I'll bet he would." Maggie eased off her shoes and used them to anchor down the edge of the blanket. "Amazing how warm it is when it was so cold this morning."

"That's Maine." One day, he'd paint her feet. Just her feet. Well, maybe her feet and her calves. Maybe her legs. The woman had gorgeous, long legs.

"Yeah, I guess so."

"Maggie?" He heard his hesitancy in his voice but couldn't bury it. "Are you going to tell me what happened in the kitchen today, or are you just going to let me guess forever?"

She shrugged and held her smile, but it was forced. "It wasn't anything important."

"I could tell. The Head Hot-Water Hoggett — who said she *never* welshes on a deal — welshes over nothing." He opened the picnic basket lid. "Makes perfect sense to me."

Maggie held out a hand. "Hush and pass the pickles."

He handed her the jar but didn't turn it loose. "You want a pickle? Then you tell me what happened."

"That's blackmail, MacGregor." The sun streaked through the oak's branches and onto her face.

"Yep, sure is."

"Charming."

"Thanks." He smiled. "MacGregor's rendition of subtle revenge."

She shifted her gaze to the tree. "I guess I deserve that."

"That's about the way I see it."

"You would. You do good nag. Unfortunately —"

"You don't have to like it, honey, just accept it. I'm going to nag until you're honest with me."

"Figures."

"I gave you my promise to always believe in you, Maggie."

He'd said he loved her, too. But he didn't. "I meant it."

Well, spit. What difference did it make in the long haul? She looked back at him. "Tony gave me a hard time."

"In the kitchen?" T.J. asked only to verify. Getting her to give in had been easier than he'd expected. Obviously, she'd really wanted to talk about this, but still had been afraid to leave herself vulnerable.

"Yeah."

That she was looking at him as if she feared he'd call her crazy had his heart aching. "Did you see him?"

"No. I just heard him — inside my head."

"You're sure it's him?" T.J. let go of the jar. "Could've been your conscience again."

"He said it was him." Maggie unscrewed the cap, her hand trembling. "I'm not sure of anything anymore."

T.J. passed her a sandwich. "Glazed ham on wheat." When she took it, he asked, "What did Tony give you a hard time about?"

She took a bite of the sandwich and chewed slowly, as if engaged in a debate with herself about whether or not to tell him. T.J. girded his loins for the battle. He really hated nagging at her, but if push came to shove, he would do it.

She swallowed and lowered her gaze to the dill pickle. "Not being honest with myself about you."

"He knew that?"

"Yeah, he did." She bit off the pickle tip then crunched down on it. "And he sure didn't hesitate to let me know it."

When she had headed for the bath, T.J. figured this was serious. But with that fifty-point threat, what could he do? She'd needed space to work this through, and so he'd given it to her.

He stretched out beside her on the thick quilt. "I have to say, you seem pretty calm about this."

"Calm? Don't be absurd, MacGregor." She finished her sandwich and finger-fished a second pickle out of the jar. "I figure I'm either having a very long nightmare, a complete nervous breakdown wherein I'm suffering delusions, or I've gone totally insane."

He put a hand on her jean-clad thigh. "Sounds like losing situations."

"Boy, you've no idea just how right you are."

He'd known from the start that she had a hidden agenda here. What he didn't know was if she'd ever be honest with him about the nature of that agenda. Just above her

441

knee, he rubbed a little circle on the rough fabric with his fingertip. "Why don't you tell me, then?"

"I can't."

He met her gaze. "Can't or won't?"

She licked at her lips. "Can't." Sending him a pleading look, she put her hand on top of his at her thigh. "I wish I could, Tyler. I swear I do. I've wished it a thousand times. But —"

"You can't." He turned his hand over and clasped her fingers. "Do you think you'll ever be able to tell me, Maggie?"

"I hope so. I really, really do. But I can't say for sure."

Why did he have the feeling that this was out of her control? Or maybe it wasn't out of her control, but something that would keep them apart? For a week, two questions had nearly driven him out of his mind. And this seemed the perfect opportunity to ask them both.

"Maggie, are you already married?"

"Geez, MacGregor. I can't believe you're asking me that. The way —"

"Are you?"

She stopped midsentence and glared at him. "No."

He started breathing again and, until then he hadn't realized he'd stopped. "I had to ask. With you not being willing to tell me what this is about, I can't help exploring possibilities."

"I can't tell you." Her voice went deadpan flat. "Can't."

He brushed at her thumb with his finger. "Are you a nun?"

Shock riddled her eyes. "Good grief! We've been to bed together, MacGregor."

"I know." He blinked hard.

"Would a nun do that?"

"I don't know." He answered honestly. "They're human, too. And, if you'll recall, it wasn't right. If you were a nun, or married, you likely would hold back."

"I am not a nun."

"Okay." This wasn't accomplishing anything constructive, except that her genuine responses had set his mind at ease on those two possibilities. Maybe it was time to just trust her. If he weren't so concerned that his judgment was sorrier than spit, he'd have done that a long time ago. But she had told him about Tony. She'd definitely been afraid of that, afraid he wouldn't believe her, and yet she'd done it. She'd earned his trust.

He kissed the back of her hand then looked deeply into her eyes. "You remember the legend, Maggie?"

She nodded, clearly offended and still

443

smarting from his questions.

Man, but he hoped he didn't live to regret this. "You remember how Collin took a leap of faith and risked what he couldn't afford to lose for Cecelia?"

Again, Maggie nodded.

"It worked for them, honey."

Her hand trembled. He rubbed it in both of his. "I'm going to take a leap of faith, too." He squeezed her hands gently. "I'm going to risk losing what I can't afford to lose. For you, Maggie."

"Tyler, don't. You don't love me. Collin loved Cecelia and that makes it different."

T.J. swallowed a knot of pure fear from his throat. "You can tell me a lot of things, sweetheart, but you can't tell me what I am and I am not willing to do. I'm taking the leap, Maggie. And I'm praying it will work for us, too."

"Oh, Tyler." Tears gathered on her lashes. "What am I going to do about you?"

Love me! his heart cried. *Just love me.* He stretched up and whispered against her lips. "I have a suggestion, honey. Anytime you're ready to hear it, you let me know."

And, Lord, but he hoped she'd let him know soon.

CHAPTER 15

Miss Hattie had been right.

Panic surged through Maggie's veins. Heaven help her, she had fallen in love with the man.

How could she have been so stupid? So blasted stupid? She stared into MacGregor's eyes, and regret washed through her as the waves washed against Little Island's rocky shore. She would hurt him, just as Carolyn had hurt him, because from all signs, whether or not Maggie believed them, Mac-Gregor really did love her, too.

He dropped his habitual emotional guard completely, and the truth shone in his eyes. "I'm going to trust you, Maggie."

Trust. Not love, but *trust.* Had Tony been right? She'd considered the possibility before, but hadn't drawn a conclusion. Had she really been like Leslie, seeing in Mac-Gregor only what she expected to see?

More certain all the time that she had,

she felt worse than rotten. She felt manipulative and underhanded, jammed by doubt and suspicion and fear into a lose-lose situation with no safe way out. Tell him the truth and lose him. Or don't tell him the truth, and lose him because she'd really never had him. Definitely lose-lose. Boy, had MacGregor nailed that one.

And maybe Tony had, too.

She hadn't seen it, hadn't considered it so much as a remote possibility, but maybe she was like Carolyn, after all. Tears stung the backs of Maggie's eyes, set her nose to tingling. She fought them. But in her mind, she imagined the cleansing and healing luxury of seeing one — only one — tear trickle down her cheek.

MacGregor sat at her side, his long legs bent and tucked. "You seem so . . . sad."

"I am."

"My trust isn't worth you being sad, Maggie. I'd hoped to please you."

It *was* worth being sad about. Few things in life were more worthy of sadness. She blinked hard and tried to steady the shake from her voice. "I'm sorry. It's a big responsibility, you know?" And a big disappointment that she was unfit to carry that responsibility.

He kissed her cheek. "It's kind of flattering that it's this important to you. But I hate to see you down."

She started to correct his misconception, to tell him the truth, but Tony had explicitly warned her not to do it. Doing so anyway could cause MacGregor more trouble, more pain. She didn't want to cause him trouble or pain. No, it was kindlier not to tell him, kindlier to let him believe a lie, than to know the truth. He'd again lose his faith in womankind. He'd be devastated that his judgment had again proved faulty. And it had. Because he couldn't trust her and he had. She'd stepped over the line and become a manipulating liar . . . just like Carolyn.

He rubbed Maggie's neck with the tip of his nose, his breath warm against her skin. "Wanna watch me try to paint?"

Her heart hurt. His request had been made simply enough, but she sensed the cry for support in it. Saw that he was leaving himself wide open, trusting her to witness his possible failure. He was living his promise to her.

Too moved to speak, she nodded.

He pressed a fingertip to her chin to force her gaze to his. "If I fail, honey, I want you to know that it won't be because I'm not trying."

"I know." She kissed his forehead, the

edge of his brow, the tender skin beneath his right eye. "Have faith in *you*, Tyler. You can do this."

He gave her a bittersweet smile that had her heart wrenching as if it were being squeezed in a vise. She sat still, watched him set up the easel, lift the canvas to it, then begin preparing his palette. Oh, how she prayed this worked. He'd lost so much already. To lose his art, too, seemed so cruel and unfair.

Life isn't fair, Maggie.

Tony? What are you doing here?

Helping. It's obvious I'm needed.

She frowned, not at all sure MacGregor needed this kind of help. *Okay, so help him — but not as you have been. I don't want to hear that life isn't fair, Tony. That isn't what MacGregor needs.*

What does he need, then?

She paused for a mere twinkling. *Unconditional acceptance — success or failure. He needs his work. He loves it. And he deserves better than he's gotten so far with this guilt business about it, too. He deserves . . . a lot better, and a lot more, Tony. So much more.*

I think what he gets depends on him, doesn't it?

Ultimately, yes. But he needs support. He needs to know —

What?

I don't know. She really didn't and that had her frustrated, searching. *He just needs, Tony. That's all. He . . . needs.*

Liar.

Her temper flashed and she spoke before she thought. *Okay, so I'm lying. MacGregor needs faith. He needs support and loving and trusting and approval. He needs understanding. He needs all that and more. But I need this lie, darn it. I've lost a lot, too. And I will not risk losing anymore.*

Think about what you just said, Maggie, mmm? Just . . . think.

T.J. watched Maggie from under his lashes, sitting on the blanket as stiff as a board, encouraging him by saying nothing at all. He fell into the old moves — squeezing the paint tubes, laying out his brushes, blending his prep colors — familiar moves, as natural to him as drawing breath.

He wanted to do this painting. He'd done it a thousand times, in his mind. Maggie. Laughing. Her head back, her eyes sparkling joy as they had the day he'd first crossed the boundary line and not blacked out.

He'd never do her justice, and he knew it. But he would pay her tribute.

Mentally seeing the blend of colors, the

intrigue of shadows and shapes and planes, he felt the fire inside him ignite. His adrenaline started pumping hard, and he reached for a brush.

His stomach twittered, then flipped, and his chest went tight. *Nerves. Pure and simple.* He looked at Maggie. She hadn't moved so much as a muscle. *Only nerves.*

Are you sure you want to do this?

T.J.'s mouth went dry. Was it his own voice, or the entity's? He couldn't be sure.

Are you? Your gift has cost you everything. Your parents. Carolyn. You could lose Maggie, too . . .

He wouldn't. Couldn't. She meant too much to him. He said he trusted her, now he had to prove it. She *wanted* him to paint. She realized how much he needed to paint. And he realized that without it he'd never feel fulfilled. His soul wasn't content, and likely it never would be. This gift was as much a part of him as his heart. She'd been right. He had to at least try.

So go on, Tyler James. Paint.

He fumbled the brush. It fell to the ground and the blue paint on it splattered across the brown grass. Glancing at Maggie, he reached down and retrieved it. She still hadn't moved.

Go on, you persistent, selfish jerk! Go on,

450

*do it! You killed all the others because you
had to have your gift. Go on now, kill Maggie,
too!*

"No!" T.J. squeezed his eyes shut. "No.
I . . . can't."

Do it!

I can't! I love her! I . . . love her.

Warm breath fanned the back of his hand,
then tender lips brushed against his skin.
T.J. opened his eyes and looked into Maggie's.

She held his gaze, kissed each of his
knuckles, the valleys between each of his
knuckles, the top of each finger holding the
brush, her own hands calm and steady,
soothing. "You can do it, Tyler," she said
softly, confidently. "I know you can."

"Maggie, I —"

"I know you can." She cupped his jaw in
her hand, smiled a serene smile that took
the breath out of him. "I believe in you."

A surge of warmth spread through his
chest then burst like an explosion. His heart
beat hard, his blood gushed through his
veins, throbbed at his temples. This couldn't
be. But it was. It was!

The magic was back.

She guided his hand to the canvas, then
released it and stepped away, returning to
the rumpled quilt. "You've got to believe it,

MacGregor." She cupped her fingers and tapped them against her chest, over her heart. "You've got to feel it in here."

MacGregor not *Tyler.* She *did* believe. Feeling slugged, and gifted with a long-sought-after treasure, he stared at her. Watched her sit back down on the checked blanket, so calm and collected and at ease. She tilted back her head and looked up at him — and he nearly came undone.

His Maggie, his adored Maggie who didn't cry, sat there with unshed tears shining in her beautiful eyes. They weren't sad tears, they were joyful ones, celebrating his victory. How he knew that he had no idea, but he did know it. And then she smiled.

His own eyes blurred at the show of emotion and support. Neither had been easy for her. Any easier than her dragging him back onto Seascape land. Yet, once again, she'd done it. His throat constricted nearly shut, blocked by a wealth of feelings that sprang from his heart which he could never adequately verbalize. He dipped his brush into cerulean blue, his favorite emotion color, then tapped the left edge into alizarin crimson — a touch, no more than a touch — then dragged the entire edge through yellow ochre. He glanced at Maggie one last time and, far too emotional to speak, he smiled then set to work.

The first few strokes were unsteady, uncertain, and unsure, but within minutes, he settled into the old pattern, working furiously, slapping paint onto the canvas then brushing furiously to smooth it into the images and shapes and shadows he saw so clearly in his mind. Every few moments, he paused and studied Maggie. She remained sitting there statue-still, her beautiful smile never wavering.

He understood now what she'd meant by his trust being a big responsibility. Her support was a big responsibility, too, and he didn't want to let her down. He *wouldn't* let her down.

And then the art claimed him, and he worked like a man possessed, his focus total and complete. And in his heart, he felt the old, creative joy well.

The moment his love for his work overtook him, Maggie sensed it. And she used the break of showing unwavering support to have a long-overdue, deep and serious discussion with her conscience. One she'd hoped to avoid, for obvious reasons, but one she'd known the minute MacGregor had told her that he trusted her, she couldn't avoid any longer.

Okay, Maggie, here's the deal. You're in love with the man, and that's a factor. You're also in a lose-lose situation here, and that also is a factor. Combine the factors, and what you've got is nothing. There it is. He doesn't really love you, just thinks he does, and there'll never be anything more for you here. There is no relationship. There is no happily-ever-after. There is no love.

True. She choked. *All true. So what now?*

Now, you tell the heart to quit aching and the regret to take a flying leap. You're no dreamer. You knew better than to ever expect the kind of love Cecelia and Collin, or Tony and Hattie, shared. So there's no great surprise in that you won't ever have it.

No, no great surprise. She plucked up a bit of dead grass and worked it between her finger and thumb. *But there is disappointment. I never dreamed of that love, but I sure wouldn't have minded it.*

It hurts so badly — even if you didn't lose your head and dare to dream, like Miss Hattie told you to do — but you'll survive. You always have, and you've never had love like that, right?

Right. But it would've been

Forget would-have-beens. They're like *almost* and *also ran.* Worthless. And forget that business that it was okay to know you

454

wouldn't have that rare kind of love before MacGregor came along because you didn't know what you were missing, and now that he has come along, and he'll be going along without you, the knowing has left a hole inside you. It just isn't so, Maggie. You still don't know what you're missing because you've never trusted MacGregor. Right now, right this second, you still don't trust the man.

So now what? I just end up empty and alone?

That's up to you. You now have the bottom line. You're going to lose him either way — if you tell him, or you don't. So the question is, do you lose him by becoming like Carolyn? Or do you lose him by being honest and retaining at least an atom of your self-respect and dignity? The choice is yours.

Some choice. Maggie fingered the nubby blanket, stared at the dancing shadows where sunlight spilled through the curled, crisp leaves on the trees and dappled the quilt. It sounded so simple, so easy. But it wasn't simple *or* easy. It was hard. To keep her self-respect, she had to go toe to toe with Tony, who'd expressly warned her against telling MacGregor the truth. She had no idea what he would do. But if she had to lose MacGregor, which seemed inevitable, then she should at least be permitted to retain what was left of her dignity and self-respect. True, after her shoddy treatment of him, both were pretty tattered, but they were all she'd have left. Tony had said he'd brought her here. Mac-Gregor had been secondary, and she felt certain Tony wouldn't hurt MacGregor — thank goodness for that. Because Maggie feared she would hurt him plenty by herself. But Tony well might hurt Maggie for defying him. Who knew what a ghost would do? Yet, to ever meet her own eyes in the mirror again, regardless of what Tony did to her, she had to tell MacGregor the truth. And that was the final, bottom line. She had to tell him the truth. Today.

Her choice had been made.

Breathing hard, MacGregor dropped down beside Maggie on the quilt. Sweat beaded at his brow, his shirt clung to his chest and back, his damp hair curled at his temples and nape, and his eyes were alight with pure joy.

Swallowing hard, Maggie brushed away an errant lock of damp hair hugging the shell of his ear. And some thought art wasn't physical.

"I thought you'd gotten a little glassy-eyed on me." He dragged a fingertip that smelled of paint down the slope of her nose. "You awake in there?"

Maggie laughed. "I'm awake."

"Then kiss me, Maggie." He rolled over her, and she lay back on the quilt and looked up at him. "We've conquered the demon."

"We have?" The sea. Warm, earthy man. Oh, but she loved the smell of him.

"Yeah." He grinned.

"I want to see it." She tried to get up.

He held her down with a hand to her shoulder. "Nope, not until it's done."

"But, MacGregor."

"Not negotiable." He slid his hand over her hair, smoothing it back from her face. "Now where's my kiss? And don't even think about welshing. I've earned this one."

"I wouldn't dream of it." She curled her arms around his neck, pulled him to her, and parted her lips to receive his kiss.

Sensations bombarded her. This was no gentle kiss. It was intense, long and hard and deep. Rather than physically depleting and emotionally draining him, working seemed to invigorate, enliven, energize Mac-Gregor. So very aware. She tasted his happiness, grew giddy with it, and shared in his celebration, promising herself that, yes, oh yes, she would tell him the truth. Today. But after the celebration. He'd waited two long years for this moment, and she wouldn't rob him of this pleasure, too.

Be honest with yourself, Maggie.

Tony. Go away! Don't you see that this is it for me? This kiss, this time with him, now, before I tell him and he hates me — it's all I'll ever have. It has to last a lifetime. Please, Tony. Please, don't begrudge me this. Please don't take it away from me.

Tony kept talking.

No! I won't let you do this. I won't. I need, Tony. I need! Maggie blocked Tony out, focused all her thoughts, her energies, her feelings, on MacGregor. On the heat, and the passion and the desire in his kiss, his embrace. *It could have been different.*

Her conscience. Thank heaven, her conscience. It could have been different, she agreed, but it isn't. Her heart ached for all the intimate longings, the lover's secrets usually whispered deep in the night, the love words spoken in tender tones and gentle words that he would never hear because she would never say them.

He kissed her back with equal ferocity, openly, lovingly, touching her in ways so achingly tender it shattered her heart. His arms trembled and he raised up onto his elbows, then looked down at her, desire glazing his eyes. "Maggie," he whispered, his voice husky and intense. "I want you."

Just this once. Before she lost him forever, couldn't she have him just this once?

It won't be right. You haven't told him the truth.

I need him! He needs me! It will be right. It will! She denied her conscience. Denied it, and reached for the buttons on Mac-Gregor's shirt. "I want you, too."

It hadn't been right.

Sitting on the dilapidated pier, Maggie propped her elbow to her knee and stared out to sea, waiting for Aaron. As the minutes passed and the trees' shadows stretched longer on the stony ground, she grew more and more anxious. She'd made a promise to herself and she meant to keep it. But she didn't have to like it and she hated, positively hated, wrecking MacGregor's celebration. For the first time since she'd known him, the man was over-the-moon happy. He'd waited two years for this day. Two years. So while she would tell him, she just couldn't tell him yet. Not so soon. Not after he'd waited such a long time for this. Hadn't he said that he'd really missed the creative outpouring of losing himself in his work? Hadn't he said that he'd come to terms with his losses and accepted that they'd been caused not by his work, but life? Hadn't he said that for the first time in two years, he felt complete and content and in harmony with himself? He was at peace. If she told him about her lies now, he sure wouldn't feel harmony or peace anymore. And he might go right back to blaming his art. She couldn't take the chance. Or the responsibility for that.

He might. And that she wouldn't let happen — she couldn't, not and live with herself. So she'd forfeit her self-respect and the little dignity she had left — for him, for today. She wouldn't ruin this for him. And if nothing else good came out of all this, at least she could take solace in that. She'd erred, but she'd also shown compassion.

"I'll make a deal with you," she said, losing the battle to curiosity. "Hot water for just a peek." She nodded toward the canvas.

"No way, honey." He set the canvas down, propping it against the picnic basket. The front of it faced the ocean, the back was stretched canvas and wood, and she couldn't see through it. "I've made deals with you before. You welsh."

He looked rather pleased at that. Should

she be pleased or offended? "It's heartless of you not to at least let me get a glimpse of it, MacGregor."

"Nope." He walked over, bent down and tweaked her nose. "Not until it's done."

She stood up. "Why not?"

He smiled, looking pleased with himself. Or maybe with her, for showing such interest.

"Anything worthwhile is worth waiting for. My bath in the garden tub, for example." He pulled her into his arms. "I can't have you thinking I'm heartless, though. How about a little compensation?"

The clock was ticking. It had to be almost five. Aaron would be here any moment, and she had to get the truth told to MacGregor so he'd have time to calm down on the boat. Once they hit shore, he'd take off like a shot, and she'd never get him to listen. Captive on the boat, she could explain her reasoning to him anyway. It wouldn't change anything, didn't mean he'd hear her, but at least she'd have the satisfaction of knowing she'd tried to make him understand. And maybe — *please maybe* — he'd only hate her a little. "What kind of compensation?"

He lifted his brows. "A kiss?"

"You get as much out of a kiss as I do, MacGregor. That doesn't seem fair."

461

"What's unfair about a good deal all around?"

A win-win situation. Oh, how she wished they could have a win-win situation. But they couldn't. She couldn't. And she couldn't wait any longer to get through her lose-lose one.

Guilt stabbed at her conscience. If she had a heart that wasn't shattered, she'd wait until they returned to Seascape to tell him. But she couldn't take that risk. The roofers had finished with the Carriage House that morning. If she waited, MacGregor could hole up in there and she'd die of old age without ever seeing him again.

Yes, at least by telling him here, he'd have a little time to adjust before he could stomp out of her life in a rage. And he wouldn't have much choice but to hear her out. That didn't mean he'd understand her rationale, give two figs about her motivation, or that he'd listen, but he would hear her side of the story and why she felt it wise to keep the truth about Carolyn to herself. Geez, how did something that started out so right, intention-wise, turn out to be so wrong?

T.J. propped his hands on her shoulders and gave her a good frown. "You know, Maggie, you don't do much for my ego."

"What?"

"I ask you if you want a kiss and it takes you forever to decide. What's a guy supposed to think about that?"

"Do you have to think anything about it?"

"You're giving me an inferiority complex. How can I not think about it?"

She wanted to razz him back, but her heart just wasn't in it. Why, oh why, had she let herself fall in love with him?

"Do you consider kissing me a chore?"

"Only when you snarl, darling. Otherwise, I rather like it."

The drone of an engine reached her ears. She turned and, as if by magic, the boat suddenly docked at the pier and Aaron stood, baseball cap shading his eyes, grinning at them. "Wow!" he said, checking his Mickey Mouse watch. "That's the fastest time I ever made that run!"

How had he gotten there without them realizing he was coming?

Guess.

Tony. She grimaced. *I should've known it was you.*

My subtle way of letting you know that it's still not time.

Not so subtle. And I've got to tell him — no matter what you do to me. It — it just isn't right not to tell him. Not anymore.

Lift not the veil, Maggie. It's not yet time.

I have to! Didn't you hear me? I can't live with me, knowing I'm lying to him.

You've always lied to him . . . and to yourself. That's the real trouble here, Maggie. Not Mac-Gregor. You.

She clenched her jaw. *I am going to tell him. That's my final word.*

I'm warning you, don't do it. You don't understand the damage you'll do.

I understand the damage I'm doing now.

Please, Maggie.

Please? The hairs on her nape stood on end. *Tony, what damage are you talking about?*

No answer.

Tony?

Still no answer.

She asked again and again, but Tony refused to respond.

MacGregor clasped her hand then lifted her onto the boat. Maggie took her seat and watched him load the gear. Should she be happy for the reprieve? Or upset?

Feeling a fair share of both, her temples started pounding, and by the time they reached the Inn she had a wall-banger of a headache, complete with an upset stomach.

MacGregor led her into the kitchen. "Why don't you go on up and lay down. I'll come up and massage your head."

"Yeah, I will." She walked straight through to the gallery, swearing her head was splitting wide open.

T.J. watched her climb the stairs and step from sight, his heart twisting inside his chest. Something was seriously troubling her. Why didn't she turn to him with it as she had with so many other troubles? Had he let her down? Failed her in some way?

"Tyler!" Miss Hattie exclaimed, the half-done canvas in her hands. "You painted!"

A smile tugged at his lips. "What do you think?"

"An amazing likeness I'd say." She looked up at him, tears shimmering in her eyes. "It's beautiful. My, my. You've captured Maggie's spirit, dear."

"It's a surprise for her."

"I see." Miss Hattie's eyes twinkled. "Well, she'll be thrilled. It's probably your best work ever, Tyler."

"I hope so." He looked down at the in-progress painting. "I'm planning to give it to her on our wedding day."

Miss Hattie gasped, looking delighted. "Your wedding day! Oh, Tyler, that's —"

"A surprise, too," he interrupted, looking sheepish. "Maggie doesn't know she's marrying me yet."

"Ah, I see." Miss Hattie's smile grew secretive and she let her gaze slide to the ceiling for a scant second, then put the canvas down and squeezed T.J.'s hands. "I'm so very, very pleased."

A bubble of pleasure burst in his stomach. "It feels good. Working again, loving Maggie. I never thought I'd feel —"

"I know, dear." She gave the back of his hand a gentle pat. "I'm so glad you were wrong."

He caught her up in a gentle hug and pecked a kiss, to the angel's soft cheek. "I'm kind of happy about it myself."

"As well you should be. A gift, be it love or talent, is a terrible thing to squander."

"It is." He sighed deeply. "Ah, Miss Hattie, it's amazing. Maggie, my work. A man could want for little more."

"True. And high time you see it, too, if you don't mind this old woman saying so." She giggled. "Now, put me down, you rapscallion. I'm far too old to be cavorting in my kitchen with the likes of you."

He eased her to the floor, grinning. "You'll never get old, Miss Hattie."

Still holding her smile, she looked around. "Where is Maggie?"

"Gone to bed with a killer headache."

"Poor dear. Too much tension, I suppose."

"Too much something. Tension. Worrying. Choose your adjective." He grimaced. "I'm on my way up to give her a massage. Maybe it'll help her relax."

The phone rang.

Miss Hattie paused, glanced at the ceiling for a split second, and her smile faded. "Would you get that for me, dear?"

T.J. frowned. Miss Hattie stood closer to the phone than he did. "Sure." Why hadn't Miss Hattie met his eyes?

He walked over then lifted the receiver. "Seascape Inn."

"Hello there," a woman said in a bubbly voice. "May I speak to Maggie Wright?"

The only calls Maggie ever made were to her mother. Had to be her — and his big opportunity to gain a little insight. Best be sure first, though. "May I ask who's calling?"

"This is her mother, Elizabeth Wright."

Ah. Good. "Maggie has gone to bed with a headache, Mrs. Wright. Should I disturb her?"

"No. No, please don't do that. I just wanted to talk with her about something."

"Is it urgent, or anything I can help you with?"

"Well, I don't know, to be honest. It is about a man I've met at my ceramics class.

He's asked for a date. Can you imagine? At my age? And I'm not quite sure what to — oh. Oh, my. It's just occurred to me that I don't know who I'm speaking to. Isn't that awful?"

T.J. grinned, leaned against the wall and crossed his feet at his ankles. "No, ma'am, I don't think so. I think it's wonderful — about the date. You should accept and have fun — so long as the man minds his manners."

She giggled like a school girl. "And if he doesn't?"

T.J. smiled into the phone. He liked her. "Well, that depends. If you don't like his mischief, let me know and I'll come down and box his ears."

"Gallant. I always admired that in a man. But what if I do like his mischief?"

"Well, then be careful and have a good time."

"You're wicked, young man. I like that, too."

Her laughter had T.J. smiling again. "Thank you."

"And now that you've resolved my dating dilemma, tell me who you are."

"MacGregor — a friend of Maggie's." He could have disclosed his intention to be her son-in-law, but that should come from Maggie — once she knew and accepted it. That could take a little while.

"Did you say MacGregor?" Elizabeth Wright sounded pleased.

"Yes, ma'am, I did."

"Oh, I'm so delighted to finally be talking with you, T.J."

Maggie evidently had more than mentioned him. That had him smiling. "Thank you." Wait. Elizabeth Wright had called him T.J. He'd not told her anything other than MacGregor, and Maggie *never* called him T.J.

"I'd hoped we'd meet long ago, but Carolyn explained how demanding your schedule was just then, and that you had no free time."

"Carolyn?" A shiver of shock splintered through him. She had to mean Maggie, of course. She *had* to.

"Yes." Her voice grew uncertain. "You are Tyler James the artist, aren't you?"

"I am." She hadn't made a mistake. T.J. stared at a small scuff mark on the floor. "How do you know Carolyn, Mrs. Wright?"

"Why, she was my niece."

"Your *niece?*" T.J. glared at the ceiling. Maggie was Carolyn's cousin? Her cousin, and she hadn't told him? He'd nearly driven himself crazy wondering if her secret was something awful like her being married, being a nun — now that was a joke — and, and all the while, she —

Birds of a feather . . .

Not his conscience. Tony. Had to be Tony. Shut up, Tony. Would you just shut up?

Truth is truth. And you trusted her. Remember now why the name Sam Grayson sounded so familiar to you?

Carolyn. Grayson had called Carolyn's apartment one night and T.J. had answered the phone.

You trusted her, and you trusted Maggie. Some guys never learn . . .

T.J. had trusted them both. Carolyn's betrayal had stung his ego more than hurt him, though her death was another matter entirely. But Maggie's betrayal devastated. And, obviously, trusting her had been but one of many mistakes he'd made where she was concerned. He'd believed in her. He'd believed.

But those days were over now.

Now, he just had to decide if he should love her or kill her.

Or just forget her.

CHAPTER 16

Something creaked.

The noise awakened Maggie and she stirred under the blue coverlet, reluctant to drag herself from that netherworld between waking and sleep where her conscience could just nag at her. House noises. Settling boards reacting to weather and temperature changes. Nothing more. Sea Haven Village, not New Orleans. No crime here.

She breathed in the smell of the sea and frowned, then forced herself beyond twilight. "Tony?" She sniffed. Flowers from the dresser's vase. Potpourri from Miss Millie's Seashore Secrets sachet, and man. The sea and man. It couldn't be Tony. Tony didn't carry a scent, only the wind and the whisper. And the warnings.

But she wasn't alone.

Someone was sitting in the wing-back chair beside her bed. She sensed it and snapped her eyes open, clutching at the coverlet. "MacGregor?" Frog-throated, she frowned at him, not sure if she should be relieved or afraid.

"How's the headache?" His expression was more grim than a death mask.

"It's gone." She shoved her sleep-tossed hair away from her eyes. "What are you doing here?"

Fully dressed in the jeans and royal blue shirt he'd been wearing earlier, he leaned toward her, his feet spread and flat on the floor, his hands clasped together at his knees. "I'm debating, Maggie."

"Debating. In the middle of the night? In my room?" She rolled onto her side and turned on the little tulip lamp atop the table beside the bed. When light spilled over his face and she saw the tethered fury burning in his eyes, she wished she'd left the light off. He'd looked grim in the moonlight, but soft yellow light didn't soften his hard expression. He clearly felt enraged.

Ignoring her questions, he enlightened her. "I'm debating on whether I should crawl into bed with you or walk out the door and never speak to you again."

"What?" Some choices. Her heart slid up from her chest to her throat. What prompted this?

A muscle in his jaw twitched. "Does Tony

come to you here?"

She grunted and sat straight up. "Are you asking me if I'm sleeping with a ghost, MacGregor?" She gritted her teeth and jerked at the coverlet. "Do you realize how absurd that sounds?"

"What around here isn't absurd?" Void of emotion, his look leveled, and chilled her to the core.

He had a point. "No." She let him hear her resentment in her voice. "Tony doesn't do that. I can't believe you'd even for a second think I'd do that, or that he would. He loves Miss Hattie, MacGregor. Have you forgotten that?"

"Okay." He let out a sigh that worried her because of the frustration she sensed in it. What had gotten into him? "Okay, Maggie."

She pestered the sheets, rubbing a bunched bit of the top one between her fingers. "Why are you considering never speaking to me again?" Had he learned why she was here? Her connection to Carolyn? Had he somehow learned the truth?

Maggie forced herself to stop this conjecture. How could he have? No, her guilty conscience was hard at work here. Nothing more.

He stared at her for a long moment. The anger in his eyes shifted to resignation. "You know I didn't want to care about you, Maggie. I suspect you know the reason, too."

"Because you didn't want me hurt?"

"I didn't want you dead."

"Like your mother and Carolyn."

"Yes." He leaned back in the chair, locked his huge hands on its padded arms. "I've told you about my relationship with Carolyn. We wanted different things. She wasn't the woman I thought she was, Maggie, and I don't think I was the man she thought I was, either. She wanted Tyler James, the glamorous façade. She had this fairytale image of marriage to a world-respected artist. But when she found out that Tyler James was only a part of me, that there was another, larger part that was just a man, well it caused some serious rifts between us."

Maggie bet it did. Carolyn wouldn't be interested in the real MacGregor. The man had flaws whereas the image was perfect. She loved perfection. Demanded it from everyone and everything.

Oh good grief. He'd told Maggie the truth from the start. Carolyn *hadn't* loved him!

"I knew we'd never be happy together, so I broke our engagement. Carolyn was devastated — not at losing me, but at losing the fairy-tale image she'd created of herself as my wife. She swore I'd be sorry. Boy, did that prove prophetic." He stood up and walked around behind the wingback chair, then propped his elbows on the back of it. "She stole the painting that night, Maggie."

"MacGregor," Maggie said, not knowing why. The pain in him was so strong, much stronger than the pain she'd felt when sitting at the turret window with her nose pressed to the glass, watching him try and fail to cross the boundary line.

Torment flooded his eyes then turned the look in them sleety and hard. "What I haven't told you before is that a few days after Carolyn's funeral, a man named Jason Carruthers called me at home."

"I never heard of him."

"Neither had I."

"What did he want?"

"He offered me the same deal for the painting of Seascape Inn that he and Carolyn had agreed on."

"She intended to sell it?" Maggie slung back the covers and swung her legs to the floor. Impossible. It couldn't be. Carolyn had felt that same lure Maggie had felt on looking at the painting. That's why she'd been obsessed with it — hadn't it?

Tony said he'd brought Maggie here. Summoned her. Maybe he hadn't summoned Carolyn. Or maybe she hadn't recognized the summons for what it had been.

"She more than intended to sell it, Maggie. She'd done it. Carruthers called me from Seascape. Carolyn and he were to meet here to deliver the painting."

"He'd already paid her?"

MacGregor nodded. "According to Carruthers, yes. And when Carolyn didn't show, he figured he'd been stiffed. So he checked to see what was happening with her and found out about the accident and her death. That's when he called me."

"Where's the money? Carolyn didn't have it, Tyler. Her account didn't have in it the kind of money one of your paintings brings."

"He stopped payment and got it back."

"Oh." This was a lot to take in. She'd really sold the painting? Good grief.

The light played shadows across MacGregor's chin and shirtfront. "People at Lakeview Gallery warned me Carolyn was a user, but I didn't want to believe them. We had a lot in common."

"You'd both lost your parents."

"Yes." He looked down at the chair seat. "Yes."

"If it helps, Tyler, I'm sure that, in her way, Carolyn did love you."

He looked up at her and the hardness in his eyes melted. "She didn't love me Maggie. Carolyn was distant, untouchable. It was part of her appeal. There was a tragic quality about her that made me want to protect her. I mistook that feeling for love. But I never, never, deluded myself into believing that she loved me. I think losing her parents so young made her too fearful to ever risk loving anyone else."

"And yet you intended to marry her."

"It's hard to explain, especially in retrospect and with distance. But, living it, I thought she needed me. My parents had died and, right or wrong, I felt so guilty about that. I came here and regained my gift, Maggie, but I never recovered my peace. Carolyn, with that tragic air, well it gave me a mission. A chance to make up for my parents' deaths. I had a purpose, you know?"

"Saving Carolyn."

"In a way, yes."

"But you discovered her tragedy was a façade to cover her manipulations."

He nodded. "That's when I broke the engagement."

"Tyler, you were willing to settle for so little."

"I didn't think I deserved more. But she

did. And she needed more than I could give her. I'm not perfect, Maggie. I'm a man. Just flesh and blood and flaws. She needed the fairy-tale image, and I couldn't give it to her."

"I'm sorry, Tyler."

"Me, too." He sighed. "I believed in her. My instincts told me to believe my friends at the gallery, but I didn't do it — until Carruthers called. Once I'd heard what he had to say with my own ears, well, I couldn't deny the truth. Carolyn never loved me, Maggie. She never even wanted me, much less needed me. She wanted the fairy-tale . . . and my art."

No wonder he'd considered his talent a curse. In using his gift, he'd lost his parents then Carolyn — only to learn that he'd never had her. Already robbed of his worth as an artist, she'd robbed him of his worth as a man. And, oh, did Miss Hattie's behind-her-hankie pleadings with Maggie to be patient with MacGregor, to be gentle with him and understanding, make sense now. She wanted Maggie to help MacGregor realize that all women weren't bent on hurting or manipulating him. That he was a worthy man. And what had Maggie done? Hurt, manipulated, lied to — and as soon as he learned the truth — reinforced what

Carolyn had done by robbing him again.

She felt sick inside.

Tell him the truth, Maggie. Lift the veil.

Maggie cringed. *Are you nuts, Tony? That'll convince him I'm just another Carolyn. I can't tell him now. Not after this. He'll be devastated. I'd rather he hate me than be devastated.*

Maggie, Maggie. You said it yourself. If your heart and mind agree on something, then you owe it to yourself to at least try. Did you think?

What?

Tony sighed his impatience. *On Little Island, you told me what Tyler needed. I told you to think about what you'd said. Did you do it?*

Yes, but I don't understand what you wanted.

I wanted what I've always wanted, Maggie. I want you to answer me. What does Tyler need? What do you need?

I don't know.

You do! Stop lying to me. Stop lying to you. Tell me what you told me then.

He needs unconditional acceptance. Truth. Trust. Maggie felt a tingle surge through her. *Is that it? Trust?*

Trust and truth, surely. But what else? Dig, Maggie! Dig deep inside you and tell me what you both need!

Maggie stared at MacGregor, stared deeply into his eyes. *Faith, Tony. We both need faith. That's what this is all about, isn't it?*

You tell me. Better yet, ask him.

MacGregor didn't so much as blink. She sensed his expectancy. He was . . . waiting.

I can't do it, Tony. I can't tell him the truth. He'll hate me!

If you don't do it, you'll hate yourself.

What is it with you? When I want to tell him, you don't want me to, and now that I can't do it, you insist I tell him. Don't you know your own mind here?

I know that your reasoning and rationale have been at odds with your heart. I know that you're still, right this minute, looking in rather than out.

Her heart and mind did agree. They both urged her, begged and pleaded with her, to trust MacGregor, to be honest with him. But she couldn't do it. She couldn't lose him. She couldn't put him through more of the same pain. She loved him, and it was better he never know it. Better that they spent their time here then went their separate ways. He'd get over her in no time. He only thought he loved her.

Coward.

Yes. In this, yes, Tony. I'm a coward. Mac-

Gregor would hate her, but for walking away from him. Not for the horrible things she'd done.

"Maggie?" Concern waffled in MacGregor's voice, and his knuckles on the back of the chair bleached white.

"I'm — I'm sorry for what Carolyn did to you, Tyler." Sitting on the edge of the bed, Maggie wrung her hands in her lap. "I know it had to have hurt something awful. But it's better that you discovered it before you married her. It would only have hurt you more later."

He stared at Maggie for so long that she half-feared he'd slipped away from her into some unseen world where she'd never again reach him.

"MacGregor? Are you okay?"

Disappointment flooded his eyes. "You aren't going to tell me, are you? Darn it, Maggie. I've bared my soul to you, and you still aren't going to trust me with your secrets."

She licked at her lips, her hands shaking, her stomach threatening to heave. "I already explained that I can't, MacGregor. I wish I could, but . . . I can't."

"Fine." He strode to the door, grasped the knob and looked back at her, his devastation carved into every pore of his face.

"I've made promises to you, given you my heart and love and trust. But even adding my soul wasn't enough. I'm sorry, Maggie, I really am. But I just don't have any more to give."

"Tyler, I —"

"Goodbye, Maggie." He walked out and shut the door.

She sat stiff as a statue on the bed, not permitting herself to so much as blink, knowing if she did she'd crumble into tears. Something was wrong here. Seriously wrong. He had been waiting for her to disclose her secrets, and he'd been bitterly disappointed that she hadn't. He'd been asking for her trust. Asking. And she'd denied him.

The temperature plummeted.

Shivering under the Arctic chill, Maggie glanced over into the dresser mirror — and saw Tony. The light from the tulip lamp reflected on his shiny buttons.

You should have told him, Maggie. It was time. I told you to lift the veil. Why didn't you?

He was right. She should have, but she'd lacked the courage to do it. She had too much to lose. Lifting her chin, she looked at Tony's reflection, and lied. *What veil?*

Oh, Maggie. His sadness etched his features and he shook his head. *Look inward for your answers and stop this. You can't lie to me, or to yourself — not here, and not anymore ever again anywhere. Don't you see that you've changed? Don't you see that in not lifting the veil, you have done to Tyler exactly that which you most didn't want to do? Like Carolyn, you've robbed him of worth, Maggie. He gave you all he had to give.*

She opened her mouth but, as she did, Tony slowly faded until all she could see in the mirror was a reflection of the wall.

Isolated and cold, Maggie shivered and huddled under the covers. But even they could warm no more than her body. Her heart felt encased in a block of ice. Why hadn't she told MacGregor the truth? Why hadn't she trusted him? He was nothing like her father — or any other man — and he'd done nothing, given her no reason not to trust him. He wasn't volatile. He didn't belittle others. And he had as much reason, if not more, to not trust her — to stay away from her — and yet he hadn't. He'd given her his trust. He'd given her . . . everything.

Lose him in lies, or with dignity.

Her conscience. Yes. And it was right. It was — oh, no. So obvious and she'd totally missed it. Faith. *Faith!*

She tossed back the covers, grabbed her robe, her insides shaking so hard she expected to hear them rattle. She slid into her shoes, half-running, half-stumbling to the door, then through the landing to the stairs. Where had he gone? To his room? The Carriage House? The only way she'd get to wherever MacGregor had gone was on a wing and a prayer.

He's on the cliffs.

The cliffs. He'd gone to the cliffs. *Thanks, Tony.*

She took the stairs two at a time, ran through the gallery, catching a single tick from the grandfather clock, then on through the kitchen and finally exited through the mud room door. She rushed on outside — and into a wall of thick fog.

She made her way around the house on memory more than sight, then crossed the lawn, unable to see more than a foot in front her. *Tony, help me find him. Please!*

Feeling a hand slide into hers, she looked to her side and saw Tony. Aged and ageless, his uniform buttons shining, though there was no light to make them shine, his smile also twinkling in his eyes. *This way.*

They crossed the craggy rocks and up on the cliff. Tony paused. *He's right there, Maggie. Two o'clock.*

She smiled. *Thank you, Tony. For everything.*

My pleasure. He nodded, then stepped back and was gone.

She called out. "MacGregor? MacGregor, where are you?"

"Maggie?" She heard footsteps then MacGregor stood in front of her, staring down into her eyes. "What are you doing out here? You forgot your coat, Maggie. You'll get pneumonia." He started to shrug out of his jacket.

The surf pounding the rocks echoed in her ears, and mist from the sea spray and fog gathered on her skin. She grabbed MacGregor's hands, locked them in hers, and nestled them to her chest. "Carolyn was my cousin, MacGregor. I came up here because I thought you might have had something to do with her death. The painting wasn't in the car at the time everything burned, and the police said no one else had been around then. But someone had to have been, and I thought it was you."

The truth hit her like a sledge. Someone else *had* prevented the painting from being destroyed. Tony!

She heard him laugh inside her head. *Nice touch, eh?*

I'll deal with you later, Tony Freeport. One man at a time with your attitudes is all I can handle. "I didn't mean to hurt you, Tyler. I

485

only wanted the truth. I'd promised my mother. Carolyn was family, and finding out the truth was my responsibility."

"So you went to the gallery to gather information and found out I was here."

"Yes, and no. I did go to the gallery looking for information. I ran into Bill there, but I didn't know you were here until you waylaid me in the hallway upstairs. Once I discovered you were here, though, I thought I might at least learn your side of the story. I know it was wrong — keeping the truth from you — and I'm sorry. From nearly the beginning I had doubts that you were involved, MacGregor. And as I got to know you, I —"

He whispered softly. "You what, Maggie?"

She looked up at him. "I knew you couldn't have been involved, directly or even indirectly."

"You knew it in your heart, but your head was a little harder to convince."

"Yes." She dragged her teeth over her lip. "And then I realized I cared for you and that terrified me. I was so afraid of being vulnerable, of needing you and you not needing me."

"And?"

"And then you believed in me and I didn't want to let you down. I realized that you were nothing like my father. That I didn't have to fear being vulnerable with you because you wouldn't abuse my tender feelings and use them against me."

"So why didn't you tell me the truth?" He frowned down at her. "I promised to always believe in you."

"That's why I couldn't tell you — at first. Then you trusted me. And then when I convinced myself to tell you, Tony told me not to do it. I battled myself over that one, and decided to tell you anyway, but then —" Shame and guilt slammed into her heart and tears burned the back of her nose, her eyes.

"Then?"

She forced herself to meet his gaze. "I can't do this." She caught her breath and held it for a long second. "All that's true, MacGregor — every word of it. But it's not the real reason I didn't tell you. I was afraid you'd hate me. I knew I'd lose you, and I didn't want to lose you."

He paused a long second, then blinked hard three times. "I have a confession to make, too."

"Really?"

He nodded. "While you were upstairs nursing your headache, your mother called. I talked with her, Maggie."

Her knees nearly gave out. "When you came to my room tonight, you already knew the truth."

"Yes." He squeezed her hands as if to prevent her from pulling away from him. "Your mother told me why you'd come to Seascape, and of your suspicions that I was involved with Carolyn's death. That's why I went to your room — to give you an opening to tell me the truth so I could reassure you that I wasn't involved."

"The veil," Maggie whispered. "I finally get it, Tyler."

Confusion put a crease between his brows. "What veil? You haven't mentioned a veil."

"I wanted to tell you about Carolyn — I started to twice, but Tony said, 'Lift not the veil. It's not yet time.' "

MacGregor frowned. "So what does it mean?"

She looked up at him, her voice softening. "Love can't be realized without trust. It's lost beneath a veil of suspicion and doubt and — oh geez, I can't believe I didn't realize this —"

"Realize what, Maggie?"

"Only faith can lift the veil." She smiled at him. "It's faith, MacGregor."

"Are you saying that you trust me, Maggie?"

"Yes."

"And does that mean that you no longer suspect I had anything to do with Carolyn's death?"

"No, I understand now. Carolyn's death wasn't mysterious at all. It was an accident — no less, but no more. She wanted the painting not for herself or for its magic, but to sell it to Carruthers." Maggie freed her hand and pressed it against MacGregor's chest. "I think she somehow knew that Seascape's true magic wasn't in the painting but in the house itself. That's why she was meeting Carruthers here. Carolyn had needed to heal. She had reserved the Carriage House suite."

"She had?"

He hadn't known that. Maggie nodded. "I knew someone had to be at the accident site or the painting would have been destroyed in the fire. I thought it was you, but it wasn't."

"Tony."

"Yes, Tony."

Finally at peace with the past, she lifted her face to the fog. "I'm sorry for doubting you."

"You didn't know me."

"Do you hate me?"

He cupped her face in his hands, his emotions trembling in his voice. "I love you, Maggie."

A lone tear trickled down her cheek. "I love you, too, MacGregor. With all my heart."

Ah, peace at last.

MacGregor stiffened. "Tony?"

"You heard him?" Maggie squeezed Mac-Gregor's waist.

He nodded.

You two really had me worried for a while there. Sorry about the blackouts, Tyler, but I had to keep you here until Maggie arrived. There was a scheduling foul-up that, um . . . Never mind. I'm just glad you managed to stay put without scrambling your brains on the rocks.

MacGregor looked through the thinning fog toward Tony's voice. "How did you do that?"

Fingers to the shoulder hollow. An old maneuver I picked up in the Army for disabling folks. Works well, eh?

"Yeah, I'd say so." MacGregor looked around for Tony but didn't see him.

"He kept you here for me." Maggie grinned. "Thanks, Tony."

Actually, I did it for both of you. You were supposed to find each other two years ago, but Maggie's mother's accident happened and

490

she needed her. Then you met Carolyn in-stead and things really got messed up. I filed a complaint with the Boss, by the way. But the damage had been done and you both had to heal before we could give this another go. Anyway, you did the work. I just assisted a little here and there.

"Thanks for your assistance, Tony." Mac-Gregor said. "I'll take good care of her."

"You will?" He nodded and Maggie smiled up at him. "Then I'll take good care of you, too, MacGregor. I'll use your razor regu-larly, to spare you from slitting your throat. And —"

"If you say you'll hog all the hot water, Maggie, I might just not ask you to marry me. The thought of cold showers for the rest of my days —"

She squeezed his forearms, her breath locked in her throat. "Did you say *marry* you?"

"Don't you want to marry me?" He frowned.

"Want to? No. You'll drive me nuts. But" — she smiled — "I insist you do, because I'd rather be nuts with you than without you." Recalling the bulletin board at the Blue Moon Cafe, Maggie twisted the smile from her lips. "Can we stay here another week?"

"I was thinking until Christmas — a Christmas wedding in the church. We both said if we ever married, it'd be in that church. How does that sound?"

Miss Millie and Jimmy Goodson had both chosen December 25th — those were the dates beside Maggie and MacGregor's names. They'd been betting on a wedding!

"What time?" Maggie asked. They'd both chosen two o'clock.

"How about two?"

"Two sounds perfect." Maggie smiled, her heart full, and watched the last of the fog roll off shore and into the Atlantic. She wrapped her arms around him and pulled him close. "MacGregor?"

He nuzzled her neck. "Mmm?"

"I think you're redeemed." She lifted her head and looked into his eyes. "Ready for that bath?"

"Definitely."

Maggie hugged him, knowing that this time when they made love it would be right.

Chapter 17

"Maggie?" Miss Hattie bustled around, adjusting the flowers in Maggie's bridal bouquet. "Where's the yellow carnation? Oh my, it must have fallen out."

"No, it didn't. It was for Tony. I took it over to the cemetery on my way over here. A little thank you for his help."

Miss Hattie smiled. "That was very thoughtful of you, dear. I'm sure it meant a lot to him."

Maggie darted her gaze around the bridal chamber, her nerves threatening to unravel. Leslie Butler, her matron of honor, came up to her clucking her tongue to the roof of her mouth and adjusted the flowing white veil trailing down Maggie's back. "You look beautiful, Maggie. T.J. isn't gonna know what hit him."

"Thanks." Maggie smiled, hoping Mac-Gregor was every bit as nervous as she was — not that there was any doubt in her mind that she wanted to marry him. She'd just prefer to do it without tripping and falling flat on her face in a church full of the villagers and her mother, who'd flown up three days ago to attend the ceremony.

"This is a little something special for you, Maggie." Leslie handed her a small box. "I bought it with the profits from that first auction."

Maggie's heart, already full, felt sure to burst. "Oh, Leslie."

"I had to do it." Leslie smiled. "If you hadn't said what you did to me that night at the Blue Moon about owing it to myself to try, I'd never have had the courage to attempt the auction. I can't tell you how much I appreciate what you did for me."

"I didn't do it. You did. I just" — Tony's words flashed through her mind — "assisted."

"Well, I appreciate your assistance."

"You're welcome."

"Oh, move over and let me in, Hattie. Beaulah's sitting in the front pew bending the sheriff's ear. It's *me,* Millie."

Miss Millie skirted around Miss Hattie and stopped in front of Maggie.

"Lovely," Miss Hattie said. "Absolutely lovely. Isn't she lovely, Millie?"

"She's lacking," Miss Millie said, then

nodded to show she meant it. "She needs this." She held up an antique lace sachet. White tulle and lace.

"It's your favorite fragrance, too, dear. Seashore."

Maggie smiled. "Oh, Miss Millie. I'm surprised you remembered."

"I said I'd make you another on your wedding day, didn't I?"

"Yes, you did." All the wonderful friends she'd made here. The love she'd found. MacGregor. Would life ever again be this good?

Of course it will, Maggie. And I echo my darling Hattie's sentiments. You do look lovely.

Tony. She looked behind Miss Hattie and saw him standing there, the yellow carnation tucked into his green suit jacket's lapel. But no one else seemed to see him. Not even Miss Hattie.

I can't let her see me. It would hurt her too much. But don't worry about us. One day, Hattie and I will be together again. Today is your day. You and Tyler are going to be very happy together, Maggie. Trust me. You're blessed with that rare love.

I trust you, Tony. With all my heart. And don't you dare laugh at me, but this trusting is getting easier all the time. She smiled, almost afraid Miss Hattie with her too-seeing eyes would sense the conversation, and Maggie wanted everyone happy today.

Tony smiled and winked.

A knock sounded at the door.

"Miss Hattie," Jimmy Goodson called out. "It's two o'clock straight up and down, and Pastor says they're waiting on Maggie. Tyler ain't looking too patient, either. Says she's got ten seconds to get up there or he's coming after her."

Miss Hattie clasped both of Maggie's hands in hers, crushing her hankie between their palms. "I'm trusting you to love Tyler well, Maggie. I've grown more than fond of the boy."

"Yes, ma'am. I will." Maggie had heard the catch in Miss Hattie's voice and it nearly undid her. "We're both fond of you, too, Miss Hattie. How can we ever thank you for everything?"

"You just did, child. And you can keep on thanking me by being happy and loving each other." The wonderful woman nodded. "Now," she cleared the rasp from her throat, "we'd best hurry, mmm? I do believe that today we're starting a new era. I just love new eras. Don't you love new eras, Millie?"

"I love antiques. And Christmas weddings. Especially ones Beaulah Favish and Lily Johnson are at solely as guests. Can't abide them being nosy and strutting their snooty ways."

Some things never changed. Maggie smiled to herself and moved toward the door, her long white gown rustling. "A new era?"

"Why, yes, dear." Miss Hattie gave Maggie an angel's smile. "One where Tyler believes in miracles . . . and so do you."

Maggie gave her a watery smile. "Yes, a new era."

Since Maggie had her mother on her side of the tiny church and Tyler had no kin, Hattie sat beside Vic on the groom's side of the center aisle. She looked up at the rugged cross Collin Freeport had hand-carved decades ago. Seeing it bathed in sunlight from the stained glass window had her feeling a little melancholy. It was Christmas, and that had her feeling a little melancholy, too. Had Tony lived, they would be celebrating Maggie and Tyler's marriage today, and their own golden wedding anniversary.

But he hadn't lived. And they hadn't shared a lifetime of love and memories together. She fingered her hankie. How joyful and loving their lives would have been.

Standing beside his best man, Bill Butler, Tyler winked at Miss Hattie then turned to watch his bride come up the aisle and join him. Such love burned in his eyes. They would have that joy, that lifetime of memories and love that Hattie had not. There was solace in that.

Maggie lifted her hand and placed it in Tyler's. The pastor began the ceremony, "Dearly beloved . . ."

Hattie let her thoughts steal away, dreaming a little herself. If only she could see Tony. Just once . . .

No. Once would never be enough. Seeing him and not being able to hold him — it would be torture for both of them. One day they'd be together again. Until then, she had to take comfort in putting yellow flowers on his grave to remind him how much she loved him still, in just knowing he was near.

He was near, wasn't he?

Tender, doubtful because she couldn't feel his presence, she let her hankie flutter to the floor.

It lay there for only a moment, then an unseen hand lifted it and placed it back in her upturned palm. Soft as an angel's breath, tender lips pressed a kiss to the back of her wrist. And inside the hankie's folds lay a single, yellow carnation petal.

Her eyes misted, and Hattie whispered.

"Thank you, Tony."

Content, her heart full, she watched Tyler and his beloved Maggie share their first kiss as man and wife and once again delighted in the magic of Seascape Inn.

ABOUT VICKI HINZE

Vicki Hinze is the award-winning author of 24 novels, 4 nonfiction books and hundreds of articles, published in as many as sixty-three countries. She is recognized by Who's Who in the World as an author and as an educator. For more information, please visit her website.

You can visit with Vicki on:

Facebook at:

http://www.facebook.com/vicki.hinze.author

Twitter at:

http://www.twitter.com/vickihinze

http://www.vickihinze.com

The employees of Thorndike Press hope you have enjoyed this Large Print book. All our Thorndike, Wheeler, and Kennebec Large Print titles are designed for easy reading, and all our books are made to last. Other Thorndike Press Large Print books are available at your library, through selected bookstores, or directly from us.

For information about titles, please call:
  (800) 223-1244

or visit our Web site at:
  http://gale.cengage.com/thorndike

To share your comments, please write:
  Publisher
  Thorndike Press
  10 Water St., Suite 310
  Waterville, ME 04901